# PASSION BEYOND REASON

Dare Trent's mouth discovered the honey of her lips as they parted beneath his kiss. All else faded as he held her tightly in his arms. Excitement exploded in his head as her body melted against his own. Time was a thing relegated to another dimension. Tenderness was a soft sensation that enveloped. Hunger was an over-riding throbbing that beat at his heart and demanded satisfaction.

Silkie didn't think. A question remained somewhere in the back of her mind, hovering, wanting to be heard and answered and it was: What are you doing? His body was steel and yet burningly alive and full with nerve-endings that touched her own and riveted her with desire.

Her body had betrayed her heart and mind and yielded to a moment's fancy. He was a rakehell, no better than Ashford really.

Other Fawcett titles
by Claudette Williams

# Song of Silkie

## CLAUDETTE WILLIAMS

FAWCETT GOLD MEDAL • NEW YORK

A Fawcett Gold Medal Book

Published by Ballantine Books

Library of Congress Catalog Card Number: 83-91139

ISBN 0-449-12660-9

Manufactured in the United States of America

First Ballantine Books Edition: January 1984

Dedicated with love and affection to my dad,
Lawrence Nissan.

# Part
# One

*Love—It holds the spring and summer in its arms,*
 *And every planet puts on its freshest robes,*
 *To dance attendance on its princely steps,*
 *Springing and fading as it comes and goes.*

—Elizabethan dirge

# 1820

## Chapter 1

*Spring* flooded Lady Augusta Melbourne's garden party with boldness. Champagne sparkled, laughter tickled the sweet cool air, and the promise of enchantment pervaded the senses. Fashionables strutted. Quizzing glasses went up and dropped with varying degrees of emphasis. Poetry was being read in one corner, gossip was being whispered in another, and all in all, her ladyship considered her affair a total success.

"Kiss me!" Zara Kane's voice was soft, urgent, seductive. Her dark blue eyes were lit warmly as she looked up into Aaron Marksbury's green eyes and discovered the fires therein. She wanted him. Oh, how she wanted this tall earth-shaking man!

He threw back his head of white gold hair and laughed as he stepped back to better view Zara's expression. Only a large oak tree blocked their movements from the rest of the *haut ton* sauntering and swaying in the distance.

"Zara, you rogue!" he teased. "You'll have all the tattlemongers at our throats yet!"

She pouted. "I don't give a monkey for such stuff!" She touched his arm and took up the hand he had dropped to his side. "Your sense of propriety is beginning to wear on my nerves."

Is that what held him in check? It was always a doubt in Zara's mind these days. Would he come up to scratch? There were some taking bets on it. She wanted Lord Aaron Marksbury for husband and lover, and wasn't concerned in what order this came about.

His gaze shifted from her lovely face to the top of her bright dusky curls. Zara was not only beautiful, she was also quite an heiress. His was a noble house but one that was in debt. His

3

investments had not yet served to alleviate his family's embarrassments and he was honor bound to marry a wealthy woman. Zara. She would answer many needs.

For one, she gave promise of being a passionate mate, a provocative and intelligent woman, but . . . and that was the problem—the "but" in his thoughts. He only knew that he was not in love with her and the thought of committing himself for life to a woman he did not love was at the heart of his depression. The sorry truth was that he was a romantic. With all his education, his sophistication, his class, still he was a romantic. It was an eccentricity he could ill afford. He should have been a cynic with all that he had witnessed.

He sighed. In the end he would ask Zara Kane to be his wife. What else could he do? It was inevitable.

"Aaron?" It was Zara, calling him to the present. "Answer me Aaron . . . why are we never alone?"

"Because, my dear, I do give a fig for what people will say," he answered with a smile and a tweak to her nose.

She leaned into the tree and pulled his hand up to kiss one of his fingers. She felt a shooting thrill tingle her entire body from this move and proceeded to lay his open hand over her full young breast. "Don't you want me Aaron? Don't you remember the time I fell into the lake and you charged in after me?"

He did not remove his hand and felt a certain urging rush through him. "We were children then. . . ." He remembered well enough. He had been hot-blooded enough to forget himself then, to reach into her wet bodice and grab hold lustily of her breast, to kiss her ferociously.

"We aren't children now," she answered huskily. The memory of his kiss that day, of his touch, was still vivid in her mind. She had been sixteen, now she was twenty. . . .

He felt his blood begin to rise. She had a way of getting to him even when he least wished her to. He brought himself closer, his voice dropping low and suddenly hungry. "Little jade . . ." he teased and bent his head to give her the kiss that now they both wanted. It was long, it was hard, and his hand found its way into her bodice again. "Ah Zara . . ." he breathed after a time, very much on fire.

"Aaron!" It was the sharp voice of Tyler Marksbury.

Zara blushed before Tyler's angry glance and she watched Aaron turn irritably to his younger brother.

"The devil!" snapped Aaron. "What in Hades do you think you are doing, Tyler?"

"Odd. I was about to ask the same of you," returned Tyler softly. "Do you know that you can be seen by half the household? If you don't care about Zara's reputation, *I do*!" He turned to Miss Kane abruptly. "Allow me Zara . . . I shall escort you back to the party and fetch you a glass of negus." To his brother he said curtly, "Lady Melbourne asked that I send you to her directly, Aaron. She wants you to meet someone."

Zara took Tyler's arm and pinched his chin playfully. "Oh, don't look so sour, love . . . it was only a kiss after all. . . ."

He relaxed enough to smile at her. He was well aware that Zara Kane wanted his older brother. He was well aware that Aaron was undecided and he was all too aware of his own feelings in the matter. "Ah Zara, it's the wrong brother you are after. . . ." It was a wistful tease.

She touched the pink ribbon of her white muslin gown and looked carefully away from his pale blue eyes. She had always been considered a sentient woman, easily swayed by her emotions, never by logic. Here was a man who would always adore her, allow her license in a marriage, and would know well what to do with her money. Aaron, though? Aaron was a dreamer, quite the opposite, but it was Aaron she wanted.

"Look there, Tyler, it is the newlyweds . . . do let us go and see them. I have been so curious to meet Worth's new bride," she said in a lively manner, neatly avoiding the issue.

"It is said that she is something of a cit," answered Tyler thoughtfully.

"Hmmm. Isn't it all very interesting?" she whispered without even looking at him. She was smiling at a passing acquaintance and because it was a male, her eyes were carefully lowered and then brought back to the man's face with mischievous amusement. He inclined his head and threw her a kiss. She giggled, saw that Tyler was looking resigned, and patted his arm. "Do you know I was told that she lived with her aunt, who ran a gaming hall some years back. . . ."

* * *

Aaron Marksbury usually turned heads. He was tall and his tight Corinthian figure was commanding in the fashion of the day. Then too, the color of his hair quite took the breath away. White gold cornsilk, full-bodied in its long, carefully clipped waves. Many a woman would have sold her soul to trade her own hair color for his. His thick brows were a darker shade and his lashes darker still. His eyes were a lake's cool green and usually twinkled. His face was chiseled in handsome lines and his lips thin and definitely sensuous.

In addition to these very enviable physical characteristics, he was the seventh baron of Marksbury Hall. True, his ancestral home had been mortgaged so heavily that he was now forced to lease it to a wealthy cit and would probably end in selling it to pay his debts. This fact saddened the *beau monde*'s mamas with daughters on the market, for otherwise he was a catch indeed. He and his younger, only brother were never omitted from the London hostess's guest lists. They were acceptable company but it was expected that both would have to make advantageous marriages.

Aaron approached Lady Melbourne and his smile was warm and friendly. He took up her white gloved hand.

"Lady Melbourne . . . your very obedient . . ." He was bowing graciously over her fingertips, dropping a light, perfunctory kiss at her plump wrist, doing what she expected of him.

She swished his gloved knuckles with her lace handkerchief and her tone was playful. "Scamp! Don't try and turn me up sweet with your tricks for I shan't have it! Now, what the deuce do you mean making love to Zara well within everyone's view?"

"I? Zara? Why, you mistake, Gussie my love. Indeed, I was but helping her with her pearls. They came undone. . . ."

"Oh-ho! A fat round-tale that! Well, let it pass." She was very near to grinning as she cut his story off and reached out to wave forward a young girl who had been hanging back behind a garden door. "I have someone here I should like you to meet." She turned her head slightly and said in an overly animated voice, "Serena . . . come here, child."

Aaron looked past Lady Melbourne's pleasantly chubby countenance and discovered a shy young thing moving daintily towards them. He felt his entire body go rigid with avid interest. He

6

heard Lady Melbourne rattling off in the background but scarcely paid heed.

"Lud, but I have been trying to get my dearest Serena to visit with me for nigh on eight months. She resides in Rye, you know . . . and what must she do when she finally arrives here but hide herself away in her room." She sighed. "I wanted her to meet you Aaron . . . so that she could see how very easy it is to get along in company." She arched a look at him. "You will see that she is properly introduced. . . ."

Serena heard her mother's dearest friend in quiet amusement. Wasn't it just like Lady Melbourne to go on in this fashion? What must this Corinthian of a man think of her? Egad, but she wished Gussie would stop her prattle. He was bowing over her hand, coming up to discover the light music of her voice. She said softly that she was very pleased to meet him and laughed to hear him babble much the same. He was leading her off and they could both hear Lady Melbourne sigh in the background with her satisfaction.

Serena's giggle was warm and lit up her entire countenance. She looked a veritable angel as she said in her quiet way, "You must think me an odd countrified creature after that introduction. Dearest Gussie, she insists I go out . . . as my mother wishes me to do."

"And you? Don't you want to?" he managed. Here was the most beautiful creature he had ever laid eyes on. Were her yellow curls made of gold? Were her grey eyes speckled with the same? Was her complexion made of cream and lush roses?

Her dark lashes brushed her cheeks and a note of sadness came into her voice. "I lost my father some months ago . . . we were very dear friends. . . ."

"So you felt it necessary to bury yourself with him?"

She put up her chin. "My inclination, sir, has never been frivolous."

"Then why did you leave the country?" He was teasing now, hoping to win her over.

She considered him for a long moment before she smiled. "My home is in the country . . . but my mother packed me off."

He gazed at her intently now. "You cannot know how very grateful I am to her that she did. . . ."

Serena found the color filling her cheeks and she looked away

7

to discover a peacock fanning his tail. "Oh look . . . how lovely . . ."

Aaron Marksbury was looking—but not at the peacock. Indeed, these words exactly fitted his sentiments. Was there ever such a sweet beauty? Had a woman's eyes ever held so much expression, so much tenderness? He felt his heart pound, his body burn, and his head was ringing and blowing away all logic.

## Chapter 2

*The* fire burned in leaping flames in the hearth. Aaron stared into its brightness and sipped his brandy. Decisions had to be made. He eased his head back against the high wing chair he had drawn to the fire. He was in difficult, dangerous waters. Debts had continued to mount. . . .

He was not a gamester by nature but he had taken what was left of his capital and had gone off to Ascot and placed his bet. It had been a risky indulgence but he had done it and fate had been kind. In the morning he would collect a hefty sum. It did not, however, solve his problems, but only staved them off for a while.

There was Serena. His adored one, his treasure. Did he have the right to ask her to join in his debts, in his worries? Her inheritance was small. They would always find themselves living higher than their means . . . such was their class. On the other hand, there was Zara.

Zara Kane's money would enable him to keep and maintain his ancestral home . . . his townhouse . . . his horses. He drained off his glass of brandy and poured himself another. She was a beautiful, hot-blooded woman who would ever try to please him. On this thought the door of his study opened and there she stood, her cloak wrapped around her, the hood low over her face. She dropped her hood and said his name softly, "Aaron?"

He jumped to his feet. These were bachelor lodgings. What was she doing here? It was unheard of for a maid of her blood, her name, to come alone and at night to a man's residence. "Zara!" His tone was reproachful, disapproving. He felt slightly heady as he moved towards her.

"No . . . don't scold me, Aaron," she begged as she moved towards him. She was desperate. She wanted Aaron, longed for him, needed him more than anything else on earth . . . and she was losing him. She had to do this thing. She was risking much, for Aaron was a romantic. He would want a chaste wife and she was no longer a virgin. . . .

"But Zara . . . you know better. . . ." What was she doing? Her dress was cut lower than was seemly, lower than was fashionable for a maid. Damn but her breasts were full and heaving with her emotions. He felt a sudden surge of desire rush through him. Here was a lusty chit. Zara had always loved him. He could forget Serena in Zara's arms. He had to forget Serena. If he loved Serena he must leave her free for better than he was. . . .

Zara felt his resolves weakening and moved instinctively into the folds of his sphere. Her hands went to his shoulders and she shivered as his arms went round her. Her whisper was low, her voice pleasurably seductive. "Don't make me go, Aaron . . . I have wanted you for so long. . . ."

The brandy was blocking his heart, whirling in his head. He gave himself over to his doubts and allowed himself to be swept up by the moment. His mouth discovered that hers was sweet and hungry. His hands yanked belligerently at the top of her red gown until he had freed her full young breasts. His hand uplifted one and he tore his mouth from hers to suckle at her pert nipple. He felt her quiver. He heard her groan and then he was lowering her to the oriental carpet at their feet.

They were on their knees as he divested her of her clothing. She worked his breeches as he slid off his linen shirt. She moved in a way that pushed out all thoughts. Greedily she bent, sweetly she took his staff to her lips. He drew in a gasp of pleasure and held her head in his hands, but as she brought him near his point he growled her name and pushed her almost wildly onto her back.

Here was enough woman to make him forget Serena. Still, his heart whispered a reproach, called her name. His head beat it off. No! He would not think of Serena now . . . not now! Here was Zara . . . his future . . . and she was pleasing to the touch. No virgin . . . but what did it matter? His thrusts were near violent as he tried to stop thinking. Zara was a passionate woman with moves enough to please the most exacting of men. Serena, oh God . . . Serena . . . but he would forget. He must forget.

He awoke with a start. The sun was blazing through his window and he sat bolt upright in bed. His hands took his face and he rubbed away at his eyes a moment before he attempted any thoughts. Zara was gone. He had seen her safely home. Odd . . . how they had talked afterwards . . . or rather how she had talked, like a happy child. He had asked her where she had received her . . . er, experience and she had cocked her head and asked him if he were jealous.

"Jealous?" He considered the word and then touched her nose. "No . . . but curious." He had known this girl since she was a babe.

She pouted, displeased with his response. "Well, I think that is rather cold-blooded of you. Aaron Marksbury . . . don't you feel even the slightest bit jealous that you weren't my first?"

He gave her an untruth and gallantly conceded that he was indeed driven by jealousy to know.

"I shan't tell you because I don't believe you really care!" she snapped, all too aware that he was merely humoring her.

He laughed. "Well, if you would rather not—"

She glanced up at him sharply. "You mustn't think I have had a great many men though. . . ."

"I don't," he said simply and kissed her ear.

"You know what Papa was before he died. He was forever bringing home a platoon of hunting-mad cronies and not all of them were old." She sighed. "He never was very strict about my doings . . . how I spent my afternoons, as long as he was free to gad about. It was inevitable that I should find myself . . . seduced."

"Inevitable?" he bantered.

She slapped his cheek playfully. "Fiend! It was your fault. After that kiss you gave me in the lake . . . well, it did awake a certain curiosity."

"Ah, so then the blame is to be put at my door?" he quizzed.

She sighed. "In a way . . . but I swear Aaron . . . I shall be faithful to you . . . I swear it."

He traced the outline of her well-shaped lips. "But Zara . . . I haven't asked for that. . . ."

She frowned. "And won't you?"

He kissed her then long and hard and he took her once more before he was to see her home. He hadn't answered though. Throughout, something was lacking. Not physically. She had a way with her body that a man could lose himself in—but afterwards when desire had been satiated and his soul called for something more . . . someone else . . . what then? It was precisely what he was asking himself now in the morning light. "What now, Aaron Marksbury . . . what now?"

Serena Parkes looked up from the letter she was writing to her mother and smiled warily as Zara Kane floated into the room. She knew they were in competition for the same man and that Zara had a ruthless streak she herself could never match. Just what was this going to be about?

Zara moved and smiled in a superior fashion, taking up the French upholstered Regency chair across from Serena and spreading her pink skirt about her as she allowed her eyes to meet those of Serena's.

"Well Zara . . . shall I ring for tea?"

"I don't think so. I won't be here long enough to enjoy a cup with you."

"Oh? Is there something then . . . in particular you want of me?"

"In a manner of speaking. I should like you to know that Aaron Marksbury is mine. I think that you should be aware of that and stop attempting to wean him from me!" It was sweetly said.

Serena felt a sharp pang shoot through her. "You call Aaron yours? But since you are speaking plainly, so then shall I. Zara . . . I have seen no evidence to prove your very strong statement."

"Serena," came the honeyed voice, "if you had been present . . . last night . . . in Aaron's study . . . you might have been witness to just how *strongly* Aaron feels about me."

Hurt and a sudden overpowering jealousy made Serena cringe. Zara Kane was a beautiful woman and Serena could picture her all too vividly in Aaron's arms. No. She wouldn't believe it. She recalled her composure. "I think . . . this is getting out of hand, Miss Kane."

"Is it? Or are you just too afraid to face things as they are?" Zara shot back at her angrily.

Serena frowned. She was not a reckless, hot-tempered being. She was not a fighter. She would not scratch and claw to stay where she was. She was soft and gentle, all too full of understanding to save herself before the wolves. She leaned forward and her voice was quiet, scarcely audible. "Zara . . . I know you love Aaron. . . ."

"Know? You know nothing of what I feel for Aaron. I would die for him. Do you understand? There is nothing, nothing I would not do to have him." Zara was on her feet, a pacing tigress. "I would move all heaven and hell to keep him from you! What will you do for him but bring him low? I have all he needs to be forever comfortable, forever powerful! You—"

"Stop it! What are you saying? I love Aaron," Serena cried, "I would do nothing to hurt him. . . ."

"Your very love hurts him!" Zara moved in for the kill. "Don't you see? Aaron has to marry a woman whose dowry will be enough to set his family estates in order! He has to . . . and would have if you hadn't fluttered your lashes his way and made him think—" She did a body spin and then stopped to compose herself. When she felt sufficiently recovered she moved closer to Serena and her dark blue eyes had melted into firecoals. Low, very low and threatening her voice came. "It makes me sick, do you hear me, physically ill to think that Aaron even thinks of you. Why . . . you are nothing! Nothing! Your sort of beauty will fade . . . and then what will he have?" She shook her head, "He will have nothing. Think about that, Serena, before you dig your claws any deeper into poor Aaron's flesh. I can give him everything . . . *can you*?" She moved to the sofa and took up her reticule. At the door she turned again for a parting smile. "Just think about it, Serena."

Serena sat for a long while and looked at nothing in particular. Her heart felt the aftermath of battle. Her head ached and her eyes felt heavy with unshed tears. Was it true? Was her love for Aaron a terrible thing? Would it in the end take him into debt? Did he have to marry an heiress? Oh no, but not Zara! She would never make Aaron happy. What to do?

She couldn't think. What she needed was a ride. She wished

she had never come to London. At home there was the sea, her horses, and a quiet life that had never in its dullness hurt her. . . .

Wade Ashford—king of all rakehells. He had not received the title without earning it! This was what Lady Bruney was advising him with a wide smile as they strolled in the park and laughed over his latest escapade.

"Do not try to convince me you were not at the heart of poor Holland's troubles." Lady Bruney laughed with a wag of a finger. "That silly wife of his would never have thought to run away from him if you hadn't seduced her."

He put up his hands. "Acquit me! For once in my career I had nought to do with it. Holland lost his countess and temper in one blow and I believe by now has found both." He clucked his tongue. "Really Sarah, I would take the credit, were it mine."

She eyed him doubtfully. "Who then?"

"Be it known that I was not the only bachelor staying with them during that week. His grin now was wide.

"Really? Who was there then? Tell me, Wade, for I am dying of curiosity and it will be such a good coup for me to be able to tell the Jersey a bit of juicy gossip for a change." She looked at him and was taken aback a moment by his expression. She followed the line of his vision and discovered Serena Parkes. "Wade," she warned, ". . . this one is definitely not in your line."

Serena slowed her mare to a walk when she saw Lady Bruney looking her way. She stopped to smile, for Sarah Bruney was a dear friend of Lady Melbourne's. "Lady Bruney," she said in soft greeting. "How lovely you look."

Sarah beamed. She liked Serena Parkes. "Hallo to you . . . and where, my dear, is your groom?"

Serena blushed. "I rather dashed off without one today . . . am I very naughty?"

"Hmmm. Just a bit, and life would never be any fun if we weren't naughty from time to time—"

"I shall go mad!" announced Wade, interrupting them. " I am in a tremble of anticipation while you two ignore me and the introduction I am entitled to!"

Sarah Bruney rapped his arm. "Villain!" She made the introduction though and added, "But take no notice of him, darling, for your mama would not want you to know him!"

"But why?" Serena's eyes were wide with astonishment.

Lady Bruney laughed. "Thats right, you haven't been in town long enough to know that Wade Ashford's alias is king of rakehells! He is the very devil of a fellow and not at all the thing for you—"

"But I protest!" cut in Mr. Ashford with a charming smile. He was very nearly mesmerized by Serena Parkes. He had had beauties in his career as a lover of women, but there was something about this one that held him spellbound. "Miss Parkes . . . as much as I do adore Sarah, she is given to a great deal of prejudice against me ever since I beat her beloved lord at faro." He turned a winning smile upon Lady Bruney. "Isn't that a fact, Sarah my love?"

He had a way with him, there was no doubt about that, but Sarah was immune to his lush hazel eyes. She was, however, amused by his audacity.

"Rogue! I know you for what you are." She turned to Serena. "He is a charming cad . . . but a cad all the same."

He laughed. "You see, Miss Parkes? My reputation precedes me. Is it fair, do you think? Shouldn't you decide for yourself what the real Wade Ashford is?"

"Oh, but I trust in Lady Bruney's opinion, sir . . . after all, my experience is not great," she teased.

"Good girl!" Sarah laughed. "Now, ignore this scamp, for it is certain he is far too devastated by you for my comfort. Oh, by the by, I had a letter from your dear mama this morning. She is hoping that you are not being tired out by Lady Melbourne." There was a tease in her voice.

"Oh, do tell her I am well and happy," said Serena softly, "She worries so. . . ."

"Lud! I have already done that! Do I see you tonight at my rout?"

"Indeed yes. Lady Melbourne tells me it is bound to be the most wondrous squeeze of the season." Serena smiled.

"That's right." She turned to Ashford and what she saw worried her. "Go on then . . . have your ride, love." Sarah sent Serena off.

Ashford watched Miss Parkes ride off. A chit worth the hunt.

There was something about her, a quiet grace that he found vastly intriguing.

"Devil!" snapped Sarah. "What are you thinking?"

"You know Sarah, you must learn to trust me more."

"With regards to myself, Ashford, I do. We have been friends a long, long time . . . but . . . Wade . . . do leave the Parkes girl alone. She is a bit of an innocent and her mama is a dear friend."

"I won't harm her," said Ashford. There was no conviction in his voice.

"Wade! I can be the very devil when I am angered. Don't toy with that child!"

"Sarah . . ." He was again clucking his tongue. "You wrong me. . . ."

## Chapter 3

*Drury* Lane Theater glittered. In its gallery throngs of English subjects crowded in to witness another of Kean's lightning performances. In its boxes, the nobility put up their quizzing glasses, scanned one another with interest and a great deal of mischievousness. Lighthearted naughtiness had carried them through the Regency. Now the Regency was at an end, King George III had died, and their regent was king.

Serena was vastly entertained as she surveyed this breathtaking world and recognized all her mother had described. The gentleman at her side had eyes only for her and was surprised himself at his interest. He found her soft coos of delight strangely enchanting and her smile radiant and most arresting. He discovered a need to make her happy, and knew that never before had he felt this way.

Serena's grey eyes laughed as she turned and touched Wade Ashford. "Oh look . . . who is that very odd woman? Goodness, just look how many people follow in her train."

Wade Ashford snorted derisively as he followed the line of Serena's chin. There stood a very fat, elderly woman whose red face appeared more so because of the white, very frilly frock she wore. "That, my love," he said dryly, ". . . is our *queen*!"

"The queen? But . . . I thought she was in Italy," Serena said in some wide-eyed surprise. She was watching her still, wondering if all the rumors were true.

"She returns to claim her throne," answered Wade.

"Who is that handsome-looking fellow with her?"

"Handsome?" returned Ashford disdainfully. "My heart breaks if you think he is handsome."

"Oh stop." Serena laughed, giving his hand a gentle rap. "Who is he?"

"Her lover, Pergami I think he calls himself. When our king takes our queen to trial—for he means to divorce her—Pergami will be named as correspondent."

"Oh my." She frowned over this. "Then I wonder at the queen going about with him so . . . openly?"

He laughed and pinched her cheek. "Indeed, my love, their games are beyond you . . . but I see Lady Melbourne returning and looking daggers at me."

Serena turned to smile at her ladyship but said, "Nonsense, Gussie likes you very well, you know."

"I do know, but she doesn't like me well enough to wish me so very close to you. . . ." His voice was low and sensual as he drew back and his hazel eyes looked full into hers. He was taken by the golden lights that glittered in the depths of her grey eyes and he had a strange sensation of breathlessness. He had to have Serena Parkes at any cost.

Serena blushed and looked away from him. Three weeks had passed since she had met Wade Ashford. In that time she had seen nothing of Aaron Marksbury. Word had it that he was in Brighton. What did she feel? Wade certainly excited her . . . yes, he did that. Amused? Flattered? Yes, all those things, and she could even be swayed romantically by him. He had charm enough but . . . that was it, the "but" in everything she did these days. Aaron. Oh Aaron. It was then that she saw Zara Kane.

Zara entered her box with a flourish of sound and movement. Her gown of bright blue was eye catching, as were her companions, the Marksbury brothers. She had one for each arm and she flaunted them in her style.

As she nodded round, she did not notice that one of these Marksburys found someone else to hold his attention. Aaron's green eyes discovered Serena in one fatal blow. He had thought he had managed to purge himself of her—and then there she was. She looked an angel in white. Blue ribbons trimmed her gold hair, but her smile, her smile was vanishing. . . . Damn! Was that Wade Ashford at her side? Fiend seize the man, was he touching her fingers to his lips?

Serena saw Aaron and her heart stopped. When it started up again it thumped twice the pace as though to make up for that loss in time. She saw now that rumor was true. Aaron Marksbury would marry Zara Kane. She had heard that he'd hurried off to attend Zara in Brighton. Well, Zara was back and so was Aaron.

Zara answered a quip of Tyler Marksbury's with a bold laugh and leaned into him seductively. Tyler's arms went round her waist and his voice was low and hungry. "You are driving me mad, Zara. . . ."

"No darling, I am trying to make you see," she answered lightly. "I don't know if you can believe me when I tell you that I like you better than anyone I have ever known . . . nay, I love you, Tyler my friend, and I would have you see that you would ever be miserable with me as wife." She indicated Aaron's unconcern with a lift of her chin. "He will never mind my dallying discreetly from time to time with someone new."

"But if you love him . . . why . . . Zara, why would you?" Tyler was frowning with his puzzlement.

She touched his lips with her gloved finger. "Because . . . I can't help it. 'Tis part of my makeup . . . but never mind . . . do look at Caroline! I declare that I think Prinny . . . rather—*our king*—is quite right for trying to oust her from our kingdom!"

Tyler laughed and whispered something into her ear regarding the latest *on dit* about Queen Caroline. Zara went into a titter that died slowly as she noted Aaron's line of vision. Serena Parkes! She had thought during these last three weeks in Brighton that Aaron had put the girl out of his mind. Her fine dark brows went up and she called Aaron to order with some bright adroitness.

"Aaron . . . darling . . . Tyler has just been relating the latest squib going about the queen . . . Aaron?"

"Has he, Zara? And what are they saying about the poor woman?"

"Let me see." She turned to Tyler. "How did it go, love? The drollest thing."

Tyler was not immune to his brother's sudden change in mood. He too had seen Serena Parkes and the effect she had on Aaron.

He avoided repeating the little piece to Aaron because he knew Aaron's sympathies, unlike those of many of their friends, were in unison with the populace and for the queen. Didn't Zara realize it would only serve to irritate him?

"Now Zara . . . I think we had better drop it for the moment . . . and look there, the queen is nodding to you."

"Yes, she is a great friend of my papa's," said Zara, making the queen a pretty mock bow from her seat. "But never mind that . . . Aaron . . . she is as bold as her attackers, but an amusing little piece has come out of it and if Tyler won't recite it for you, I will."

"Do then," said Aaron softly and he managed to tear his gaze away from Serena's lovely form.

She put her gloved finger to her lip. "Now, let me see . . . ah yes.

> Most gracious queen, we thee implore
> To go away and sin no more;
> Or if that effort be too great;
> To go away at any rate.

With this Zara burst into mirth and attempted to wield Aaron into the same mood. It did not serve. He frowned darkly.

"It is amazing," Aaron said reproachfully, "how very cruel we humans can be to one another."

"Tyler," said Zara, ignoring this, "you know what your brother needs right now? A drink . . . do be a dear and fetch him a bumper of ale so that we may be comfortable."

"I think not!" snapped Aaron. He stood up and made Zara his bow. "If you will excuse me but for a moment . . . I see a friend I should like to pay my respects to."

The lights had already been dimmed, but at these words the curtain was drawn. Zara said lightly, "Leave it be, darling . . . it isn't the time."

He looked long at Zara Kane before he accepted this and took up his seat once again. When next he chanced to glance across the wide gallery to Lady Melbourne's box, Serena was gazing raptly at the stage, but Wade Ashford had eyes for no one but Serena. Inwardly, Aaron cringed.

What Tyler Marksbury thought about all this he kept to himself. Aaron was man enough to control his own fate and if he were hurting, it was his own fault. Guiltily Tyler conceded that fate had not helped their family by driving them into financial distress. Now he would have to leave England to look for a new life and perhaps the means to some success. Zara? She would never be his, and this was a heartache he looked to time and distance to heal:

Unfair? Well, life held no guarantees. Perhaps Zara was right, perhaps she would only find and give happiness with Aaron. He looked from Aaron to Serena and sighed. No, Aaron would always remember Serena Parkes and it would gall in the end. There was nothing Tyler could do. He looked to Zara and without realizing it there was a plea in his eyes.

She saw it there at once and took up his hand. Her whisper was soft and low. "Dearest Tyler, you will forget me. . . ."

"Never, my love." He kissed her hand and wondered that Aaron did not care.

## Chapter 4

*It* was the morning after this interesting display at Drury Theater that Wade Ashford found himself being shown into Lady Melbourne's elegant morning room. The sun streamed into the room in bright straight lines and her ladyship made certain her back was to the window as she received her morning caller. Her brow was up as she allowed Wade Ashford to take her hand and drop a perfunctory kiss upon it. He was looking well in his cutaway coat of dark blue and his waistcoat of embroidered ivory silk. Now, just what did he want with her alone, for that had been the request she had received from him last night. She had agreed out of curiosity.

"Gussie"—his hazel eyes gleamed as he caught her expression— "you look enchanting this morning."

"Nonsense. I look just as I feel, quite haggard. Now, out with it, rogue, and no fustian if you please. What do you want with me?"

"You may have noticed my very keen interest in your houseguest?" he said gently, taking up the seat she indicated and crossing his legs.

"Ha! Interest? You have been dangling after Serena in the most marked way I have ever . . . well, I've been wondering to what purpose, Wade, for I didn't think you would dare bring low someone directly in my charge."

"As to that, Gussie love, I would not have allowed it to weigh had I that end in mind for Serena." He smiled at her ladyship's shocked expression and conceded to her, "I am, you will admit, many things, but I am also honest. However, that is not the case here."

"Oh? What then is the case?"

"I intend to make Serena my wife," he said softly and there was, Lady Melbourne noticed, a strange light in his eyes. Its intensity made her shiver.

"I suppose I am to be transported by this piece of foolishness?" she scoffed.

"As it happens, your reaction hardly concerns me," he said on an amused note. "I am merely advising you of my intentions, so that you may write to her mama."

"And what if I object?"

He laughed and it was a harsh sound. "Why should you? I have a bloodline as noble as your own. My estates are in order and I am considered one of London's wealthiest men. No, you will not object."

She frowned. It was true. To object solely on his reputation would be ludicrous. He was one of the grandest marriage prizes in all of England. "Wade . . . if you believe that in Serena you have found a biddable girl who will . . . be a wife to you, a mother to your children, and sit back and overlook your indiscretions, you are gravely mistaken. She will hurt as another . . . less sensible maid might not. . . ."

"Don't be maudlin, Gussie. I don't plan on hurting Serena." He sat forward suddenly in some animation. "Oh, I know what I am, and no, I don't promise to change . . . I don't think I want to change, but believe me, Gussie, I shall care for Serena and make her happy. She won't want for anything."

"Wade . . . I don't know what to say to you."

"It doesn't matter. You see I mean to have her." He got to his feet.

As he took his leave, Lady Melbourne felt a definite chill rush through her. No good would come of this. It was certainly a problem and there was only one thing to do at the moment. Hurry off a letter to Serena's mother!

The next week found Aaron Marksbury seething with irritation as he watched the love of his heart become Wade Ashford's latest flirt. How could Lady Melbourne allow it? And Serena? Why did Serena sit transfixed on every word Ashford uttered, for hadn't he seen them driving in Ashford's phaeton this morning?

Hadn't she been all eyes for Ashford? What to do? He hadn't the right to do anything.

Zara. She was his future and Serena would have to be relegated to the realm of dreams. Ah, but it was proving to be more than his flesh and blood could bear to watch his gentle Serena warm beneath Ashford's experienced hands. Ah Serena . . . have you so quickly forgotten? This question kept him very near the edge—and ready, all too ready to explode.

And just what did Serena think of all this? She had put it all in its proper place because such was her nature. She couldn't divide things into black and white; she was one to always note the varying shades. It didn't take the hurting away but it eased it. She knew that Aaron Marksbury had no choice. He would have to marry Zara. She wished it weren't so, but there was nothing she could do to change this and so she accepted it. No fighter to challenge the gods was Serena. She cried only to herself and attempted to make the best of what was left to her.

Wade Ashford happened and while she did not love him, she had to admit that she found him exciting. He was all that she was not—and what was more, he had set out to win her. Too often she found herself shocked by a nature he could not hide from her all the time, and she would hold something of herself back from him. However, his methods were insidiously and relentlessly taking a grip on her. More and more she found the pain of losing Aaron lessened when she was with Wade. All these things, however, were brought to a climax one evening at Lady Bruney's soirée when Aaron Marksbury found himself confronting Serena.

There she was, within his reach, a kiss, oh God, a kiss away, and he thought he would burst. She looked away and made to pass him. He stopped her, held her arm, and drew her out the garden door at his back. "Serena . . . Serena . . ." It was all he could say. Her name was scarcely a whisper but it shouted his helplessness.

She was surprised at the anger she suddenly felt. She couldn't understand—she thought she had carefully, logically tucked it away. She looked at him levelly and her voice was a soft and yielding answer. "Yes, Aaron?"

He was beside himself. "I am crazed . . . Serena . . . forgive me."

"There is nothing to forgive." It was almost a sigh. What had she hoped? It was useless.

"Is that what you believe?" He was desperate and he drew her further outside. "Damnation! I know what I am . . . but Serena . . . Ashford is worse! Believe me . . . don't you know what he is after?"

She puzzled up. "I rather thought I did?"

"Then you're a fool!" he snapped. "He wants you, but not as his wife! Oh no, Wade Ashford is not about to marry you or any other sweet young thing."

She lifted her hand to slap his face for suddenly she felt as though more than her heart were breaking. She stopped herself in midair, turned, and started to walk off. She felt all of youth's dreams crack within her soul. Hope was dashed. . . .

Aaron reached out and held her, turned her towards him, and she looked up at him with her open grey eyes—soft, gentle, and honest. She was not a fighter, but she won him with that look. He collapsed into it. "Serena . . ." His voice was a tender call.

She wanted to ease away, say goodbye and find a corner in which she could recover. "Aaron, what I do should not concern you. You have no choice . . . I know that. You must marry Zara." And she would have been less than human if she didn't accuse—for the memory of Zara hissing her relationship with Aaron came sharply to mind. "After all . . . I understand that you are already much in accord with one another." There was a touch of hurt in her voice.

"What in hell do you mean? I haven't asked Zara to marry me."

"Haven't you? It is expected that you will . . . especially by Zara . . . after all, Aaron . . . a man of your stamp doesn't usually seduce a maid in his own study unless he means to marry her. . . ." There, it was out, and as as soon as it was, she flushed with her confusion. She was at odds with herself. What was she doing? What sense to all of this?

His hands went through his white gold hair. "Serena . . . everything I have done . . . I've done to get you out of my mind . . . my heart. . . ."

"I see," she said quietly and again started to move off.

He hadn't released her arm and this time he pulled her up against him. Her grey eyes discovered the fire in the depths

25

of his dark green eyes and she melted as he pulled her into his embrace.

"Serena . . . I don't have the right . . ." With which he proceeded to take it. She was everything to him. All questions were resolved as his lips took hers, as their souls mingled, as their hearts sighed to one another in the spell of that moment.

When at last he allowed her breath, she sank against his chest and said in a small voice. "Don't you want me, Aaron?"

"Want you? Of course I want you. With all my heart I want you, but how can I condemn you to a life without the luxuries we have been taught to need?"

"Condemn me? My darling, you are all I want and we could be comfortable in the country . . . I know we could. . . ."

London had always been his base, his source of entertainment. Rye was another land, another way of life, and he wasn't sure he wanted that way of life. He needed to think, so he turned away from her. His winning at Ascot had encouraged him to place a rather hefty sum at the gaming table at White's, and amazingly enough he had won. His financial condition had improved slightly, yet he knew this was but a temporary state of affairs. If he put Zara aside he would be committing himself and Serena to a life of debt. If he didn't, he would be relegating them both to misery.

"I want more for you, Serena," he said on a whisper, afraid to look into her eyes. "Another man, a better man than I, can give you so much more. . . ."

She couldn't stop the words. They were out just as she realized their meaning. "Ashford can give me more. . . ." It was said quietly, sadly.

Aaron made a scoffing noise. "It is not your hand he is after!"

"You mistake, Aaron," she said softly. "Ashford has in fact come up to scratch. Lady Melbourne says it's a miracle. He has applied to her and awaits my mama's response before putting his question to me." She put up her chin, "You see, he behaves just as he should."

"Hell and brimstone, Serena! You are pushing me to the edge. He won't make you happy . . . you can't mean to have him . . . Serena, look at me!"

"Then who, my darling, shall I marry? Will you hand pick

the fellow?'' She shook her head. ''I think not. If I marry for love, it will be you. If not, it must be Ashford, for I find him attractive, amusing—''

''Stop it!'' he cut in and it was an anguished cry. Serena and Ashford? He would see her in debtor's prison first! ''Serena, I hope one day you won't hate me for this night's work. Say you will marry me . . . quickly, now, before my better sense throws you away on purer intentions!''

She went into his arms and her voice was nearly a sob. ''Yes, oh yes, Aaron . . . I will marry you.''

In spite of his doubts he felt a wild elation surge through his body. Zara! A voice pounded her name. What a scurrilous thing to do to Zara. She had expected. . . never mind that! Zara would manage. She was strong and resourceful. Zara would mend. He pushed these self-recriminations aside and took Serena's hand.

''Then come with me, love, for I mean to tell the world here and now!''

She laughed and attempted to hang back. ''But Aaron . . . how outrageous! You haven't even applied to Lady Melbourne . . . my mama . . . Aaron . . . think.''

''I don't want to think! If I take a moment and constrain myself to thought, Serena . . . I would be ruled by good sense and now, now, I want to be ruled by my heart!''

''Oh Aaron,'' she sighed. 'Tis most improper.''

''That's right! I am a most improper fellow, but look''—he kissed her hand—''see my prize!'' With this last he pulled her along and headed straight for his hostess, Lady Bruney.

# Chapter 5

*Sarah* Bruney saw Aaron pulling Serena along in his wake. They were both laughing and looking radiant. It immediately worried her and she cast her faded brown eyes round the room. There was Wade flirting mildly with the Jersey and Zara dancing with Tyler Marksbury. She felt her heart quake. She didn't know why, but at that moment she was filled with a sense of foreboding.

"Sarah!" It was Aaron running his hostess down to earth, but his voice was a joyful sound. "I have something I wish you to do."

She smiled at him and attempted to depress her sinking feeling. "Do you, scamp?"

"Yes, and you shall call me scamp no more, for I mean to settle my racketty ways and behave as I should."

"Really?" She glanced at Serena. "What is this youngblood blubbering about, do you know?"

Serena nodded and her voice was a soft whisper. "I am afraid I do."

"Ah, so then, now it is my turn. Explain, Aaron." She was smiling but inwardly feeling more and more uneasy.

"Aaron . . . Aaron," said Serena, tugging at his sleeve. ". . . there is Gussie . . . do please motion to her first."

"Yes, my love," agreed Aaron as his eyes beckoned Lady Melbourne to their circle. As she approached, he felt he could hardly contain himself. "Gussie," he said all too loudly, ". . . Gussie, wish us well."

"I do," said Lady Melbourne brightly. "Always have."

"No, no, you silly love," cried Aaron, "you don't understand. We have decided, Serena and I, that we are meant for one

28

another. Gussie . . . you wouldn't say us nay . . . would you?"

The truth dawned on Lady Melbourne. She was as astonished as she was pleased. It was sudden, it was unexpected, it perhaps was unwise, but it certainly got Serena out of Wade Ashford's clutches! "Yes, yes, of course I wish you well. How utterly marvelous. Say you nay? How could you think so?" She was putting her arms about them both.

Once again Aaron Marksbury was turning to his hostess. "Sarah, indulge us . . . have your musicians make the announcement now."

They were creating no little stir. Someone, in fact, had overheard them and it was quickly being whispered round the room to various individuals and causing a hubbub of some account. Ashford directed a look of inquiry at Serena and took a step forward, just as Zara had noticed that Aaron was holding Serena's hand. They were standing beside one another when the music stopped and one of the players received the attention of the room. His announcement set up a round of applause and much commotion, but Zara Kane felt her world crumble beneath her feet and Wade Ashford's fists clenched at his sides.

Lady Bruney managed to get to Ashford and touched his tight arm. "Don't mind it, darling, she was really not in your style."

"Oh but she was . . . she most definitely was, and Sarah . . . I don't mean to let it end here."

"Wade! Think first." There it was, that sixth sense of hers, warning of something she couldn't quite see.

He was already moving towards Serena, closeted round by maids and dowagers giving her their felicitations. Somehow he created his own path. There was a hush as he came to face her.

"A word with you, Serena?" It was a low, odd sound, nearly a growl in his throat.

She felt a sense of compassion and put her hand on his arm. "Of course, Wade."

"You know that you have quite broken my heart," he said on a reproachful note.

Serena knew him better than that. "No sir, I think not, though you are balked at not getting your way."

29

"What, Serena, don't you believe I have a heart?" He was frowning.

"Yes, Wade, I do and it was hardened long before you ever clapped eyes on me."

He pulled a rueful smirk of his lips. "So then not breakable, eh? You mistake the situation."

"You will manage without me, Wade. . . ."

"No, my pretty, I shall not." He bowed his head and backed away and she stood for a moment looking after him. Something in his tone frightened her, but then Aaron was at her side, pulling her towards the dance floor.

Zara Kane clutched at Tyler Marksbury for support. She watched as everyone buzzed round the happy couple and she felt her body go rigid with humiliation and defeat. How had this happened? When? And then a slow, burning rage seethed and saved her from breaking down. She heard Tyler at her side, saying her name, calling her to reality, and she went into his arms. She looked up into his face and her blue eyes were dark with her rioting emotions.

"Get me away Tyler . . . quickly."

"No my love." His voice was soft, soothing. "Think again."

"You must Tyler . . . I can't face . . ."

"Yes you can. If you left now you would give the tattlemongers more meat to chew. I shan't allow you to be the brunt of their gossip."

"Ha! Your brother has already done that quite nicely."

"Zara . . . oh God, Zara . . ." His heart was breaking as he drew her closer still. "Look at me! Zara . . . *see me*! I love you, love you past thinking. Don't you know? Haven't you seen how I feel about you . . . how I will always feel about you?"

Suddenly a wave of ragged despair and angry spite shook her into a new plan to save herself. "Do you *really* love me, Tyler?"

"Thunder and turf, woman . . . are you really asking?"

"Do you love me enough to marry me . . . take me away with you to that New World you are always talking about?"

He felt a rush of excitement. She didn't love him, he knew that, but he was a man in love. He believed in love and therefore the hope that he could make her love him was strong within him. "Egad, Zara! Need you ask?"

"Then go there . . . announce our betrothal . . . at once!" Her eyes burned with purpose.

He frowned. "But why, Zara . . . why like that?"

"Do it, Tyler! If you want me, do it for me now. Save me, Tyler, oh please . . . you have always been there for me—be there for me now and you shall have me and my wealth. We will build an empire together in that heathen country you want so much! I shall make Aaron rue this day, I swear I shall!" She held his shoulders and her face was a mask of determination. "Oh Tyler . . . marry me and take me away from London so that I may never see his face again!"

Tyler frowned in spite of his victory. Here was Zara and she was really going to be his, but . . .? Never mind his fears, it would work out in the end. It had to. He would make her forget his brother. Tyler was a second son with a dim future in England. In America he could do as he pleased, and now with Zara as his bride the entire world was opening up for him. He would do as she asked and the *haut ton* of London would breathe heavy with the news.

Zara Kane swished her wispy black peignoir round her as she reclined on her settee and awaited her guest. Her father—away from home more than ever now that she was safely engaged to Tyler Marksbury—would not be home for hours. Tyler was not expected as he had gone to Southampton to make arrangements for their sailing. What Wade Ashford could want, she had no idea, but she planned on amusing herself with him. She was in a dangerous mood these days, restless, hungry, and hurting for Aaron.

Ashford was shown into her bedroom. His dark brows were up in rueful wonder. He had heard many things about Zara Kane, and when he saw her now he knew most of them had to be true.

She watched the tall, arrogant man make her his bow. He looked a dashing blade in his brown cutaway coat and his fashionable skintight breeches and hessians. She wondered how it was they had never crossed paths in the past.

Ashford inclined his head. "It is so good of you to see me, Miss Kane. I hope I am not . . . inconveniencing you." He looked round and was surprised that no chaperone was present.

She noted this at once and laughed. "Haven't you heard, Mr.

Ashford? I am the *beau mond*'s outrageous pet. I have done without a bothersome duenna for a good number of years now.'' She indicated a chair not very far from where she reclined and waited for him to be seated. ''Now''—her tone was provocative— ''. . . how may I . . . help you?''

''Why do you assume that I have come to you for help?''

''Am I wrong?''

He smiled. ''No, you are quite right, but I think we may help each other.''

''Hmmm, yes, I think we may,'' she said and her meaning was clear.

He laughed outright, quite amused with her boldness. She was a saucy piece and it did his ego some good at the moment. ''If it were possible to end Aaron Marksbury's alliance with Serena Parkes, would you wish it?''

She directed a level look at him, ''Why should it matter to me what Aaron and Serena do with their lives?''

''Ah, I see that I was mistaken.'' He started to get to his feet.

She stayed him. ''Fie on you sir. I did not say you were mistaken. Do sit and tell me what you have in mind.''

''What I have in mind is to marry Serena Parkes,'' he said roughly, ''and one way or another . . . I shall!'' He studied her a moment. ''That would leave you with Aaron.''

''Would it? But I am engaged to Aaron's brother and we set sail in a week's time.''

''Then before the week is out, Serena Parkes will be my wife.''

''Why tell me this?''

''Because I need your help in the matter.''

''Really?'' She leaned forward.

''Would you be willing in this regard?''

She eyed him. ''How much would be expected of me?''

''Serena will be your sister-in-law. It would be natural for you two to get together and make amends . . . perhaps at some lovely country inn. Indeed, I know of just the spot,'' he said steadily.

''Do you? Such a marvelous notion, Mr. Ashford.'' She was caressing her long, well-shaped ankle with her bare foot, arranging her legs invitingly, swaying them. ''. . . you must tell me more . . . after . . .''

He got up and came to the settee where his hand went to the

silken string of her negligee and gently pulled it down. "It will be my . . . pleasure, Miss Kane." He looked back a moment towards the door.

Quietly she said, "My servants are well trained. No one would dare disturb us. . . ." She didn't have to say more. Ashford's sensuous mouth was already closed over hers.

He felt a violent need to take and it ruled his body. Serena Parkes would pay for this week of aching, but not until she was his wife, and damn it all, he would have her for wife. In the meantime, this one would serve. . . .

Zara Kane teased his manhood with her deft handling. She laughed low and wickedly as he shrugged out of his clothes. Fleetingly she thought of Tyler, who loved and trusted her . . . Tyler. No! Tyler need not know. He wouldn't know . . . she thrust herself into Ashford's embrace, felt and reveled in the fire of his touch. His features blurred and she saw Aaron . . . felt Aaron . . . but no, those moments were gone. . . .

"Make me forget, Ashford," she whispered as his hands ran over her satin skin. "Work me well and make me forget . . . for a time."

"Pretty woman . . . you won't have to forget Marksbury. Within the week, he will be yours again!" growled Wade into her ear just as he poised himself to enter her.

She groaned and opened to receive him and his pact.

## Chapter 6

*As* Serena left Lady Melbourne's townhouse and approached
Zara Kane's hired coach, she had an odd feeling of wariness.
What was this? Nonsense, that was what! She chided herself. Zara
was soon to be like a sister to her, for within the next week that
was what they would be to one another. She must forget her last
meeting with Zara. Yes, they would start over. Zara was right,
this luncheon she planned was a perfect notion. So why this
awful feeling of dread?

Zara watched as Serena approached. It made her almost ill to
think she had lost Aaron to this soft fluff! Really, the woman
was nothing more. A wisp of a girl with no taste! Look at her
bonnet—a simple chip straw, and her spencer, indistinct in its
shade of blue . . . and then Zara found Serena's grey eyes.
Damn, but it was infuriating! Yes, she could see her Aaron, and
she would always think of Aaron as hers, falling into those deep
grey eyes. It made her nearly lose her composure. She smiled as
sweetly as she could. "I am so glad you could join me, Serena.
We have a great deal to discuss, you and I."

Serena's response was genuine. "Yes, so we have." It was an
honest and grave reply, though amiable. She could not help but
notice that Zara was looking her best in a wide-brimmed pink
silk bonnet. Its huge pink feather curled round the woman's ear.
Zara's dusky auburn curls peeped out teasingly and her blue eyes
were rich with color. She could see why Aaron had cared for
Zara. The woman was a striking beauty . . . but cold . . . why
did she receive this feeling of bitter hatred from Zara? It pervaded the air too sharply to be ignored. Oh, but stop, she told
herself. She was being fanciful. Serena steadied herself and

attempted a smile. Wasn't it Zara, after all, who'd requested this meeting, insisting they should be friends in light of the future?

"You must be so happy, Zara . . . Tyler tells me you love the sea and how much you both are looking forward to this voyage."

Zara eyed her sideways. "As to that, we three—Aaron, Tyler, and I—were great sailors as children. We often sailed my father's sloop in those days, but as to living in that heathen country . . ."

Serena laughed and it was a bubbly sound that went through Zara like a knife. She could imagine Aaron responding to that laugh.

" 'Tis no heathen country, Zara . . . and you will be going to New York, won't you? Quite a sophisticated city, I am told."

"Yes, well I shouldn't be surprised if it turns out to be amusing, but there is no reason why we must live there, after all . . . and once Tyler has had his fling, I daresay inside of this year, we shall be returning." She paused a moment, noticed that the coach had already reached the outskirts of the city, and then proceeded, "That is why it is so important we become friends . . . Tyler and Aaron have always been so close. . . ."

"You are, of course, quite right," said Serena, her hand moving impulsively to touch Zara's.

Zara had all to do to keep from jumping away. Serena's touch made her want to scream, to lash out, but no, she controlled herself. She mustn't be connected with the day's deed. . . .

Lady Bruney touched her husband's cheek affectionately as they stepped away from the orphanage they had just been visiting.

"You are a love," she said with a sigh, "but do you think we may enlist enough subscribers to this cause of ours?" She did not hear his assurances, for her thoughts were immediately snatched away by the sight that met her eyes. Her mouth fell open and she stood clutching her husband's arm so that he was constrained to object.

"Oh . . . sorry . . . but darling . . . do look there, do you see who is in that coach?"

"Eh?" He looked in the direction she had indicated and grunted.

"No, no, you don't understand, do you? That is Zara Kane and Serena! *In the same coach!*"

Evidently his lordship could not see what there was in this fact to astound. Impatiently she stamped her foot at him and delved into further conjecture as he led her to their waiting curricle. "But John . . . what are they doing together . . . and where are they going . . . and for that matter . . . what are they doing in a hired coach?"

"Shall I answer you in order?" he returned with a twinkle lighting up his eyes.

"Oh, do be serious! John . . . it is very odd!"

"As they are about to each have a Marksbury man, I don't see what is so very peculiar about their being in one another's company," he suggested idly as he sat back and motioned for his driver to turn the curricle about and return to London's center.

"Oh, for goodness' sake! You know as well as I do that Zara Kane wanted Aaron . . . that she loathes poor Serena." She shook her head. "And why should they be taking the Charing Cross Pike? Where are they going?"

"Perhaps they are visiting some of the Marksbury relatives together . . . for tea or some such nonsense?"

"No, no . . . Marksbury has no relatives just outside London . . . and oh John, I daresay I am being silly, but it strikes me as terribly strange. In fact, I have the shivers!"

His lordship of Bruney touched his lady. "Now, now, don't be a widgeon. There is nothing so very odd in two ladies taking a drive together to straighten out their . . . differences, is there?"

"Oh, do you think that is what it is?" said Lady Bruney, her brow clearing considerably.

"Indeed, I do."

Lady Bruney sighed. "You know, John, you will laugh at me, but I can't help thinking it would have been better for everyone concerned if Serena had married Wade Ashford and Zara had taken Aaron and not Tyler Marksbury."

"Do you, my love? I must disagree with you in this. I know you have a fondness for Wade, and indeed, if I didn't know more of him than you do, I too might find him an engaging rogue . . . but I think Miss Serena Parkes has done the right thing."

"Oh, I don't know. I have known Wade a long time, darling, and Serena could have been a turning point in his life." Then more thoughtfully, "she still may be that, and *not*, I fear . . . to the good!"

\* \* \*

Wade Ashford moved restlessly as he sat on his horse and waited. Beside him was a brute whose grisled face and broken teeth were only half hidden by the dark scarf and covering he wore. The day was a bright one and the trees were all the concealment they had from the road. It had to be done though and he couldn't trust the job to tobies. . . .

"Oi don't loikes this waiting, oi don't!" snapped the highwayman at Wade's side. "It ain't whot oi be used to, robbery in dayloight!" He shook his head. "It don't make no sense, it don't!"

"You are being paid well for your part in this and as long as you do as I have asked, no one shall get hurt, including ourselves!"

"That may be, but ye be a flash covey, whot da ye care for sech things?"

"Never mind! You just keep a sharp eye to the road."

"Aye—" He stopped short and cocked his head as they heard the sound of carriage wheels. It was a road that was scarcely traveled since no posting inns could be found along its badly rutted path, which was precisely the reason Ashford had instructed Zara to take her charge in its direction.

Wade pulled his dark silk scarf up and over his nose. His hat was angled low over his eyes and his gun was held in readiness. Damn, but he could already feel a swelling of bitter satisfaction surge through him. Before long Serena Parkes would be his bride and hell, he meant to make her rue the day she scorned his suit!

Inside the hired carriage, Serena sat frowning. She didn't like this. They were too far out of London and why such a terrible road? She had been joggled and tumbled over the roughest of bad thoroughfares and to what purpose? Why had they turned off the Charing Cross Pike? Just where was this country inn Zara was taking her to?

"Zara?" It was a hesitant sound, for Serena did not wish to offend now that they were attempting a friendship. However, she could not help herself. "I think this inn of yours is perhaps a good deal too far away. Why don't we leave it to an afternoon when Tyler and Aaron might join us?"

"Nonsense . . . and besides, we are almost there."

"Yes, but Aaron will be expecting me at Lady Melbourne's at three o'clock and faith . . . 'tis past one already."

"I am certain it won't be long and we needn't stay more than an hour or so. You will love the inn's gardens . . . we can take lemonade outside . . . don't worry, Serena." Zara was just beginning to feel some uneasiness. Soon, it would be soon. Oh God, would Aaron suspect her part in this? It didn't matter! This loathsome creature beside her would be Wade Ashford's bride. Aaron might no longer want her, but at least he wouldn't have Serena!

The postilion saw two highwaymen coming at him fast. What to do? He knew it would come to this! He had told Miss Kane at the outset that this was no direction to be taking. Flash mort! Look what she had gotten him into.

"Up!" growled one of the two highwaymen. "Hands away . . . that's right and don't even think it m'friend! That barking iron of yours won't do you any good as my comrade here has his gun leveled right at your head."

"Oi don't want no trouble, guv," breathed the driver.

"Good, then I shall relieve you of your pistol." Wade moved up in his stirrups and took hold of the heavy thing before he flung it into a nearby clump of bushes. "There . . . now, shall we see your cargo?" He went round, bent low over his saddle, and managed the carriage door. His smile beneath his mask was wide and his eyes were glinting with their changing lights. "Well, well . . . now just what have we here?" His voice came in drawling accents. "Out, my darlings . . . out so that I may have a better look at you. . . ."

At sixteen a boy has many dreams and for young Harry Harbootle, one of those dreams revolved round his father's farm. He meant to modernize it, improve it, build it up, and make it pay. Yes, by God, and he knew just how he was going to do that. It would take more than hard labor—it would take the application of his mind. With this plan he set out that day to visit with Farmer Wendell.

Mr. Wendell was a shrewd fellow, but there was something the Harbootles had that he wanted badly enough to take the edge off his bargaining power. Harry smiled to himself, for if Wendell only knew it, Tess was his for the taking. Aye, Harry's sister was all that Wendell thought about these days, but Harry wasn't just giving her away now that the year of their father's death was at an end. Oh no, if Wendell wanted her he was going to have to sell his used machinery at a reasonable price.

A frown came to Harry's eyes, for Tess did not want to wait. She wasn't in love with farmer Wendell, but she wanted to be comfortable all the rest of her life and she saw marriage to him as a way of obtaining that desire. She would wait, though. After their talk that morning she had promised.

Harry sat his unsaddled cob horse well as they plodded over the badly rutted road, and he turned off into the woods that would cut down the distance of the winding road by a good half-mile. When he was once again emerging onto the road, the sound of heavy horse's hooves and the dust they had left behind brought him up short and wary. "Now what was this?" Cautiously he moved forward and then he quickly darted into the woods again to watch a carriage with two ladies of quality alight at the order of a highwayman. "Coo . . ." he breathed and waited.

## Chapter 7

*Lady* Bruney waved her husband off and looked up to find Tyler coming down the road, his arm linked through his brother's. Both seemed in gay spirits. Ordinarily she would have smiled at them and motioned her driver to proceed on their way. Today she couldn't help herself. Meddlesome? It occurred to her that she was behaving in a manner most odd, but she couldn't help it.

"Aaron . . . Tyler?" she called brightly.

"Oh bother!" breathed Tyler beneath his breath. "I believe the Bruney summons us."

"Buck up, old boy, she isn't so very bad." Aaron grinned as he returned her salute and began steering his brother her way. "We'll just pay our respects and move on." They approached her carriage and Aaron took up her hand. "Hallo Sarah, and don't you look fetching in that pink fluff." He kissed her gloved hand as he spoke.

"La . . . but you must tell me how you managed it!" she exclaimed, getting right to the heart of the matter that held her curiosity.

"Must we indeed?" Tyler laughed, exchanging glances with his brother and taking her hand as well as making a mock bow.

Her brow went up imperiously. "Don't play off your boorish manners with me, Tyler! It won't fadge. I, of all people, know what a softie you are . . . now tell me!"

"Right, ma'am, and gladly," said Aaron at once, ". . . but what is it we must tell you?"

"Why—how you managed to get those two lovelies of yours together?"

This time the brothers looked long into one another's eyes.

However, as brightly as Aaron's green eyes filled with happy wonder, Tyler's blue eyes clouded over. Aaron grasped Lady Bruney's arm. "What do you mean . . . are we speaking of Zara and Serena?"

"Well of course . . . didn't you know? I have just seen them riding off together in a hired chaise."

"Riding off? Hired chaise?" returned Tyler somewhat sharply. "Where did they go?"

"Well, I don't know, but they were on the Charing Cross Pike . . . at least I saw their coach turn off onto that road." She shook her head, "You mean . . . you didn't know they had made it up?"

Aaron was overjoyed, for Zara was a guilt that weighed heavy on his mind. If she had finally accepted his Serena, why then they could be comfortable again. Tyler did not, however, see it this way. He knew Zara too well. Zara hated Serena . . . and Zara had not mentioned any intention of going off in Serena's company. A dark foreboding took strong hold of him and he began making his apologies to Lady Bruney.

"Why, that's right! They were to have lunch together today . . . why didn't I remember . . . Aaron." He turned to his brother. "Do you know, if we collect our horses, we can surprise them. . . ."

"Can we, old boy?" Aaron was surprised but he was also being pulled along and waving, to Lady Bruney's astonishment. Under his breath he said, "Slow down, Tyler . . . we were most rude to Sarah . . . taking off like that."

"Aaron, don't argue with me . . . we have got to get to Pall Mall and collect our horses. Thank God I hadn't sold mine yet. We are going to have to cover ground and will need fit animals!"

"But . . . Tyler," Aaron started, "what the devil is it? What is wrong?"

"Wrong? Damnation, brother, Serena and Zara . . . *together*! That is what's wrong!"

Zara watched with pleasure as Serena went weak with fear. It was with an effort that she kept the sneer from her face when Serena clutched for her hand. With a sharp curtness she disengaged herself.

"Stop it, Serena . . . just give them whatever they want," Zara snapped as they jumped lightly to the ground.

Serena pressed herself against the carriage doors as she heard the driver beg the tobies not to " 'urt the loidies none." She blinked with fright as she watched the darkly clad rider dismount and move towards her.

"My, my, a fine selection I have here," said the toby moving at her. His hand went out and played with one curl. As she cringed he felt a burning anger rush through him and he was snatching for her arm, whipping her up tightly, bringing her body up against his.

"Oh no," he hissed low in his throat, ". . . I don't mean to let you get away this time."

Serena's grey eyes opened wide because she thought she heard something familiar in his voice, in the glint of his eye, but how could this be? And what did he mean? Pacify him, humor him, that was it. "Please," she said softly, attempting a half-smile, "we don't mean to put up a fight. Indeed, we are in no position to do so. Could you just take whatever jewels we have on us and leave us be?"

He laughed harshly. "You don't understand, love! I mean to take the most precious jewel of all." With this he was bending and swiftly, unceremoniously hoisting her over his shoulder.

Serena screamed and he laughed all the louder. She attempted to pound at his back but found herself in a precarious situation and her efforts were inept and inadequate to the task. She wriggled and he slapped her on the rump. She felt the world whirling round in her brain. This could not be happening. All her life she had been pampered, petted, and bred to be a lady. Fine—what did a lady do in such a situation? At last, exhausted and frightened, she fainted. Wade threw her roughly over his horse's withers and mounted to take hold of his charge.

A moment later he was tipping his hat to Zara Kane and turning to charge down the country road. His toby accomplice would have to be paid off and then it was to the cottage where he would keep his prisoner overnight. In the morning? A simple but quite legal wedding. Again his laughter rang out and it was filled with exultation!

\*　　\*　　\*

"Whot the bloody 'ell?" breathed Harry Harbootle as he sat on his horse and wondered what he should do. He glanced towards Zara Kane and watched her shoot out and order her driver to turn the carriage about and head back for London. "Whot then, does the fancy mort leave t'other to go to the devil?" He shook his head and then, without a moment's hesitation and without sleuthing out his motives, he charged through the thicket of the wood, blazing a trail parallel to the road.

His cob horse was a sturdy beast and not more than fifteen hands, so it was well able to take him through the heart of the low hanging trees. As he caught up to the two hard-riding highwaymen, he was able to slow his animal to a jog. Jest whot was all this? Well, it was plain as pikestaff that the little slip of a maid was no match for her attacker. Aye, and whot's more, she was noble blood, she was. Mayhap there might be a reward in this. At least it would make up for the time he was losing.

Ashford pulled up and turned to his henchman. "This is where we part, my friend."

"Aye . . . if ye'll be handing over the blunt ye owe me, flash . . . thats jest whot oi'll be doing."

Ashford laughed, went into his pocket, and produced the gold coins, slapping them into the toby's hand with some force. "There, though I can't say you deserved it. You did no more than hold the driver at bay and I don't think he would have meddled . . . but never mind . . . I'm pleased enough with this day's work!" He watched the highwayman take a wooded path and disappear, and then he looked down on the limp form. She was small and delicate and so very helpless.

Serena stirred and groaned and he lifted her into a sitting position in front of him. His horse objected beneath him and he laughed and brought the nervous animal under hand.

"Ah Serena . . ." he whispered, "we don't have far to go."

She came back to consciousness and stared hard at his face before her hand went to her mouth and then pulled away at his scarf. "Wade!" It was an accusation.

"Yes, love . . . but we have no time for talk now." He urged his horse forward.

"Wade . . . what are you doing . . . why . . . why?"

That was all Harry Harbootle heard before he saw the rider turn off the road and take a narrow dirt trail. Hell, that was the old Wendell cottage the highwayman was heading for! The Wendells had abandoned it some years ago when they moved to the big farmhouse they lived in now.

Right then, whot next? Aye, take the road up to Charing Cross, that was the ticket. Fetch the magistrate . . . and he devoutly hoped the magistrate would believe him!

Exhilaration tinged with a shade of fear filled Zara Kane. Her driver whipped his horses over the rutted road and as she felt the carriage lurching with the speed she wanted to laugh. Serena was now Ashford's prize and Aaron would never have her! It was a victory indeed. Everything had gone as planned and now, now there was only the moment of explanation to face. Somehow she must make it turn out right. . . .

Even as she schemed, the sound of thundering hooves came to her ears. She held her breath. What was this? Instinct answered her and she bit her lip as her coach came to a sudden halt. Before she looked out her window, something inside told her what she would find. *No!* Oh God, she prayed, not when she was this close.

Tyler and Aaron Marksbury were jumping off their sweated horses, taking large, forceful steps her way. Aaron was pulling open her door, taking her by the wrist, and roughly yanking her to her feet and out of the carriage. Tyler was looking a cloud and not saying a word.

"Aaron . . . what do you mean by this . . . Tyler . . . see how your brother uses me!" She attempted to enlist Tyler's sympathy but she could see from his eyes that he knew what she had done.

"Where is she, Zara?" snapped Aaron. "I won't stand for any of your games, so quickly, where is she?"

The driver frowned and thought to answer at this point since the lady seemed reticent on the subject. He cleared his throat and attempted to gain some attention.

"S'cuse me, guv . . . but oi was jest on me way to the magistrate's in Kirkwell, oi was . . . to tell 'em, ye know . . . and mayhap now ye might be able to help and 'ave done wit it?"

"What in hell are you blabbering about?" thundered Tyler.

Aaron was looking at Zara's face and his lips were set hard. Again his voice slapped at her. "If you have harmed Serena—"

He was cut off by the sound of the driver's voice as it slashed through him. "Abducted she was," said the driver, shaking his head. "Odd that, fer they didn't bother wit anything else . . . didn't prig me ready . . . nor the lady's sparklers . . . no, it was off wit 'tother loidy . . . like as that was whot they came for. . . ."

Aaron was breathing hard as he took a step towards Zara, but Tyler took hold of his arm and his voice was sharp. "I will handle this, Aaron!"

"Will you? Then do it, or I swear Tyler . . . I won't be responsible for my actions!"

Tyler rounded on Zara. "Give it up . . . whatever you have done, give it up."

Her voice was a tumultuous breath of harshness. *"No!"* Her eyes snapped fiercely.

"Damn it, woman! What do you hope to gain?" Tyler had her arm and stopped her from moving away from him. "Aaron? Do you think Aaron would have you after this piece of folly?"

"What do I care for that? He won't have her . . . and that is all that matters now!".

Aaron was shoving his brother aside, taking Zara's shoulders, shaking her with a force that sent his hat flying, sent his white gold hair into wild profusion round his handsome head. His green eyes blazed as he accused, "Bitch! I may suffer over this, but Zara, I swear it, if Serena is harmed, you won't live to see my suffering! Now where is she?"

"Guess . . ." Her voice was low, full with spite. "Can't you guess? Who but myself would want her out of your hands?"

Tyler's heart sank but when he saw his brother raise his hand to Zara he stepped in between. "Aaron . . . no . . ." Then he was pulling Zara away, out of range, turning to her, his eyes pleading. "Zara . . . why? I thought . . . I thought when you agreed to marry me . . ."

She softened. She could see the pain in his pale blue eyes. "Tyler . . . this doesn't change anything between us"—she touched his cheek— "I needed to get back at him. this was a way. . . ."

"Tell him, Zara! Tell him what you have done with Serena." Tyler was pleading now.

"No, never."

Aaron was again stepping towards her menacingly and Tyler

again took a stand in between. "Out of my way, Tyler, for I mean to make her tell me, even if I have to spill her blood."

"I can't let you do that, Aaron."

Tyler wasn't put to the test of proving his warning. Instead, he and Aaron exchanged surprised glances when at that moment a scraggly youth on a cob horse stole the scene. Breathless and filled with the importance of his news, Harry Harbootle charged forward.

"Sirs! Sirs!"

Serena was a gentle soul. She was frightened by her present situation but there was an anguish behind the leer on Wade Ashford's countenance that drew out her compassion. Her voice was soft and only quietly reproving as she stood up to him and asked, "Wade . . . I don't understand . . . why?"

"Don't you?" He couldn't bear it when she looked at him with her grey eyes wide. He wanted her and that was all he would allow himself to feel. He moved forward and roughly took up her slender arms and yanked her into his embrace. "I have to have you, Serena! That is your answer!"

"But . . ." She tried to reason. It was all he allowed her for he was crushing her into his arms, up against his hard lean body. His lips bruised her own with the force of his emotions and she knew that no consideration for her would weigh with him now. Instinct instructed her to struggle, yet her character forbade her from violence. She could have kicked, screamed, fought at him, but she did not. She simply did not respond and it infuriated him to brutality.

"Feel! I want you to feel what I feel . . . raw passion, Serena, and don't tell me you aren't capable—"

"Oh, I am . . . but not for you," she answered softly.

"If you can feel it for *him* . . . damn it then, you will feel it for me." He had the collar of her gown in his grasp and was in one harsh, swift moment tearing it lengthwise and away from her.

Serena gasped and her hands flew to cover herself, but he was flinging the gown away, grabbing her wrists, dragging her towards the cot in the corner of the cottage. "Hell and fire, woman . . . I am going to make you want me when I'm done!"

"Wade . . . please . . . I beg of you—" Serena cried. All her dreams were being attacked, her future hurled into a sea of

46

flames. She had to stop him, but how? The room began to reel in beat with the heavy drumming in her ears. She couldn't bear his touch. It had to stop . . . stop . . . oh, Aaron . . .

He had thrown her onto the cot but even before he was on her he saw her black out and felt her go limp. "No . . . damn it, Serena, you can't escape me that way!" he shouted in high rage. He took up her shoulders and shook her into wakefulness. "Serena!" She would not stir. He looked round frantically and discovered a pitcher. He took four swift strides, had it, and went towards the water pump. A moment later he was splashing water onto her face.

She gasped and blinked as she opened her eyes to the water. Oh God! He was still here. She was still here. The nightmare was real and unending. . . .

He laughed boldly and bent over her, ignoring her pleading, her protests as his hands sought her breasts, as his mouth took the sweetness of her flesh.

Then all at once Wade Ashford felt himself flung up and away, felt his head meet the hard wood flooring with a resounding force that jolted his senses. He heard a low animal growl as he was caught by his lapels and brought mightily to his feet. Dizzy from the attack, he attempted to focus and saw before him Aaron Marksbury. His green eyes were like two bolts of flame. His lips were set in determined lines and his face read kill.

Savagely Aaron began pounding into Ashford. He only knew he wanted him dead. Nothing else mattered at that moment. He never felt his brother tug at him, demand that he release Ashford. Ashford had dared to touch Serena and Aaron had to obliterate him.

"Aaron—" It was Serena clutching her gown round her, begging him to hear her. "Stop . . . Aaron . . . don't."

"Damnation Aaron . . . think of Serena . . . of the scandal!" shouted Tyler.

Serena's hand was on Aaron's arm. He felt her touch and turned to encounter her eyes. All at once he was dropping Ashford and taking Serena into his arms, while both of them cried.

# Chapter 8

*Zara* Marksbury held her cloak tightly around her as she leaned over the poopdeck and contemplated the last few days she had spent in England. Hell! They had been hell and somehow she had risen up out of it and was now in purgatory. What had Byron written when he had left England? Ah yes, it so fitted her aching heart:

> *Tis done—and shivering in the gale*
> *The bark unfurls her snowy sail;*
> *And whistling o'er the bending mast,*
> *Loud sings on high the fresh'ning blast;*
> *And I must from this land be gone,*
> *Because I cannot love but one.*
>
> *And I will cross the whitening foam,*
> *And I will seek a foreign home;*
> *Till I forget a false fair face,*
> *I ne'er shall find a resting-place;*
> *My own dark thoughts I cannot shun,*
> *But ever love, and love but one.*
>
> *Twould soothe to take one lingering view,*
> *And bless thee in my last adieu; . . .*

Bless thee? She nearly cried out now in the anguish these memories dredged up. "*No*," she said quietly and shook her head. "Not I, Aaron Marksbury, not I. Ever will I curse you and yours and wish your life a hell!"

Now, here she was in this heathen country. It wasn't even

New York City. Nothing had gone right. The tail of a hurricane had struck and they had been diverted from their original course. The captain had thought it best to pull into Sag Harbor. She sighed with resignation and the depression brought on by the last few tedious days. All around her the sailors were at their various tasks and she watched them absently. So much had passed during what seemed more like a cavity in time than reality. Tyler. Thank God for Tyler. He had supported her throughout and in his own way he had understood as no other could.

Aaron was relegated to another domain, surrounded by bitterness and undying passion. Serena. The name delved deep and raked up hatred, resentment, and dark desires for revenge. Wade Ashford. Contempt. Had he been quicker, smarter . . . but that was over.

America! Oh faith! England was left behind. She stared at the unfamiliar surroundings of her new country and felt a deluge of depression overtake her. She detested the sight of the rugged land and its wild people. Look at them! The women . . . what were they wearing? Dowds, every last one! She needed to scream her vexation. This was not what she wanted, not what she planned. . . .

Revenge. The thought that one day she would have her revenge eased some of her suffering, calmed her. She would make Aaron bleed . . . oh yes, in some way.

She looked round then at the sound of approaching footsteps. Tyler. Here he came with that silly lovesick look lighting up his blue eyes . . . blue, not green like Aaron's . . . never mind! Poor Tyler, he was really just a babe. No more than two years older than she was, but he was a friend. Damn, but she needed more than that and his touch did nothing for her. *nothing!*

Wade Ashford meandered into White's with audacious boldness. Six weeks had passed since the day he had lost his pride and Serena to Aaron Marksbury. No one knew. Aaron and Tyler had decided it would best serve Serena to keep things quiet . . .

He had retired to his country estate to heal his wounds, but now he was back and he meant, in slow degrees, to have his ounce of blood. He strolled into the card room, nodded to passing acquaintances, and stopped to watch Aaron Marksbury's happy countenance. Hatred welled inside him. How could he bear it? He wanted to destroy . . . but no, not in the conventional way. That would be too easy. He was a patient man, and could bide his time.

What was this? What was Marksbury at now? Good God! The man was a fool! Would he overextend himself? Was this the moment Wade had been looking for?

"Egad, Aaron!" cried Lord Wembly, "you can't mean to back the black man!"

"And why in thunder should I not?" demanded Aaron amicably. "I have got five hundred little gold guineas that say I do!" He looked up and found Ashford contemplating him. He sucked in his breath and looked away. Men crowded in and around Aaron and Wembly.

"He don't stand a chance against Stone and well you know it!" exclaimed Wembly.

"How can you say so? If I knew that, I wouldn't be willing to put up the blunt, now would I?" returned Aaron on a friendly laugh. "He'll beat Stone . . . depend upon it!"

"You must think this black extraordinary," said Ashford quietly.

The room's buzzing stopped on the instant. Though no one knew for sure, they had vague notions about the rift between Marksbury and Ashford. They felt the hostility and waited for its outcome.

Aaron squared up and glared. "I have watched the black and I think he is going to win."

"Right then, I'll take you on that wager . . . but let us make it interesting, shall we?"

Aaron frowned darkly. He had been keeping his bride in style by betting wisely and winning more than he lost. He was already dipping deep by betting the five hundred he had offered up as a wager.

"What did you have in mind?" he snapped.

"You know what I want, what I will always want." It was a quiet hiss.

Hell and fire! The man needed blood letting! He had to be careful. No hint of Serena's name must come into this. Even so, Aaron took, without realizing it, an ominous step forward. Wembly held him in check. "Damn your eyes!" spat Aaron on a low note.

Ashford sneered. His hazel eyes glittered as he surveyed the reaction of his peers. They were shocked, thrilled, surprised, expectant. They were hoping it would come up. They wanted to hear Serena's name, see a challenge issued. He felt a wave of disdain shoot right through him. With his disgust with mankind, he felt justified.

"For wishing to back Stone?" he said baitingly.

"What is your wager?" returned Aaron harshly.

"Not cash . . . no, how very dull . . . let us say instead . . . a piece of property . . . perhaps your townhouse?" Ashford said on a low, sweet note.

Aaron contemplated this in the space of a moment. He had managed to maintain Serena in London. It was a small townhouse but it served them well and she loved it. "Against what, Ashford?"

"It seems to me when we were up at Cambridge that you had a love of the sea." He thought about this. ". . . weren't you one of the unholy three always vanishing with Captain Pierce's sloop?"

Youth recalled nearly brought a smile to Aaron's lips. Ashford's face banished it. "So?" He shook his head. "What has that to do—?"

"I have a yacht I never use that is worth a tidy sum. What do you say? My yacht against your townhouse?" He didn't want Aaron's house. He wanted to break him. He wanted Serena to find herself married to a penniless gambler. He wanted her to regret . . .

"Done!" declared Aaron. He couldn't lose. He had watched the black's science. The man had more than brawn, he had quick technique. He had watched Stone and the old pugilist was no match for the black. He would win. He had to win.

Tyler was as excited as a babe receiving his first shiny toy as he led his wife down the long thousand-foot wharf, but Zara was repelled by it all. The scent of whale oil clung to the air, infiltrated the senses and repulsed her. Everywhere men were busy with the rush of their industry. Here were the warehouses, the oil cellars, the cooperages, and the smithies. Every single cap-covered male head moved purposely as they attended to their chores. Seamen were a dense mangle as they worked the ships alongside the wharf.

The hotel was pointed out to them and they walked the short distance to Main Street. There stood the village's American Hotel, a building of weathered brick ornamented by gothic columns and a covered porch.

Zara grumbled ill-naturedly as she looked over the basic structure and advised her husband that she wouldn't set foot in it, let alone sleep there. He laughed and stroked her as he pulled her along. "It's here or the street, my love."

So it was that she allowed Tyler to lead her within, where they were greeted cordially by the clerk. Rooms were procured for their night's stay, for they meant to hire a poste chaise to take them to New York in the morning. However, Zara became increasingly obstinate when they were told there would be a fifteen-minute wait until their rooms were readied.

"Bother!" snapped Zara, out of temper and nearly out of control. "Well then, show us to your private parlor, we'll take tea."

"I am very sorry," apologized the clerk, who was somewhat overwhelmed by Zara's queenly air. "Our only private parlor has been bespoken already." He felt himself go hot with embarrassment for the woman looked as though he had slapped her.

"Drat!" Zara breathed, incensed. She turned to her husband. "Tyler, do something!"

"Dearest—" He attempted to soothe her nerves.

She cut him off sharply for she would not be humored, "Tyler, I am tired and would like a cup of tea . . . *now*!"

"But madam . . . I should be happy to have a tray brought to you at once," offered the young clerk.

"Oh? And where would you have me served?" she snapped on a sardonic note. "Here? In your lobby?"

"Dearest," attempted Tyler on an assuaging line, "why don't I have you seated comfortably—"

"Tyler!" she cut in, "I want my room and I want it now!"

Tyler Marksbury turned to the clerk. "Am I to understand that the only place of quiet you have available has been already occupied?"

"Well no . . . but Captain Trent said that he would be here at five and it's nearly that now—"

"So, the private parlor is available!" Zara closed in. "Show us there at once!'' At which point she turned and received her first impression of Captain Arthur Trent.

Striking. Her eyes clicked with interest and it rushed through her senses that this was a tall, broad-shouldered, and ruggedly good-looking man. He was dressed in a careless fashion, though his garb depicted his seafaring rank. She felt his eyes sweep over her and she stiffened as he smiled.

''Is there some trouble here, Saunders?'' Captain Trent inquired easily.

Saunders looked at Captain Trent with relief. The captain was one of the hotel's regular boarders. Being a man of some means and authority, he would know best how to deal with this Englishwoman. ''You see, captain,'' started the harassed clerk, ''Mr. and Mrs. Marksbury have just arrived and their room is presently being prepared for them, but . . . they wished to retire to our private parlor for refreshments and I was attempting to explain—''

''Ah, I see,'' said the captain, cutting him off and turning to smile amicably at Tyler Marksbury. He could see very well that the attractive Englishwoman was in a state and he took pity on her husband. ''Sir, won't you and your wife join me in the parlor? There is ample space for us all.''

Tyler Marksbury flushed. ''I take it, then, that you are Captain Trent, and while I do thank you, I must decline. I am certain you reserved the room to be private. . . .'' He felt his wife's eyes burn through him and inwardly he winced.

''Nonsense. I only hope you won't find my conversation tedious, for I am due there for a business matter,'' said Trent graciously, including Mrs. Marksbury in his smile. He had by now assimilated the fact that Zara Marksbury was not only a dark-haired, blue-eyed beauty, but that she was something of a vixen. He felt ready sympathy towards Marksbury. It was inevitable, or perhaps it was fate that Tyler would give in.

Some hours later at dinner, the banker, young Jim Falkes, was shaking his head over Captain Trent's proposal.

''I don't know, Arthur.''

''How can you say no to me, Jim? Haven't you heard what I have been saying?'' returned Captain Trent impatiently. ''I mean to add three more whalers to my line. I have thoroughly investigated the temper of our times and I tell you, lad, I believe whalers will pay off handsomely.''

Again Jim Falkes shook his head. ''That may be so, but I don't know that you need another three.''

''The two that I have now aren't enough. Good God, man! Sometimes they are out to sea seven months at a time. When I have two fully rigged whaleships out that long the turnover isn't enough, but think what returns you'll get on your loan if I have well-timed vessels coming in, one after the other . . . *think*, Jim!''

''He can't.'' It was Zara's voice. ''He is a banker and as such has no imagination. They deal in facts, realities, not in dreams. My husband however . . . he has the cash to invest and the inclination to dream.'' She turned to Tyler. ''Isn't that so, my love?''

Tyler Marksbury moved eagerly in his chair and sat forward. He had been listening to Arthur Trent intently for the last hour. Zara had realized his interest. He touched her hand as he spoke. ''Zara has been reading my mind.''

''What are you saying?'' returned the captain, frowning as he turned to contemplate this new turn of events.

''Why, only that we don't need Mr. Falkes here. We—you and I—could, if we wanted to, build a small fleet of whalers.''

Trent fell upon Marksbury at once, and as the two men discussed, debated, and explored, Zara watched them.

She had been sitting quietly all evening, watching Arthur Trent. She knew nothing of the whaling industry. Less did she know or care about the figures they were tossing about. She only knew that she wanted more of Captain Trent. She had glanced at Tyler. He was excited and speaking intelligently about the big ships. This would be a wise investment. Yes, she was quite pleased.

A black bruiser faced the champion pugilist Stone Hurst in the final round. Stone was faring poorly, for Aaron was correct in saying that the black knew his science. He blocked, he hooked a heavy right, and he danced in a way Stone had never seen. The champion stood bloodied, breathless, and dazed as the black landed him a final blow.

The shouts, the cheers, the cries of disbelief went round in deafening display as Aaron turned to find Ashford standing in angry, mute incredulity. He had lost again. Wade Ashford's wrath seethed and burned in his brain. Aaron had bettered him again! He didn't give a fig about his yacht. He never used it, but losing once more to Marksbury was almost more than he could bear. All the old resolves were renewed with vigor, and as he signed over his sailing vessel he swore silently once more to be revenged.

# Chapter 9

*Captain* Trent watched as his hard-working, muscular men toiled away at the first of the new whalers he had put into production. He bellowed out his orders with enthusiastic glee and his dark eyes were lit with excitement.

"Do you see Zara . . . can you see her take shape . . . take form?"

Zara saw a great deal through his eyes. She was beginning to love the might of this new world she had plunged herself into. Power. It was all around her and she felt a part of it.

"The keel, Zara, is the backbone . . . the focus of the ship. She'll take her strength from the keel."

"Yes, Arthur, I see," she said quietly. She watched him move and again felt the growing need, the irrepressible hunger. She found the way his greying dark hair fell to his neck nearly hypnotic and restrained herself from reaching up to touch it.

His eyes were shaded by his thick dark brows, by his curling black lashes, but Zara knew something of the passion in their depths. His passions? One—more than anything, more than anyone—was his son, his Darrow, his Dare.

The eight-year-old boy held this big man's heart as no other could—running amok through the timber, mimicking his father, laughing with the laborers and seamen. Yes, Darrow filled his father's eyes and when it was not Darrow, it was the sea. Those were Arthur Trent's passions; he was a widower and that third love of his was gone.

Two years. The thought flitted through his head as he caught Zara's hand and led her along to better view his creation, his wondrous design. Two years he had been a widower. Out of the corner of his eye he could see Zara's dusky short waves flying in the wind, freely, wildly, and he checked his thoughts. He turned and caught her expression as she swayed towards him. Damn but he wanted her, was drawn to her, and it was good to have her at his side, listening, admiring. . . .

Her dark blue eyes sparkled at him. "It's marvelous seeing your model come to life. Oh, Arthur, I am so excited . . . what shall you call her?"

"Why, what else but the *Zara Sail*," he answered at once.

She squeezed his hand. "May she bring us luck."

"She will. Ah, Zara . . . do you feel it?" he asked suddenly as his eyes drank in the vision of what was to be.

"Not as you do, Arthur," she answered softly.

"She is a complex being. Every line in her forest rigging is a strength or a weakness. Every angle, every curve in her hull has something to say about the ship's way with the sea. This keel, this is the center of it all." He sighed and avoided her eyes. "Tyler should be here . . . it's his ship too." He moved abruptly away from her. He liked Tyler. What was he doing, wanting this woman, his partner's wife? He was a cad. It was something that stuck deep in his conscience, because at heart Arthur Trent was a good man.

She laughed lightly. "You know Tyler has no understanding of ship building. He is enjoying overseeing the building of our estates. They will be beautiful . . . our two houses, side by side." She glanced provocatively up at him.

"Aye. Tyler doesn't take to the sea, but he'll do well for us at home. That man of yours is as sharp as any blade when it comes to dealing!"

Darrow was waving to them. She touched Arthur's arm to bring his attention to the boy and felt a shooting bolt of excitement rush through her. He felt it too. She could tell by the way he looked, by the way he breathed. She didn't love him. There wasn't anything of that left in her heart, but she wanted him.

"Zara . . ." he started. He could feel his body tremble. What was he going to do? He needed to caress her body, feel it against his own. He couldn't say more than her name and then there was Darrow calling him away.

"Papa?" Darrow had his mother's Irish blue eyes, bold and rich with expression. He was eight years old and already an opinionated little devil. He adored his father, he was fond of Tyler, and just a bit infatuated with Zara. All very confusing emotions at his age, for he was also aware of things beyond his ken. He spent a great deal of time with the seamen and was subject to overhearing their jests, their discussions, and their flirtations with the passing women.

He could see that Zara and his father were a bit closer than they should be. Never mind—they were adults, they knew best. It was what he told himself but he did still feel guilt when he thought of Tyler. "Papa," he repeated, out of breath, for he had scampered up the steep hill. "Come quick . . . they are out of scarf joints."

"Out of scarf joints? Impossible, lad."

"That's what I told them," the boy said as he dragged his father along, "but they can't find them."

Zara laughed and found Dare taking up her other hand. Together they went to investigate and again she met Arthur Trent's eyes—this time in mutual amusement—and she knew it would be soon. Ah yes, he had the look.


While Sag Harbor, Long Island rocked with the union of Tyler Marksbury and Captain Arthur Trent, many changes were taking place in Aaron and Serena's lives, the first being the death of Serena's mother. Serena's parents had lived comfortably in their country cottage just outside of Rye, overlooking the English Channel, and title of this cottage as well as a small living came into Aaron's hands through Serena's inheritance. They took on the quiet life, but while Aaron was mindlessly in love with his wife, he found he needed more than their happy home offered. He needed the pitch and fever of London. He needed the gambling that had been a source of income for him, that he truly enjoyed. He sat pondering this problem in the small but cozy study of the cottage and Serena's delicate brows drew together as she leaned over to touch his hand, "Aaron . . . you regret selling the townhouse, don't you?"

"Eh? Oh, a bit, but never mind, at least we have the yacht. It's too bad you don't enjoy the sea, darling. I do wish you would come out with me more often for a sail," he said wistfully.

She sighed. "You know it makes me ill."

"Odd that. I mean . . . with you living by the Channel most of your sweet life." he tweaked her nose affectionately.

She put up her chin. "As to that, my fine sir, I lived in the heart of Romney Marsh, surrounded by smugglers, but that didn't make me one of them!"

His green eyes clicked with interest. "Smugglers, you say? I rather thought that passion wore off after Waterloo."

"Ha! Why, the Marsh still has its *gentlemen*. Never say you haven't heard of the Aldington gang?"

"No . . . can't say as I have," he answered on a grin. "Who may they be?" He was enjoying the roundness of her grey eyes, the excitement in her voice.

"Aaron! Why . . . there hasn't been such a dangerous pack of scoundrels since the Hawkhurst clan. Faith—everyone knows about the Aldington gang."

"Well, I don't, so tell me." He put his arm round her and drew her close.

"Their cargo is, I think, for the most part brandy, though I've heard they deal in tea and tobacco as well, not to mention some very fine lace. In fact, Mama told me that Papa was moved once for reasons I have never understood—to lend them his aid and they left Mama yards and yards of the finest lace that I have ever seen in or out of a customs house!"

He laughed. "Why Serena, you surprise me. Now, just how did your father help these blackguards?"

"Oh, but we in the marsh don't think of them quite as blackguards." She frowned over the problem.

"Don't you?" He was amused by her contradictions.

She wrinkled her nose. "I can't think why, for they are a terrible set, really. Papa used to say men like the Aldington crew existed because of the way our seamen were so brutally used when the press gangs came round. He said it was the press gangs that squeezed the law out of our marsh riders."

Again Aaron chuckled, but he pursued. "Yes, I can well understand that, but Serena . . . *how* did your father help them?"

She was pleased enough to entice him out of his moodiness and she lowered her voice to a whisper lest the servants overhear.

"We have a secret door in our underground storage room." She allowed her eyes to convey that this was an extremely thrilling circumstance.

"A secret door?" He felt a boyish sensation of excitement touch him.

"Hmmm, yes. It goes underground, you see, to a cave that is halfway up the cliffside. Papa let them store their kegs there once when the dragoons were hot in pursuit."

"Why Serena, you astound me! Show me this cellar door at once!"

She frowned. "Oh dear, the thing is, Aaron, that I was never quite sure where it was."

"Come on then and we'll find it!" he announced in some high glee as he took up her hand.

Off they went to the storage room below ground level and discovered an amazing quantity of empty barrels, cobwebs, old and damp-ridden articles of antiquity, but nothing could they find of a cellar door.

Serena sighed and left him to continue the search, for she was weary of it. This he did by plopping himself into a thinking position on a discarded Windsor chair. His eyes scanned the room and came to rest on the fireplace for no other reason than it was directly in front of him. A fireplace. In the cellar? Odd that, but then if the house dated back the four hundred years Serena insisted that it had to its credit, perhaps . . .? Well, well? He stood up. Certainly the house's Tudor facade marked the habits of that period. And then he recalled reading about the hiding places in such old cottages and how so very often they were near the fireplace.

With a rush of anticipation he moved quickly across the dimly lit room and put down his branch of candles. Wine racks and wooden crates were hurriedly heaved out of his way and there he stood, staring at the ancient, weathered, and undersized panel he had uncovered. He opened this easily and with an intake of breath he shoved a candelabrum into the dark hole. "Egad!" he hissed in excitement, "true . . . it's really true."

After a moment he was taking the stairs and rushing towards his wife, his voice as vibrant as a youth's. "Serena! I say, Serena!"

Five months had passed since the *Zara Sail* had first been started. Sag Harbor buzzed with the activity this had created. Blacksmiths hummed as they prepared the harpoons that would be needed. Blockmakers smiled as they made the pullies for the rigging. Coopers went about in happy glee as they prepared the barrels that would be needed, and masons drew up plans for the decking.

Already they had seen the arrival of one of Captain Trent's whalers. It had come into dock heavily laden with whale oil and whalebone and had landed the company of Marksbury and Trent a hefty profit. This set the oil refinery into motion in the small town. All these things kept Sag Harbor's men employed and fed and therefore well pleased with the new company of Marksbury and Trent.

Tyler rarely visited the shipyard, but the day was cool, crisp, and inviting so he set out on his expedition with some enthusiasm. Sweet autumn filled the breeze and touched the salt air gently. Tyler had an illustration of the inner workings of the whaler in hand, and, curious about its actual design, made his way to the *Zara Sail*. Well, he thought as he stood and gazed at the vessel, here she is. A ship. His first. Three masted, nearly three-hundred tons and built to take five whaleboats, thirty-six men, and a three-year voyage if need be. It was impressive.

The hatch coamings had been fitted, the *dogs* had been driven into the beams, and the pine planking had been tightly sprung into place. She was ready for the hot tar!

Tyler could hear the peculiar ring of the caulker's mallet as he made his way through the ship. Such a sound it made. What had Zara called it? Music, ship music. Indeed, so it was. He glanced up the hill and saw his wife. Her short and dusky curls were blowing freely in the wind. Her muslin gown was whipping round her trim figure. She looked happy. And why not? She was in love again. Not with himself, he knew that. It was Arthur. It was his partner, his friend. He could see it, feel it, and it hurt so much more than he thought possible. He turned away. This was not something he could easily contemplate, dissect, and rationalize. He worshipped Zara. There was no reason in the world he should. She was selfish, egotistical, loose moraled, and she was a wonder. Yes, she was his wonder, his heart, and so she would always be to him.

Her laughter thrilled him, even more so when he knew he had brought it on. So he worked to make her smile and thought it all worthwhile when that smile rested on his face. Her waywardness, even her whims—all of them he held to be the acts of a spoiled child—more often amused than annoyed him. He loved everything about her, everything! The way she would suddenly kiss him and, oh yes, she would kiss him and make love to him with an ardor that nearly always convinced him that she cared. In spite of the fact that he was nearly sure she had become his partner's mistress, she never withheld herself from him. She was as passionate a bed partner as she had been in the beginning. What could he do? He loved her.

He moved absently among the workers. His mind warred with his problem. Would she end up leaving him? He couldn't bear it if she were to go. He would rather she went on having Trent and remaining here with him. A perfect little *ménage à trois*. And the thing was that he admired Arthur Trent and adored Trent's rambunctious son, Darrow. So, how to handle this?

As these questions hovered about his head, blurred his vision, troubled his heart, he didn't see that something had gone wrong on the open deck above him. He didn't see the hot tar pit's footing had broken loose, that it was toppling over and that *he was just in its path*!

Zara looked down the hill and discovered her husband going on board the *Zara Sail*. "Look, Arthur . . . there is Tyler. Let's go down and give him a tour. He would like that."

Trent was ever surprised by Zara. She was like no other woman he had ever known. How she handled her infidelity was something that always set him back. Only an hour ago she had lain in his arms, touching him, loving him. What sort of woman was this? How did she manage to look Tyler in the eye? He knew damn well *he* was having a hard enough time of it!

"Why don't you go on, Zara. I want to ride into the village and see if my shipment of oakum has come in yet."

She pouted. "Very well, but I think you should want to go over the ship with your partner."

He looked at her a long moment but refrained from giving her the first answer that flew to his lips. "You know how I feel about Tyler. He is a good man and I respect his ability to deal with our suppliers—a surprising thing, considering his youth and his aristocratic background."

"What does that mean?" she returned in some surprise. "A

nobleman is brought up to handle his own kind as well as his inferiors!"

Trent laughed. "Always the grand duchess." He flicked her nose. "I have no doubt of that, but trade was a forbidden thing to a nobleman in England . . . is so still, in fact. You mustn't forget my grandfather was a mighty member of the *haut ton* of London. I have heard the rules mentioned often enough."

She changed the subject and brought it to what interested her most. "Shall I see you later . . . at dinner?" In reality she was making a demand, not asking a question.

He knew it and it was what he liked least about her. For contrariness, he shook his head. "I think not. I want to run over to Sawyers and set up the list of seamen we need for the *Sea Horse*'s next voyage. She'll be ready to go in a few days."

She glared at him for a brief moment. Her ego felt slighted, not her heart. Zara's heart had been broken by Aaron Marksbury and its pieces were buried deep. Tyler was wrong in thinking she was in love. It was no such thing. She shrugged to display her indifference and moved away from him, down the hill without another word.

Arthur Trent watched her. A quick thought flashed through his mind. Better to back away? Yes, but oh how he loved the feel of her passionate body, the way she moved beneath him, atop him, the way she had of teasing him into a frenzy of desire. Zara filled a void in his life. There would never be another who could take the place of his darling Molly, but Molly was gone and he would never remarry. So here was Zara. A feminine light in his life, in Darrow's life, for the boy seemed quite taken with Zara Marksbury. It was always "Zara . . . Zara . . . and Zara" on the boy's lips.

What to do? An interesting question with no easy answer. And then a small voice at his back called his name.

"Papa . . . come on then!" It was Darrow, beaming wide.

Zara waved her hand and attempted to get her husband's attention, but he seemed in another world and didn't see her. She puzzled. Poor Tyler. Did he know? She tried desperately to keep her infidelity from him. Not because she was afraid of repercussions because, indeed, she wasn't. In truth, she had no desire to hurt him.

She was helped on board by one of the seamen and condescended to throw a complimentary jest to some of the masons as she made her way across the unfinished deck towards her husband. A sudden scuffling sound of horror on the poopdeck above caught her attention and her hand flew to her mouth. The large cast-iron pot that held the bubbling tar was tilting, shifting, and she could feel her body go rigid as she realized that Tyler was directly in its path!

Without thinking, without feeling, without a moment's hesitation she was moving. She screamed his name and dove at him. He turned with a look of amazement and received her barreling into his chest. They hit the rail, tumbled and rolled. Zara held fast to his arm, tugging at him, pulling him out of harm's way as the tar came sizzling, pouring, steaming where they had been only a moment ago!

She was up in a thrice, hurling abuse at the men above, taking command in her indomitable manner. "What in thunder are you fools doing up there? Why wasn't that pot secured? Damn you all! I won't have such carelessness on our ship!"

Tyler righted himself and touched her arm gently. "Zara . . ." His voice was full with emotion, gentle with wonder. Zara had thrown herself into danger to save his life. She could have left him where he stood. She could have been his widow, his beneficiary, once again the ruler of her accounts, her life. He thought he knew her—but did he?

"Oh, my darling," she said at once, taking his embrace. She could see some of the hot tar covered his boots, had splattered up onto his pants legs and her own gown. "Are you alright? Come . . . let's go home." She was in full command.

He was touched by her genuine concern. The full impact of what had just transpired had not been absorbed yet but he felt an engulfing emotion cause tears to well up in his eyes and constrict his throat. He was unable to speak as she took over and led him away to their waiting carriage. There she took up the reins. He made no objection. "Oh Zara," he breathed suddenly, "you do care for me."

"Well, of course I care, Tyler. What a very odd thing to say."

He smiled but there was a sadness in his eyes as he asked on a meek note, "Then . . . you won't leave me?"

She stopped the carriage and turned full to him. "Tyler Marksbury, what maggot have you in your head?"

"I . . . you see, I know how you feel about Arthur . . . I can't say as I blame you." Had he no pride? He turned away. He had lost his pride when he gave her his heart so long ago.

She took his hand. "I don't love Arthur and what is more, I never shall. He is amusing . . . only that. Tyler, listen to me. You have something no other man shall ever have from me."

"And what is that, my dear?"

"My friendship, my trust. Whatever I become, whatever I do, I shall always be a faithful, loyal friend to you. I offered my heart to your brother and when he took it . . . he destroyed it for any other . . . but all else is yours, only yours, Tyler. Leave you? No, my pet, I shan't leave you."

He kissed her hand fervently. "Will it be enough for you, Zara?"

She drew on air. "In the end, Tyler, that is all one human being can give to another . . . friendship." She touched his cheek. "Don't work yourself up over my indiscretions . . . they are nothing next to what we share . . . a past, a future . . . Tyler . . . we laugh together. We smile across a room at one another and know what is in each other's mind."

He buried his head in her shoulder. Perhaps now was the moment to bring it up again. He kissed her neck, her ears, and heard her low chuckle. "Zara . . . I want a child," he whispered.

It was a small price to make him happy. "Do you, my love?"

"You know that I do . . . Zara?"

"Yes, I know that you do . . . and I suppose that time has come. . . ."


"That's a lad," said Aaron Marksbury as he shoved a few coins into Jim Lyons's damp hands. "Go on now . . . get yourself home and out of sight. That was the last of the kegs." Aaron stood and waited and young Jim hurried out of sight. He watched as the youth made his hasty way down the dark cliffside to the beach below. Damn! but they had done it! They had actually accomplished a successful crossing! He turned with his candle and made his way along the passageway to the dark hidden door that would lead to the stairs and eventually to their cellar. This attained, he stood for a long moment and breathed a heavy but satisfied sigh. Home. It was good to be home, but Serena . . . oh Lord, what would Serena say?

This was a question that he found answered all too soon for his comfort. He made his way to their bedroom and there he stood on the threshold. Serena sat on the windowseat, tapping her fingers against the pane. She turned round sharply when she heard him and her grey eyes glinted as she opened her arms and went careening across.

"Aaron," she cried as she flung herself against him. Then more softly, reproachfully, "Aaron . . ."

"Serena love, what are you doing still up?" He bent and tweaked her nose.

She put up a brow. "The fire was nearly out. I . . . I got up to stir the embers and noticed you were still not home. Oh Aaron, I have not seen you since yesterday morning."

"Dearest love . . . what is this?" he chided. "I told you that I was going over to Calais . . . that I might wait for the tide to be with me before I returned."

"Yes, you told me." She turned from him then and said in a low voice, "I went for a walk earlier this evening . . . along that stretch of beach." She could almost feel him stiffen. "That's right . . . you remember . . . that spot I love so well. Aaron, do you know what I saw?"

"Serena—" he started.

She cut in at once. "I saw my husband captaining a question-able group of ruffians. Do you know what they were doing? Why, of course, what any gentleman with a pack of scoundrels does on a night in Romney Marsh—hauling wooden kegs which I must assume were filled with French brandy and which, I might add, I am quite certain did not first go through the custom house." She stopped and glared at him.

"Serena . . ." He reached for her.

She moved out of his hold. "We have a customs house in Rye, you know. If you wanted to bring French brandy back with you from Calais, you could have done so without breaking the law."

"Serena . . . don't."

"Oh, of course, I was forgetting, that wouldn't quite meet with your standards of excitement, now would it?"

"Serena . . . please." He tried. What seemed a profitable,

thrilling adventure had been reduced into a shameful crime. He felt himself humbled. He adored his Serena and she was finding him worthless.

Serena saw him dashed and went into his arms at once, her anger beaten into concern. She wanted him to be happy! But this? What could she do about this?

If he had married Zara he would have been in London with horses, gambling, and all that a gentleman enjoys. If he had married Zara he would be riding to hounds, attending routs, and boxing with all the bucks at Jackson's. Now all he had was this cottage, the yacht, and a pile of debts. It was her fault and she felt it. "Aaron, I . . . I am so sorry."

He looked at her full and then took her roughly into his arms. "Sorry? Why are *you* sorry?"

"You should have married Zara Kane . . . you would have been . . . so much better off." She started to sob. "You . . . wouldn't have to resort to . . . to *smuggling*."

He threw back his head and laughed suddenly. "Silly peagoose! I think I was made for smuggling. I've always been something of a sailor, and with the yacht and living in the midst of the Aldington gang it was inevitable that I should end up as one of them." He was teasing now, but she looked sharply at him and there was genuine fright in her eyes.

"No . . . oh no, Aaron . . . never say you are traveling with their set."

He chuckled and flicked her nose. "No, I haven't that much ambition." He sat her down on the bed. "Look Serena . . . I made a trip to Calais, picked up a few kegs of brandy . . . on which I shall make a handsome profit."

"You won't do it again?" she begged.

"Not often. I do promise that . . . I won't do it often." He kissed her nose and then her lips. His kiss became more insistent, more purposeful, and as his hand pulled away her nightdress, it occurred to him that Serena needed a baby to occupy her time. That was it . . . *a baby!*

# Part
# Two

*One fatal remembrance—one sorrow that throws*
*Its bleak shade alike o'er our joys and our woes—*
*To which Life nothing darker nor brighter can bring,*
*For which joy hath no balm—and affliction no string.*

—Thomas Moore

## 1843

## Chapter 1

*On* a cliff's edge, mesmerized by the glory of the sea, touched by its mysterious beauty, unaware of her own, stood Silkaline Marksbury.

The storm had whipped up suddenly, swiftly, and her gold-flecked, gray eyes scanned the rising breakers before her hand went to her forehead in deepening concern. Where was he? He should have been back hours ago! The early signs of the gale were already moving in threatening blasts. The sea was foaming in its rage, the wind was taking her unhampered waist-length hair of white-gold and slapping it around her neck. Her dark wool cloak was wrapped around her tightly, but even so, the swirling gusts pulled at it and thundered at her delicate figure.

Her father had been due in from Calais some time ago. Had he decided to stay the night in France? Had he suspected foul weather? She cast this consideration aside. No, he wouldn't leave her to Wade Ashford another day! He had to return this day and satisfy Ashford's note or they would lose their vessel, their cottage . . . oh faith, where was he?

She inspected the heavens with a sinking heart. The quiet grey of the morning had turned into a blustering mass of darkness and already she could feel the rains coming. It would be worse, so much worse in the Channel. What to do? Go back to the cottage and wait. She couldn't . . . she just couldn't. It was here she had always come to watch for her father. It was a very special spot, this cliff's edge, and the moment brought back engulfing memories of her mother.

More often than not they had waited here together, comforted one another whenever he had been detained. Now her mother

71

was gone and how could she bear it if she were to lose her father as well? No! He had to be safe, he just had to be.

"Silkie!" It was a rude awakening. A voice that ranged sharply through her mind. It was firm and self-assured. It was the enemy. Her father's enemy. He had come on them suddenly last year after her mother's death and he was always there, hovering in the background.

She turned sharply, prepared to do battle. How dare he follow her here? But Wade Ashford was up to anything. Why? How often she had asked her father why, but he had always refused to discuss it. "What do you want?" She was already stepping away from his advance. "You have no right following me everywhere I go!"

He sneered. The years had increased his bitterness, added lines of dissipation to his lean, hard, and bold face. His hazel eyes were stern and full with their misanthropy. His auburn hair was laced with grey. The twenty-three years had left their mark. He was fifty, and although there was still that rakish attractiveness in his style, the bitterness was too deeply etched to ignore. Here was Serena's daughter and he meant to have her—and in having her, some of the revenge he desired against Aaron Marksbury. He had finally found the way. His gloved hand reached out and grabbed hold of her arm, bringing her up against him. "You little fool! What are you doing out here with this storm pending?"

"That is *my* business!" she snapped and attempted to pull out of his hold.

"Is it?" His arm encircled her trim waist. He was molding her against him and with his free hand he took her hair and held her rigid so that she could not struggle without pain. "And all that *you* do, my dear, is most definitely my business. Hasn't your father explained that to you yet?" He bent his head and his mouth closed roughly, hungrily on her cherry lips.

She struggled, she bruised against him, and her foot lashed out effectively and found its target. First his shin, but as he still held on to her, she then brought the heel of her boot down on his toes. He released her with a sharp cry and as he snarled and went for her again, he was stopped by a firm voice at his back.

"Well, there you are, Miss Silkie!" It was Kora, the Marksbury's housekeeper, but for more years than she could remember, Kora had been a part of the Marksbury family. She was large and plump and always an anchor in rough waters.

"Kora." Silkie was already running to her, taking up the housekeeper's pudgy hand.

"That's right, fie on you. Didn't you remember you were to try on that hunting coat so that I could repair last season's damages?" she clucked. "Come along."

They turned and started down the path, leaving the cliff's edge and Wade Ashford at their backs. He stood and slowly a smirk lifted his thin lips. Well, well, Kora meant to set herself between, did she? Never mind, Aaron Marksbury would not be back in time to deliver and then . . . then Silkie would be his!

Evening came to the villagers of Rye with some excitement. A flurry of activity ensued, for never before had they witnessed the spectacle of an American clipper ship towing in one of their own vessels. Whispers soon foamed into a fever of exclamations and nodding heads as the scanty and badly injured crew of the *Silkie* was landed and the doctor sent for. The Americans were greeted with hearty hospitality not, however, given without its measure of wariness, but given nonetheless.

Aaron Marksbury was carried off his shattered yacht, and while the vessel he had dubbed the *Silkie* looked as though it would do well enough after some repairs, he did not. He was given over to the doctor's hands and the villagers clucked and sighed. Silkie was the village pet. They had watched the lovely girl dance and play at her mother's side. They were proud of her and they loved her, for she had endeared herself in many ways to most of the village's lifetime inhabitants. What would Silkie say to see her father in such a state? At once the hushed cry went up: What would Silkie do? And then they looked up with some amazement as the American captain took control.

The American captain? Curious to be sure, thought more than one seaman as they watched Darrow Trent. Rye's inhabitants were cautious by nature; for too many centuries their village had been the center of Romney Marsh and the smuggling that went to and fro. They appraised him openly. His manner was arresting yet easy. There was no mistaking his air of command. His years seemed lean for a man of his bearing, but that same bearing seemed awesome in his overpowering height and athletic lines.

The ladies of Rye were quick to discover that the captain's eyes were bright aqua blue, rich and full with promise. Their interest mounted as they noted his dark black hair that fell in glistening waves round his handsome head and curled round his neck. His clothes were damp and in some disarray from the storm's work, yet it was obvious they had been cut by a tailor of

73

no mean standing. The barmaid came forward to offer her help and caught her breath when his eyes twinkled at her. He smiled and she jumped to his bidding.

His orders were crisp, clear, and effective. His crew made short work of all he required so that the men of the vessel *Silkie* were seen to immediately. It didn't take much longer before he had the *Silkie*'s captain well laid out with Doctor Baskins in attendance, and not many moments after that before they were making their capable way to the Marksbury cottage at the top of the grassy downs.

Kora opened the cottage's front door wide and gasped. Her plump, work-roughened hands flew to her full cheeks. "Oh no, oh no . . ."

Silkie was at her back and then pushing forward to see her father. Everyone else blurred before her vision. Her father was deathly white and though his eyes were closed, he was mumbling something she could not hear. "Papa . . ." It was a low breath of air as she bent towards the stretcher on which he lay.

"If you will instruct my men where you wish his lordship taken, ma'am?" As the captain spoke he took into account that this was the finest piece of female flesh he had witnessed in many a month.

Silkie was dazed with the sight of her father. She heard Trent but ignored him without realizing it as she turned to the doctor, a familiar anchor in dire straits. "Doctor Baskins—what . . .? How?"

"There will be time enough for you to speak with the doctor later," said the captain briskly. He was tired and short on patience. In addition to that he was not used to finding himself ignored. "Now, where shall my men take your father?"

Silkie snapped round, surprised and even just a bit annoyed by his tone. "Upstairs, please." She watched them move after Kora, who hurried them upstairs and once again turned to the doctor. "Tell me what has happened." She was touching the elderly physician's arm, looking pleadingly into his faded blue eyes.

Doctor Baskins heard the terror in her voice and put a comforting arm round her small, delicate shoulders. "Now Silkie girl, this isn't like you. I've got to go attend to your father and you have to attend to your guest. I must tell you before I go up that this American . . . Captain Trent is responsible for saving your father's life. He towed in your father's yacht, managed to find me at farmer Cubbin's. "He glanced at the tall American so that Miss Marksbury was given the moment to nod at him. ". . . that's right and then he pulled his men up, for they are tired and hungry, you know, and mayhap Kora might find them a thing or two in that kitchen she runs.'' He was patting her hand, moving towards the narrow flight of stairs, gently rebuking her, bringing her to a sense of herself, quieting her fears. Silkie was a favorite. He had brought her into the world. He had seen her mother out of it and now he just couldn't be certain what Aaron Marksbury's fate would be. Things did not look good.

Silkie turned back towards the American captain in some confusion. All she wanted to do was rush up the stairs after her father, but courtesy demanded she attend to the captain and thank him. She discovered the captain was studying her and she presented her hand. ''I am so sorry . . . I am Lord Marksbury's daughter . . . and you are—''

''As the doctor informed you, Captain Trent,'' he said, inclining his head slightly, wondering where his hat had gone to.

Her brow rose with this and then she discovered his blue eyes. How dare he appraise her with such openness, for that was just what he was doing. She inclined her head. ''Do forgive me, I was a bit dazed and did not catch your name, but I am better now. Won't you come with me to the study? There is a fire there where you may warm yourself, for I see that you are quite damp.'' She was telling herself that she should be thanking him. The doctor had said he saved father's life. . . .

Kora appeared in something of a bustle. ''I've sent those men of yours to me kitchen, captain . . . I hope you don't mind, for they should take some hot soup and warm sweet buns before they make the trip back to town.'' She touched Silkie's hand. ''Take the captain to the study, darlin' . . . I'll bring in something for him to eat.''

Damn, thought Captain Trent. All he really wanted to do was return to his vessel, take a quick survey of what damage she had sustained, have the cook put something substantial before him, and drop on his bed! Now here he was and by some miraculous coincidence, he had saved Tyler Marksbury's elder brother! He sighed over the thought and put out his open hand for Silkie to lead the way.

She took umbrage. Who the deuce did he think he was? He looked bored, weary, and scarcely able to conceal the fact that he considered this nicety she was extending to be something of a strain! She nearly stomped forward and still she was reminding herself that he had fished her father out of the sea and brought him safely home. Her father. Dash it all! She wanted to go up to her father.

They went down the long, dark corridor to her father's quiet study. For no reason at all she felt herself hot as she realized she was going to be alone with this man, and when she stopped at the large gold-brocade-upholstered wing chair that her father usually occupied she attempted to recoup herself. The captain immediately flustered her with his deprecatory cough, reminding her that he was awaiting her before he seated himself. She plumped herself down and took in some air before asking earnestly, "While we are waiting, captain, would you tell me what has happened . . . how my father was injured?"

He frowned. Of course she would want to know, and he softened. He took his time, however, for he wasn't sure just how much she knew about her father's illegal activities at sea. Her father—his partner's brother—a noble gentleman *was a smuggler*! Trent and a hefty number of his crew had witnessed the crew of the *Silkie* drop their contraband on the sink line into the Channel.

She became irritated with the delay. "*Please,* Captain?"

His dark brow, a straight impressive line, took on an arch, but he did not say anything to this. Instead he attempted a kind tone: "We were hit by the gale in the middle of the Channel. Ours is a clipper, well able to sustain the winds, but your father's vessel could not withstand the storm. Some of the timber came down and your father was caught directly beneath it . . . he was sent reeling overboard. I went in after him and we towed the *Silkie* in."

She closed her eyes and pictured this all too well. When she opened them again it was to find the American once again studying her. "I see," she said softly. He had saved her father, had risked his life to do so. Why then did she feel so hostile towards him? She brought her grey eyes to his face and quietly, sincerely said, "Thank you."

He looked at her full. Damn but there was something, perhaps the gold in the very depths of her grey eyes, that caught and held his attention. "It was only what any man of honor would do."

The door opened and Kora saved her mistress from having to reply by coming in with a flurry of apologies for the meager fare and setting it on the dark wood coffee table in front of the captain's knees.

"Tch, tch . . . that is no fire," she reprimanded, looking at the diminishing flames. As she went to the hearth, picked up the poker, and kindled the flames, she said, "Your men are settled in the kitchen, sir, and making do with the pot of soup I reheated for them. I hope the ale is to your liking. I thought it would go down better with that cold chicken than wine."

"It's marvelous, Mistress Kora," said the captain at once and his smile enveloped her.

She beamed, pleased that he had heard and remembered her name, and she was not immune to the charm of his smile. "Well, that's it, eat hearty." She threw a log on, looking sideways at Silkie. "You too, lass . . . I brought out your favorite cake . . . have it, with the captain, for you didn't eat dinner . . . and the doctor may be a while yet with your father."

"Thank you Kora . . . but I really am not hungry just now." Silkie felt subdued and strangely betrayed. This was absurd. She didn't like Captain Trent. Why, she couldn't say. He seemed arrogant and too self-assured and . . . rakish somehow—and here was her own Kora, taken in by him! And there was that inner voice, nagging, saying over and over, he saved your father's life! Oh, she hated to be in such a bind, beholden to someone she did not trust!

"Well then, child, I'll just go and see how those poor men be doing and what else they might be needing. You call me if you have a need."

Captain Trent watched Silkie, for she had lapsed into silence. He nearly swallowed his meal of cold chicken, bread, and ale whole, for he was a hungry man. Still, all the while an eye moved over Silkie's face. The girl got up and unconsciously began pacing. She was worried about her father. Again he softened towards her. She was haughty—at least she had been to him—she was distant and uncommunicative, but she had suffered a shock. Damn, but what was it to him? He had suffered a grueling day and he was feeling its strain. Just what had he gotten himself into? Fiend seize it all!

He sat back and released the sigh of a man who has just eaten and wants only his bed. Strange. Here he was on the other side of the Atlantic, far away from the scheming Zara and her delectable daughter, and who must he yank out of the sea? Who indeed but Zara's brother-in-law! What next lay in store?

# Chapter 2

"*What* next lay in store?" An interesting question and one that coincided with Zara Marksbury's as she contemplated her daughter's movements across the Long Wharf. Her dark brow went up as she eyed Blaine brightly waving to that young captain, Dennis Werth. Nothing she had said to Blaine detracted her from her purpose. She could see that her usually obedient child meant to be stubborn in this regard. Well, well, she would just have to handle it!

And Zara Marksbury was well equipped to handle it. She had become, in the twenty-odd years that had passed, Sag Harbor's ruling mistress. She led the fashionables of Long Island with an iron hand. All matters of society were deferred to her judgment, and all of Sag Harbor's elite bowed before her. How could they not? Her husband was one of the wealthiest men on Long Island. He and his late partner had attained a position of might and something of a kingdom. This was in no way affected by Arthur Trent's death, for Darrow took on his father's shares with a zeal. In this year of 1843 Sag Harbor saw their first clipper leave for the Far East with Darrow as its captain.

Zara had not been pleased. The timing was all wrong. She wanted Blaine and Dare to make a match of it—and how could they when Blaine blushed for this Werth fellow and Dare didn't bother himself over it?

As her thoughts tumbled and collided, her kid-gloved finger went to her lips with her speculations. She was going to have to take charge of the situation, and soon. At that moment a young sailor moved near her and as he scanned her face he brazenly tipped his hat in her direction. Zara's dark blue eyes glinted appreciatively and she gave him the glimmer of a smile. She sucked in some air as he threw her a kiss and then sighed, for Blaine was moving onto Werth's vessel and she would have to hurry if she were going to manage the affair. The sailor gave her a disappointed glance and went about his business, for Zara was, even in her forties, still quite a striking beauty.

True, her dusky curls were now tinged with silver, but she kept them cropped in elegant waves. Her blue eyes had darkened with time into fine, bright sensuous features. A perceptive mind might, if it looked too deeply, be repelled by what it found in the recesses of Zara's eyes. To most men, however, they held the promise of experience—and that was a lure indeed.

Dennis Werth's hazel eyes lit up when he looked down from his whaling vessel and found Blaine coming his way. She looked stunning with her auburn waves bouncing at her back. Had she come alone? A slim hope was dashed as he looked past her and found her mother in the distance. A frown brought his light brown brows together, but he made his way towards Blaine and bent over her outstretched hands.

"I wasn't sure you would be able to get away," he whispered as he came up from her hands.

She indicated with a movement of her head that her mother had accompanied her. "I didn't really . . . Mother is not far behind, but Papa says you are to come tonight! You will . . . won't you?" Her blue eyes pleaded, her mind reeled. How she loved the way his light brown hair swept over his forehead, the style of his straight nose. . . .

"Blaine?" It was her mother calling. "Blaine? Ah, there you are," Zara said, coming upon them briskly.

Werth had time only to squeeze Blaine's gloved hand and say softly that nothing could keep him away before he turned and made a polite bow to Zara Marksbury. "Good day to you, ma'am."

Zara could have snubbed him, but she knew better. Instead she smiled sweetly. "The same to you, captain . . . getting ready for another voyage?"

"That we are, though I plan to put in at New York first and visit with my father."

"We will see you before you leave, won't we?" returned Zara easily, offering her hand in dismissal.

"I would count myself immensely unfortunate if you didn't, Mrs. Marksbury, and as I have some business still to finalize with your husband, I trust that I may be allowed to pay my respects to both you and your daughter at that time?"

Zara Marksbury wanted to shove him into the brine. Instead she smiled, inclined her head, and took up her daughter's arm. "Come, child, I promised Mrs. Alexander we would be in for tea."

Dennis Werth watched Zara lead her daughter away, not at all fooled by Zara'a cordiality. She was not going to allow him to court Blaine openly. He sighed. Zara Marksbury was a dangerous woman and his father's small business could be hurt if he crossed swords with her. But he had to have Blaine. A problem indeed. Tyler? Would Tyler lend his aid? Never against Zara. It was a well-known fact that Tyler Marksbury never went against his wife's will. Dare Trent? He and Dare had been at school together and were considered friends. Could he count on Dare's friendship? Perhaps. After all, they had never been close. Their paths had taken them in different directions. Ever since Dare's father had died and Dare had taken over his father's shares in the company of Marksbury and Trent, Dare had been known for his fairness. And yet . . . Blaine would inherit her father's fifty percent in the company one day. A very interesting circumstance and one that might sway Dare towards her. Damn, but he wasn't giving her up. Not without a fight!

Hell, but she was a fine-looking wench! It flitted through Dare's mind as he watched Silkie pace. "It won't do you any good, you know," he said in a patronizing tone, hoping to divert her mind.

She turned and frowned at him. "What won't?"

"Expelling all that energy in the pursuit of nothing," he answered. "Come on . . . sit down, the doctor will be here soon. Eat the cake Kora brought you if only to please her."

She smiled. "Faith! I won't have to do that when she finds you have wiped your plate clean. You must have been half-starved."

"I was a man fully starved, thank you!" he retorted in good

humor. He was grinning now and she caught a glimpse of the boy in the man.

Kora popped in her head at the study door. "Captain, your men said they would be . . . piking off to the village and your clipper unless you sent word for them to wait."

"Thank you, Kora. Tell them to get as much rest as they can for we shall have our jobs cut out for us on the morrow, I'm certain."

"Right then," she said and was gone.

Silkie looked at him. "Your men must be exhausted."

"Poor devils, they've earned their rest. We've had a hellish day, all of us."

"I'm certain you have . . ." She stopped and then looked straight at him. "However did you manage to spot my father's yacht? How did you—"

He cut her off but tempered his answer carefully. "There really isn't much to tell. Sometimes it's nothing but lady luck at work."

"Yes, but . . ."

At this juncture Dare found himself saved the necessity of a reply by an interruption that occurred out in the hall. They could clearly hear Kora's voice raised in some heat.

"I am sorry sir, but I must ask you to stop at once!"

The words did not deter Wade Ashford. At last he meant to have his ounce of blood. "Stop? Oh no, I don't think so, and not by *you*!" he answered easily and his gloved hand went to the study door.

Kora put her buxom body in his way and he sneered as he reached round roughly and pushed the door open. "Out of my way, woman, for I mean to see Silkie now!"

Captain Trent had risen to his feet, his brow lifting with interest when he heard Ashford's use of Miss Marksbury's first name. There was a familiarity here. What then? A lover come to make up a lover's quarrel? An odd hour for that. He stood waiting, and as he watched Silkie blanch and then color up, his curiosity increased.

Silkie felt her heart sink. Was Ashford here already? Did he expect her to pay him his due this very night? Not this night. He couldn't expect her to do so, not with her father unconscious abovestairs? Not even he could be quite that cruel. She looked at the captain. Oh faith, that this should be happening with this American here! It was humiliating.

She went forward and at the doorway said quietly to Kora, "It's alright Kora . . . really . . ." She touched the housekeeper's arm gently.

Kora eyed Ashford before turning to her mistress. "If you say so, child." She looked towards the captain and there was something in her dark eyes that called to him.

The captain was not proof against her silent plea and his expression answered her. Thus reassured, Kora left them abruptly, though she mumbled beneath her breath and her opinion of Wade Ashford and his behavior was all too apparent.

Silkie's dark lashes brushed her white cheeks before she was able to meet Ashford's gaze and then she had to take in air quickly for she could see that he meant his worst. "Mr. Ashford . . ." she started, not moving for him to pass by her as she still hoped he would not enter the room any further. "My father has been injured at sea. He was brought in just a while ago. The doctor is with him now . . . and my housekeeper was only trying to tell you that now is *not* a good time for an interview."

Ashford inclined his silver-tinged auburn hair, his hat held in his gloved hand, and then he brought his hard hazel eyes to her face. "I am sorry to hear it. However, as you know my legal note with him falls due as of midnight tonight, if it is not paid before the hour—"

She stopped him. "I can't believe you won't wait till morning . . . until I have had a chance to speak with him, provide you with your miserable payment. . . ."

His eyes flickered from her outraged countenance to that of the enigmatic expression on Captain Trent's face. He hadn't noticed there was anyone in the room. This must be that American captain he had heard about in town. He felt a moment's irritation before he resolved to ignore the Captain's presence and proceed.

"You can't believe I won't wait?" He shook his head and reached to touch her cheek, sneering ever so slightly, ever so perfectly when she stepped away from his touch. "But dearest, you have so often said you know me for what I am."

She held herself erect. "Then I am to take it you are here to conclude your business whether or not my father is well enough to answer to you?"

"That's right. You see, love, it isn't *his* answer I want, but yours." His meaning was clear for he spoke on a low note and his sharp eyes peered intently into hers.

Silkie's grey eyes flashed before her lids closed and she collected herself. Ashford was a scoundrel. She knew this, knew what he expected. He left nothing to the imagination. If she wanted to spare her father his cottage, his yacht, all he had left to him, she was to promise herself to Ashford. Mercy! The man had not even given his word that he would marry her. . . .

"Oh, I know you Ashford," she said on a low sardonic note, "yet, even so, hopes die hard."

"Well then, pet?" He was indifferent to her cut and determined to bring things at last, at long last, to his goal.

She took to pacing, forgetting Trent's presence. Indeed, in that moment Ashford and Silkie saw only each other, the first with intense anticipation, the latter with dread. Silkie's hands came together before she stopped her movements and glanced at Ashford's face. Her voice was low and in spite of her pride there lingered a plea. "You know, of course, that the cottage and the yacht are worth twenty times more than the miserable note you hold?"

Wade Ashford's laugh was short, clipped, and very nearly triumphant. He inclined his head. "I know. It was what made my wager with your father . . . er . . . so very interesting. Marksbury could have refused it."

"Could he have done so? I think not!" she snapped. "We both know what trinket you held . . . and that you counted on the storm to weigh down his chances of winning!" The man was a swine! Here he was, pinning her against the wall, with her father helpless abovestairs, and a stranger hovering. She had hoped the captain's presence would deter Ashford to some extent. Evidently, she was wrong.

Indeed, Wade's sharp eyes caught much of the captain's cautious movements in the background. Trent seemed impassive to the proceedings. Still, Wade tried to get Silkie alone. "This is . . . I believe, a matter that you and I should discuss in private, my dear."

She took a step backward. It was an instinctive movement that she was scarcely aware of. "I think not, sir!" she snapped and the sharpness with which she flung the words at him brought her eyes contemptuously to his face. She was finding a courage she hadn't been hitherto aware of possessing. "I have, after all, until midnight before I must give myself over to you!" Her cheeks burned, but if this glaring blackguard meant to shame her before all the world, he might as well start now.

His eyes narrowed. "Ah Silkie, my dear, you can't go on fighting me forever. It won't serve your interests in the end, you know."

"Nor yours!" she riposted on a low angry note.

Wade's hand reached out and held her arm. "You wanted that London season as much as your father wanted it for you! If your father had won our wager, you would have had it. I didn't think you could be such a poor sport." It was a taunt.

That was it! Dare Trent had stood for all he was going to. Damn, but he wasn't used to fading into the background. It wasn't his affair, he had told himself. This was no doubt a lover's quarrel. Still, the girl looked genuinely distressed. An inner voice kept telling him that he was tired, it kept telling him he had done enough for one day, but this did not satisfy yet another voice that answered—the chit is in trouble!

She was the niece of his partner. She was therefore something of a connection, though she did not even know this yet. He took a step forward, silently, he hoped, making it clear to the English roué that he offered Miss Marksbury his protection should she need it. Ashford couldn't do more than bandy words with her while Trent lingered at Miss Marksbury's side, now could he?

It was then that Ashford made his first serious error. When he attempted to put hands to Miss Marksbury, Trent drew the line and stepped forward. "I think, sir, you have bothered Miss Marksbury enough for one evening." His voice was cool and full with self-assurance.

"You know nothing of the situation and I would suggest you stay well out of it," returned Ashford with more harshness then sense, for he was irritated by the captains interference in the matter.

Trent was somehow between Ashford and Silkie and he turned to her, saying quite blandly and not in the least bit perturbed, "Do you want the dog thrown out, Miss Marksbury?"

"Yes," she snapped. What more could Ashford do? At least she had until midnight.

The door opened as Ashford took a step sideways to better consider Captain Trent, and the doctor, his coat slung over his bent arm, came into the room grumbling in his manner and avoiding Silkie's eye as she ran to him.

"Doctor . . . my father?" Forgotten were Ashford and Captain Trent.

# Chapter 3

*Doctor* Baskins's blue eyes were faded with age, hardened by time and the passing of too many good people he had cared for. Tortured by the helplessness of his profession, lines were deeply etched in his heavily jowled countenance. Concern brought gruffness to his voice. He took up Silkie's hands and squeezed them as his brows drew together with his words. "Lordy, lass . . . what shall I tell you? The truth? I don't have it all. I just don't. Your father has been badly snabbled this time. It wasn't enough that he had to be railed . . . no . . . he went and caught as bad a chill as ever I've had the misfortune to treat. You are going to be in for a bad time of it, my dear. . . ."

She looked unwaveringly into his eyes. "As though I care a fig for that! Just tell me what to do!"

"He will need tending. I've already spoken to Kora . . . you'll share the time with her for we can't have you coming down ill as well . . . and then, lass, I'm not promising anything. His fever will have to break, but he has suffered a concussion as well . . . and, well, I just don't know. . . ."

"Doctor Baskins?" She stopped as her throat constricted on the words forming in her mind.

He patted her hand and then put her away from him. "I've never minced matters with you, my dear, and I'm not going to start now. I just don't have any answers for you. Go on up to him now . . . go on, but don't expect anything. He is delirious and probably will be until his fever breaks." He shook his head. "Just keep him comfortable."

"Yes of course." She was nodding, hurrying towards the

door now. Upstairs her father lay . . . and there was a chance . . . no, she wouldn't think that, couldn't think of that.

The doctor turned to the two men standing before him. Wade Ashford, eh? Well, well, the doctor had a pretty fair notion what that chap was doing here. Ashford meant to have Silkie Marksbury and made no secret of it. Shameful! She was a lady born and bred and it was certain Wade Ashford meant to ruin her. A vulture was what the man was . . . nothing better, but that made no odds, for what could he do? Again Baskins felt a bitter helplessness shake his soul and put him out of temper.

Remember. He had to remember what Aaron had been mumbling about upstairs. Did it mean something? A wager with Ashford. Yes, something about a wager, but Aaron had been barely coherent. Blast and double blast! What could he do?

"So then, Mr. Ashford, I didn't think to find you here," said the doctor, shrugging himself into his coat.

"Didn't you?" was all the reply he received and that with something of obvious disinterest.

"No, no I did not, and what is more, I think whatever business brings you here can wait for the time being. His lordship is indisposed as you must have already gathered and his daughter is in no fit state to attend to her father's affairs tonight!" snapped Doctor Baskins.

"I don't mean to set up an argument with you, doctor, but my concerns . . . are none of yours," replied Ashford blandly.

The doctor started to put up an admonishing finger in response, but the captain loomed on the scene and took over in his quiet but commanding fashion. "I think Mr. Ashford, that I was about to show you out a few moments ago as that was what Miss Marksbury wished."

"Were you indeed?" Wade Ashford's brow was up but his voice resumed a cautious note as did the set of his gaze. "But I have no intention of leaving."

The captain grinned in answer to this but there was no friendliness in his smile. "Then I suppose it is left to me to persuade you otherwise." He took a menacing step forward.

"Damn your American boorishness!" hissed Ashford all at once. "Who the devil do you think you are?"

"A friend of the family, sir. My partner in America, you see, is his lordship's brother and I intend to stand buff in his stead." There it was—quietly spoken, evenly said, powerful in its impact.

Wade Ashford was silenced and furious. Here was an unexpected jolt! Never mind. What did it matter? It didn't. Of course it didn't. He would still go through with his plans.

"Very well, Captain Trent. I will leave now, but at midnight I will return with a bailiff and then *Miss Marksbury* will answer to me . . . one way or another!" He turned round sharply, took up his hat and gloves from the sideboard, and was off.

The doctor watched Ashford's departure before breathing a sigh of relief and turning to Trent. "He will be back and there will be the devil to pay!"

"Will there? I fancy I could deal with the devil better than with that one!" The captain laughed on a rueful note.

"Aye, you have a point there." The doctor was shaking his head. "I've got to be going now . . . there is that Rawlings child I must see."

"Yes, but doctor . . . before you go, just what have I walked into here?"

"Trouble, lad . . ." The doctor sighed in response as he made his way to the hall.

Trent followed him. "Well, that is plain as pikestaff . . . but if you could take a moment to expand on that statement?"

" 'Tis a bit of a tale and I haven't the time." He gave the Captain a considering look. "Ask Silkie . . . she'll tell you what she knows—which isn't much—but it's more than I have." He looked up to find Kora coming towards them. "Kora love . . . the captain will be putting up here for the night . . . see to it that a room is made up for him."

Kora looked doubtfully from one man to the other. "Of course, Doctor Baskins . . . but . . ."

" 'Tis best, Kora darlin', for that cull Ashford means to be back with a bailiff and your Silkie will be needing an able-bodied friend. Depend on it!"

Kora's soft brown eyes opened wide. "The scoundrel." She looked then at the captain. " 'Tis welcome you are, sir . . . I'll just see to it that your room is made ready."

"Don't go to any bother, Kora." The Captain smiled. "You must be exhausted."

She beamed at him. " 'Tis no bother, sir, 'tis a pleasure." With that she bustled off, for there was something reassuring in the captain's presence. Surely Ashford would be helpless against such a man?

The captain saw the doctor off and then stood in the cold, dark hallway and frowned. The devil! What the bloody hell had he gotten himself into? Damnation! Brimstone and fire! He could have stood and cursed himself and the entire list of events from the moment he had opened his eyes some thirty-two hours ago!

He couldn't just walk away and leave his partner's niece in such a miserable state of affairs. Could he? No. It was really none of his business. Yes, but damn, he wanted to plant that fellow Ashford a steady facer! His lips curved ruefully. What, was he setting himself up as a good Samaritan? Lord! It was all very well to fish a man and his crew out of a murderous sea, but this? This was diving a bit deep.

Zara Marksbury pressed her hands together with some degree of satisfaction. As usual, her ball would open the fall season. She hadn't been able to wait any longer. She had wanted Dare to return, to be here for Blaine, but she just wasn't able to put if off any longer. Her gown of gold satin swept the floor elegantly as she glided down the hall, calling last-minute orders to her retinue of servants. Her home was ablaze with light, nearly overpowered with the scent of hothouse blooms, and sparkling champagne awaited her guests.

She looked in at the library and found Tyler, pensive and standing near the fireplace, a glass of brandy in his hand. When had she ever seen him in these last years without a glass in his hands?

"Darling?" she said gently, hoping, sincerely hoping that he was not already too deeply dipped. She moved towards him, a slight frown marring her perfectly groomed countenance, and her hand touched his. "What is it? I rather thought you were looking forward to this season's affair?"

He looked long into her dark blue eyes and very nearly cried. Instead, he said, "I am, my love, very much."

"Then, put this down and come with me . . . our guests will be arriving soon . . . and Blaine will be coming down. Wait till you see her. Oh Tyler, she is ravishing!"

He smiled and gave his wife his bent arm, his voice soft. "Like her mother."

"Ah Tyler, I do love you." It was lightly said and just as quickly forgotten as she clucked at a clumsy servant passing by.

Dennis Werth's silk top hat was held in a tight grip on his lap. He sat tense and forward in the back of the hack carriage that lumbered up the brightly lit drive of Marksbury land. His hazel eyes scanned the Georgian—styled estate, noting that its structure was as elegant in taste as was Zara Marksbury. Damn, but the woman took on the role of a duchess!

Torches blazed their way up the winding drive and in the rich dark sky a crescent moon hung intimately. He thought of Blaine. Saw her face there in the velvet heavens. Certes! He loved her, wanted her, and, by God, he was going to have her! What he needed now was Blaine's promise that she would wait for him, have no other till he could return and claim her for his own. This trip would be one step nearer to the riches that Zara Marksbury demanded for her daughter. Yes, this voyage had to be the answer . . . and by the time he returned, Dare too would be back in Sag Harbor. Dare. Would he be friend or rival?

It was hard to know what to do. Blaine was so very near to Dare . . . a perfect mate, for that would seal the business and put it into Dare's hands. Still, Dare was his own man. He wouldn't be pushed into anything by Zara, would he?

In a few days Werth would be bound for New York and then the high seas, after whale. Thank the Almighty, Tyler had seen fit to issue him an invitation to this ball. How could Tyler Marksbury not do so? Tyler and Denny's father were old friends and Tyler was not about to slight the son of a friend. Of that Denny had been certain.

The hack pulled up to the wide entrance and waited as giggling maids were helped out of the carriage in front of him. All of Suffolk's fashionables clamored to this ball. It opened the season and one had to be seen there. Even the villagers looked forward to it and talked about it weeks before and then for long weeks after. He sighed. She was a powerful woman, this Zara Marksbury. How would he ever manage to get Blaine alone tonight? He certainly had the will, but how would he find the way?

*   *   *

Silkie put a handkerchief soaked in rose water to her father's forehead. She had been tending him for hours and his fever seemed to have quieted. He no longer mumbled but her mind reeled—she had never before seen him in so weakened a condition. What would she do if she lost him? A hand touched her shoulder and she looked up into the plump gentle countenance. "Kora . . . he seems better. . . ."

"That he does, child, and I will sit with him . . . but first, let me take you downstairs. You'll be wanting to say goodnight to that nice American captain before you get some sleep yourself."

"What? Is he still here?" Silkie was surprised.

"Queers me that he is, but I think he wanted to satisfy himself about that blackguard before he turned in."

"What? What do you mean?"

Kora patted Silkie's drooping shoulders and released a sad sigh. "Ah darlin', I don't remember things here ever being at such a pass and Lord knows it pulls at my heart to have to remind you, but . . . Ashford did say he would be back at midnight and . . . well, it is close to the hour now." Kora was shaking her head, straightening Silkie's flaxen waves with a gentle smoothing of her hands. "That American, he means to be there with you, though I don't know what he can do. Decent sort he be . . . for he is fagged to death and this is none of his affair."

"Gracious . . . I had forgotten Ashford." Silkie was on her feet, squaring her shoulders. "Don't you worry, Kora. I am prepared to handle whatever the scoundrel means to level at us."

"He is a devil, that one. Listen to me, child, I know what he means to trade off with you. It's not marriage he is after . . . but, you might get it out of him if he thought you still would choose to be out on the street rather than go into his protection." Kora was eying her young mistress steadily.

Silkie's dark brows went up. "Can it be that even you believe I might accept any proposition from Wade Ashford?"

"You might, for he does mean to use your father in this," said Kora softly.

Silkie bit her lip. Yes, she would rather be out in the cold then in his charge, but how could she condemn her father to such a fate?

"Right then. I will go down and await Ashford's arrival . . . perhaps he can yet be put off till the morning." She cast her father a long loving look. "By then . . . my father may be better."

Kora also looked at Aaron Marksbury and then ushered Silkie towards the door. "Go on and don't worry, I'll watch over his lordship."

"Thank you Kora," said Silkie as she squeezed the housekeeper's hands, "Just what . . . oh what would I do without *you*?"

"Tosh." Kora gently pushed her off. "Go on now, love, you'll be wanting to speak with the captain, so off with you."

Dare Trent's handsome head had fallen onto the sofa back. One of his legs was stretched out towards the dying fire, the other, with knee bent and twisted at the ankle, was in an awkward position, but he was sleeping soundly and unaware. He hadn't meant to doze off, but contemplation of the crackling flames, his fatigued condition, and the quiet of the room had sent him off into a series of wild dreams. Oddly enough, Silkie's image was at the heart of these fantasies and thus it was that as he reached for and received her in his arms she felt suddenly, vividly, very real, very tantalizingly alive. He pressed her to his hard, lean body and groaned. Was that her voice asking for release? But why? No, not when it felt so good . . .

Silkie had found the captain in his awkward sleeping position and though it brought the color to her cheeks, she bent over him and gently attempted to rouse him. The next thing she knew she was in his arms and experiencing a wild surge of blood speed through her limbs.

"Captain . . . let me go, wake up . . . captain . . . please . . . you are dreaming!" Silkie's attempt was near useless as she found herself appropriated.

"Sweet darlin'," he murmured and kissed her throat. "Damn, but you feel so good . . ." he was saying in soft tones.

"Captain!" It was a desperate cry.

He was moved to open his bright blue eyes and he saw her face as it came into focus. He frowned. Where the hell was he? That's right . . . England . . . Marksbury . . . that's right. Had he just been holding her in his arms or was that all part of his dream? He brought himself up and shook the last remaining dregs of sleep from his head. "I *am* sorry," he apologized.

Silkie attempted to cover her discomfort by averting her eyes. Her cheeks felt hot and she burned from his touch. Ridiculous girl, she scoffed at herself. A quick glance told her that her gown was askew and she smoothed it over with a quick, quiet motion. Where was her voice? Stuck in her throat, that's where! She managed to bring the words to her lips. "I . . . I didn't mean to startle you, captain."

He looked up at her and his eyes twinkled appreciatively. "I was dreaming, my girl, but *you* can wake me anytime—"

"Yes, well . . ." She cut him off quickly, finding this line of conversation was doing nothing to restore her reserve. "I think you might be more comfortable in the room Kora has prepared for you."

Damn but she was an incredibly lovely creature. No time for such a thought, he reprimanded himself. He was here for a reason. Ah yes, the Ashford fellow. Still, he tried to assuage her sudden tension with his ready charm. "Comfort is not something a sailor ever looks to and your sofa has served me well." His smile swept her face and invited her to sit with him. He noted that her cherry lips parted and he felt a sure hunger well up within himself. Such lips, just made for . . . but never mind that now. "Won't you sit with me a moment, Miss Marksbury? I have something I must own before any more time elapses."

"Have you?" returned Silkie with some surprise.

He smiled easily and his hand made a waving motion over the worn yellow cushion at his side. "Won't you sit with me, Miss Marksbury, so that we may discuss this?"

She was amazed at the change in him. Earlier that evening he had been curt, arrogant, and impatient with her. Now he seemed disposed to charm. Why? She thanked him with an inclination of her head and sat instead in the wing chair opposite, noting with some satisfaction that this irritated him. "Right then, captain, I am sitting."

"So you are," he allowed and his good humor saved the moment. He allowed her one of his boyish grins before adding, "And so very prettily, Miss Marksbury."

She was not immune to his smile but for no reason she could readily understand, she set herself off, put up a wall of protection from him, and answered on a slightly reproving note, "It appears that you Americans are quite adept at flattery. Now if I may know what it is that you wish to tell me?"

"We Americans are quite adept at many things, Miss Marksbury," he picked up and his blue eyes were twinkling audaciously, defying a smile out of her. He won it and then proceeded. "Right . . . the point, you wish me to get to the point?" He sighed. "When we came across your father's yacht tonight . . . it was floundering in the storm . . . and as you can imagine . . . there was no time to consider anything but that fact. It wasn't until later that I was told your father's name, you see . . . when we had landed in Rye."

She leaned forward on her chair. "And I am very grateful to you, captain. Do not think that I am not—"

"It's not your gratitude I want. . . ."

Her brow went up. She was swiftly learning to be quite cynical about men. "Oh?"

He laughed. "Miss Marksbury!" He pretended to be shocked. "We are not all of us Wade Ashfords waiting to pounce."

She made him an apologetic countenance. "I have interrupted you, sir. Won't you proceed?"

"Right. It was in Rye when I discovered your father's name and realized that we are connections of a sort."

"*What?*" It was nearly a shriek.

"You see, your father is my partner's brother."

"Uncle Tyler . . . Uncle Tyler is your partner?" What did she know of her father's brother? So little. Her father and mother had never really told her very much about him. Now here was this stranger claiming a connection. It was startling.

He misunderstood her amazement and took offense. He felt himself bristle. Didn't this English wench think an American good enough to be connected to her family? "Tyler Marksbury and my father were partners in a whaling industry they set up in Sag Harbor some twenty-three years ago. I inherited my father's fifty percent when he died four years ago."

"Whaling? Uncle Tyler is in whaling?" She was clearly astounded.

"Are you shocked? Don't you approve?" said the captain on a hard note.

"I am amazed . . . you see my father never said more than

94

that Uncle Tyler was a shipbuilder in America.'' She took a moment to digest this and then quickly asked, ''Were you coming to Rye to visit with my father?''

He shook his head. ''I didn't even know Tyler's brother lived here in Kent County. This isn't my first trip to England. I was stopping over on my return from the Far East. I have friends just north of Rye, in Playden, and meant to spend some time with them before returning to Sag Harbor.''

She discovered his eyes in that moment and their rich, deep blue color. It sent a thrill through her body, but she hadn't long to contemplate the fineness of his eyes or the information he had just imparted to her, for she could hear someone at the front door of the cottage. She bit her lip. It was midnight and no doubt this was Wade Ashford come to collect his due!

## Chapter 4

*Kora* opened the door wide and stood aside. There was nothing that she could do to prevent this and she knew it. Even so, there was the fierceness of spirit that lent itself to her glance as she met Ashford's hard scrutiny.

"You will inform Miss Marksbury that I am here with the bailiff as I promised and that I should like a private audience with her." His tone was as hard and uncompromising as his words.

"Miss has been waiting for you in the study, Mr. Ashford, and will receive you there." She threw a haughty look at the young clerk who blushed beneath her scalding glance. "Your bailiff can wait here." She indicated a hard Windsor chair propped against the papered hall wall.

Ashford's eyelids brushed his cheek acquiescently and the bailiff went to the chair and sat. This accomplished, Kora turned her back to Ashford and led him once again to the study door. She opened it, but stood back in the hall and allowed him to pass through.

Silkie looked up, her grey eyes dark with her trouble, her chin held high with pride, her hands folded in her lap in an attempt to stop their trembling. "Well, Mr. Ashford, right on time," she said dryly.

Wade Ashford stopped short when his quick appraisal found Captain Trent, and his brows drew together in irritation. He said on a low note, "You knew, of course, that I wouldn't be late for such an important event. I've waited more than twenty years for this moment. However, I am surprised to find the American here. I think now you really must ask him to leave us."

She started to answer but Trent was before her. He had gotten to his feet and positioned himself neatly between Silkie and Ashford. There was a purpose in his eye though his demeanor appeared pleasant enough. "Mr. Ashford?" He saw that Wade ignored him and sighed on a mocking note. "You don't respond to your name, I see. Well, I have observed that you are not deaf and must assume that it is rudeness that moves you. I can get your attention by the use of other means at my disposal." It was calmly said but there was no mistaking his meaning.

Ashford directed a measuring look and said on a sneering note, "I consider your presence here an intrusion and as such do not feel I need accord you the slightest courtesy."

"That really is too bad, but then I must suppose you have not yet realized just what my being here means to you," said the captain easily, his fingers picking up a book on the sofa arm table, his blue eyes looking down at it for a long moment before he brought those penetrating orbs up and leveled a hard glance at Ashford.

"Damn your impudence!" responded Wade angrily. He was out of patience now. He was the American's senior by more than twenty years and felt himself the American's superior in every way.

But Dare Trent's thirty years had been well spent. He had handled men in every clime and knew well what sort he was now up against. "Indeed, you may wish to do so. However, it won't help you in this instance." He put the book down hard. "You see, I have decided to back Lord Marksbury and finance this venture he had with you." He smiled. "That's right, Marksbury's note is mine and I have the means to satisfy it."

Wade Ashford sucked in air. "You never ever saw Marksbury until today . . . you have nothing to do with this affair!"

"True," said Dare softly. It was, however, only money and perhaps the easiest solution to resolving the problem and getting out of it. He answered Ashford glibly though, because he didn't like the man and was pleased to get the better of him. "A whim . . . yes, call it a whim."

"May you rot in hell! A whim! Why? Because you want her? Is that it?"

Trent foresaw a touch of scandal. No sense in that. He shook his head. "As it happens, Ashford, his lordship's brother is my partner and friend in Sag Harbor."

"Tyler?" Ashford's voice was nearly a shriek. He was taken aback, speechless for the moment on one thought. Out of nowhere came this barbarian. Out of nowhere Tyler had thrust himself between. How could this happen now, now when he had nearly brought his plan to fruition? He calmed himself, but his agitation was apparent all the same. His voice came in dangerous waves. "Trent, you are intruding in something that goes beyond your understanding, something that does not in any way concern you. Stay out of it, for I warn you, I am not a man that other men cross . . . mark me!"

Trent's ire was up and his eyes sparkled militantly with the challenge. "And I am not a man other men threaten!" All at once he was smiling, but there was no friendliness in the curve of his thin, sensuous lips. "We are well matched, Ashford, and I grow more intrigued with this every minute. Stay out of it? No, I think not." He turned then to Silkie whose eyes were open wide as she silently took in the proceedings. "Miss Marksbury is, I realize quite weary from the day's events and I believe that we may excuse her."

She took the cue and got to her feet. When she brought her eyes to his face they were filled with her gratitude. She wanted to say something but he silenced her with a finger to her lips and a soft smile. "I look forward to seeing you in the morning when we might find your father much improved. We will talk further then."

"Good night, captain . . . and thank you." She dropped him a curtsy and turned to find Ashford sneering. "Goodnight, Mr. Ashford."

He allowed her to move off with only a nod but as she reached the door he called out on a hard note, "It isn't over yet, Silkie, depend upon it. I don't give up that easily. Oh no, not quite that easily."

She brought her pretty head round. "I know that, Ashford, and will be ready." With that she left the room.

Wade turned to Trent. "How do I know you can handle the sum involved here?"

"You don't right now, but I will sign whatever documents your clerk has handy here and I believe my clipper which rests in the harbor should be collatoral enough until tomorrow morning."

"And you will have the cash in the morning, no doubt," Ashford snapped.

"That's right, no doubt about that at all." Trent smiled and moved towards the study door in dismissal.

Gone! It was all destroyed in the flash of a moment. Ashford's realization came as a swift, slashing stroke that went right through him. He had brought Marksbury to within an inch of ruin. He would have seen Aaron Marksbury whipped and brokenhearted all in one final blow. He would have been cleansed . . . but out of nowhere came this stranger, arrogant and cool. Damn his soul, he would make Trent pay for this night's work. All this year's plans and in walks this American, catapulting those plans out of sight.

He inclined his head slightly as he passed the captain. "You know, of course, it does not end here." It was a statement, not a question, but Trent's brow went up confidently.

"Doesn't it, Ashford? I think for you it does, but we shall see."

The crescent moon's soft ivory beckoned as did the irrepressible glitter of the stars, but the two youths in the darkness of the conservatory did not observe the night's beauty. They were too involved in one another and the sadness that had brought them to this moment. Parting. It is a heart-rendering thing that leaves one empty and drained.

Denny Werth's fair head was bent in passion and concern. His hands gripped Blaine's soft bare shoulders, his hazel eyes pleaded. "I can't go without your promise. Why won't you give it to me . . . Blaine, is there someone else . . . is it Dare?"

She bit her rosy lip and her deep, ocean blue eyes were filled with her misery. How could he think that? "My darling . . ." Her voice was scarcely audible for she was on the brink of tears. "How can I explain to you . . . what can I say? There is no one but you . . . Denny, I love you, only you, but Mama will never allow . . ."

He pressed her to him in a crushing embrace and looked up at the heavens. There had to be an answer! Then all at once he had it. His eyes glistened with the sudden notion and he held her away from himself so that he could watch her face when he told her, begged her: "We don't need her approval, Blaine. Sail away with me tonight! I won't wait till morning. I will have my men put to this very night and we'll be in New York by tomorrow afternoon. Blaine . . . we can be married before the week is out.''

An elopement? My God! What was he asking of her? No decent girl eloped! ''Denny . . . how can you ask me to do such a thing?''

He frowned in some consternation. ''Blaine . . . don't you trust me? You'll have a separate cabin . . . I won't come near you . . . I swear it!''

She laughed in spite of her unhappiness and touched his cheek.

''As though *that* worries me. No Denny . . . I can't elope with you. It's no way to start a marriage. It isn't what I want . . . Denny, I can't do that. It would break Mama's heart.''

''And doesn't she break yours?'' he growled.

She stopped to consider this and said on a low, sad note, ''She doesn't mean to . . . she loves me . . . and Papa . . . Papa loves me. Denny, maybe Papa will be able to change her mind.''

He couldn't bear it any longer. He had to convince her to come away with him. He had her in his arms and his kiss was as hard and hungry as the raw helplessness he felt. He had to have her. She had to promise to wait for him if she did not come away with him tonight. How was he going to convince her? He felt her melt against his lean, youthful body when suddenly a voice struck through him like the quick, cold slashing of a sword. He felt Blaine break away from him in guilty fear as they turned to face Zara Marksbury.

''My, my,'' said Zara on a soft and amazingly calm note. Her hands were folded in the crook of each elbow. Her dark brows were up and her countenance was rigid with disdain.

''Captain Werth, I shall say nothing to you but that I think it prudent you leave my house at once.'' She didn't wait for a reply but turned to her daughter. ''Blaine, please rejoin our guests at once.''

''Mama . . .'' started Blaine on a frightened whisper.

Zara was not moved by the terror in Blaine's eyes. She was scarcely touched by the fact that all color had drained from her daughter's face, and it wasn't because she did not love her child. Zara had a plan for Blaine, a plan that would make her daughter happy and achieve an end. At least this is what Zara Marksbury believed. Anger did not touch the command though she was impatient with the situation she had discovered. Indeed, secretly she applauded Blaine for having passion in her blood. However, she must teach Blaine to use such passions, not be used by them. And here was a passion that must be thwarted immediately.

"I don't mean to stand here and argue with you, child. Please do as I ask." Zara's voice came like a quiet blast of frosty air.

Blaine had never been strong enough to withstand her mother. She felt her knees go weak and her will vanquished. She dropped a dutiful curtsy and fled the room. She didn't dare look at Denny's drawn, unhappy face. She didn't dare meet his questioning eyes—for then surely she would break and be undone! No, now she would attend her mother's guests as she had been bidden, but later, well, that was something else. Later she meant to attend to her own needs!

Zara had dismissed Denny Werth and every inch of him recoiled from her granite eyes, but he held his ground. He had to make the attempt, didn't he? Softly he said, "Mrs. Marksbury . . . I must apologize . . . and have only the excuse that I love—"

She cut him off with a harsh, biting laugh. "Yes, I know, you love my daughter!" She shook her head. "Selfishly, you love my daughter, a euphemism for what you really mean, which is you *want* my daughter!"

He frowned. "Well of course I want her! There is nothing wicked in a man's wanting the woman he loves. Can it be that you don't realize I wish to marry her?"

"Oh, I understand that very well!" Zara Marksbury was in command and very cool. She pulled herself up to her ample height and stared hard at him. "But what can you do for her? Your father's company is a small one . . . scarcely able to hold its own." She shook her head. "We have better plans for Blaine's future and if you really cared for her, you would not wish to stand in her way."

"I am quite able to support a wife in some comfort, Mrs. Marksbury."

"Not in the comfort and grandeur Blaine of Marksbury is

entitled to enjoy. This is not something I mean to discuss with you. I am, in fact, quite surprised that Blaine did not inform you that she will in the very near future be announcing her betrothal to Captain Trent.'' The words were meant to pierce and they did, overwhelmingly and straight to his heart.

Dumbly he repeated in a voice that he just managed to make audible, ''Darrow and Blaine? Neither one ever mentioned to me . . .''

''No, I don't suppose they did, but it's a fact. It was all arranged some years ago when Darrow's father was still alive. It was Arthur's fondest wish, for he adored Blaine and of course it would mean the uniting of the business. . . .'' Her voice trailed off as she watched the impact of her words. Excellent. Dennis Werth appeared beaten at last! ''Now, if you will excuse me, Captain Werth, I must return to my guests.''

He said nothing but accepted this final dismissal as he took polite leave of her. There was nothing to do but call for his hat and greatcoat and somehow put Blaine out of his heart . . . but how?

Zara watched him go and her mouth twisted into a smile. That was easy enough. A man, real man would not have been so easily taken! Fool! Blaine was well rid of him . . . and once Dare was home again she would forget all about her quiet, fair Denny.

## Chapter 5

*Aaron* Marksbury opened his eyes with a start. The faded and heavily molded ceiling was a cloud of strange patterns. He frowned and attempted to understand what he was looking at. Slowly it took shape and his features relaxed. He was in a room, not the wild sea. He lifted his head, felt the weight of his injury, and dropped it back down at once, but he had quickly seen enough to tell him he was in his own room. How?

Think! The storm . . . yes . . . they had been caught by the storm. He remembered that, but all else seemed a blank. How did he get home? He felt a flush steal over him and he groaned, for his thoughts had brought him to the realization that he was in pain, a great deal of pain. There was something wrong with his body. He could scarcely move. His middle . . . what was wrong? Ribs. Had he broken his ribs? He groaned again.

Silkie had relieved Kora during the night. She sat in an upholstered wing chair beside her father's bed. She was in her nightdress with a blanket pulled up to her chin, and she had dozed off only an hour past. Her dark lashes fluttered and then she was jumping to her feet.

"Papa?" Her blanket fell to the floor as she went to his bed and touched his forehead. Was the fever gone? To be certain she touched behind his ears. Cool. Yes, yes, he was cool enough. "Oh Papa?"

This time his lids snapped open alertly and he saw Silkie's tears streaming down her soft cheeks. In spite of his pain—and it was considerable—in spite of his disorientation, he smiled. Here was his Silkie, his and Serena's only child. Lovely, gentle Silkie. Wrong. Something was wrong. He wasn't sure how he knew this, but it flooded almost overwhelmingly into his mind. He was supposed to do something for Silkie. What had it been? He tried to speak and discovered that while his lips seemed to move, they did so without discipline and the sounds that he emitted were mumbled, garbled. It was too much of an effort and with a sigh he gave up trying. She would understand. She always did. He closed his eyes.

"Poor Papa . . . that's right, darling, you rest. 'You've had a bad accident at sea . . . but you shall be better presently." She stroked his forehead and while he was still quite warm to the touch, she was certain the worst of his fever was over. She watched him a long moment in thought. Should she send for Baskins? The good doctor would prod and push at him and probably bleed him as well.

She glanced at the mantleshelf clock. With an uplift of one dark brow a weary sigh escaped her lips. The hour wanted five minutes to six. It was early, but at least their groom, Joseph, would be up and about and in the stables. Flossy, their one serving girl who came daily from the village to help Kora, should be down in the kitchen. She would ask Flossy to go to the stables and send Joseph to fetch the doctor.

Her pink wool wrapper was slipped on and loosely tied at her waist before she took the back stairs to the kitchen below. The aroma of brewing coffee and hot buns reminded her that she hadn't eaten since high tea the day before. Lord! She touched her flat belly and was suddenly ravenous. The arched doorway leading to the roomy kitchen was always a welcoming, beckoning sight. It was a large bright room, made so by her mother, who had installed an oversized window and took to growing herbs and flowering plants on all available shelf space. The room's dominating force, however, was its huge red brick hearth where a multitude of cast iron and copper pots hung in serviceable and ornamental array.

When Silkie first entered she saw that Kora was nowhere to be found and then she stopped short. Seated at the large dark oak table with his arm neatly wrapped around Flossy's youthful waist was Captain Trent. A quick frown fluttered Silkie's features and was just as speedily dismissed. She pulled her wrapper round her more tightly and nodded. "Good morning, captain. I didn't expect to find you up and about so early."

Flossy turned a bright red, adjusted her mobcap round her short brown curls, moved out of his slackening hold, and would have then escaped the kitchen had her mistress not called her attention.

"Flossy?" Silkie's eyes appraised her as she never thought to before. Woman looking over woman. The girl was about her own age and fair. Silkie wondered at her for she had always assumed that Flossy and Joseph would make a match of it. Well, well, the captain, it would seem, was very much like all his kind.

"Yes, miss?"

"Would you mind running over to our stables. I want Joseph to take the cob and fetch Doctor Baskins."

Flossy bobbed a curtsy. "Right away, miss."

"Has your father taken a turn for the worse?" The captain was on his feet, pulling out a chair in an invitation to Silkie to join him at the table.

She eyed the chair, the hot buns, and the pot of coffee. She was hungry. She took a seat opposite him, politely refusing the chair he had pulled out for her at his side. "No." It was said with a smile. "In fact, his fever has broken . . . and I hope this means no more complications. . . ." She poured herself a cup of coffee and turned round as Kora bustled into the room from the yard door.

"Kora!"—it was a more joyful tone than she had used with Trent—"Papa is better! The fever broke and I've sent for the Doctor."

"Praise be!" sighed Kora, coming over to give Silkie's shoulders a squeeze. Then she eyed the captain's empty plate. "Would ye be wanting more eggs, sir? I can have them readied in no time."

He put up his hands. "I've eaten enough to last me the rest of the day, Kora my darlin'. No, I've got to get down to my clipper and have things in readiness for Mr. Ashford." He was getting to his feet again, looking down at Silkie, smiling. "I hope I may call on you this afternoon to see how your father goes on?"

"Of course, captain, and I believe you and I have business to conclude. . . ."

He chuckled. "I am no Ashford, Miss Marksbury. That can wait until your father recovers sufficiently to handle the matter."

She took umbrage. Why she should she didn't know. Why, in fact, she should feel irritated with him was a question that suddenly popped into her head. She should feel grateful. Grateful—yet somehow she didn't—she only felt obligated and that ruffled her feathers. "Don't you think me capable?"

He glanced at her in some surprise but his charm came to rescue the moment. "Precisely why I prefer to give myself over to your father's hands. I have no doubt I would be safer there."

His smile disarmed her and she relented. "Well, I don't want to keep you now, captain, but we will discuss the matter later, for I am afraid I really cannot let it rest."

He inclined his handsome head. "If you like."

Flossy then reentered the kitchen with a generous swing of her well-shaped hips. Dare was in the process of taking up his captain's hat and managed as he did so to give the girl a flirtatious wink, which accorded him a blushing smile. This trick was not lost on Silkie, who watched with some surprise. A sharp word sprang to her lips but she restrained herself and merely directed Flossy to help Kora. She then turned and watched Captain Trent take his leave. A tingle of emotion touched her when his blue eyes glinted but quickly it was gone. Her father. She had better return upstairs and see to her father. . . .

Dare Trent had been exhausted and well satisfied enough to sleep deeply before his early rising that morning. Things had not been so with Wade Ashford! In fact, Ashford had not slept at all. He was too pent up with agitation, too frustrated to let his mind relax, and too bitter to put things into proper perspective. He was up and pacing the oriental rug of his library before dawn, pounding the rich velvet upholstery of his Regency desk chair, staring out the bow window onto quiet Rye Avenue.

His valet Tatem entered cautiously and set down a tray of his employer's usual morning fare. He could see that the master of his household was in a fit of temper.

Ashford's eyes lit on the tea and crescent roll. Meager board for an Englishman, but he watched his weight and rarely succumbed to sirloin and eggs in the morning as did most of his cronies. Hell! In a spurt of irritation he pushed the tea pot away and said harshly, "Get this slop away from me! I want a pot of coffee, and Tatem, have my horse groomed and brought round in thirty minutes.''

"Very good, sir,'' Tatem answered with a bow of his balding head. His narrow drooping shoulders unbent as he hurried to do his employer's bidding.

Ashford resumed his pacing, this time stuffing the soft crescent into his mouth and chewing viciously as he moved. Damn Darrow Trent's American soul! By all that was holy, if Trent were one penny, just one penny short, he would move in on Marksbury. . . .

But there was no doubt that Trent would come up with the cash, so another answer must be found. The answer to his dilemma lay somewhere in his brain. Silkie had to be his! Her mother had escaped him, but Aaron Marksbury's daughter would not! One way or another, even if he had to resort to marriage, he would have Silkie. She was Serena's daughter and he would take her right from under Marksbury's nose. He would take her and make her life a living hell. Yes, damn it all . . . finally he would watch Marksbury suffer. His brows drew together, sternly, even more stern than they had been a moment before. Silkie came to mind as an entity. For a moment he saw her—not Serena's daughter, not Marksbury's treasure, but the innocent girl—and he felt a moment's flitting regret. It was a private thought and one he did not like to own. She was always so cool, so angry with him. Her grey eyes would darken and their gold lights would flicker when she was in a passion. How she could rage, this one, so unlike her gentle mother, and it had been the soft and gentle mother who had stolen and broken his heart.

He recalled the first time he had ever laid eyes on Serena, how he had felt when Lady Bruney introduced her to him. He remembered how completely she had caught his attention with her quiet smile and her gold-flecked eyes. No woman before her had ever drawn out his feelings, no woman since . . . but that was over. Hell and fire! Look what she had done to him! She had humiliated him publicly, taking Marksbury over him. Now her memory only served to harden his resolves. He needed one thing only and that was revenge. He would have it through Serena's daughter. She was all that Aaron Marksbury had left in this world and . . . hold a moment . . .

There was something in that thought. Aaron Marksbury had

not a *sou* to fly with. It was a fact. The man was in debt and there had to be a great many other debts. How serious? Tradesmen's bills could be considerable. Oh, he was certain Aaron knew the trick of dealing with many and paying some, but even so . . . If someone were to pay off all those debts and hold the notes as a total sum . . .

Slowly, very slowly, his lips curved and the expression they formed was enough to make a kind man shiver. That was it, by God! Here was his key. It would mean a quick trip to London, for he wanted his solicitor to handle this and make it all quite legal.

"Tatem! Tatem!" he called.

As the valet hurried, now laden with a pot of hot coffee, he raised his eyes heavenward and breathed to himself, "What now?"

# Chapter 6

*Blaine* pushed the dark hood away from her head and took a long deep breath. She had never done anything like this before. It was inexcusable, she knew that. The looks she had received from the seamen above deck had been enough to tell her that. She could turn round . . . she could take the companion stairs and rush away. No, she could not. Her hand went to the captain's latch and with a strength she never knew she had, she opened the door and stepped within.

Denny Werth started up from his desk chair with a muffled sound. Blaine. Blaine was here. He went to her without thinking, without a moment's hesitation, and she was in his arms, sobbing his name. All the evening's irritation, frustration, and rage dissipated in that embrace. Emotions flickered and melted into one.

"Blaine . . . my darling . . ." He whispered words of enchantment as his kisses covered her face, her eyes, her neck, and then he was taking her sweet lips.

She didn't resist. This is what she had come for, wasn't it? The question in her mind was scarcely heard as she responded to his ardor and then he had her shoulders and he was pushing her away.

"Go home darling . . . now . . ." It was a ravished sound for the resolution had been torn from him.

"But . . . don't you want me?"

"More than anything . . . I want you, but Blaine, you shouldn't be here, you know that, I know that . . . and I . . ."

She touched his lips with her fingertips. "This is the only place where I should be, *with you*!"

He held her close and closed his eyes. What should he do?

Take her home? "Did anyone see you leave . . . won't they miss you?"

"I waited till the last guest had left . . . no, they don't know I have left my room and shan't miss me. My maid has instructions not to serve me my morning chocolate until past nine . . . and it's nearly three now, Denny . . . so we have time together." Her meaning was clear. She felt bold and brazen and so natural with him. It was wonderful and she felt herself slipping away into another realm. "Oh Denny . . ." She was up on tiptoes, putting her nearly at his height; she was a tall girl like her mother.

"Then we sail together in the morning!" It was a desperate statement, for he could see in her eyes that she would not agree.

She didn't. Instead, she shook her head. "I can't do that, Denny, I won't do that to my father . . . but I am here now to show you that I will wait for you to return."

This time when his mouth closed on hers it was with a sense of exultation. This was not how he had wanted their first time together to be, with a parting in the morning, but it would have to do. As he lowered her young, responsive body to his captain's bed, he pledged his love. Their promises were whispered in the fever of their time.

Dare Trent's cabin was a bright airy room, accented by the skylight above. Its wainscotting was dark and rich, its furnishings sturdy, uncluttered, its four-postered bed just scarcely smaller than the one in his room in his home estate. There was a floral-designed carpet covering the highly polished floor and its colors of gold and brown were picked up and repeated in the rich hangings round the bed.

He sat at his small but serviceable desk with a metal box in front of him and counted out the gold he would need to cover the morning's transactions. He frowned. It would leave him sadly depleted, but he didn't mean to remain in England more than a week anyway. Tyler would have expected him to help his brother, wouldn't he? Of course he would. Even if there had been a rift between them—and there was no saying that there had been. Yet why had he hardly heard Tyler speak of his brother? Why had he never mentioned Silkie's existence? Silkie? Now that was a wench worth possessing! Damn, but he wouldn't mind finding her grateful. He laughed at himself. Since when did he need to buy a woman's attentions, and why should he stoop to that now?

Wade Ashford. What a devil! Why was he out to ruin Aaron Marksbury? He wanted the girl. That was obvious, but there was more to it than that. There was a mystery here and it was damn intriguing. Well, what had his father always said to him? "Dare, if you ever meet the devil, go straight forward, and if you have to, cut him in two and go between the pieces." Well, it would appear as though he were doing just that.

He could hear his men working above, repairing the rigging, chanting, "Whiskey Johnny." They were dreaming of going whaling, no doubt. His vessel was a clipper, not a whaler. It was built for trade, built for speed. Its lines were lean and its action was swift, but his men were whalers, every last one. The long journey to China had left them anxious, restless, and yearning for the chase. He sighed, for he had never really taken to whaling. He was a romantic at heart and there was something in his soul that regarded the great whales with admiration and a revulsion at their destruction. Even though it was the mainstay of their business . . .

A knock sounded at his cabin door and without looking up he called out, "Come in."

Wade Ashford, clothed in a fashionable if somber gray and a many-tiered greatcoat, entered, his top hat and gloves in his white, long-fingered hands. "Good morning, Captain Trent." And although a sneer played about his thin lips, he managed something of a nod in his greeting. Why not? He had not been altogether defeated, had he? No indeed, only delayed.

Dare got up and stood aside, his hand making a sweeping indication as his spoke. "Good morning to you, Mr. Ashford. You will find there the sum due to you as well as a receipt upon which I will need your signature."

Ashford inclined his head as he moved forward. His hand took up the gold and dropped it into the leather pouch he had brought along. Trent's lips curved. "Aren't you going to count them, sir?"

Ashford released a short snort. "No, for we both know I don't give a monkey for the money!" He shook his head before bending it to sign the prepared receipt. "You have proven to be a singularly onerous fellow, captain." He looked up from his name on the paper and found Dare Trent's blue eyes on his face. He smiled dangerously. "I trust you will not again find yourself . . . inclined to put yourself in my way."

Trent's smile appeared friendly enough but his intimates would have immediately recognized the warning contained therein. "Mr. Ashford, I doubt that our paths shall again intersect, as I mean to spend my time in the company of my partner's brother and his lovely niece while I am in England."

Impudent savage! "That could prove tiresome . . . for both of us, captain."

"Could it? You will find that I do not tire easily, Mr. Ashford." Still he smiled.

"And I am a patient man, willing to bide my time, while on the other hand, your time in England will end. What then, captain? You will sail for home . . . and leave the Marksburys to me, and by then, if I have been frustrated by you, my temper might unwittingly be unleashed on them. I think you would be better served to stay out of a matter that you know nothing about."

Trent walked determinedly to his cabin door and held it open for Ashford. "There are, I believe, always answers to such problems, and if a person applies himself, he may find just the answer he needs. Depend on it, Ashford, I won't be leaving Rye and the Marksburys until an answer has been found."

Ashford's sneer distorted his face. His hazel eyes blazed with sudden explosive hatred. "Damn your interfering soul! One way or another, Captain Trent, I will complete my business with the Marksburys. And if you are in my way, I shall know well enough how to remove you!"

Captain Trent's blue eyes glistened and his smile was very nearly a grin. "A challenge indeed, and one for which I can give you an immediate answer if you like." His meaning was clear, for an honest fight would be welcome.

That was not what Wade Ashford had in mind. He released a half snort. "When I strike, captain, I don't mean for you to be in a position to retaliate." With this parting note he made his exit and took the companion stairs to the top deck.

Dare Trent stood for a long moment. Hell and fire! Just what had he gotten himself into? Well, there was only one way to find out—and that was to go visit Miss Marksbury and ask her straight out. Maybe that was too bold for the English but it was the only way he was going to find out what Ashford was about, and why. However, right now he was going up and looking to his sails.

The storm had done its work and he was sure that the right fore topmast could not be salvaged. He moved to where it lay in a heap and examined it. His first mate, a round-cheeked, wiry-haired, husky man in his late fifties ambled over. "Don't think we should bother mending it, cap . . . do you?"

Dare shook his head. "Agreed, but I want four of our best seamen working aloft today on that foresail. They'll have to make fast the earings and draw up the sail's upper corners as taut as they can get them."

Forbes nodded. "Aye, then." He turned and signaled one of the men. "You there, Jimmy . . . take three more and up with you to the yardarms." He turned back to Trent. "I'll see to it, cap. You can depend on me."

Dare Trent put his large bronzed hand on his first mate's shoulder. "I know I can. I've got to ride up to the Marksbury cottage and I don't know when I will be returning."

"Don't worry about a thing, . . . I'll see to the men. They won't get testy with me around." It was said with a low-throated laugh.

"That's a fact," returned the captain as he pulled on the greatcoat he had brought topdeck with him and made for the gangplank. He would visit the livery and see if he could hire a mount. Silkie popped into his brain and brought on a frown. Thunder and turf, there was only one way he knew of forgetting about a wench—and that was to have her! That thought brought on a smile. A wide smile!

Silkie had donned her riding habit of dark brown velvet. It was an old one and simple in style but its lines showed her own to advantage. Its matching top hat sported an almost new, flowing white silk band that she had indulged herself with some months ago. She had pulled her flaxen hair tightly away from her face and piled it high beneath the slightly angled top hat. Riding her grey at a jaunty pace across the open field, she could see the weathered grey fence coming closer, and started to check her gelding with gentle hands and soft tones. "Easy, Rocket . . ."

She was riding sidesaddle and was never as comfortable taking a jump as she was when riding astride. She managed, however, to time it properly and it was smooth and exhilarating. "Good boy!" she said and opened him up again.

Her father was resting comfortably, Kora was taking charge of the household as usual and it left Silkie free to take this ride and collect herself. Not her thoughts, not yet. Now all she wanted to do was ride and forget everything but this feeling. It was the only thing that helped when all the world seemed out of balance, this oneness with her horse, this glory of riding with the wind. She sighed and started to slow their pace. Rocket had been hers for five years. He was a valuable animal because he was a marvelous hunter. She could get a good price for him, but selling Rocket was something she couldn't bear to do.

She recalled the first time she had borrowed Blaize Fenton's breeches and gotten on Rocket's back. He had bucked her off almost immediately. She hadn't given up. Instead, she nearly bloodied Blaize's nose for his teasing and up she went right onto Rocket's back again. It had taken months and months, for the grey gelding had been only three years old and quite green. He had cost her father very little, but now he would fetch a price!

Ashford. He was the cause of all this grief—well, not all of it, but certainly a good part of it. Wade Ashford? Darrow Trent? Two entities that would have to be handled, but how? Her mother had rarely spoken about Tyler Marksbury, and though when her father mentioned Tyler's name it was with affection, somehow she had sensed that a cloud hung over the memory. Why? It had something to do with Wade Ashford. She was sure of it. When her father was fully recovered she was going to make him tell her why Ashford was hounding them.

Darrow Trent. The name brought forth his image. She could see him all too well. His blue eyes glistened with their full rich color, with hidden thoughts, with taunting. He was a flirt. Yes, he had saved her father's life and yes, he had come to the rescue again with regards to Ashford, but there was something about him that she could not trust. He was dangerous. She was sure of it. Just look how easily he flirted, one minute with her and the next with . . . Flossy. Why, he had only met Flossy that morning and already . . . but she wouldn't think of Darrow Trent. He was too self-assured, too arrogant . . . he saved your father's life. She grimaced, for this was true and it was a fact she could not ignore. Oh, but it irritated her to be in such a position!

She missed Blaize. He had been away now for more than a year. His letters had stopped coming over six weeks ago. He had probably forgotten her . . . and then she blinked! She had to, for she could not believe her eyes. Blaize? Was that stylishly clothed, lean young man riding towards her really Blaize, or was it her dream following her into reality? There was no mistaking his horse. His horse, of which he was struttingly proud, was a black and white American and could not be easily taken for any but Sir Blaize's Daring Paint. She put up her hand and waved frantically. Here was Blaize, her childhood friend. Her confidant and, in the recent past, her knight in shining armor! She was nearly twenty; he was twenty-two. That he should find his way to her heart was rather inevitable, as he was in his fashion a fine-looking man in his prime. Once again she was racing her horse across the dark moors and this time calling out his name, "*Blaize!* Oh . . . Blaize!"

Sir Blaize Fenton looked at her and grinned. So here was his Silkie. He always thought of her as his. They had been through so much together. The time in India managing the estate he had inherited had left him hungry for England, for his home, and now, watching Silkie coming rushing towards him in her rough and tumble way, for her as well!

They were off their horses in an instant and in one another's arms. It was the embrace of friendship, for nothing else had developed before he had left and they'd had too many years, too many childhood scrapes, for it to mean more now, though Silkie did find herself blushing almost shyly when she looked up at his angular face. This was soon dispelled when she noted that his thick crop of ginger locks had been cut in the latest fashion. She squeaked and pulled off his top hat. Her gloved hand went to her cherry lips as she stifled an unladylike giggle. With her free hand she pointed. "Oh Blaize . . . look at you!"

"I'll have you know it is all the crack in London!" he returned hotly.

"London? You went to London before you came here?" she asked archly, and then because of his expression of guilt, she gurgled and clapped her hands. "And that is another thing, Sir Blaize, why haven't I received a letter from you in over—?"

He was laughing now, taking up her shoulders, all too aware that she was playing a game with him. Silkie was his playmate, his friend, and yet somehow . . . different. "Brat, you are more a rogue now than when I left you!"

"When you left me I was not yet eighteen! Remember? You left one week before my eighteenth birthday. Now I am very nearly twenty!" She paraded herself before him. "A woman, you know . . ."

He reached out and took hold of her arm and drew her to him. "A minx is what you are . . . but a beautiful one. . . ." He grew suddenly thoughtful, "If you weren't my own dear Silkie, it might prove interesting to make love to you in the grand manner, as they do in Paris."

"Oh Blaize . . . would you? I mean . . . really, it's the very least a friend can do!"

He caught her and, as he had so many times in the past, he swatted her rump. It was only afterwards that he thought it was not quite the thing to do now, but then she was giggling and taking to her mount, stopping to cuddle Paint's nose. Over her shoulder she called out, "Come on! Oh Blaize . . . I am so happy you are home."

## Chapter 7

"*There*," said Kora as she pulled out a chair and waved her hand for the doctor to sit down. "Make yourself comfortable and admit that you've never tasted an apple tart the likes of mine!"

He smiled, but it was an absent gesture as he sank heavily onto the wooden structure. She had poured him a tall mug of coffee and was watching him with concern. He warmed his fingers round the mug and released a long, unhappy sigh. "Its not good, Kora."

She nodded. "Aye . . . I saw it in his eyes. I've never seen his lordship laid so low. It's a wonder the child hasn't guessed. She believes he is on the mend."

He shook his head. "That is my fault. Didn't think there was any sense in worrying her now. His fever did break and normally that would be a good sign, but his internal injuries are extensive and he has been coughing up some blood." Again he was shaking his head.

"She should be told, Doctor Baskins, she has to be prepared. . . ."

"Not just yet."

Kora's work-worn hands clasped her plump arms in some distress. "Whatever will the lass do?"

"What she needs to do is get married," answered the doctor emphatically. " 'Tis all a girl has to worry about and Silkie is beautiful enough to make a match of it."

"Ha!" snorted Kora, moving to her pots and stirring the soup she had started earlier. "You don't need me to tell you the way of the world, doctor. A girl needs more than beauty."

"Well and she has that. She comes into a small dowry when

117

she is five and twenty . . . and she certainly has the breeding . . . the noble bloodline.''

"Aye, she has all that and no one to sponsor her. Where are these single, eligible men? And her dowry may be one thing, but she doesn't have the ready money to put down for the sort of affairs and routs it needs to catch a marriage prize! It's why his lordship accepted the curst wager in the first place." She bit her lip, thinking perhaps she had said too much.

"What's that? So there was a wager. Tell me, Kora, was Silkie to be Ashford's bounty if he won?''

"No, his lordship would never . . . but Ashford had it in mind to use his lordship's debt . . . if debt there would be, to persuade the child . . . well . . . to . . .''

"Yes, yes, I am no dunce," said the doctor, frowning darkly. "The man is a cad!''

"So he is and means ill by his lordship even if he has to use the girl to accomplish his deed." She drew in breath and let it out. "The captain . . . the American may have staved him off a bit, but more than that I very much doubt.''

"As usual, Kora, you are probably right." He mused this over while he listened to Kora's clucking as Flossy reentered the kitchen laden with silver.

Flossy complained, "But Mistress Kora . . . ye did tell me only the pieces that looked tarnished.''

"So I did, girl, and if that is all you found, then you weren't really looking, now were you.''

"I swear . . .''

Kora took the girl's hand and pulled her along. "Do you now? Well, we will just go have a look.''

The doctor allowed their chattering to fade as his thoughts turned to Silkie's future. He was fond of the girl and it grieved him to find her in such a dilemma. What to do? Just what could he do? Nought, that was what!

Silkie rattled off to Blaize, telling him all that had happened in the past year in vivacious style until she came to the subject of Wade Ashford. Her grey eyes grew stormy then and her voice lowered a note. "He has done everything he can to ruin my father . . . and Blaize, he means to, even if he has to . . . to . . .''

"To what?"

"To marry me and I despise him . . . but . . ."

"Hold just a moment there, Silk ole girl. What are you talking about?" He was looking at her, wide-eyed.

"Wade Ashford. I am talking about his intentions, and furthermore, he doesn't want to marry me. He would much rather take me on as mistress. . . ."

"Devil you say!" He was incredulous. "Come on, Silk . . . he can't mean to do that. Why . . . you are a Marksbury after all. Blood you know . . . gentlemen don't go about seducing gentle-born maids, even if they are rough and tumble." He was grinning at her, attempting to lighten the look on her face.

She grimaced at him. "So much for your worldliness! Blaize . . . oh never mind." She urged her horse off and took the field in a canter.

He called her name and followed after her. "Hold there, brat, and tell me . . . go on . . . do."

She slowed her grey to a jog, adjusted her leg which had begun to ache, wished silently for a moment that she were riding astride, and then drew breath, "Well then, Mr. dandy . . . for I have now had the opportunity to appraise your style of dress. Your father would have taken a whip to you were he alive to witness the stripes on your waistcoat."

"What?" He looked down at his open greatcoat and then with a grin added, "Don't you like my sporting colors? It's all the crack in London, I do assure you."

"Is it? Well, maybe you should go back to London then, for it won't do in Rye!" With this she giggled until he called a halt to her laughter.

"Enough I say! I want to hear more about this Wade Ashford. Heard of him, you know. He is a man about town . . . a high flyer. Top sawyer. Well known in all the clubs. A gamester and a Corinthian." He thought about this. ". . . can't say he is well liked though. In fact . . . I am pretty dashed certain he is not!"

"Well then, so you see," she retorted. "He is a scoundrel and out to do Papa harm."

"But why?"

"I don't know exactly. An old grievance, I imagine." She didn't want to tell Blaize too much about something she herself was uncertain.

Blaize's light brown eyes surveyed her face. "An old grudge, eh? That seems to ring a bell . . . something my father told me once . . ." He shook his head. "Wonder what it was? It's there, though. I shall think on it." He patted his horse. "Eh, Paint old boy, think we can take the next fence and show this chit how 'tis properly done?"

"Oh you fiend! How dare you, when I am riding sidesaddle?" Silkie fumed.

"Can't you do it?" he taunted.

"Not as nicely as I can when I am riding astride. Then, my dear fellow, I can take anything you aim your horse at!"

"Let's see what you can do!" He laughed and animated his gelding toward a greying three-railed fence surrounded by high weeds, shaggy bushes, and prickly vines. Paint's ears flickered as he willingly took his cue and his rider timed him towards it. However, a rabbit chose that moment to come hopping out of the weeds growing round the fence. Paint objected to the sudden movement by throwing his head up, and as he shied to the left he stuck in the ground, absolutely refusing the jump. Sir Blaize landed very neatly on his animal's neck just in time to see Silkie taking her fence in fine form.

She screeched with merriment when she reached the other side and turned her grey round to point at him as he adjusted himself back into his saddle. "Ha! Fool! Couldn't you feel Paint start to stick?"

He didn't bother to answer her. He was in something of a dither as he turned his horse back far enough to head for the fence again.

"Damn you, old Paint! You are going to take this fence and you are going to take it *now*!" At this juncture he cropped his horse on the rump with enough emphasis to get the rear legs to drive him forward. Up and over they went in marvelous form.

"That's better!" he said with some satisfaction, patting his horse's neck as he brought him up to Silkie.

She inclined her head. "Bravo, Sir Blaize," she teased him, "now what were you saying about my jumping abilities?"

"Do shut up," he said.

She laughed happily. "Oh it is good to have you home!"

\*　　\*　　\*

Dare Trent's dark brows veered darkly over his bright blue eyes as he pulled up the bay hack he had leased just a short while ago. He was in time to watch Silkie greeting Sir Blaize and he was frozen with interest. Why it evoked such rigid attention was a question that irritated him, so he shoved it aside as he observed them from the top of the hill.

Damn but she looked ravishing in this new and carefree manner she had with the English puppy! He felt a moment's envy. He had not yet been able to arouse her in such a way, and he was quite used to arousing every woman he had ever bothered with.

Their play sent a mixture of emotions through him, and reminded him that he still had not had a woman since setting foot on land. Then he watched with interest as Blaize caught Silkie by the arm and gave her rump a familiar thump. Well, well, the two were lovers then? It must be so, for she allowed this liberty with some enthusiasm.

Right then, that explained why she had not shown any interest in flirting with him. She had a prospect. Odd that. Why hadn't she applied to this fellow for help against Ashford? Now here was a question that needed asking. Damn, here he had rescued her father, rescued her from a prime rough situation with Ashford, and all he had managed to get from her was the smallest of smiles! Just look what she gave that puppy!

He watched them remount their steeds and head in an easterly direction, evidently towards the Marksbury cottage. Well, he would give them enough time to reach it and he would follow. The thought of interrupting them in her home rather pleased him, for he found himself suddenly in a strange mood. Hell! He was going to go call and see how his partner's brother fared and how Miss Marksbury meant to deal with Ashford in the future.

Blaize and Silkie were laughing as they sauntered into the kitchen, their riding gloves and hats in hand.

"Oh doctor," said Silkie, going forward to take his arm, "how is Papa? Isn't he better? How quickly will he recover completely?"

"Now Silkie, these things can't be rushed." He patted her hand. He had been on his way out and he moved towards the door when his faded blue eyes fixed on Blaize Fenton, grinning widely at him. "Why . . . if it isn't the whippersnapper come home!" He reached out and took Sir Blaize's outstretched hand and clasped it warmly. "How are you, lad? How did you like that devilish country you went to? Come back rich as a nabob?"

Sir Blaize snorted. "I didn't like it and I don't seem to have a head for business. I'm thinking of selling my interests in India."

"Are you? Well, don't know much about such things myself." A thought came to him and he turned to Kora with a speculative look. "Well now . . . Kora dear . . . you know that matter we discussed earlier?"

Kora was by this time taking Sir Blaize's shoulders in her hearty grasp and planting a kiss on his lean cheek. She turned to the doctor at this. "Yes?"

"Seems to me the answer might be right under our noses," answered the doctor. "Got to lope off now." Then to Silkie, "Just see to it your father is kept warm and comfortable. There isn't much more you can do . . . and only give him the laudanum at night."

He was gone in that instant and Silkie turned merrily to Kora. "Shall I go to Papa now?"

"No, love, the doctor left him sleeping. I will look in on him in a moment. There is a fire lit in the study. Take Sir Blaize in there if you like and I'll bring in some hot scones and tea. I've got clotted cream for you, Sir Blaize . . . just the way you like it." He was a favorite with her, for she had watched him grow and play at Silkie's side. It was good to have him home again, and the doctor had put a notion into her head.

"Do you still know the way?" teased Silkie as she led him through the kitchen doors to the long corridor.

"Move over, brat, and see if I don't!" he chuckled as he passed her.

"Rude!" she called after him. "And do you know you still have a pair of cat sticks for legs! What you need, Sir Blaize Fenton, is fattening up. You are too skinny by half!"

He opened the study door and made a low mocking bow. "As I am a gentleman, I shall ignore your discourtesies"—he waited for her to pass through, then closed the study door—"until I have you alone!" With which he turned on her and made as if to do her injury. She was quick to run to the fireplace and pick up a poker.

"Down brute! Down I say!"

He sank onto the sofa, putting a hand to his heart and then to his head. "Home for just a day and already wounded to the quick!"

She laughed, put away the poker, and dropped down beside him. "Oh Blaize . . . it's wonderful . . . you being here again. But you know, you have let Paint go to fat over in India. Didn't you work him?"

"Well, not very much . . . too hot!"

"Yes, but here it is nearly hunting season and he won't do in his present condition, you know."

"Hmmm . . . but that is another thing," he said thoughtfully.

"What is?"

"Well, I don't know if I shall be here for the start of the hunting season.

"What?" she ejaculated.

The study door opened and an imposing figure, captain's hat under the armpit and gloves in hand, stepped forward. "I hope you don't mind," said Captain Trent. "Kora sent me directly in . . . she said there was no need to announce me." He hadn't missed the easy intimacy the two on the sofa seemed to share, or the fact that Silkie sprang guiltily away from her young man.

## Chapter 8

*Silkie* tried to compose herself beneath Captain Trent's even gaze. Why his presence should intimidate her, she could not say or begin to understand. It was an annoying fact and she ignored it as she made the introductions. Sir Blaize immediately fell to questioning Trent about his travels in the Far East.

Silkie listened to her friend conversing easily with Trent and felt an almost irrepressible irritation. Why did Trent have to come just now? Immediately she reproached herself. After all, he had saved her father's life. He had rescued her from Ashford's clutches. Oh faith! She would have to repay him the two thousand pounds! However could that be done? She wanted to broach the subject with him but couldn't very well do that with Blaize present. Her friend might feel it encumbent upon himself to hand over the money on her behalf . . . indebted to one and then to another was not what she had in mind. So she listened to them converse and finally, when there was a lull, she said carefully, "Captain . . . I want to thank you for what you have done for us."

"Do you?" He inclined his head and there was the slightest mocking gesture in the movement. "Kora tells me your father is resting comfortably now, and while I have no wish to disturb him, I am anxious to pay my respects to him."

"Oh yes. I am certain he will want to hear all about his brother." She smiled now.

Kora appeared with a tray piled high with an assortment of delectables. This she set before them, chastizing Sir Blaize as he rubbed his hands together with anticipation of his attack on the food.

It was nearly six in the morning and a bright sun was peeping through Captain Werth's cabin porthole. He was watching Blaine as she slipped into her simple gown of brown muslin. How could he bear the next few months without her? He moved forward and reached round her, holding her back tightly against his lean hard chest.

"Ah Blaine . . . there is still time. We could sail off together, now, right now."

She bent her neck to his kiss and then turned round to face him, to put her hands to his cheeks. She was a woman now, his woman, and the memory of their night together would serve her until his return. "Give me these months to change my mother's mind . . . and if she doesn't, the next time you leave Sag Harbor, my love, I will leave with you."

He kissed her then but she was pulling away, taking up her cloak. "I have to hurry . . . before they discover I am not in my room."

"When will your maid go in to wake you?" he asked anxiously.

"Oh, because of the ball, she won't come in till after nine . . . but I want to get into the house undetected and the servants will be up by now." She giggled. "I shall have to climb the trellis and I haven't done that for years."

"I don't want you doing that," he said sharply. "You could fall."

She laughed and started for the door. "Don't worry, my Denny, from here on out I can do nothing wrong! You have given me . . . *magic*!"

With this she was scrambling up the companion stairs, across the deck, past his busy crew, noting as she smiled at them and they smiled back that she wasn't in the least ashamed. It was an amazing realization. She hurried through the town, taking a shortcut to the woods and then down a woodland path to the outskirts of her parents' Georgian-styled estate. She stopped there for breath and thought further. Perhaps it would be better to saunter in the front door and say that she had simply risen early and taken a morning walk. Yes, her mother might be suspicious, but it would be safer than attempting to sneak into the house. Oh Denny, come back soon, before this new courage dissipates. . . .

*     *     *

Sir Blaize licked off some clotted cream and jam from his spoon, downed the last of the scones, and sat back well satisfied. However, as he looked up, he also discovered the time on the mantleshelf clock wanted ten minutes to twelve noon.

"Egad!"—with which he jumped to his feet—"have to run, Silk!"

"Oh no, Blaize, not so soon," she wailed as she watched him take up his things.

He bent to her and took up both her hands in a warm clasp. "You will, of course, convey my sincerest regards to your father and tell him I shall be up to visit with him as soon as that old rascal Baskins gives me leave." With this he was chucking her beneath her chin. "Now don't fret, brat, I'll be back."

He was turning to the captain. "It's been a pleasure, captain. I can't thank you enough for all the help you have been to Silkie and her father. They are my dearest friends and I appreciate what you have done as though it had been done directly for me."

"Beast!" pursued Silkie, pulling at his sleeve. She hadn't told him that the captain had paid her debt to Ashford and she hoped Trent would make no such slip. "You could at least promise to return and have dinner with me."

"Can't," he answered merrily, "I'm promised to friends in Hastings." He put up a finger. "But if you are very good and don't plague me, I shall come for you tomorrow and take you to Rye. We can lunch at the Mermaid Inn and hobnob with the smugglers." He then remembered that her own father could be labeled thus and coughed deprecatingly as an apology. "Er . . . well . . . I'll be piking off now, Silk."

She walked with him to the study door and planted a tender kiss on his cheek. "Till tomorrow then, Sir Blaize." Her tone was mockingly formal.

"Brat!" he answered and was off.

She turned to find the captain surveying her thoughtfully and it was then that he asked quietly, "So, you do know then?"

He had been quick to see the look that passed between Sir Blaize and Silkie when the lad had made the slip about hobnobbing with smugglers in the Mermaid Inn. The puppy knew about Lord Marksbury's seafaring ventures. If the boy knew, then so did the girl!

"I have never considered myself dense," returned Silkie,

attempting to sidestep the question, "But I must ask you to clarify things for me. What is it you want to know?"

He smiled to himself to find her ready to boldly challenge him to withdraw. That was, of course, what she was doing. Enough! He had put himself forward for these Marksburys and he was going to have his way now! "What I am asking is whether or not you are aware what games your father plays at sea?"

She put up her chin, for her pride shot to her defense. However, one look at his demeanor was enough to tell her he would have his answer. "Games? You mean, do I know that my father has been . . . free trading?" she answered him levelly, feeling her cheeks burn even as she tried to sound casual about it. "Yes, I know it."

"Bravo, little girl," he said with ever the slightest of sneers. "You do it so well, but then you have been bred to behave as though anything, even smuggling, is your right!" Now why was he taking this attitude with her? He didn't feel harshly about smugglers.

"I have never questioned what 'rights' my father chose to take on as his," she answered quietly.

"Ah, then you don't approve of your father's pastime?" He clucked his tongue. "Or do you?"

"Stop it! How dare you? What do you know of our lives and why we do what we do?"

"I know that the landed gentry get bored from time to time and indulge themselves in games of highwaymen, smuggling, political intrigue. . . ." he taunted.

"I don't know what you think you know, Captain Trent, but my father risks his life so that we may put food on our table. He may be a baron, but a title is an empty thing if there are no funds to support it." She was seething now. Why was he making her defend herself and her parent to him?

He goaded her on purpose. He wanted to know something of her life, what she thought, how she felt. "So a baron of noble blood turns to smuggling," he said softly.

"To smuggling, to gaming . . . to anything that serves!" she hurled at him angrily. Here she was in heated defense of what had often brought a tinge of shame to her cheeks.

"So that the noble house of Marksbury can keep up the facade of aristocratic life? You English and your class distinctions. The *haut ton* may not dirty its hands in trade, so to keep your stable filled with blood mounts and your tables covered in linen and your children clothed in silk—''

She cut him off sharply, her temper at a new height. ''You may not have noticed, captain, but *our* home is not overflowing with servants, our table fare is simple, and my clothes are rather outdated and worn.'' She turned away from him for she felt a surge of tears. She bit her lip. She would not break down in front of this boor!

He wanted to stop. He could see that he had touched a raw spot, but even so he delved further. In her wrath she had forgotten to keep up her wall. He was finally seeing a real person and he wanted to see more. He teased her on. ''Still, in your carriage house you have a neat and well-sprung curricle, a coach, and a high-perch phaeton. In your stable, there are three blood mounts, one a grey gelding which I am certain is a valuable hunter.''

''Our carriages no longer have horses to draw them and are up for sale, and while Rocket, my grey hunter, is certainly valuable today, he was not some five years ago when I first got him. He was green and . . . and why I should bother telling you this?''

Suddenly he was standing so very close to her, towering over her, and she was taking a step backward. ''I . . . I . . . what do you know about such things. How would you recognize a hunter? I daresay you don't even know what riding to hounds is in America!''

He laughed at that. ''I am afraid you are out there. Riding to hounds has quite a following in Long Island and I am an avid subscriber to the sport. Do you use the grey in the hunt?''

''Of course. I had my forehead bloodied by the time I was fifteen, though I can't say I cared for that very much.'' She eyed him curiously. ''Do you have the red fox in Long Island?''

''We do, though the going is quite rough with the coverts so heavily protected by dense forests. You've got the open fields which give you the long and marvelous chases. We have to contend with thick brush and woods.'' He was reaching out for a stray length of flaxen hair. Its color had caught his eye and he felt transfixed by its brightness. He was touching it gently, curling it round his finger while his eyes sought and found her deep grey pools.

She was suddenly held captive by blue. The color mesmerized, the expression hypnotized. She felt her knees wobble but that was something she didn't have to worry about because she was upheld by two strong hands. Gone were her legs, but she was floating towards him, discovering viselike arms that held her stable and sent her sensations soaring. What was this? What was happening? Then his lips touched hers and she was sure she had stopped breathing.

Dare Trent's mouth discovered the honey of her lips as they parted beneath his kiss. All else faded as he held her tightly in his arms. Excitement exploded in his head as her body melted against his own. Time was a thing relegated to another dimension. Tenderness was a soft sensation that enveloped. Hunger was an overriding throbbing that beat at his heart and demanded satisfaction.

Silkie didn't think. A question remained somewhere in the back of her mind, hovering, wanting to be heard and answered. What are you doing? she asked herself. His body was steel and yet burningly alive and full with nerve endings that touched her own and riveted her with desire. Had his kiss lingered into two? Were her hands gripping his arms or pushing him away? Stop, Silkie, stop! It was a cold command from the recesses where will-power lingers forever waiting to be called upon to act.

She managed to break away and was hit with the coldness of stark reality. "Captain . . . don't . . ."

He reached for her again. "Ah beauty, sweet life, why should I when you really don't want me to stop?" His tone was caressing but his words had been ill judged. They hit her like a slap.

She bristled and took instant offense. "Oh, but you are mistaken, sir! I was but momentarily caught off guard and did not wish to offend someone who has been so kind to my father. After all, you did save his life and we are in your debt. I was merely allowing you . . . a show of . . . gratitude," she said sweetly.

"You give your kisses in lieu of payment then? I should have realized," he said with some contempt.

She looked at him boldly. "I have little else to offer these days, sir." Her ire was up and she was astounding herself with her audacity. What did it matter anymore? Why should she care what this brazen American thought of her? "However, when my father is well enough, he will advise me how to go about obtaining the cash you were kind enough to advance Mr. Ashford on our behalf.''

He took up his hat from the wall table and inclined his handsome head. ''I will bid you good afternoon, Miss Marksbury, but please rest assured that I mean to present myself to your father as soon as he is able to receive visitors.'' As a parting note he added, ''You know, little vixen, it's no wonder Ashford thinks he may have you in the end. You do lead a man to that conclusion!'' With that parting statement he was through the study door and gone before she could think to answer him.

How dare he? Did she deserve it? She had let him kiss her. Oooh! The gall of the man! He'd had the effrontery to take her in his arms . . . but she had let him . . . oh faith! She could still feel his touch. Her body burned with his touch and it was a mortifying realization. How had she let him? He had taken her by surprise, but never before had she felt like that.

Her body had betrayed her heart and mind and submitted to a moment's fancy. He was a rakehell, no better than Ashford. She moved to the mirror and inspected her reflection. Ha! One moment he wanted Flossy, the next herself, the next after that another, no doubt. A dangerous flirt! That was what he was—and she was in no mood to subject herself to such as he.

## Chapter 9

*The* meet! A shrill undertone of excitement permeated the air and invigorated the subscribers of the Kent hunt. They had been waiting for the summer to pass, to proceed to this moment, their first meet of the season. Everyone was elegantly and neatly dressed in their formal hunt attire. The huntsman in his scarlet coat was calling his hounds round with a short blast of his horn. Silkie, herself in the correct black jacket and yellow waistcoat, was sitting her Rocket sidesaddle, watching with avid interest.

A week had passed and her father wavered on the edge of getting better. Every day she would go to him, care for him, and look for a sign of improving health—but she could not find any. She was by nature an optimist and assured herself that all he needed was time. She hadn't been sure she would attend the meet today, but her father had insisted. He was a bruising rider-to-hounds sportsman himself and he wanted her to represent them at their first meet of the season.

She glanced sideways at Captain Trent, mounted on her father's chestnut hunter, Ajax. He was studying the proceedings, listening to the comments, looking over the hounds. She wasn't sure what to think of Captain Darrow Trent. He was a puzzle. After that day when he had kissed her she'd thought about him more, much more than she should. He had visited her father the very next day and every day after that, and she was forced to continue her polite yet aloof relationship with him.

Blaize was gone only a day now and already she missed him. He was off to Cornwall and hadn't even been able to tell her when he would return. It was ever so vexing for she had never needed him more.

However, this sad thought was interrupted as Master Rush came by. She watched as the captain tipped his hat and listened to the polite and correctly brief greeting that passed. She had introduced them earlier and she was relieved to find that the captain knew just how to get on.

Master of fox hounds is a term given to the man who is in command of the hunt in the field and kennels. To the hunt of Kent, Master Rush reigned supreme. Beneath him is the huntsman in charge of the hounds, assisted by two whipper-ins.

Silkie watched Rush as he approached. She twinkled at him, for she was a favorite and took full advantage of this fact. "Good morning, Master Rush."

His eyes were blue and faded with his age but he glittered before her smile; he was the best at what he did and very much a ladies' man as well. "That it is and I believe we have a good scent day in store for us. But tell me, this American of yours, will he be able to keep up or do you think you will be constrained to keep him company at the back of field?"

She laughed, for although he spoke in a low tone she was fairly certain by Trent's rueful expression that he had heard him. "Oh, he has told me that he is a devilish rider to hounds at home and received his colors when he had been no more than a boy, so I rather fancy he will be at your back just as he should."

"Good." He wagged his finger at her. "I know how much you dislike the sidesaddle, but do try and stay on your animal," he teased.

"Ha! Have I ever disappointed you? I am always up front . . . spurring you on. If there is mud to be cleaned off, my dearest Master Rush, it will be my hand brushing it off your shoulders."

"Naughty puss!" He was well pleased with her response. He moved on to further mingle with his chosen few, leaving Dare to grin at her.

"Lord, but he is something of an old rogue, isn't he?"

"That and more! Master Rush's sense for the hunt is almost mystic at times. There is no one like him, and he has been master of our hunt forever. I know he is nearly seventy, but to me he is ageless."

Trent shook his head. "It is a wonder that at his age he can keep up."

"Oh, he never tires. At the end of a hunt day I am dragging my feet, but not he!"

"Hush love," said Trent suddenly, "I believe he has called the huntsman for the hounds."

She looked at him sharply. He was doing that more often than not recently—calling her by endearing terms. She would not have it and so she had often told him, but now was not the moment. Indeed, she heard the master repeat, "Hounds, please!"

A quiet aura that held a fever pitch hung over the collected field. The moment had arrived. However, a young gentleman in scarlet, whose experience had won him the position of whipper-in with the hunt, came up behind Silkie and whispered, "Silk . . . eh girl, do take this, for we may need you to help with the hounds. James hasn't returned from London yet and with your father out . . . it goes to you." He handed her the whipthong.

It wasn't the first time she had helped with the hounds and knew well enough what was to be done. "Of course," she said at once, taking up the thong and smiling at him as he hurried his horse off.

The field moved in behind the field master, as the huntsman with his hounds around him had already begun following the senior whipper-in whose job it was to maintain the pack. The lad who had just given the whip to Silkie caught up and moved into position behind the pack and received from the MFH a dark look for the delay.

Unlike the field master who must stay in front and control his field, the MFH may go anywhere he pleases and deems worthy. Thus Master Rush went on ahead in the distance and at some pace.

Darrow Trent watched in some fascination before turning to Silkie. "He seems a knowing one alright. Why, I could have sworn he was sniffing the air!"

"He probably was." She laughed. "It is because of Master Rush that we have such an enormous membership. Over one hundred, you know," she said proudly.

Then suddenly she was sitting very still. "Famous!" she cried on a low, exultant note. "Did you hear?"

A hound had given tongue!

"I did. Do you know your hounds? Is that one a babbler . . . or is it a reliable cry?"

Again the hound spoke and it was a thrilling sound picked up by yet another hound. Silkie answered in some excitement, "That was Warrior and *he* is no babbler! Get ready, Captain Trent, for you are in for quite a chase!"

He grinned. "Don't think you will lose me. Your father says this big hunter of his can jump anything in sight as well as put turf behind him for hours!"

"Right then, but do watch for the bogs. You will know them by their reddish color . . . we have lost some horses in them from time to time."

"Aye, we have them at home as well." But there was no time for more.

The staff was already in full chase and the field at their backs was opening up into a gallop. They were off and it was a glorious sight that most of the farmers had come out to witness. More than the villagers, farmers, and townspeople had ridden out to see the riders to hounds in action. At the top of the crest, astride his bay gelding, was Wade Ashford.

They would be gone for at least four or five hours. Time enough to find his way to Aaron Marksbury's bedroom and have a chat with him. Indeed, Wade had been sharpening his teeth for the moment. He was now fully equipped to take on Marksbury and finally bring him low. He frowned over this, for it was rumored that Marksbury had received his death sentence. He hoped not!

That wasn't what he wanted, not now . . . now he wanted Aaron alive and fully sensitive to his daughter's plight. He wanted to watch Aaron suffer.

He gave his bay a hard kick and off he cantered towards the Marksbury cottage. He would have to get past Kora, but there was very little she could do to keep him away from Marksbury. Slowly, very slowly, he would tell Marksbury what lay in store. Silkie would be his! Damn, but that was a thought. Silkie? Yes, indeed, he would know just how to use Serena's daughter.

Aaron lay back against his pillow and found himself drifting into another world. Was it a dream? He seemed to be moving in a fog and there was Serena, an arm's length away. She was smiling to him, beckoning him, and it was good, so good to see her again. He moved towards her and put out his hand. Her fingers came towards him and he heard her say his name. Why couldn't he reach her? She was right there. . . .

A voice intruded sharply. Hateful voice, despicable image. There was Ashford, as he had been twenty-three years ago. Ashford reaching for Serena . . . but it wasn't Serena . . . it was Silkie . . . Silkie . . .

"NO! I won't let you!" It was an anguished cry from a broken man.

"Won't you?" Ashford's sneer was marked but he was disturbed. This was not how he wanted to find Aaron.

All at once Aaron was awake. His tired green eyes centered and fixed on Ashford's face. No dream. Here was Ashford. Here. What did he want? Silkie had told him that Trent had advanced him the two thousand on behalf of Tyler. Tyler? Trent seemed sure that Tyler would not wish to be repaid. Was this so? He was so tired, but here was Ashford . . . threatening.

"You see, Aaron . . . I have brought up all your notes. It comes to quite a hefty sum. Ten thousand pounds, as a matter of fact. I mean to bring legal action against you . . . that is, if you don't cooperate."

"How do you wish me to cooperate?" He pulled himself into a sitting position. The doctor had said Aaron had cracked his ribs and had wrapped him up, but it didn't help. Something inside was wrong and there was pain, so very much pain . . . it was hard to concentrate on anything. He wanted his laudanum. He reached for it, but Ashford's hand closed round the bottle and put it out of proximity.

"No, I think not. I want you coherent. I want you to understand."

"What do you want, Ashford? What could you possibly want now?"

"You know what I want," hissed Wade Ashford, suddenly baring his hatred. "I want you to rot in hell and I want you to do it while you are still breathing."

Aaron managed a rueful smile. "Be content then."

"No, you don't know the extent to which I want you tortured. I mean to have Silkie. Did you know that? Yes, I mean to have her still. That is not at an end."

"She won't have you. She loathes you."

"She loves you, though. She will come to me to keep you in

this house and out of debtor's prison. You see, I mean to hold that over her head.''

"You are too late . . . I am dying, Ashford, and shall do so before you can have me ousted from here. . . ."

"Do you think so? Silkie does not. She thinks you are on the mend. I could have her tonight if I wished.''

"I will kill myself first,'' breathed Aaron.

"You haven't the courage for that. You are many things, Aaron Marksbury, and perhaps you may once have been noble enough to do that, but not now. Now you are a sick old man and yes, you are dying, but you shan't until you have seen your sweet Silkie ruined at my hands!'' With this Ashford had risen and found the door. It had been pure good luck that Kora had been in the storage room when he had stealthily made his way within. He wanted out before she found him.

Aaron said nothing to this. He watched as Ashford left and he sat very still with his thoughts. Then he knew. It was as though Serena whispered to him and told him what he must do. It was a villanous thing to do to someone who had saved his life, but it had to be done. He reached for the bellrope and winced, for it brought on a wave of maddening pain. When Kora finally appeared he said hoarsely, "Send Joseph to me . . . at once, Kora, for there is much to be done!''

## Chapter 10

*Silkie* and Darrow Trent burst into the Marksbury cottage. It was a joyful entrance. They had hunted for nearly six hours behind a superbly organized pack of hounds and had the thrill of riding across good country, watching a well-trained pack of hounds hunt a swift and cunning fox, and staying at the front of the line.

Theirs was the exhilaration of two young people who have put their skills to the test and come out victorious. It boosted their egos, made them nearly bosky with delight in themselves and the sport—but mostly with themselves for having survived the danger.

They were laughing over some of the lighter moments of the day. There had been Squire Ralph Aldershot who had gone headlong into the stream. "Did you see him fly?" cried Silkie dissolving into wicked mirth at the memory. "Someone called out, 'Aldershot's come to grief!' but no one stopped."

"No one had to. He was up and chasing after us all, determined to remain with the hunt." Trent laughed.

"Never mind, his horse did!" She shook her head. "And what about that silly boy, Skippy Henderson. He was getting to be a bit of a bother when we were going through that thicket. He cut me off several times and seemed almost giddy about it. Then what must he do but turn round to tell me he was having a splendid time and *wham* . . . that branch wipes him right off his horse . . . I laughed so hard I thought I might go over myself."

She sank down with a happy groan onto the yellow damask sofa in the study and stretched out her hands towards the blazing fire Kora had prepared for their return. "Oh, but Dare . . . I really did think it was all over for you when I heard you cursing away and turned round to see you holding your left leather and stirrup in your hand! Your face . . . your face looked so comical!''

He dropped unceremoniously down beside her and without thinking his hand rested on her knee. ''Have you ever tried to reinsert your stirrup leather into its fitting while at a full gallop, my love? 'Tis no easy matter, let me assure you!''

''Oh, but you were marvelous . . . though there was that moment when we lost Master Rush and the staff over the hill. There we were with no one . . . not a soul on the field behind us . . . no one in front and no one in sight. I didn't know how they could have vanished so quickly.''

''Well, that particular part of the country was densely wooded. 'Tis a good thing you know your territory. Quite frankly, with the sun gone, I couldn't tell our direction.''

''Truth is, Dare, I couldn't either, for I only hunted that part of the country once before. We were in Sussex by that time. I gave Rocket his head and he found the staff for us, you know.''

''Clever little bird!'' said Dare, pinching her chin. ''Lord, but your face is smudged.''

She laughed and touched her hair. Its waves were in a tangled heap around her neck where some of the remaining strands were confined in a netting somewhat worse for wear. Her clothes were soiled, her black hunting coat torn in yet another spot that she proudly displayed to him and said t'was the sign of a true hunter. ''I'll just go up . . . see my father, wash up a bit, and return . . . we can dine in here if you like, by the fire. It will be nice . . . and I am sorry about the tea . . . I really couldn't stay. I wanted to get home to Papa.''

''Never mind the tea. I would much rather have dinner with you here . . . by the fire, which is an excellent notion.'' He was looking at her softly. ''Go on then.''

''Right.'' What was this she was feeling towards Dare Trent? Friendship? Had the day done that for them? Had the common bond of fox hunting brought them closer, made it possible for her to see another aspect of this complicated man? He was still a rogue and a devil with women. Flossy had tittered about Captain Trent's taking the Rye women by storm. Careful, she told herself. He was far too handsome, far too charming to allow to get too close!

Kora met her outside the study door and touched her hand. "Silkie, love?"

"Hallo darling. We have had a marvelous day."

"You deserve it, child, and I don't mean to ruin it for you but—"

Silkie's eyes opened wide with sudden fright. "What is it? Papa, is Papa worse?"

"No . . . well as to that . . . he seems about the same . . . only . . . something is wrong. I don't know what it is. He had a visitor . . . I haven't been able to find out who it was . . . but after that he sent for Joseph and had him fetch his man Fletcher."

"His first mate? Why?"

"I don't know. He is up to something and he won't tell me. Thought mayhap you might pry it out of him for it has me that worried, it does."

"Alright, dearest, I shall speak with him now," said Silkie. Kora was hardly ever wrong, but this time she must be. What could her father possibly be involved in when he was abed and not well?

A moment later she was kissing her father's forehead. He opened his green eyes and smiled. His Silkie. Everything had been all settled. She would be angry. Good God! She would be furious, but she would be safe.

"Papa. Kora tells me you have been up to mischief."

"Nonsense. Here I have been all day and if it's bobbery I have been at, it's been in my dreams. Tell me about the hunt."

"Oh, it was glorious!" She sighed. "Perfect. One of those really perfect days. We had a run, Papa . . . I thought I wouldn't last. Really, my legs were starting to give out—one leg did in fact go numb on me sidesaddle—it just wasn't made for those really hellbent rides."

"How did Dare like our English hunting?"

"He was marvelous. He is a famous rider, Papa. His seat is really to be admired. He says that his hunt in America is traditional and not unlike our own."

"Do you like him, Silkie?"

She wrinkled her nose. "Sometimes I do."

He sighed. "You'll ask him to stay the night."

"What?" She eyed her father thoughtfully. "Why?"

"I didn't want to worry Kora and I don't want to worry you, but Ashford was here today and I didn't like the sound of his . . . threats. I would feel better if Dare were here tonight."

"*Ashford was here?*" she returned sharply. "Fiend seize his soul! How dare he bother you! What did he want?"

"You," said Aaron simply. "When he knew that Dare was in your company he seemed to back off . . . that is why I should like Dare to stay the night . . . you will ask him, Silkie?"

"If it relieves your mind, of course, Papa."

"That's a good girl. Now you go wash up and then keep our Captain company . . . I'm a bit tired."

She kissed him lightly, stroked his cheek, and left him alone. Ashford! Why must they always be bothered with Ashford? Silkie had questioned her father about it and all he had said was that they'd been rivals for her mother, that Ashford had never gotten over the loss. Still, it didn't seem enough cause for the quantity of hate that Ashford felt for them. Then there was Dare Trent stepping in between, refusing to take her note for the two thousand. What had he said? "Your uncle will reimburse me . . . you may issue your note to him if he wishes." Right then, so he had saved her father, saved her, and had for the last week managed to keep Ashford away. He would leave them soon, return to America, and then what would keep Ashford leashed?

Indeed, where would they be once Dare returned to America? Blaize was in Cornwall attending to relatives, but he would be back soon, wouldn't he? Blaize. Could Blaize ever think of her romantically? She had certainly thought of him in that vein . . . at least this week she had. It was an interesting dream, the thought of marriage to Sir Blaize. They were such good friends. Faith, but they would deal famously together . . . wouldn't they? Passion. Would there be passion in that union? Perhaps.

Two hours later the word passion crept into her mind again but it was put there by a pair of sparkling blue eyes that nearly took her breath away. They had broken all conventional rules and had taken their simple but hearty meal on the hearth rug. Kora popped in and out, but for the most part they had been alone and their conversation never lagged.

Suddenly, with the intensity of his gaze, they were silent. She knew, she just knew what was going to happen next. She had to stop it from happening. He was a rakehell. Hadn't Flossy named those whose hearts he would be taking back to America with him? Did she want to be one of the casualties?

No, she did not, yet when he reached for her shoulders, she made no move to stop him. Indeed, if she were honest with herself—and she usually was—she would have had to admit that she wanted him to kiss her.

Kiss her? He wanted more than to kiss her. She had freshened up, but she had undone her yellow waistcoat and unbuttoned the white linen shirt she was wearing. He could see her full breasts heaving with her sudden shortness of breath. Her white gold hair fell in silky torrents round her shoulders and her grey eyes held the promise of pleasure. Kora could step in on them, but he didn't care. He had to have her in his arms and he had to have her now!

His fingers closed on her small shoulders and easily, deftly he slid her into his embrace. As his mouth found and parted her lips, his hand slid to her waist and held its trim line before moving to her hip and then back to her tight small rump, bringing her in even closer to his body. He was on fire and he couldn't think. Was that her voice asking him to stop? Was it his own telling him he must stop?

What was happening to her? She couldn't fight him, didn't even want to. She had wanted him to kiss her again . . . ever since that first kiss she'd had from him, she had wanted this moment. Oh God! What was he doing? His hands set her flesh on fire. Her blood bubbled in her veins and her arms went round him, held onto him lest she lose herself, but it only made that loss a certainty.

He heard someone at the study door. How he did, he couldn't know, but he realized that Kora was coming and quickly set Silkie from him with a rueful smile. "I think, little pet, your Kora comes to fetch you to bed."

Kora came in clucking her tongue. "Do you know the time, Silkie love? Why its near midnight . . . those hunts seem to last longer and longer . . . you must be done in, you poor child." She turned to the captain then. "Your room is ready for you, sir, whenever you wish to retire. I've put a hot brick in the bed for you so I think you'll be comfortable."

Earlier, Silkie had asked him to stay and he had been more

than willing. He got to his feet and reached down for Silkie's hand. She was trembling from their encounter but she gave him her hand though she wasn't able to meet his gaze. "Up with you, minx," he said to her lightly. "Kora is absolutely right, you know . . . you have had a long, hard day. We both have and what we need now . . . is *bed*." With this last he looked intently into her grey eyes, his meaning all too clear.

Beneath her breath she nearly shouted at him, Devil, now don't prod me too far! Then in a bright voice she said, "Goodnight captain. Come Kora . . . we'll let the captain relax a bit with his cognac."

Captain Darrow Trent watched Silkie leave. Damn, but she was the finest piece of flesh and blood . . . and he couldn't remember ever wanting a woman before as he wanted Silkie. She was, of course, not to be had. After all, she was Tyler's niece, and probably a virgin. He didn't tamper with virgins. At any rate he would soon be leaving and he believed in playing fair. Hit and run was not his style.

He would leave her in peace . . . a kiss . . . he had taken a kiss. Damn, but she had felt wondrously good in his arms. He wanted to keep her all night, hold her, make love to her, teach her passion. How her body had warmed to his touch. . . .

Forget it! She is not for you so get her out of your system. You will be off for home and . . . and *what*? Blaine? Will you fall in with Zara's schemes and marry the pretty Blaine? Certes! That was something he didn't want to think about.

Ashford. Trent was here at the Marksbury cottage for the night because Silkie had said that Ashford threatened her father. Well then, what the bloody hell were Silkie and her father to do when he departed for America? Perhaps Sir Blaize would return to look after Silkie.

This thought gave him no comfort. Odd that. The notion of Sir Blaize looking after Silkie annoyed him to the point of exasperation. This was absurd! Everything that had happened to him since he had entered English waters had been utterly ridiculous. He would sail for home and put his life into order and forget this Marksbury and his bright-haired, grey-eyed daughter.

## Chapter 11

*Joseph* Linch was the Marksbury's groom. Tall, fair, wiry, and gentle-handed with a horse, he had twenty-two years to his credit. Aaron Marksbury had found him in the gutters of London when he had been no more than twelve and had brought him home to Serena, saying, "What can we do for this whelp, darling? He is dirty, ill-mannered, and I think ready to meet his maker . . . but there is something in his eyes . . . I don't know . . . what do you think?"

Softly she had taken the boy and tenderly she had cared for him and before long he was putting on weight, teasing Kora in the kitchen, and worshipping both Lord and Lady Marksbury with a loyalty he had never been called upon to prove. However, things were at a sad pass at Marksbury now and his love had been called upon by his lordship. He stood outside the Mermaid Inn and bit his lip, just a bit frightened that the crewmember of the *Silkie* would not agree to fall in with his lordship's scheme.

He went inside and looked round the crowded room until his large pale eyes found the lordship's first mate, Harley. Here was a brute of a fellow. Unshaven, unkempt, and something of a boor. Could he be trusted in this task? Possibly. Harley looked up and saw Joseph eyeing him. Eh? Whot was this? He motioned for the lad to approach.

"Sit ye down, boy!" he said loudly, pulling out a wooden chair and giving the boy a sharp penetrating appraisal. "Tell me 'ow our lordship is. Doing better, is he?"

"I think so . . . he sent me here . . . to get you . . . he wants to see you, Harley." This huge man always made Joseph just a bit nervous. Joseph had spent too many years of his youth working and groveling to a man who had looked so much like Harley. Even their voices had the same hard ring. "It is important, so can you come . . . *now*?"

Harley looked at the men at his table. Most of the crew of the *Silkie* had already recovered from their mishap at sea. It had been the captain who had sustained the most serious of the injuries.

"Aye . . . I can do that . . . but he has never had me up to the house afore . . . we usually meet at the cave." There was doubt there, for his occupation had long ago made him suspicious.

"He can't get around and this is about something different."

"Is it now? Whot might he be wanting?"

Joseph felt like crying. A man wasn't supposed to do that but what his lordship had told him had gone down hard. "He . . . he thinks he is dying . . . and he needs your help. He said that was all I had to tell you . . . he said you wouldn't let him down, you have never let him down."

Harley went thoughtful. No, he wouldn't let Aaron Marksbury down. A flash cove Marksbury was, but a better, braver captain he had never had. They had for the past ten years been something of a team. Seaman and gentry outwitting the dragoons. They had been through a great deal together and Harley's life had been . . . easier. At least since he had teamed with Marksbury he always had shelter, food, and drink. . . .

"Let himself down? Aye, I think not!" he said levelly and got up from the table. "Come on then."

Together they had gone to the Marksbury cottage and quietly they had gone to his lordship's room. Harley was at first astounded to hear what his lordship wanted but as soon as it sunk in, a slow grin made its way across his grizzled face.

"Aye, m'lord . . . I think I know jest the vicar we need . . . not your respectable sort, you know . . . but he'll do."

"It must be legal!" returned Lord Marksbury with some concern. "Everything hinges on its being legal, Harley."

"Don't ye fret it, m'lord. Legal it will be."

"The license . . . you'll have to rush over to Hastings and obtain the license . . . can you do it?"

"Aye . . . leastways, *I* can't . . . but I know the cove what can . . . have faith in me, captain. I won't let ye down."

"No, I didn't think you would."

It was past midnight and as Joseph entered the study he remembered the pact he had made with his lordship and Harley those many hours ago. It was wrong. This American had saved his lordship's life. Captain Trent was a decent sort and Joseph liked him . . . even if he did flirt outrageously with Flossy. He sighed. It was for Miss Silkie's sake. That made it right. The American was just finishing off his cognac when he looked up and encountered Joseph.

"S'cuse me, Captain Trent. 'is lordship thought ye might indulge 'im with a nightcap in 'is room."

Dare Trent eyed the lad speculatively. Now, what was this all about? He had spent a long, eventful, and most enjoyable day, but all he wanted now was his bed. However, he had promised Silkie that he would stop in and see her father before he retired for the night. He supposed his lordship was just reminding him about their late "date." "Yes Joseph, I was just on my way up."

Joseph could only nod and lower his eyes as he turned away. Well, what the deuce was wrong with the lad? Dare Trent frowned over this question as he followed the younger man out of the study. It wasn't the first time this day that Joseph had behaved oddly. The lad was usually bright and full with nonsensical conversation, but when Trent had entered the stables with Silkie after the hunt, he noticed that Joseph was strangely silent. He could find no ready answer so he shrugged it off and put it to moods. No doubt Flossy and Joseph had had a lover's spat.

He went upstairs, stopped outside Aaron Marksbury's door, and knocked. Aaron had been waiting and he put on a smile. To the door he called out, "Come in."

The Captain went within and his smile was genuine. "Did you wish to see me, my lord?"

"Ah, Dare . . . such an appropriate name. Here . . . sit beside me," said Aaron on a low note. "That's right." He watched as Dare took up the wing chair and tried to relax. Something, Dare knew not what, was making him uneasy. "I had Joseph pour us two glasses of brandy . . . 'tis the best I have in the house. I didn't send it down for I particularly wanted to take a glass with you and toast your first English fox hunt."

"How kind of you, my lord," said Dare. He really didn't

want another drink for he was tired and ready for bed, but there was nothing for it. He couldn't decline without appearing rude.

They sipped the dark, smooth brew and all the while Aaron kept up an easy flow of conversation, talking about hunts past, incidents where they had nearly lost a rider who had come off near the cliff's edge. Quietly and in gentle tones Aaron Marksbury spoke until he saw Dare Trent's head begin to droop.

"Dare?" he said softly. No response. He smiled. "Dare? Dare Trent?" Still no response. Fine. The drug had taken its effect and Captain Darrow Trent would sleep soundly for many, many hours.

Joseph, who had stood by the door, came forward. "Would you be wanting anything else, my lord?"

"Did you do as I asked? Did you put the sleeping potion in my daughter's hot chocolate?"

"Aye, oi did that before Mistress Kōra took it up to her, but oi don't know if she drank it."

"Well, that we shall have to leave to chance . . . and if she didn't we'll have to switch to our alternate plan."

"Aye . . . but it's that bad oi feel . . . Miss Silkie . . . she's going to 'ave me skin."

"Don't worry, Joseph. She will know you were only obeying my orders. Go on now, get a couple of hours' sleep and then when Harley arrives, bring him up here."

Sleep. It should have come easily, peacefully, drowningly for Silkie Marksbury. She had certainly sustained a long, exhilarating day. But instead, Silkie tossed, she turned, she pounded her pillow, and finally in some exasperation she got to her feet and paced!

The fire in her hearth was dying so she went to the grate and placed another log on, playing with it until it ignited. She then sat and brought her knees up so their peaks reached her chin. She hugged her calves round and swayed on the hearth rug. This was absurd. He had kissed her. So, he had kissed her! Faith! What was that? It hadn't been her first kiss . . . nooo . . . not her first kiss.

Wayne Van Buren had given her that very first grownup kiss two years ago when he had come down from Oxford to visit with Blaize. Blaize. Oh Blaize. He had never even tried to kiss her.

Never mind. That was silly—Blaize trying to kiss her, ha! Kisses? Oh yes, there was that friend of her father's . . . hmmm. Lord Ashbrow. A bit of a rake he had been. She had been amazed at his audacity and just a little dazzled by his attention. He had been interesting but his kiss had done nothing for her. Odd that, it should have done, for he had been experienced enough. And then Wade Ashford had come along!

He was hateful, was Wade Ashford, but Silkie was ever honest with herself. Thinking about it now she realized all too well that Wade Ashford's kiss had certainly awakened a certain heat in her. It was, of course, humiliating to discover that her blood could be aroused by a man she despised. Logic came to her rescue. She told herself she was twenty and on the verge of womanhood. Of course she wanted a man; it was the natural order of things. Wade Ashford was a villain but he had a certain sensuality that had been all too apparent during his pursuit of her. She could be aroused—but it had nothing to do with love. Ugh! Wade Ashford. She didn't want to think about him or his kisses. Who then must she meet? A swaggering, conceited, arrogant American cavalier with easy manners and a cool command. Had he the power to make her weak kneed or had that been just her own awakening desires? Famous? She pulled a face over this. It was simply famous! Here she was on fire—for she had to admit that Dare Trent's touch, his lips, his embrace had set her to burning—and there was nought she could do about it!

His aqua blue eyes reached deep within and drew out a response she was loath to admit feeling. His hold on her was vividly recalled. His lips on hers had melted her resistance and cut up her peace. She chided herself. Nonsensical girl. He will be off for America soon. You were simply excited by the hunt, he shared that excitement with you, and . . . and . . . that is all. It was his ability to ride to the hounds which you admired, not his character. Forget him!

You should know better. Didn't you always promise yourself you wouldn't paint a picture round a man? Didn't you always promise yourself you wouldn't expect a man in shining armor because he doesn't exist, not anymore, not today—and Captain Dare Trent is no knight. He saved your father, yes, and he is a bruising rider to hounds, and yes, very good-looking, but he is an

outrageous flirt and will break your heart if you let him . . . so
. . . just don't let him!

She got up and spied her mug of hot chocolate. No doubt it
was cold by now. Never mind, it might help her to sleep. She
walked over to it, took it up, and took a long gulp. Another
followed and still another before she noticed that it left a bitter
taste on her tongue. She wrinkled her nose and looked at it. The
milk didn't seem curdled and it hadn't tasted sour. She took
another sip and decided to leave the remaining dregs on her
nightstand. She drew in a deep breath, lifted her covers, and
plumped herself down. How was she ever going to sleep when
her mind was so confused and rattled? However, no sooner had
this question been asked of herself when she felt a heavy drowsi-
ness overtake her. Ah, sleep at last.

Later, much later, her bedroom door was opened and the
shadows of Harley and Joseph carrying another large dark form
moved in her room. She didn't hear them though and she didn't
see them either. They did stop and hold their breaths when she
tossed under her covers. A moment later they were breathing
easier and tiptoeing out of her room, part of their job completed.

Silkie's dreams were heavily plotted and filled with more
action than dialogue. Real? Ah, so much felt so real. There was
a hand on her waist . . . it was Dare's hand and he was pulling
her closer, closer . . . but he didn't try to kiss her. He held her
tightly and it was wonderful. She snuggled in his embrace and
the dream scattered with the deepness of her sleep.

It was morning and past eight o'clock when Lord Marksbury
summoned Kora to him. She came in flushed for she had been
baking since seven.

"What is it, my lord? Are you not well?" asked Kora when
she entered his room and found him looking haggard and frowning.
Quickly she sent a glance to Joseph in the corner of the room.
The boy was fidgeting and appeared ill at ease.

"Kora, I didn't want to trouble you . . . but we have something of a problem to deal with this morning. I need Joseph with
me . . . so I hope you won't mind taking the dog-cart and going
into town to fetch me the items I have listed here." He handed
her a slip of paper.

"Well, of course, my lord. 'Tis no problem . . . would you be wanting me to wake Silkie?"

"No! I mean . . . the girl is no doubt tired after her marvelous day yesterday."

"That she should be!" returned Kora, putting on her face, for she had never approved of his lordship's teaching Silkie to be a fox hunter.

Some minutes later they watched Kora take off in the dog-cart, clicking and clucking as she made her way down the drive. Something was very odd. She didn't know what it was, yet she felt in her bones that something was not right. She shrugged this off. If only Flossy would do as she was told and polish the cabinets correctly. . . .

Harley waited in the stables with the Reverend Andrews. Here was a little man who licked his lips too often and whose bloodshot eyes explained why he no longer had a parish to call his own. He followed Harley into the house and up the back stairs past a grumbling Flossy who did not witness their arrival. A soft knock at Marksbury's bedroom door sent Joseph flying to open it wide and stand aside for them to enter.

The small reverend clapped his hands together and smacked his lips; he was already itching for his drink and wanted the business over with. "Well, well, well . . . now where is the happy couple?"

"Shut yer mummer, Andrews!" snapped Harley. "We'll be takin' yer there when his lordship is ready."

Aaron Marksbury looked the small man over and raised a brow at Harley. "Are you certain he is legally capable of performing the—"

The reverend made a deprecatory cough. "Er . . . I am fully qualified and legally recognized as a man of the cloth, my lord." He sighed and raised his hands a bit dramatically. ". . . a few setbacks I have encountered . . . were at the heart of my—"

"Too fond of his whiskey!" put in Harley, cutting the man off.

"That is a fact, my lord," agreed Andrews. "It was my predilection for—"

"We know, Andrews! 'Tis a wonder his lordship hasn't passed out from that cheap firewater you've got in ye!" said Harley in some disgust. Then to Marksbury, "Would ye be wanting me to lift ye to Miss Silkie's room now, m'lord?"

"Yes, thank you, Harley . . . if I could just lean on you."

It was not easy going. Lord Marksbury found that in spite of the fact that Harley took nearly all his weight, every step was extremely painful. He was out of breath and his cheeks had paled with the effort, but Joseph soon opened Silkie's door and Aaron was placed onto Silkie's settee as he waved Joseph to the hangings.

Joseph pulled them wide and allowed the bright sunlight to come streaming harshly into the room and illuminate Silkie's bed. No one gasped. No one felt the least bit of outrage. A father, finding his trusted male guest in his daughter's bed, should have been riveted by the sight, yes? No—for this father had created the scene.

"Silkie!" called Lord Marksbury. "Silkie!" His tone implied anger.

She stirred. Was that her papa calling? Why did her limbs feel so heavy? Well, she would open her eyes first. No! It was impossible. She closed them and then opened them again. Beside her, lying on his side, his one arm flung round her waist, was Captain Dare Trent!

She went bolt upright and stared down at him. What was he doing here? Was she in her room? She looked around and gasped, "Papa?" There was Joseph, and a man she knew as her father's first mate . . . and still another, a stranger. Where was she? Her room, this was her room! "Papa?" she repeated.

Aaron Marksbury discovered that theory put into practice could be a most difficult thing. Here was his daughter, his jewel, floundering in shame. What had he done to her? How could he proceed? Wade Ashford will destroy her if you do not, came the sharp answer. He cleared his throat. "Silkie . . . don't worry, my pet. I have arranged for everything to be set to rights immediately."

# Chapter 12

*Dare* Trent's brows veered into a frown. He had been holding a most delectable prize. He had won her fairly in a game of chance and he had meant to have her . . . but somehow she had slipped away. His dream ended abruptly as Silkie shot bolt upright. Had he heard another man call her name? Silkie? Yes, damnation! Someone had called Silkie away and he would see the fellow pinked before he would give Silkie up to him! Damn, but it was difficult to move. He moaned, reached, and found Silkie's thigh. A smile spread over his countenance and once again he held fast and drew her to him. This time she would not get away.

Silkie found herself in the captain's steel-hard grip, and what must he do but pull her down beside him. She flushed and struggled. Oh Lord, but this was a rare set-to! Here was her father and all the world watching the captain attempt to make love to her in his sleep and she not knowing how he had gotten into her bed! Mercy! What must they think? What could they think? Famous! What did she think? "Stop it, captain!" she cried and pushed at him as she tried to release herself. "Stop it . . . please . . ." She was wrestling with him now. "Oh faith! Trent . . . stop it, I say!"

Dare Trent finally roused. Silkie's tones got through the fog in his head and fluttered his thick dark lashes. His bright blue eyes discovered Silkie's flaxen hair tickling his shoulders. His dark straight brows moved with his surprise and he started to prop himself onto one elbow as Silkie escaped and moved away from him. He opened his eyes wider and felt the room spin. Damn! What was the matter with him? He must have really had more to drink than he had realized.

What was she saying? Who was she talking to? He saw Aaron Marksbury on the settee, Joseph holding up a wall in mute discomfort, and a large, rather burly seaman beside Aaron. "Certes!" he breathed out loud, "what in blazes?" He returned his gaze to Silkie. "What is going on?"

"You are daring to ask me? How did you get into my bed?" she shot at him and turned a furious shade of red. Oh God! She pulled the covers round her at this juncture and moved off the bed to stand beside her nightstand.

He discovered that his breeches were still on, but the black riding coat, with the yellow waistcoat as well as the shirt he had worn for the hunt were missing. He frowned and discovered these articles on the floor with his boots. He was trying to remember, when Aaron Marksbury's voice split the air in sharp resonance.

"Captain! I am amazed that you saw fit to take advantage of my state of health, my hospitality, and my daughter! You may do such things in America without impunity, but not in England!"

"Papa . . . no . . . you are wrong. . . ." Silkie shook her head and her grey eyes were filled with confusion, "It is not what you think! Nothing happened. The captain must have had too much to drink and wandered in here by mistake."

"My dear child, we discovered you . . . in his arms," said Aaron quietly, and he put up his hand to still the flow of words that would have poured out from both the captain and Silkie. "Let me explain. I was unwell during the night and Joseph was kind enough to sit with me as I didn't wish to disturb either you or Kora. He was on his way up from the kitchen where he had raided the larder on my instructions. What must he see but your door slightly ajar; he moved to close it and heard the captain . . . laughing inside the room. He reported this to me . . . but it was too late . . . we knew this from the silence." He bowed his head. "I don't blame you, Silkie love, you are an innocent and he is a charming, sophisticated man. No doubt you felt you owed him a wealth of gratitude." He eyed the captain. "However, I had not offered up my daughter to your bed, sir, and therefore you must pay the price!"

"Hold a moment," said the captain.

"No, you must do that. You see, summing up the situation I realized what had to be done and I sent for Harley here. He went for the reverend who is waiting by the door . . . and they obtained the license.''

"The license?" ejaculated the captain. He was beginning to feel a trickle of fear. He got to his feet, discovered that his legs felt rather strange, but managed to stay there.

Lord Marksbury ignored the captain for a moment and gave his daughter a long look of sad conjecture. He carefully avoided her eyes for he was feeling all the anguish of a parent torn by what he knew he had to do for the future of his offspring and the doubt that goes with the decision. He found refuge in parental command.

"I trust, Silkie, that you may take a moment to don your wrapper and tidy your hair?" He put up a brow to indicate that he would stand for no argument.

She made some exasperated noise but did as he asked, grumbling all the while as she hid behind her embroidered screen and brushed her hair into some semblance of order. While she was at this, her father sent a look of disgust to the captain who was standing still naked to the waist. "Captain . . . may I suggest that 'tis time you displayed some . . . er . . . modesty?"

Dare Trent was not moved to blush. Oh, there was a bright flow of color in his cheeks, but that was due to his extreme irritation. However, he bent, swept up his shirt, and while he proceeded to slip it on and see to its buttons, he again tried to speak to Silkie's outraged father. "My lord . . . if you will only let me think for a moment."

"Think? There is no longer any need for that!" snapped his lordship. Here was the man who had saved his life and look what he was doing to him. Well, what was he doing to him, he asked himself, forcing him into marriage with the finest woman in all of England! No harm in that . . . no harm. "Indeed, you should have thought, but since you chose to act without that aid, you must now pay the price. The fact that I am for life condemning my child to your care—"

"What?" shrieked Silkie coming away from the corner behind her screen. "What are you saying, Papa?"

"Andrews!" His lordship's voice was beginning to show the strain he was feeling in body and soul. He couldn't look at Silkie. "Andrews . . . 'tis time we got on with this blasted ceremony.''

"Papa . . . no!" cried Silkie. She put her hands round his face, attempting to force him to look at her. "I did nothing. . . ."

He did look at her then. "I know, my dearest heart . . . just . . . trust me. . . ." he whispered.

A terrible fear gripped her heart. What was this? What was he saying? She got to her feet and her voice was low, her chin high. "I shan't sign that special license you have procured, Father."

"You needn't, my dear. You are underage. My signature is all that is required."

"And what of mine?" snapped the captain. "I am *not* underage."

"We have done what is necessary, sir, and your signature will not be required. The license was taken out by me as father of the bride. It is quite legal, I do assure you." He turned to the fidgety Reverend Andrews who had already produced his flask from his pocket and was taking a swig of the brew contained therein. "Andrews!"

"*Certes!*" thundered the captain, "he may damn well begin, but not with me!" With which he started for the door.

It was at this point that Harley stepped forward and as he did so he brought from behind his back a large and formidable horse pistol. With an amicable grin he brought the weapon up and aimed it directly at the captain. In a perfectly friendly tone he said, "Don't make a ha'porth o'difference to me if ye makes me use this or not, coz ye see now, I mean to see ye do whot his lordship wants."

"Well then, sailor, you may as well use that barking iron you have, for it will be the only way you can keep me here. Though I don't know that a dead man will be of any use to his lordship and his daughter!"

"Oi wouldn't be shooting ye dead," said Harley, shaking his head. "Now whot good, like ye said, would that do? I disremember ever 'aving done sech a thing before, but oi thinks I could manage to put a bullet in each of yer legs . . . aye, that would keep ye here." A flashing smile spread across Harley's face.

The captain was for the moment at a loss—he could see that the seaman would certainly carry out his threat. Damn, what was he up against here? All of them were unprincipled rogues! Because he discovered himself caught, he breathed fire. "Damn your soul!"

"Aye, but t'was damned ever afore I seen yer face, captain, sir," riposted Harley merrily.

"Enough!" snapped Lord Marksbury, feeling that the captain needn't be so badly used. "Andrews . . . do get on with it."

The captain turned to Silkie. "He wouldn't shoot his own daughter." It was almost a plea. "You could leave."

"You are right, captain," she returned, throwing the air of defiance round the room. "I don't think anyone here would put a bullet in my leg." With this she started for the door.

"Joseph," said his lordship softly.

Joseph felt his heart sink. He couldn't believe he was reaching out for Miss Silkie's arm, that he was holding her tight. He ducked her blows and caught her other arm and held both behind her back.

"Please, Miss Silkie . . . don't make me hurt you . . . please." It was Joseph's whisper and he was nearly moved to tears.

Silkie went rigid with shock. She stood perfectly still and Joseph dropped his hold. She looked round at her father's face, at Harley, and then at Joseph, but it was Joseph's eyes, his drawn countenance, that finally told the story. What she had suspected a moment ago came into focus. This was her father's doing! All this was her father's doing!

## Chapter 13

*It* was over. Last night he had been a free man . . . this morning? Fiends seize these Englishmen! He turned ferocious blue eyes on Silkie, who stood mute and stunned across the room from him. The reverend had gone through the motions and the couple had not even been standing side by side.

"Do you think, madam, that I shall call you wife, or treat you as such?" He made a strangled sound deep in his throat at the idea. "Not for a moment will I accept this . . . this farce of a marriage!"

What? What was he saying? She looked up at him still too stunned to comprehend all that had happened. *Wife?* Faith! Was she this man's wife? Had it all really happened? Joseph and Harley had carried her father, exhausted, to his own room. She had stood riveted, unthinking, unfeeling, a statue enduring what couldn't really be, and now this arrogant American was railing at her. "This . . . this was not my doing," she started.

"The hell it wasn't!" he snapped in wild irritation. "How did they get me into your bed without your realizing it? Do you sleep that soundly, madam?" He moved towards her now and reached for her shoulders. He was shaking her. *"Well?"*

She pulled out of his rough clutch and stamped her foot at him. "I don't know! I just don't know. . . ." Tears were at the rim of her grey eyes, and they spilled over as a sob caught in her throat.

"Oh, that's right! Go ahead, take refuge in tears as do all your kind!" he spat at her in some impatience. His hand was tearing at his dark glistening locks and he was pacing in something of a frenzy. "Why? What I want to know is, why? Wouldn't that puppy, what is his name . . . Sir Blaize, wouldn't he come up to scratch?''

She shook her head because she didn't want to cry and couldn't yet make a sound. She turned away from him and once again found his hold on her. This time he was taking her arm, pulling her to him. ''Answer me, by God!''

''Stop it! I don't want to be married to you either. Why, in spite of the fact that you saved my father's life, I disliked you from the first. So don't flatter yourself, captain, this was not my idea!''

Pique. Was it possible that through all his wrath, his agitation, and his concern that his ego felt pinched? ''Really, madam?'' He walked over and bolted the door. ''Well, we shall see about that!''

''What the deuce are you doing?'' she shot at him. He was stripping off his shirt once again and moving towards her in a fashion that ticked off a tingle of fear in her spine.

''Why . . . only what I have been accused of. I am doing that which brought us to this pass.'' He had her roughly in his arms and as his mouth closed angrily on hers he felt a sudden surge of excitement move him. Slowly, expertly he molded her to his hard, muscular frame and his kiss evolved from its brutal beginning into a touch that drew out her soul.

She felt his crushing embrace and started to fight him when his mouth bruised her own, and then something happened and she felt her body respond against her will. No! She brought up her hand and pushed ineffectually at his hard chest but it only served to spur him on. He had her wrapper in his hand and in one stroke it was off her shoulders, hanging from her elbows.

''Captain! Stop this . . . do you hear me,'' she cried when he allowed her breath. ''I don't want you! I won't have you.''

''Too late, my girl! You took my name and now you shall have all that goes with it!'' So saying, his hand tugged at her flimsy nightdress and in a swoop exposed her full young breasts. He groaned and his hands devoured.

She trembled in his arms, beneath his touch. She saw his head lowered, saw him take her nipple to his lips and she closed her eyes. This couldn't be happening. Everything about the morning had an unreal aura to it. She would wake up. This was a dream, brought on by his kiss last night. His kiss last night? That was it, she *must* be dreaming, for that was the last thing she remembered. Her legs . . . what was happening to her legs? Her calves were no longer able to support her thighs and her legs were crumbling.

"Damn, but I have wanted you," he groaned as he scooped her up and carried her to the bed. ". . . and by all that is holy, I mean to have you, here and now!"

What was it she had once read? "Those whom the gods wish to destroy, they first made mad." Was that what was happening? Was she being punished? Was she going mad? Just what was happening?

"Captain . . . you must not . . ." she tried in a faint voice.

He had already put her down on her covers and as he hovered over her he was aware of the tenseness in her slim and alluring form. He was moved by anger and his lips curved into a sneer. "Oh, but I must and I shall." His voice lowered into a harsh whisper. "Didn't that devil Andrews pronounce us man and wife?"

"And didn't you disclaim it?" she cried. "Captain . . . *think*!"

"Not now, sweetings, this isn't the time." He was fingering her long white gold hair, brushing it away from her breasts, away from her neck. He discovered her grey eyes and knew that in their depths he had awakened something of desire. It urged him on for his manhood exulted in the knowledge. He bent to her delicate ears and he told her how long he had wanted her, how beautiful she was, how right she felt. He was nibbling at her throat, parting her thighs, touching her pleasure points with expert skill, and he was caught up by a bevy of sensations. He hadn't had a woman in a long time and by damn, he was going to have this treacherous creature!

Silkie discovered her body was on fire. Everywhere his hand strayed, she burned, oh how she burned for more. Thoughts flickered and they were entwined with guilt. Somehow she felt guilty for their present predicament. She had been an unwilling party in her father's scheme, but because she knew now that her father had engineered the marriage, she felt responsible. Unconsciously she thought to appease this man with the magic touch and she gave herself for a moment to his kiss—and in that moment was lost.

It was, of course, the end of all her secret fantasies, the end of a young girl's dreams, and the quick, hard stab of reality. No marriage for love. No flowers. No words of tenderness . . . no white gown . . . no wedding ring. Only this sudden passion. Here she was being seduced, allowing herself to be seduced by a man pronounced her husband. He was intent on taking his conjugal rights and years of dreaming were rudely ending.

"Ah babe, that's it, come to me . . . feel for me. . . ." he said on a provocative note, spreading her thighs further apart as she moved and responded to his touch. His fingers discovered the honey of her womb and played there gently, enticingly. She gasped and the sound of her pleasure fevered him, hurried him. He saw the passion darken her grey eyes and he groaned as he released his manhood and placed it at her opening. "Now, sweetings . . ."

She went rigid with sudden fear. What was he doing? This was going too far . . . he was entering slowly and she made a protest, pushing at him, but this only served to engender a stronger movement from him that sent him deeper, harder into her honeycomb.

She released a small, frightened scream of pain as his thrust split and ended her virginity. He answered her with soft words of reassurance and then he was again plunging deeper, rotating harder, working her away from her fear into a realm of pleasure. She held to him tightly as her blood bubbled and her mind discovered it had no will whatsoever against such a force. She was sent into a spinning pitch of sensation and then as she peaked and reached her climax, he allowed himself his own with a long satisfied groan.

They lay there for some moments wrapped in one another's arms, each with thoughts much alike. What had happened between them? Why had it happened and what now were they to do?

Sir Blaize approached the Marksbury stables in an uneasy mood. Something was wrong, but what it was he couldn't quite guess. Then he saw Wade Ashford already at the cottage door. Hurriedly he dismounted and gave his horse over to Joseph.

"Is Miss Silkie within?" he inquired hastily as he patted Joseph's shoulder with a friendly greeting. He was already moving towards the cottage.

"Aye," said Joseph uneasily. Sir Blaize. He had forgotten

about Sir Blaize. Should he tell him that Miss Silkie was now Mrs. Darrow Trent. Coo! No, he wasn't about to do that. How could he?

Wade was standing impatiently at the front door, staring hard at its dark Tudor lines before he reached out and banged at the knocker again. Where was Kora? What was afoot? He heard a sound behind him and turned to find Sir Blaize coming at him in a bit of a hurry. They had never been introduced, but he knew something of the young man. Word had it that Sir Blaize and Silkie might make a match of it one day. Ha! He would make damn well sure that never happened.

"Hallo!" said Sir Blaize in an amiable fashion. He knew all too well what Wade Ashford wanted at Marksbury and he would thrust a spoke in his wheel if he could. He had cut his trip shorter than he had intended because of his concern over Silkie and her father. "Isn't Kora about?"

"Doesn't seem to be," said Wade curtly.

Sir Blaize reached for the latch. "Might be open." Sure enough, it was. He smiled and moved aside to allow Ashford to enter, after which he followed. It was then they found Captain Dare Trent smashing down his peaked captain's hat onto his dark locks. He stopped short when he discovered the presence of Blaize and Ashford and while he accorded the lad a brief nod, he only glared at Ashford and said, "What in hell do you want here now?"

"I don't think, captain, that is any of your business," returned Ashford quietly, curbing his temper.

"Oh, but you mistake!" sneered the captain. "Everything that concerns the Marksburys is *my* business." It was clear that while Trent considered this to be a fact, he was not finding it a pleasant one.

"What is it? What is amiss?" asked Blaize, for this was something that moved him to instant concern.

"Amiss? Now what the bloody hell could be amiss?" returned the captain sardonically. "Or did you know how I would be repaid for my kindness?"

"Fiend seize it, captain . . . what are you talking about?" demanded Sir Blaize.

"Didn't you want her, Blaize, lad? Is that why they settled on me?"

"Want her? Silkie, you mean?" Sir Blaize was blushing. "We're friends . . . just that, but what has that?" He took a step forward. "Slap me if I know what maggot is in your head, sir."

"The maggot is not in my head, but in theirs, and damn if they didn't get away with it! Prime planning it was," said the captain harshly as he remembered the events of the morning. "I wonder if they would have served you in the same manner." He mused out loud then, looking at Sir Blaize, he shook his head. "No, I don't think so."

"Are you queer in your attic?" asked Sir Blaize, for he felt as though he had been dropped in the middle of a raging sea.

"If anyone would have told me I would wake up and find myself a groom at a wedding, I would have thought . . ."

"Groom?" snapped Ashford, suddenly feeling a chill come over his spine. "Will you stop talking in riddles, captain?"

"Riddles? Well, here is a riddle for you," said the captain. "Tell me . . ." Then, changing his mind, he shook his head. "Forget it. My bride tells me she will have herself divorced from me by this afternoon! That is what she is doing right now, getting dressed so that she can go into town and see her solicitor!"

"What?" ejaculated Sir Blaize.

In a low-keyed voice Ashford spat, "Are you trying to tell us that Silkie is your wife?"

"She is that, though she don't mean to remain so," returned the captain ruefully. "Imagine that, married and divorced, all in a day's time and without even trying."

Ashford felt as though he had been stabbed through the heart. "NO!" It was a shriek that came from the very depth of his being. He felt himself plunged into the past where there was only pain. Somehow, from his sickbed, Marksbury had managed to outmaneuver him again. This was impossible. Ashford nearly brought up his fists as he lashed out, "You lie! She couldn't be your wife. What about the banns? There was no posting of the banns."

The captain eyed him thoughtfully for a moment, "That's right, Ashford, no banns. Marksbury obtained a special license . . . but make no mistake. Silkie *is* my wife and she is under my protection." He didn't know why it was but he wouldn't have Ashford come near Silkie.

"Damn you and your protection!" snapped Ashford. "Do you

think that makes a lick of difference to me? Do you? I have waited too long to allow you to stand in my way.''

''I am in your way though, Ashford, and I mean to stay there,'' returned Trent carefully, meaningfully. This was absurd. When Silkie had lashed out at him and cried that she would have the marriage annulled, he had been pleased enough. So why then was he standing buff for her now?

Ashford started for the stairs and Trent grabbed his arm, pulling him round roughly. ''Where in hell do you think you are going without my leave?''

''I have business to conclude with Marksbury, and not you, not anything you can do, will stop me,'' hissed Ashford.

''*Really?*'' challenged Trent. ''As it happens, my . . . er . . . father-in-law is too ill to see you or anyone else for that matter, and it would afford me great pleasure to vent my bad temper on you.''

Ashford nearly forgot himself. His fist was brought back but Sir Blaize took hold of his arm. ''Mr. Ashford . . . this is not the place . . . step outside with the captain if you wish to brawl.''

Ashford shot the lad a glaring look of hatred. ''Brawl? I don't brawl, puppy! When I fight, it is to the death.'' With this he pushed Sir Blaize out of his way and stomped out of the house.

Blaize shook his head. ''I'd watch out for him, captain. He is the sort to exact his revenge without heed to honor.''

''Aye, I've got his measure.'' He looked at Blaize penetratingly. ''And yours, I think. You stand the Marksburys' friend, don't you?''

''Yes, captain, and I find all this . . . hard to believe.''

''Nevertheless, 'tis true. They managed to drug me and put me in Silkie's bed. She couldn't have slept through it all . . . so she must have been a party to it . . . and if Ashford is what moved her to it . . . Well, to some extent, I might even understand . . . but never, never can I forgive them this morning's work!'' He moved towards the door. ''Should her solicitor wish to see me, I will be on my clipper . . . for within a week's time, I mean to sail for home.''

Captain Trent stepped out into the sunshine and found Kora standing in mute vexation; Ashford had swept roughly past her only a moment before.

"Ooh, may faith preserve us," she breathed on a low note of worry. "He means ill by us, he does."

The Captain was studying her face. He came up to her and touched her shoulder, bringing her full attention to himself. His voice was dry. "Tell me, Kora, did you know?" The notion that she had been a part of the morning's affair was something that disturbed him.

"Know?" She puzzled up at him. "Lordy, know what, captain?"

His brow cleared but his smile scarcely curved his lips. "No, of course you did not. The very reason you were sent off, in fact, must have been to keep you well out of it."

"Sent me off? Pardon, captain, I just don't understand what you have fixed on."

He touched her chin lightly and there was not the usual twinkle in his eyes. "Kora, Lord Marksbury managed some heavy manipulation this morning. Indeed, quite remarkable for a man in his condition. I shall allow your mistress to recount all the lurid details, however, suffice it to say that the end result of the affair is that I find Silkie is my wife." With this he tipped his hat and left her standing, her hand clasped over her mouth.

She turned to the open door and found Sir Blaize staring at her. "Well now, what is all this?" she demanded.

"Don't know, but I tell you what, Kora, I mean to find out," he said as he turned for the stairs.

# Chapter 14

*The* crew of Trent's *Seamaid* was proud of their vessel. They enjoyed the stares and open admiration they had been receiving these past weeks while they whipped the clipper into shape for their trip home. However, this morning more than a few of the clipper's sea worthies were grumbling as they went about their business, due no doubt to their captain's hard mood.

"Aye, but he had no call to tell me I was a whipstraw and lazy to boot!" complained a youth as he stretched out a length of canvas and made ready to repair its rent. "I was only checking out the wind and having a bit of a laugh with Tom . . . I meant to get right back to work."

"Sneck up, lad!" riposted the elderly seaman he was addressing his complaint to. "I've sailed many a bark in my time and let me tell you, Captain Trent is jest about the fairest I've ever had the good luck to sail under! Why . . . I could tell you stories that would make that frizzy mop of yours stand out straight! Lord bless ya, laddie, a bark now and then from a captain t'aint nothin'."

"Aye . . . well he had no call," answered the youth sulkily.

"Didn't he now? Well, you and Tom were laughing up a storm which wasn't too bright considering the way capt'n came charging on board this morning. Fit to kill he was, but you had no better sense than to put yourself forth and call out his thunder! When I sailed the *Rainbow*, I saw a man flogged for less than that."

"The *Rainbow*? You sailed the Rainbow? Lordy, but my pa says she is the fastest clipper out of New York."

"Eh? Does he now? Well, well, you go home and tell him

there's a faster one and it's this here *Seamaid*! You tell him that and what's more, laddie, you are sailing under the man who designed her!'' At the boy's startled expression, he nodded triumphantly. ''That's right. Bless ya, boy, don't ya know nothin? Hardly used, eh? Well, sail another bark and see what treatment is doled out to the men!''

''Yeah, well . . . I dunno.'' returned the youth, still unconvinced.

At that moment Captain Trent came round the bridge and discovered the two deep in conversation. He frowned, for he had just come down hard on the boy Jim and his friend Tom for larking when they should have been working. He was surprised to see that the older seaman, Barney, seemed also inclined to laziness this morning. It was irritating in the extreme, but Trent controlled himself and merely raised a brow.

Barney's eye twinkled as he lifted up the ropes he had just completed and shuffled off, calling the younger crewman to hurry up with the canvas. Trent said nothing to all of this as the lad scurried off, tripped, blushed profusely, stammered something incoherent, and shot out of sight. The moment did something to ease Dare's agitation and he sighed long and heavily. Had it really happened? Was he really married to Silkie Marksbury? Silkie? No longer a Marksbury but a Trent? Damnation! Three hours ago he had been a free man. Now what was he?

He had a throbbing in his head that was proving to be exquisitely painful. A solution to the problem must be found, but he couldn't think. Hell and brimstone, just what was he going to do? Hadn't he left Sag Harbor and Zara's clutches? Hadn't he escaped marriage to Blaine? How the hell did he end up in this state? At least marriage to Blaine would have consolidated the firm, brought it all eventually into Trent hands.

This was absurd. There had to be an answer. Then, without reason, Silkie's face came to mind. The feel of her long, flowing cornsilk hair touched his nerves in a manner that sent a shiver up his back. The fresh fragance of her body suddenly engulfed him, and her grey eyes growing dark with a passion he had aroused in her reminded him all too vividly of the moment he had taken her . . . *enough*! She was just a woman, only a woman, and as such had her place, had her use. . . .

A discreet cough at his back brought his head round and he found his stocky and bright-eyed first mate. "Yes, Forbes?"

The older sailor held up a sealed ivory envelope. "This was brought round last night by a lad from the Prendergast people."

"Oh?" Clearly his response questioned why it had not been brought to him earlier.

"You were in a mood . . . a rare mood this morning, capt'n, and they said it wasn't urgent and didn't need no reply . . . thought it best to leave it till you were feeling . . . er . . . more the thing."

"Oh, did you now?" But he was taking up the envelope, breaking the seal. He allowed Forbes much license—they had been together a long time and Forbes had been his father's first mate as well.

Fleetingly he thought of the friends he had visited only days before, George and Mary Prendergast. When he had been with them at their Playden Estate they had made him promise to come back before he left England. They would be in London by now . . . enjoying the season. He sighed and looked down at the delicate writing.

Dearest Dare,

We are off to London and I have scrawled our address below.

You promised us a few days and I am writing you this epistle to recall you to that promise, as George assures me you have a dreadful memory. Prove him wrong, for we have a wager. I win a small bundle if you make good your promise—and if you do, I shall share it with you.

Godspeed,
Affectionately,
Mary

London? It was just what he needed to rid himself of the shoe-pinched feeling. Yes, by God! London. Certes! He would show his new bride just what she had bought herself. Fiend seize them all, they may have forced him into this marriage, but by all that was holy, he meant to show them just what he thought of such a trick. His clipper was coming along just fine and in no time they would be taking the Atlantic for home. There was nothing to keep him kicking his heels here in Rye. A bride? Ha!

"Forbes . . . I'll need a poste chaise, for I'm off to London, but before you arrange it, have my steward pack my things."

"Aye, aye, Capt'n . . ." He stopped and frowned. "Oh, by the by, that fellow Ashford?"

Ashford! Damn the man, for it was Ashford who had indirectly caused him to be in this predicament. "Yes, what about him?" It was an impatient question and truth to tell, he wasn't really interested in the answer.

"Well . . . the thing is . . . you had your sights on him a while back, so I been keeping m'own clappers that way . . . and the thing is, he took off for London too."

"Did he? When?" Trent was suddenly interested.

"That twiddle-poop of his . . ."

"That what?" Amusement lit the captain's blue eyes.

"Er . . . gentleman's gentleman, they call 'em here," drawled Forbes in an exaggerated mimickery. "Well, the thing is . . . saw that . . . er . . ."

"Yes, yes, his twiddle-poop."

"Right, rushing about town this morning on some errand for Ashford and he let it slip that they was off for London."

"Well, well," mused the captain out loud and then to himself. Had the tenacious Ashford finally given up on Silkie? Ironic that, if it should be the case. He shook his head. Marksbury had speedily, treacherously forced marriage on him with Silkie to avoid Ashford's hold on her—and here was Ashford off for London and seemingly no longer interested. Damnation and may all of them rot! He wasn't going to think about this any longer. Not now. He was bound for London and some frivolity and then . . . And then he would see who was married, that's what! There had to be a way out of this. At any rate, one way or another he would see himself a free man and to hell with the Marksburys.

Silkie stared at her reflection in her gold-edged looking glass. Was she someone new? Dare Trent had rushed her body and her senses and she was a virgin no longer. Did it show? The thought and the memory of his touch brought the blush to her cheeks.

Faith! It hadn't been her fault . . . had it? Of course not! He forced himself on you . . . wouldn't listen . . . it was nearly rape. . . .

Wasn't it? Honesty brought to mind the manner in which her treacherous body had responded to his handling. She closed her eyes and took in air. She had let him. Perhaps in atonement for what her papa had done. Perhaps.

With this she plopped the forest green velvet top hat onto her head of flaxen curls, which she had piled high and full. She was dressed in her forest green riding habit and meant to go into town and see her father's solicitor. There had to be a way out of this mess. There just had to be! With a final look at herself she went to the door, again took in a steadying gulp of air, and made her way to the stairs. Halfway down she stopped short to find Kora and Sir Blaize on their way up.

Oh no! Blaize? How could she face him after the morning's mortifying work? Again, color flooded her cheeks. What would he say? What would he think of her, of her father? She breathed his name. "Blaize . . . oh Blaize."

"Silkie love," Kora said, going before Blaize and taking her young mistress's hand. "What is this? What has been going on here?" She led Silkie down the remaining steps, glancing at Sir Blaize who turned and followed them.

Silkie looked from Kora to Blaize for she didn't know how to start, what to say. Blaize saved her the trouble. "What is this nonsense Captain Trent is blabbering about a marriage?"

"Y-es . . . oh yes . . . 'tis true," whispered Silkie, for she discovered that her voice had nearly disappeared.

"What?" shrieked Kora and Blaize in unison.

"Don't tell me you are married to the captain?" expanded Sir Blaize in disbelief.

Silkie nodded her head, found her courage, and added, "But not for long! I mean to go into town and do something about it at once!"

"Hold there a moment, girl," said Blaize, taking up her arm and steering her to a hard wood bench propped against the wall. He pushed her forcefully onto its polished seat.

*"Explain!"*

She bit her lip. "I don't know how."

"You don't know how? Damn it, girl, if you were married to

168

the captain against his will . . . ." said Blaize on a note of impatience.

It pinched at her. "Did he say that?"

"Something to its like," responded Kora quietly. "So, start if you will, at the beginning. Your father asked me to run an errand in town for him. You were still abed?"

"Yes, that I was," said Silkie on a sour note. "With Captain Trent asleep beside me." She saw Sir Blaize's shocked expression and suddenly found relief in laughter. She burst into uncontrollable mirth which rocked her body for a time. She managed after a few moments to sober, since neither of her companions seemed amused. Wiping a stray tear from her eye, she again took on a grave expression, sighed, and said as evenly as she could, "You see . . . 'tis not what you think. I am persuaded Papa got him drunk . . . or . . . drugged him . . . which he must have done to me as well."

"Your father got you drunk?" expostulated Sir Blaize. "I don't believe it! That is fustian, girl, and well you know it!"

"No, no, of course he did not get me drunk. I think he must have put a dose of laudanum in my hot chocolate . . . just to make me sleep deeply."

"But why?" cried Kora.

"So that I would not awaken when they carried in the captain and put him in my bed." She looked hard at Kora. "Harley and Joseph were in on the game, Kora."

"Mercy!" breathed Kora. "Never say they did that?"

"How else could he have gotten there?" Silkie asked with a shrug.

"Well, he could have walked there, love." answered Sir Blaize on a sardonic note, but as he saw her ready to clout him for this response he quickly put up an apologetic hand. "But of course . . . *you* would have sent him on his way. Well then . . . proceed."

"You must not think poorly of Papa . . . Blaize . . . he must have thought us to be at a desperate pass." Her grey eyes filled suddenly with tears.

Sir Blaize reached for her shoulders and gave them a brotherly squeeze. "Aye, depend upon it, that was his frame of mind." Then gently, "Go on then, girl."

"Yes, well . . . we woke up suddenly with Joseph and Harley

and Papa making . . . accusations at the captain . . . and this little, awful man who stood by . . . well, he was the minister . . . and Papa had a license of some sort that precluded the need of posting of the banns.''

"A special license," said Blaize with a shake of his fair head. "Aye, he was desperate, indeed . . . for I'll warrant a Marksbury was never married by one before."

"Oh my poor child," cried Kora, dropping onto the bench beside Silkie and taking up her hands. "So 'tis true . . . my poor dear.''

"What is worse is that Dare thinks I was a willing party to this dreadful thing.''

"How did they force him to it?" asked Blaize with some interest.

"That was one of the worst things, for they threatened to . . . to put a bullet in his leg . . . oh Blaize . . . it was the most humiliating thing.''

"Lord yes!" agreed Blaize with some ready sympathy for the captain.

"What can I do?" asked Silkie on a forlorn note.

"Buck up, ole girl. I ain't accounted the best of my kind, but you know I'll stand buff for you. Mayhap we could obtain a quiet little annulment for you?" This last was said more to himself than to her.

She brightened. "Oh . . . do you think so?"

He regarded her for a long moment. "Perhaps . . . if it is what you want?"

"What I want? Of course it is. How can you ask?"

He pulled at his lower lip thoughtfully. "It's just that now and again I rather thought . . . but never mind that now. Happen, it was a good thing I changed my mind about my trip and turned back!''

"Oh yes, Blaize. I thought you wouldn't be back for weeks." She touched his gloved finger and pulled at it as she was wont to do whenever she found herself in a worry and he was within reach.

"Wouldn't have been but got to thinking about that fellow Ashford, and then when I reached Eastbourne and by chance discovered he had purchased your father's notes—"

"He what?" riposted Silkie in surprise.

"Aye. The man is a devil. I wouldn't be surprised if that is what he has been doing, taking on your father's debts to himself so that in the end the total sum will fall due to him and not to the individual tradesmen originally involved."

"So that is it," said Silkie with some understanding at last. "Ashford must have gotten to Father . . . threatened him."

"Aye. Only one thing left to do now," said Blaize.

"What's that?"

"Go up and speak with your father." He took up her hand. "Come on."

"But Blaize."

"Made up my mind to it. Annul your marriage to Trent . . . let the captain off the hook and replace him with myself as your husband."

*"Blaize!"*

"Think we should deal famously together. Don't you?"

"You have never had any notion of getting married."

"Yes I have, only meant to do it when I had a few more oats sewn and some more years under me belt. Don't mind it though . . . rather like the notion, in fact."

"That's doing it rather too brown!" she returned. "And . . . anyway, you . . . you don't love me. . . ."

He studied her for a long moment. "Could, you know." He touched her nose. "Now, upstairs with you, Silkie m'girl. I mean to speak to your father and set things right and tight." He looked at Kora. "You had best be getting some hot tea readied for your mistress—I have a notion she will be needing it after this session!"

Kora was obliged to do as he asked and a moment later Blaize and Silkie were entering her father's room. They found him resting quietly, though his brows were drawn in discomfort. His lids fluttered open as he heard their steps and his green eyes were touched with pain. He managed a smile. "Ah, you here, young man? Come to scold me, have you? Yes, I can see that you have. Well then . . . go on, I suppose you think you have a right."

"It isn't my place to scold you, my lord," said Sir Blaize gravely. "I am surprised though . . . I would have thought you trusted me."

"What has that to do with anything? My trust in you is not pertinent to the situation."

"If you had trusted me, you would have taken me into your confidence, and I would have been honored to offer Silkie the protection of my name."

His lordship smiled sadly. "My dear boy, don't you realize I thought of that?" His lids drooped. "I am afraid you don't understand the man we are dealing with. Had I married my Silkie off to you, she would have had to stand back and watch Wade Ashford destroy you both . . . no, you just don't understand. . . ."

Blaize was a youth and much of his ego was ruffled by that statement. He pulled up his shoulders. "I think I do understand, and you have underestimated me, my lord."

"No . . ." It was an effort to speak, but he had to make these children see. He had to take some of the confusion out of his daughter's eyes. ". . . it is you, in your inexperience . . . who has underestimated Ashford. There is no other like him . . . except the devil himself." His words were scarcely above a whisper, yet somehow they held the might of his convictions.

Blaize frowned. "Tell me, sir, if you will, how legal is this marriage between your daughter and Captain Trent?"

"Quite legal . . . I saw to that." A smile lit his lordship's faded green eyes but no amount of effort on his part brought it to his lips.

Blaize gave this last statement his consideration before replying. "Right then, my lord. I suppose there is nothing more to be said on that score. Legal it may be, but so shall it be undone. I want you to know that I intend to accompany your daughter into town and visit with your solicitor . . . or mine and—"

Marksbury attempted to get up. It was an impossible task for his broken rib had slipped and splintered with his early morning exertions and it had punctured a lung. Still, in his great agitation, he made the attempt and was thrown into a fit of coughing. His daughter rushed to him and smoothed over his brow until he was quieted. He tried to speak and felt his body racked over with an agony he had never before encountered. His head screamed with pain and his limbs begged for release. Still, for love of his child, he composed himself and managed faintly, "No . . . you can do nothing . . . she is underage."

"Oh Papa . . . I don't want to trouble you when you are suffering, but how . . . how can you do this to me? I don't want this marriage you have forced on me . . . please try and understand." The plea was in her grey eyes as well as in the touch of her hand.

"I do, my Silkie . . . I do . . . but Ashford will ruin you if he can. Now . . . you will leave England with Trent . . . away from Ashford . . . yes, your mother would be pleased . . . Trent . . . man enough . . . man enough." His words were scarcely audible and he felt something warm and sticky in his mouth, flooding his nostrils. What was this? Not yet . . . he couldn't go just yet. . . .

Sir Blaize was pacing now but these last words filled him with a surge of displeasure. "Trent is man enough? Am I not? My lord, am I not?"

What did the boy want of him? He was depleted. His body was torn apart and there was nought left him to fight with. Still, because he was able to draw breath, he said, "You are a boy . . . not for you to . . . take on."

Silkie was looking at her father strangely. Something was wrong. She was losing him. Suddenly nothing else mattered. Not her marriage to Trent. Not Sir Blaize, not Ashford. "Papa . . . Papa . . . shall I get the doctor . . . *Papa*?"

His lids drooped. "No . . . no . . . too late." He opened his eyes and looked long at her troubled countenance. "Do you know . . . in . . . many ways . . . I have . . . failed."

"Don't say so, Papa . . . no . . ."

"But . . . not . . . in . . . this last . . . not . . ."

"Hush, Papa . . . you have to rest now." Tears were forming in her large grey eyes. A sudden terrible realization gripped her heart and she fought against its truth.

Then all at once, her father reached out his hand and grabbed hold of her wrist. "Silkie . . ." It was a hoarse sound but it rent through her heart. "You will go with Trent . . . you will . . ."

"No . . . Papa . . . I can't." She was crying now in some agitation.

"Child . . . promise me . . . while Ashford . . . lives . . . you . . . stay with . . . Trent . . . I would have . . . your promise . . . ."

"How can you ask it of her?" put in Blaize, staring down

hard at Marksbury. However, his color drained from his lean cheeks for he culd see that his lordship was in a bad state.

"Promise . . . Silkie?" Something inside of him was bursting. He knew now that the warm, sticky fluid was blood; he could taste it as it made its path down his tongue onto his lips. Oh God, pain, so much pain. . . .

What was happening? She was killing her father. He had worked himself into a frenzy. What was that . . . blood? No, oh no! "Papa, *I promise* . . . Papa . . . don't die . . . Papa . . . forgive me. I promise, I'll do anything, only don't die . . . Papa . . . please . . ." Her words came between heart-rendering sobs. Tearing through her body, they took hold of her and split her in two.

He heard her promise and closed his eyes. Now, now she would be safe. Trent was just the man to see her safe. He was tired, so tired, and there was Serena whispering his name, touching his forehead. She was pleased with him in this last act. Yes, it was good to know he had done the right thing by their daughter. He could feel Serena reaching out her hand and he stretched and went to her.

"Ah . . . Serena," he whispered as he left his pain behind.

Silkie was calling to him still but he had taken his last breath. It couldn't be. She didn't want to believe it and she held his face. "Papa . . . don't do this . . . don't die . . . Papa . . . for me, don't die." It was a child begging.

Blaize was on his knee beside her, pulling her away, holding her close. "Its over m'girl . . . all over . . : shhh Silkie . . . shhh . . ."

"Oh God, Papa!" It was a woman coming to grips with reality, and then, as she succumbed to her loss in her friend's arms, it was a woman-child, grieving.

## Chapter 15

*A* popular pair with the *beau monde*, George and Mary Prendergast's opening townhouse ball was sure to be a success. Nearly everyone on Mary's list was present and in a festive mood. She looked round her full ballroom with a satisfied sigh, pleased with the results of her efforts. George towered above her dainty frame and chuckled as he bent and pinched her cheek.

"Well puss, you have outdone yourself. All our guests seem to be enjoying themselves immensely." George turned as a jolly fellow clapped him on his broad shoulders and passed a quick jest before he returned his attention to his wife.

His lady's dark eyes traveled to their friend Darrow Trent's merry antics, and she pointed her chin in his direction. "Yes, aren't they just!" Her tone ever so slightly disapproving.

George's hazel eyes followed her lead and his brows of dark ginger drew together. "Eh? Never you mind. The poor man has been through something of an ordeal and it will do him no harm to let off some of his hot steam."

"If I thought that was all he was doing, my love, I wouldn't have given him such a setdown earlier," she said doubtfully, "but the thing is that he is in terrible straits and this is no way of alleviating one ounce of his troubles . . . not really."

"Gave him a setdown, did you?" Her husband zeroed in on that. "How did you do that, darling?"

"Oh, it is all very well for you to take an odiously light attitude on the subject, but it won't do, George, and so I tell you to your head!"

He sighed. "Well then, goose, what would you have me do?"

"For one thing, curb Dare's drinking! He has been in his cups for nearly two days . . . and flirting outrageously with the Lady Sophie.''

''What is that to say to anything? Everyone flirts with Sophie!'' He grinned.

She eyed him for a moment. ''Even you, George?''

''Well, she is a beauty and rather demands it of one . . . but how could I flirt with her? I haven't looked at another woman since the first moment I saw you.'' He was still grinning.

''Really, darling?'' She was momentarily diverted from her purpose.

''Really.'' He saw her satisfied and could not help adding, ''Besides, I don't relish the beating you would administer to me if I did!''

She released her fist and neatly found his almost flat belly. He grimaced and bent over in mock pain before he found his coat sleeve shaken by her satin-gloved fingers. ''Stop it, beast, and do be serious!'' she admonished severely. ''Something must be done!''

''Indeed, for I believe you are crushing my coat sleeve most dreadfully, dear, and if I am to continue looking my best—''

''Lobcock!'' she returned. ''Oh . . . look . . . you don't think Dare is really taken with Sophie . . . do you?''

Her husband did as he was commanded and discovered his American friend nibbling at Lady Sophie's dainty ear. ''No, no, of course not! Besides, he is safe enough from the widow—he is a married man you know!'' This he found so vastly entertaining that he went off into a peal of mirth for which he was soundly scolded.

Dare, unaware of Mary's grave concern regarding his behavior, was doing all he could to put the memory of his strange wedding out of his mind. It was proving to be a more difficult task than he anticipated.

Lady Sophie was the *haut ton*'s scandalous widow. Her indiscretions were the talk of London, but were winked at by society. This was due to the fact that her bloodline was exceptional. Daughter of an earl, she had married one of the wealthiest men in England, who died shortly after the marriage. She was just thirty, wore her dark curls cropped round her high-cheekboned and beautiful face, and had a wit to match her good looks.

Dare had not been in Mary Prendergast's home above forty minutes when the widow had paid her friend a visit and come beneath his appreciative notice. He had not been in London more than a week and already he was pointed out as Sophie's new flirt. It was natural that two such striking creatures were attracted to one another. Lady Sophie's charms were enough to please the most exacting of men, and Dare Trent found nothing to fault himself in whiling away the night by waltzing Lady Sophie round a room.

What he chastized himself about had nothing to do with Lady Sophie. It was when he looked into her inviting eyes and discovered without logic and beyond his control that he was seeing a pair of gold-lit grey eyes instead that he became irritated. It was when he took Sophie in his arms and bent to kiss her painted lips that he recalled the sweetness of another mouth, a pert nose, a heart-shaped face, the softness of flaxen, cornsilk hair . . . oh God! Damn it all to hell! Silkie, Silkie, Silkie. The touch of her provocative, innocent body responding beneath him brought a fresh rush of desire. Even the luscious Sophie had not yet made him forget Silkie.

Fiend seize it all! He would forget her—had to forget her—for he meant to be rid of her and the abominable marriage deed that made her his wife. He looked now at Sophie, smiling at his side, and he bent to nibble at her ear.

"Sophie . . . shall we find a reason . . . and be off?"

She gurgled with pleasure. It was exciting having this handsome American pay her tribute. He was younger and he was being nicely received by the *beau monde*. American he may be, but he was a prize. Every matchmaking mama in the room had her eye on him, for it was rumored that he was vastly wealthy. However, she had to be careful. Lord Briton was on the verge of proposing to her. He was away in Northumberland on estate affairs, but he had given every indication of his intentions before he left. Briton was a jealous man and he would not stand for it if she were to bestow her favors elsewhere just now. Still, she wanted this rugged American. Her hand walked up his muscular arm. "Dearest Dare . . . how can we leave, the ball has only just begun." Her voice was low and husky with desire.

"You have developed the headache, sweetings . . . and being a gallant, I shall . . . be honored to see you safely home."

She tittered. "And set every tattlemonger present to wagging their tongues. Thank you, no. That won't serve."

"What then?" he growled playfully as he took her waist and led her to the dance floor. "For I tell you frankly, I have to have you . . . and don't mean to wait any longer."

"La, captain, you set me to panting," she answered him, but even as the tease was in her voice, her eyes told him that this was very nearly true.

"Would that I may, Sophie." He answered her in form. He felt an absurd restlessness take hold of him again. It wasn't the first time he had been touched with this sensation. Every single day, no matter what he was at, he felt as though it weren't enough, weren't where he should be, and always he felt dissatisfied.

She sensed something she couldn't quite pinpoint. Was he losing interest? Had she kept him at bay long enough? "If you like, Dare, you may come to me tonight . . . after the ball. My maid will let you in, but you will have to come to the rear entrance . . . do you mind?"

"Mind?" he answered promptly and as was expected, "how could I, if it leads to your bed!" Damn but that was cutting to the point. Why had he done that? It wasn't his style. Never mind. She was no innocent to be frightened off.

She wasn't. Quite the contrary. She felt her blood surge and a tickle of anticipation rushed through her. "Indeed, Dare, that is exactly where it will lead."

She glanced across the room then and found Mary Prendergast looking right at her. Ah, the staid Mary did not approve. To her longtime friend she shrugged her shoulders and was rewarded with a rueful smile in return, and then she saw Wade Ashford enter the ballroom.

Wade Ashford's mood the past four days had been terse and irritable. All he wanted to do was return to Rye and institute his plans for Marksbury's ruination. He had the means as he had already warned Aaron and, by damn, he meant to carry them to fruition! He was itching to be off when his agent sent him word that his estates in Nottingham needed his personal attention.

Reluctantly he had presented himself in the north and put away all these bothersome matters as speedily as he could. His return to London that morning found a reminder from his secretary that he had promised to attend the Prendergasts' ball. Fiend seize it all, why had he accepted the invitation? Ah well, perhaps it would do him some good. Perhaps it would ease the tension stiffening his neck and making his lower back ache so miserably. In this frame of mind he donned his black cutaway and delectably threaded white satin waistcoat and proceeded to the ball.

His quizzing glass found many of his cronies present and in good stead he hailed these fellows and endured the usual amenities. He was already beginning to feel the old sense of boredom descend upon him when to his amazement, he discovered Captain Trent flirting outrageously with the Lady Sophie. Well, well, he thought, and was not unamused. So Trent had left Silkie and her charms and had already found another. Excellent! Well pleased by this circumstance, Wade found Mary Prendergast and in his leisurely fashion made his way to her side.

"Ah, Mary, my beauty, you are as ever quite enchanting," he said as he bent over her gloved hand. As he brought his hazel eyes to her face and discovered the twinkle in her dark eyes he was reminded of his old friend, Lady Bruney. But Sarah had died five years ago and left him more alone than ever.

Rumors surrounded Wade Ashford's head. There were those who called him a hardened rake, others who said he was in league with the devil, and still others who said he was, in fact, the very devil himself. Few gave him their trust and friend was not what his intimates called him; he never allowed any too close. Even so, he was *ton*, the very pink of *ton*, and accepted by all the London hostesses.

Mary Prendergast was always disturbed by him. Perhaps it was the sadness she could sense behind the cold hazel eyes. Perhaps it was because he seemed so very, very alone. She knew all the gossip that hung about him, had even recently heard Dare speak of Wade's envolement with the Marksburys in Rye, and still she found pity in her heart for Wade Ashford. Lines of Byron's from "The Corsair" nearly always came to mind:

> *His heart was form'd for softness—warp'd*
> *to wrong;*
> *Betray'd too early, and beguiled too long.*

There was a story there in Ashford's soul, but what it was she could not say. She responded to him easily and her smile was sincere.

"Wade! No wonder they call you dangerous. There are few who could turn a compliment just as you do." She allowed him to take her hand and added lightly, hoping to draw him out, set him at ease, "I am so very honored to have you here, my buck. I am told you no longer condescend to attend our frivolous town affairs."

"How could I keep away from any event which finds *you* its mistress?" His eyes flirted with her, his voice implied more than the words.

She laughed. "You are irreclaimable! Beyond my help—"

He cut her off shortly. "The sad thing is, that is true . . . all too true."

"Oh Wade . . . what you need is the love of a good woman." She attempted to tease him away from the sudden bitterness that lit his eyes.

"That's right, but there I am in Rye, surrounded by smugglers and rurals, and you staunchly refuse to run away with me." He found her dimples enticing and lowered his voice. "Ah Mary, would that we had met long ago."

"Nonsense . . ."

He took her other hand and drew her closer. "Say you will leave that big and clumsy fellow you married. Say you will run away with me!" He had raised his voice as he heard George coming up behind them."

"Unhand my wife, you cur!" This from George in mock rage.

George Prendergast did not like Wade Ashford. He did not share his wife's sympathy for the man and knew too much about him to ever be in a position to extend friendship. At the same time, he was a man of amiable qualities and a kind nature that allowed him to flow with ease at such moments.

Ashford answered him promptly, "Dash it, George, you do have an annoying habit of keeping close watch on this sweetness of yours!"

"Eh, with rogues like you about, it's no wonder!" answered George at once.

"Well, I can't whisk her off willy-nilly beneath your very nose, so do go away!" countered Ashford merrily enough.

"Precisely why I mean to keep me nose right where it is!" riposted George with a solemn nodding of his head.

His lady laughed deliciously over all this and it was not surprising that no little attention was drawn their way. In fact, Captain Trent, just finished at the waltz with Sophie, looked round and discovered with some surprise that Wade Ashford was holding Mary's hand. His dark-winged brows took flight, accentuating their thick, fine shape. His aqua blue eyes studied the scene thoughtfully and Lady Sophie had leisure to note that he was one of the finest specimens of male flesh and blood she had ever encountered.

In a corner of the ballroom, not so very far from Ashford's group, sat an elderly baron attempting to make love to a lady in puce. She was not much younger than he but every bit as game, and they were enjoying the sport when he heard Mary's sparkling laughter and looked up. "Egad!" he exclaimed. "Look there . . . 'tis Ashford!"

"So it is," said the woman in puce, putting up her glass to be certain.

"But . . . don't you see . . . then 'tis true!" answered the elderly fellow with a shake of his white head. "Didn't half believe it when old Holland told me, for the fellow is daft and always gets his stories wrong . . . but Ashford wouldn't be here if it weren't true."

"Yes, but Alfred—" the woman in puce started.

He patted her hand and cut her off. "Wait for me, little bird, I just want to run over and hear for myself if this thing with Ashford and Marksbury is finally ended!"

"Yes, but . . ."

"Hush now, darling . . . I'll be back," he promised her as he took up his ebony cane and began hobbling towards the group in which Ashford was a present member.

Ashford groaned as he discovered Sir Alfred making his way through the crowd towards them. "We are about to be visited by Sir Toad-Eater." He nodded his head in Alfred Irskine's direction whereupon Mary was moved to giggle—for Sir Alfred was at that moment taking up his cane and waving it through the mesh of people.

"Oh stop . . . Wade . . . he seems to want *you*," she said on a laugh.

"Thank the good Lord," responded her husband. "He nearly chewed off me ear this evening. Think I'll lope off."

"Oh no, you don't," said Mary, taking up his sleeve and pulling him back to her side.

"Old fidgets like Irskine remind me why I prefer the company of smugglers and rurals," said Ashford.

"Hush, he will hear you," cried Mary, very sure that Ashford meant to be unpleasant to the elderly man. In the corner of her eye she discovered Trent. The Captain had every appearance of making his way towards them and she bit her lip. Oh no, this was going to be trouble. What to do? She looked up at her husband and attempted to catch his eye, but he seemed intent on looking in another direction. Didn't he realize their ball was in very real and imminent danger? She was quite exasperated when all George would do was call out jests with his intimates.

"Tallow-faced fool!" snorted Ashford as Sir Alfred Irskine came up to them, breathing hard.

"There you are, Wade!" said Sir Alfred bringing his cane down and resting on its wide handle. He drew a long gulp of air. "Blister it! Not what I used to be." Then, impatient with himself, he hurried on, "Want to talk to you."

"Do you?" asked Ashford on a dry note.

"Now, you ain't got no call to come on puffed up with me! Knew your father . . . and have always had an interest in you, so come down out of the boughs."

"I wasn't aware that I was in the . . . er . . . boughs," said Ashford blandly.

"No, I'd warrant, in fact, that you are feeling better than you have in years!"

"Would you?"

"That's right! I know you been fretting yourself to flinders these twenty years over that business with Marksbury."

"Is that what I have been doing?" There was a warning note in Ashford's tone.

"Ah? Playing at ducks and drakes with me, eh? Don't like me talking about what is your business. Well, that may be, but you made the feud almost public with your gull catching . . . and now that your arch enemy—"

"*My what?*" Clearly he would take no more from Sir Alfred.

This was a gross impertinence and he would suffer it from no one.

"Starched up about it, ain't you? Damn, but I thought you would be dancing a—"

"Would you get to the point or do you mean to stand here and bleat at me all night?" snapped Ashford, for he was now losing control.

"Well, bless me . . . bleat, is it?" returned the elderly man, slightly hurt. He stopped then and put a finger thoughtfully to his long and angular nose. "Can it be that you don't know?" This he found hard to believe—Ashford was accounted for his sharp omniscience. "Of course you know. You're always up to every rig . . . stands to reason you would know."

"Hell preserve my sanity!" raged Ashford, ready to take the man by his lapels and shake him. "Will you tell me what you are talking about?"

"About Marksbury, of course," returned Irskine, "Good God . . . you . . . you don't know!"

"What about Marksbury?" This came from Captain Trent who had just arrived on the scene.

"Who the deuce are you?" returned Irskine, looking Trent over from head to foot.

"An excellent question!" drawled Ashford. "Ignore him, Irskine. Now, what do you think I should know about Marksbury?" Once again he was in command of his voice. Something inside of him was suddenly on edge. Damn, but this Trent was an impudent fellow!

"Well, but I was certain *you* would know . . . and mind now, I can't be certain for it was Holland who told me and you know old Holland, he is forever getting his—"

"Irskine!"—this from George—"spit it out man . . . spit it out."

"Right then, it appears that Marksbury has gone to ground."

*"What?"* This from Trent and Ashford in one voice.

"That's it, he died some days ago, according to Holland . . . injuries he sustained during an accident at sea . . . so then, Ashford, your feud is at an end?"

Ashford could not answer. He stood stunned by the news. NO! It couldn't be. Not now, not when he was so close . . .

Robbed! Oh God, it wasn't fair. First Silkie married to Trent and now this. . . .

"Lord Marksbury is dead?" repeated Trent, his brows drawn in a severe frown. Silkie, Silkie was alone. It was his first thought. "Are you certain?"

"As I said . . . got it from Holland . . ." started Irskine.

Trent was already turning to Mary and taking up her hand. "Mary, you understand?"

She knew just what he meant: He would be off. "Godspeed Dare . . . and don't be too hot at hand."

He kissed her gloved fingertips, turning to George who held his shoulder tightly. "You'll take care of your treasure and perhaps the next time I shall see you, George, you will be stepping onto our dock in Sag Harbor."

"You are a rascal, Dare, that you are . . . but as Mary says, godspeed!"

Then there was Sophie, standing in mute disbelief. What was this? Could it be that he was leaving? Why? What did Marksbury's death have to do with Darrow Trent? "Sophie," he said softly, bringing her hand close to his chest. "I've got to run . . . I'm sorry. . . ."

"Indeed, captain, you should be." Pride prompted her to put up her chin and turn round. She walked towards a group of gentlemen and was quickly hailed.

Without another word, the captain was off to pack his bags and collect his horse. Ashford was for a while heedless of what went round him. He was trying to assimilate the fact that Aaron Marksbury was dead. Dead. "Hell and fire!" he breathed at last. "You won't escape me so easily, Aaron . . . no, not by dying. You have left your mark upon the earth—you left me Silkie!"

Mary heard this last though it was uttered beneath his breath. She reached for his arm. "Wade . . . stop a moment . . . think . . ."

"Stop?" He shook his head and there was a bitter curve to his thin lips. "I think not. The problem is that I have waited too long, but no more . . . I shall wait no more!" With this he stomped off.

Mary turned to her husband who seemed oblivious to what had just passed before him. "George . . . I have this terrible feeling that . . ."

George Prendergast put a finger to his wife's mouth. "Aye, lass, but 'tis none of our concern, is it?"

"No, but . . ."

"No, and we are helpless to do anything about it, aren't we?"

"Well, I suppose, but . . ."

"Then, my dear, we had best attend to our guests, which *is* our concern." With this he was off, doing just that, and she stared after him a moment thoughtfully before sighing and following suit. It occurred to her that her large and docile husband was not so oblivious, after all.

# Chapter 16

*It* was past midnight and the dim firelight in the Marksbury study was enough to give a warm and comfortable feeling to its occupants. Silkie, her black mourning gown spread out around her slim form, sat on the hearth rug, her back propped up against the sofa. Her long flaxen hair was loose and in flowing waves around her shoulders. Her grey eyes were bright with the flickering flames in the grate and her thoughts were suspended in space. The moment was peaceful and she wanted no more than that.

Sir Blaize, his waistcoat unbuttoned, his dark superfine cutaway discarded on the sofa, his shirt sleeves rolled to his elbows, sat across from her. His fair auburn-lit hair was spread across his forehead, his dark blue eyes moody as they surveyed Silkie. What was it he was feeling? Had he always felt this way? Was it wrong? Egad, but she was beautiful. He looked away from her and contemplated the fire.

"It will go out soon if I don't add another log . . . perhaps 'tis time you bid me goodnight and let me lope on home."

"Ha! I like that," she answered at once, "I begged you to go home earlier but you wouldn't rest until Kora had finished baking those gingerbread cookies. Wanted them iced too, as I recall, and stuffed yourself so you couldn't walk, let alone mount your horse!"

"Saucebox! Never say so, for I'll swear I didn't eat more than a dozen or so." He chuckled.

"And that wasn't enough, but you made quick work of that bottle of wine I brought up from the cellar."

"Have done! A man is entitled to have a glass of brandy with his gingerbread cookies."

"A glass? More like two bottles, for don't think I didn't see you slip off for another," she bantered.

"Well, it served . . ."

"It did that. Lord, but I have never seen you so bosky before, not even at Holland's ball two summers ago when you and Skip discovered an abandoned smuggler's keg." She stopped suddenly, remembering her father.

He hurried her on, "Bosky? I was not! I will have you know I hold my drink very well!"

"Do you indeed? I have for the past two hours been plying you with one cup of coffee after another and I shall tell you to your head that you were dreadfully foxed, Blaize, and not fit company for a lady!" The tease was in her grey eyes, the smile on her cherry lips.

"Well, I did it all for you," he countered.

"What? Oh you . . . you . . . that is doing it a bit brown, don't you think?"

"Had to get you to smile again," he offered with a shrug. "It worked."

She reached over and touched his hand. "You looked a veritable moonling, wobbling from side to side with the silliest grin on your face. When Kora came upon you I nearly burst, for nothing would satisfy you but to plant a kiss on her cheek for the cookies. There the two of you were running about the room like lunatics! Oh, my side still aches from laughing."

"Oh Silk . . . you have got the most beautiful smile . . ." he said on a dreamy note, ". . . it starts in your eyes . . . and lights up your face and then touches your lips . . ."—he frowned then—". . . confound it, why did I never notice that before?"

"Don't be absurd," she admonished and put up a warning finger. "And don't think I can be taken in by your nonsense."

"It isn't nonsense. Oh, I know I have been hounding you to marry me . . . to forget your promise to your father . . . but Silk, it's made me realize that I *want* to marry you." His Silkie. He had come to think of her as his mascot. As an adoring fan that would ever be at his side. Perhaps in the recesses of his mind he thought one day he might marry her, when he was ready . . . and now, now that she was beyond his reach, he discovered that he had to have her!

"First of all, I am already married."

"Spare me! We both know we can find a way out of that if we try."

"I don't know that we can, but secondly, I shan't try. Not just yet."

"Your father was ill, Silk . . . he didn't realize what he was making you promise. You can't mean to stick to it . . . ah Silk, you are hipped now, blue-deviled, but eventually you will want to get on with your life. How can you if you are married to a man whose home is across the Atlantic Ocean? Think, girl, even if you don't wish to marry me . . . you might want someone else one day."

She turned away from him and composed her thoughts into an answer. "Blaize, we have been through this and I have asked you to stop picking at me. I don't know what I am going to do . . . I only know that at this moment in time, I cannot contemplate the thought of breaking my promise to my father."

"He wouldn't have forced you to it had he known that Trent was going to treat you in this offhand manner! Lord, Silk, married is he? That is a jest! Off he goes without even advising you. No doubt having a bang-up time in London and who knows when he will return and ship off to the States."

"Stop it! Remember, Blaize, the captain was tricked into marrying me. Even worse, he thinks I was a working party in my father's game. He thought . . ." She closed her eyes. Yes, Dare had thought she had tricked him as well and he had proceeded to demand his conjugal rights. He had forced her to the bed, but during that time together she had responded in a way that even now brought the color to her cheeks. It was a lowering thought, for he had still picked himself up and left her. It was a shock to her sense of self, to her ego. He had taken her intimately and he had not been moved to care for her. Enough! She wasn't going to think of that now.

"Ah . . . my poor Silkie . . . but how he could have thought anything disfavorable about *you* is beyond belief." He had released a long and weary sigh, saw the expression in her grey eyes, and moved forward onto his knees, "Don't cry Silk . . . not about Trent . . . he is a beast."

"He isn't . . . not really . . ." She trembled, drew on her inner self, and controlled the tears.

"Come on then . . . it's time you went to bed. . . ." However, he fell forward at this juncture. Nearly crushed beneath his weight, she giggled and pushed at him.

"Get off . . ."

"Why? I rather like it here." He grinned.

She wrestled with him and managed to throw him onto his back but his arm had her waist and he held her fast, whereupon he proceeded to haul himself up. She choked with her laughter as she beat at him and then suddenly he was very still and looking long into her grey eyes.

Dare looked up at the full moon and grimaced. Well, that was it, of course. A full moon! No doubt that was what had moved him to this insane act. Almost four hours had passed since he had taken to horse. It was nearly one in the morning and he was dust covered, stiff, and out of temper.

He had no sooner heard that Silkie's father was dead when he'd been overcome with this impetuous desire to rush headlong to Rye and see . . . his wife.

Like a crazy man he had taken one of George's fittest hacks, promising to have the horse returned with a servant at a later date. The poste chaise he had hired for his trip to London was instructed to take up his luggage and follow him to the Marksbury cottage on the morrow, and off he went in the dead of night. Absurd! And now here he was. Marvelous.

He contemplated the dark stable and carriage house. No doubt Joseph was fast asleep in his quarters above. He dismounted and heaved out a bellowing cry: "*Joseph!*" He slapped at the dust covering his greatcoat and arched his back before stretching out. "*Joseph!*"

Sleepily the young groom stuck his head out of the loft window and called groggily, "Aye . . . who's that?"

"Captain Trent. Come on then . . . get down here and take my horse." It was not Dare's habit to be so coldly inconsiderate to his servants, but he still blistered with the memory of Joseph's part in the events that caused him to be a married man.

Joseph hurried below and outdoors. He wasn't able to meet

the captain's eyes and took up the reins, "He is in a bit of a sweat, captain."

"That's right. Best rub him down and don't let him drink any water till he is cooled off . . . you might put a flake of hay in his stall as well."

"That I will and bless me, I know better than to give a horse water when he is hot," returned Joseph, slightly affronted.

"Do you? But then . . . there were a few things I thought better of you and have since been proven wrong," said the captain quietly.

Joseph bit his lip and said no more as he led the horse away. The captain called him to a halt. "Joseph . . . I hear tell this is a house of mourning."

"Aye, Captain Trent. That it is. The black wreath hangs on the door for his lordship and my mistress is sorely grieved."

Dare made no reply to this but turned and made his way up the sloping drive towards the cottage. It was a ridiculous hour and he was certain he would be waking Kora.

Kora was at that moment buttoning her brown wool wrapper. It was sadly worn and she found another seam that needed mending as she moved down the hall. It was certainly late, far too late even for Sir Blaize to be alone in the study with Silkie. The fact that Sir Blaize so nicely picked up Silkie's spirits had allowed Kora to go off to her own quarters to change and leave the young couple for a time without her supervision, but enough was enough! She shook her head as she padded towards the study door. Really, young Blaize—even Silkie should know better. Ah well, they had been friends for so long they probably wouldn't even think the proprieties would be attacked by their easy behavior.

She put her hand to the study door and heard Silkie giggle. It made Kora smile to herself. At last. She hadn't heard the girl laugh in days. Silkie had been cloaked in dolorous forlornness since her father's death and it had worried the housekeeper. It was at this moment, however, that she heard the front door knocker sound. A puzzled frown came to Kora's countenance. "Who on earth?" she said out loud and moved towards the door.

She undid the latch and cautiously opened the thick oak door a crack. Her eyes took in the captain's large frame as he stood within the torch's beam of light. She opened the door wide saying, "Why, mercy, Captain Trent!"

He was surprised that she was so quickly on the scene but said, "I am sorry to disturb you at this hour, Kora, but I have ridden all the way from London . . . I only just received the news that his lordship died, you see."

"Och, sad is to tell," she answered, shaking her head. "But never say you rode on horseback from London. Why, it must have taken you nearly five hours . . . and in the dark?"

He grinned. "I had the moon which afforded me light enough to find the road and my time was not quite five hours." He shrugged off his dust-covered riding coat. Even in the dim candlelight it was obvious to the housekeeper that the captain was dressed quite elegantly.

"Why . . . bless me . . . don't you look fine."

Again the boyish grin came to his face. "Er . . . I was at a ball at the time . . . and didn't stop to change." He went serious then. "I wanted to get to Silkie."

She nodded in understanding. "Worried about her, were you? The poor girl. She has had a bad time of it . . . well, captain, if it's Silkie you want, you'll be finding her in the study. I'll just go make you some hot cocoa . . . it will go well before you go up to bed"

He smiled at her. "That's a love, thank you."

She beamed beneath his charming blue eyes and hurried off. He turned and made his way down the dark corridor to the study door. At its latch he stopped and heard Silkie cry out, her voice a mixture of pain and wailing, "No . . . please . . . Blaize . . . I beg of you . . ."

## Chapter 17

*Shock?* Anger? Surprise? Wrenching jealousy? All very interesting emotions, especially when they bombard a man in the space of a moment. Dare Trent stood a moment, feeling what he had never felt before, and reason left him. Emotion ruled. He surveyed the scene that met his eyes. There lay his bride, flat on her well-shaped back, Sir Blaize straddling her across the belly with the obvious intent of tickling her unmercifully.

That they looked like veritable children never occurred to him. That it was an act of innocence was a thought he would have scorned had it come to mind. This, perhaps, was understandable. After all, one must remember that the captain had been through something of an ordeal since the moment of his marriage. Furthermore, he had as a boy never experienced the friendship and companionship of a rough and tumble girl and did not fully understand Silkie and Blaize's relationship. In addition to these facts, he had spent a grueling trip in the dark, damp night air. What he had wanted was to come home to a young woman, console her, and then—in the most amicable manner, of course— divorce her.

What instead did he find? His young wife giggling and wailing pleasurably at the hands of another man! It was the outside of enough and not to be borne! An amusing scene? To an indulgent parent perhaps, but not to a husband, even an unwilling one.

"No doubt," he said in a loud dry voice, "I intrude." His tone froze the couple. "However, I fear . . . at the risk of rudeness, that I must."

The two on the floor very naturally jumped apart with Sir Blaize rushing to his feet. Silkie was not far behind him. Guilty?

They appeared so. This further irritated Captain Trent and his sneer rose contemptuously.

"Dare," breathed Silkie, "what . . . what are you doing here?"

"I do make you my apologies, sweetheart," said the captain on a sarcastic note. "I hurried to your side the moment I got news of your father's death. I had ever good intention of consoling you. Of course, I didn't then realize Sir Blaize was in town."

"Captain . . . you mistake . . ." said Sir Blaize, stepping forward, his cheeks red hot.

"Do I?" Dare Trent's expressive dark brow was up.

All at once Silkie understood what Dare was thinking and her temper flared. She stepped between her friend and her husband, her grey eyes blazing with anger, her hands on her hips and her voice as sharp as her words. "How can you? Why . . . you stand there in self-righteous indignation . . . when you should be thanking Sir Blaize for standing by me this week! Where were *you*? Off you went without a word . . . and then you dare . . . you dare to think . . . why . . . you are nothing but an American boor!" So saying she turned to Sir Blaize, who was protesting feebly, begging her to calm down. "I am sorry for Captain Trent's rudeness . . . and shall be pleased to receive you in the morning, Blaize, should you choose to honor me with a visit." Her hand was extended to him.

Her gave her the high sign, hoping this would soothe her before he bent over her hand. "Good night Silk." He turned to the captain and nodded. "Captain . . . I'll . . . er . . . let myself out."

"Yes, I fancy you know the way," returned Trent.

"I should," managed Sir Blaize, "I have been in the habit of coming and going here since I was a boy." With this he strode emphatically forward and left husband and wife to eye one another ferociously.

Silkie put off her glaring and took a step to pass Dare. Unwise. He reached out and with his large, strong, and ungloved hand grabbed firm hold of her upper arm. "Just where do you think you are going, madam?"

"Why, where should I be going but to my room." She had

her chin well into the air. "Goodnight, captain." Her eyes swept his hand and her well-shaped brow was up.

He did not release her. "I think not. There are still a few things I want to say to you."

"Well, I have nothing to say to you." She was once again staring hard at his intractable face and in the depths of her grey eyes he could see shooting flames of red.

As she tried to yank herself out of his hold he felt himself overcome with anger and he pulled her forcefully up against his chest. His face was drawn in hot rage and his lips were near, all too near her own. "Haven't you, my dearest wife? I come home to find you in the arms . . . *Certes*, on the floor, being straddled by another man, and you say you have nothing to answer for? Well, damn it, I mean to teach you that I expect better behavior than that whilst you wear the name of Trent!"

She bit her lip because she could for a fleeting moment see his point of view. It was, however, absurd and so he should realize. Blaize was her friend. They had done nothing wrong and besides, it was nothing to him. Off he goes to London without even advising her where he had gone or when he would be back. How dare he? "You . . . you are insufferable!" was what she managed to return to him.

"And you, my . . . wife . . ." he drawled in low-keyed heat, ". . . are unbearably beautiful when in a rage." So saying, he found her tightly in his embrace. His mouth once again discovered that hers was sweet and he lost himself for the moment in a kiss that set his blood to flowing wildly through his veins. Had a woman ever filled him with such desire before? Damn, but he wanted her. It was all he could think, all he could feel. Gone were any other considerations in the headiness of their touching. He wanted her. His hand strayed from her back to her waist as dimly he was aware of her struggling to be free of him. No, by God, not yet . . . another kiss . . .

She was pressed suddenly against his hard, lean body and to her supreme annoyance she felt an all-too-real tingling along her spine. She wanted to forget everything and lose herself to him, but she couldn't. He didn't want her. Her father had tricked him. What had he been doing in London? Had there been other woman there? "Stop it," she breathed, but her voice came without fury. Indeed, it was hard to speak for she could find no air in her lungs.

"The hell I will," he whispered seductively in her ear. "Ah babe, Silkie babe, you are my wife . . . remember." He wanted her to think of the last time she had been in his arms, and proceeded with his gentle but mesmerizing lovemaking.

She was melting to his touch and her body wanted more. Her mind, however, proved to be strong in the struggle. "Your wife? By force, my captain . . . in every way by force." She was pushing against him ineffectually for the blood burning through her limbs was urging her to succumb. Pride found its way. How dare he? How can he? Didn't he leave for London hours after he had stolen her virginity? Didn't he leave without a word? She made a fist and pounded at him—the question angered her to a frenzy.

His ego pulled at him. Pique. Was she fighting him? Damn the woman! She had tricked him into his present predicament. She was his wife through a shabby trick and yet she would resist? Certes, but he wanted her, here and now, but not this way. He set her from him and his sneer was marked across his handsome countenance.

"Very well, madam, have it your way."

"I certainly hope I shall," she answered at once, confused ever so slightly to find herself free of his arms. For a moment she thought she might tumble, but quickly she regained control of her senses. "Just as I hope that together we may find a way out of this marriage."

"Oh, we shall that," he answered with his head cocked and his eyes cold. "Tomorrow we will pay a visit to your solicitor . . . that is if you have one."

"Indeed, captain. In the meantime, I am certain Kora has seen to your room if you would like to retire." She hurriedly made her exit, not waiting for his reply. She nearly ran down the dark corridor and took the stairs so that when she reached her room and bolted the door she was quite out of breath. She stood for the longest time, listening, trying to catch some air and afraid to move. Would he follow her up? Would he again try to . . . to ravish her? Oh faith, Kora, Kora, please steer him to the guest room . . . please know what to do. . . .

Kora was in fact somewhat aware of the captain's mood and

haggard state of mind and body. She went to him as though all were well. Her voice was cheery as she dropped him a perfunctory curtsy. "Well now, captain, 'tis that tired you must be. I've put a hot brick in your bed and a tray of hot chocolate and biscuits on your nightstand." She had already turned to lead the way out of the study.

He stopped her, for her attitude amused him and served for the moment to assuage his ruffled temper. "Well, apple cheeks, tell me, if you will, how did you know which bed I would be occupying tonight?" He couldn't help teasing the middle-aged housekeeper and as he did, watching her reaction, brought a smile to his hard expression.

"Ha, as to that, t'was plain to me, seeing as I'm not a green miss, captain, and so I will have you know at the outset," she answered at once, showing him that she was not one to be handled by his charm. "The way you stormed my Silkie tonight, mercy, t'was clear what room you *wouldn't* be having the use of!" So saying, she neatly preceded him out of the study.

He stood a long moment, the smile widening across his face as he watched her move with her single candle down the hall. Then, with something of a sigh, he snuffed the table candelabrum and took up a single one in a pewter holder. The thought came to him fleetingly that Silkie was his wife, and if he wanted the use of his wife. . . ? Hell, that wasn't how he planned his life. That wasn't how he wanted a bride. Not by trickery, not by force. In the morning he would find a way out of this situation. That's right, and then he would be off for Sag Harbor and . . . and then what? Zara Marksbury. Zara and her plans to have him wed to Blaine. Oh God, what a mess!

A neatly styled traveling carriage was wielded through the narrow arched opening of Rye's ancient grey stone landing gate. Its high-fashioned painted yellow wheels clanked over the cobbled street as the carriage's perfectly matched greys brought the coach to its destination.

Tatem glanced up at his master's lodgings with something of a weary sigh. Why must they have traveled in the middle of the night? But then, quality was ever odd about things, weren't they? Crazy the lot of 'em, for want of steady business. That was their trouble. All they was brought up to do was play and nose about with their cronies. Mad, all of 'em, that's what!

The coach slowed to a stop and Tatem was already alighting and rushing orders at the groom before he took the steps to Ashford's front door and disturbed the footman. It was nearly dawn and there was every good chance Ashford would sleep till midday. At least that would give them some time to put things in order.

Wade Ashford stirred himself. He had not been asleep but dwelling on many disturbing thoughts; they had taken him to another realm. His legs had been stretched out on the seat opposite him and when he brought them down he discovered sharp pins and needles in his feet. He shook, stretched, and stamped his feet before he attempted to bend and step down from the carriage.

He watched his wiry valet rush about, efficiently handling underling servants and waking the household staff. He was a good servant, his Tatem, but hell, why shouldn't he be? He was paid enough for his services, wasn't he?

Ashford passed his footman, noting the sleepiness round the elderly man's eyes and his brow went up. He expected his staff to be in readiness for him at all times. After all, since he demanded very little of these people, the least they could do was look lively. No, they would rather rush about in their nightclothes and make it obvious how inconvenient his arrival was to them. Damn their souls! It furthered his irritability, but dissolved his guilt.

His library door was held open for him and he went within to find Tatem already building a fire in the grate. Ah, that was what he needed. Some bread, cheese, wine, and a roaring fire. He repeated the fancy to his valet who immediately unbent and hurried to do this bidding.

"Tatem," he called after the valet in an afterthought. "Have cook bring me what I want and you . . . go off to bed. You have had a long night and I can manage on my own."

"But your clothes, sir?"

Ashford nearly smiled. "I assure you, Tatem, I know the knack of undressing myself."

"Yes sir, thank you, sir," said the man, wondering silently at his employer's sudden generosity.

Ashford moved to the fireplace and took up the wrought-iron

poker. He played with the kindling wood until the flames were bolting high and bright before he allowed himself to slip into thought again. Well then, here he was, on a whim, back in Rye!

Why? Hell, fire, and the devil, what was he doing here now? What was the good? All revenge on this side of hell was lost to him, wasn't it? Marksbury had been buried and what was worse, the man had gone to his grave thinking he had beaten Ashford! Oh but it rankled! God, how it rankled and rubbed, leaving him sore and hot with frustration. Silkie? There was Silkie, married to Trent! Another slash in his gut. If there were an afterlife—and there had to be—he would chase Aaron Marksbury's soul to hell, but first, first he would seek out his revenge on Silkie and that plagued interloper, Trent! He had to—it was his only outlet. But how? He would have to find a way.

## Chapter 18

*Mr*. Brumby's wide large hand strayed to his full head of white hair and he ran his fingers through the soft tresses without putting a one out of place. He clucked his tongue, took up the brass letter opener from his desk, and shot Silkie Marksbury a disapproving look that halted her distressing speech. Mr. Brumby was at sixty a man who believed in the holiness, the steadiness, the unbreakable rules of the marriage rites. Divorce? It was an ugly word. Still, as Silkie Marksbury's solicitor—as he had been her father's before her—it was his legal duty to aid her in whatever legal endeavor she required. In this case, divorce. It nearly made him shudder. He closed his eyes for a moment and gathered his resources for a reply.

"We have, as you must be well aware, something of a grim and, for me, heinous task ahead of us," he said after a long pause.

Silkie's grey eyes looked quickly at her husband. He was seated beside her, and from his profile she could see his determination. Once again she looked at Mr. Brumby and said with as much composure as she could muster in the awkwardness of the situation, "Nevertheless, it is a task that must be accomplished."

"I am certain that you feel so, Mrs. Trent, in spite of the fact that you father . . . willed it otherwise." He put up his hand to halt her from sending him one of her hot, quick replies. "However, other than the obvious problems that present themselves in this sort of . . . er . . . affair, there is one that is very nearly insurmountable."

"I take it, sir, that you are referring to the fact that my . . . wife, is underage," said the captain quietly.

Mr. Brumby shot the captain a long hard look. No fool here, he thought fleetingly before he steadied his answer. "That is precisely so, captain. Your wife, my late client's daughter, is underage and therefore some delicacy attaches itself to this particular situation."

"I don't see why it should," put in Silkie, her cherry lips forming a pout. "After all . . . I am very nearly twenty . . . and besides, doesn't being a married woman enable me to handle my own affairs?"

Mr. Brumby cleared his throat and leveled a severe look at Silkie Marksbury. A child. Look at her, sitting there in her fine grey feathers, pouting and carrying on! Well, she was ever a headstrong chit . . . and the marriage was, after all, forced on both Silkie and this American. He sighed and then directed a look at the captain, ignoring Silkie's outburst. "*You*, I am persuaded, will understand what I am talking about when I say that an annulment is not, in this particular case, available in the ordinary sense."

The captain inclined his head. "You are speaking, I take it, about the signing of the separation deed?"

"Ah, if that were so, it would be no very difficult thing. No, what we have here is the fact that you have taken a minor as your wife and in the eyes of the law, have in that vein accepted guardianship over that minor. Now, you wish to declare the marriage null and void. Very good, sir, but there is the problem of who is to stand buff for the minor. You?"

The captain's hand went to shade his eyes as he considered the truth and the complication of this. Silkie poohed such stuff away and sat forward on her chair. "This is all nonsense. I don't need anyone to stand buff for me! I will sign the annulment papers myself."

"My dear child. It would be assumed that you were . . . er . . . coerced into doing so and that might cause both the captain and yourself some problems in the future. No, if this thing is to be done, it must be done clean."

"What are you saying? I just don't understand," returned Silkie, her lovely brows drawn in an inquiring frown.

"That is doing it up a bit sweet, isn't it?" demanded her

husband, suddenly out of temper. Look at her, feigning innocence. She knew this all along! Damn her and her father!

She put up her chin and ignored him as she once again directed her question. "Mr. Brumby . . . please, just what do you mean?

"It is really very simple, my dear. As a minor, a . . . divorce would be almost impossible. An annulment is, on the other hand . . . within contemplation, but only with difficulty. You see, it could be said that Captain Trent took you under his protection and then discarded you." Embarrassed, Mr. Brumby turned beet red, cleared his throat, and then proceeded. "Therefore, in order to preserve his name, and, I might add, your own, certain prerequisites must be followed."

"Such as?" she pursued.

"Applying to the man who would be your legal guardian had you not married Captain Trent," answered the lawyer gently.

In some exasperation Silkie forgot for the moment the grief of her loss. She only knew she had to get out of this hateful marriage. A voice whispered that she was abandoning her promise to her father. It was pushed aside in the irritation of the moment, "What you are saying"—she put to the lawyer, her ripe lips drawn in a frown—"is that the captain is not only my husband, but my guardian as well, and because of that fact, we can not obtain an annulment until I come of age." She shook her head. "All in the name of propriety, no doubt!"

"No, no, my dear, that is not what I said, though, if a guardian had not been appointed, that is what I would have been saying."

"What? What do you mean?" cut in Silkie, for the word guardian sliced through her agitation.

"If you will but calm yourself, child, I shall attempt to explain," said the elderly man, one white brow up as he waited for her to sit back in her seat. She did so and after he cleared his throat in the manner he had acquired over the years of getting full attention, he said in a patronizing tone, directed only at Silkie, "What I had said, my dear, is that, had you *not* married the captain, you would have had the guardian your father stipulated in his will."

Once again Silkie was at the edge of her chair and cutting him off. "My father never—"

"Enough!" said Mr. Brumby, "now hush, child, and let me finish." He waited a moment in open challenge, saw that while she was bursting to say something she seemed willing enough to keep quiet, and then resumed, "Your father decided some six months ago to appoint a guardian for you in the event of his death. He wrote to your uncle Tyler, who signed the necessary documents agreeing to your father's request. However, Aaron was never really happy about this arrangement, said something about being worried that you would not be welcomed by your aunt Zara . . . your uncle's wife."

"Papa never told me," she said quietly and fell to brooding. There was so much she did not understand, so much that her parents had withheld from her, and now here she was in this muddle and not knowing what to do.

The captain had been sitting back, thoughtfully contemplating his wife. Damn but she was a picture. Her flaxen hair was tightly wound at the nape of her neck, nearly hidden by the black and grey confection of silk on her head. Her black cloak was severe and, he noticed suddenly, quite worn, as was the dark grey gown she wore beneath it. He guessed it had been her mother's, for it was outdated. It brought on a feeling of irritation. His wife shouldn't be so shabbily dressed. His wife? Hell! Not by his choosing! Conflicting emotions tore at him. He found her grey eyes, discovered the gold flecks, became absorbed in the pain he found in their depths. Certes! What was he doing? Allowing himself to be taken in by a beautiful woman? Hell no! He got to his feet, suddenly irritated beyond endurance, and extended his hand in abrupt dismissal of the elderly magistrate.

"We have, I believe, nothing further to discuss. You will prepare whatever affidavits and documents necessary for us to present to my wife's uncle and we will have them signed upon our arrival in Sag Harbor."

Mr. Brumby frowned at the younger man. This was very curt and almost rude of the lad, but, no doubt the captain had reason enough for his behavior. "Indeed, Captain Trent, all the papers will be prepared. When do you plan on departing?"

"If all goes well, the day after tomorrow," answered the captain, easing the abruptness of his manner with the charm of his smile. He turned and bent an elbow to Silkie. "My dear?" he said lightly.

Her grey eyes came up to his face in sharp inquiry, surprised and just slightly disconcerted, for he had not behaved so solicitously all morning. She hesitated in her confusion and he chuckled. "I am not a monster, after all, only a man in need of my freedom."

She was charged with the sting of his words and her chin went up in defiance. "Do not for a moment believe, captain, that you do not have it. The law may consider you my husband, but I definitely do not!"

"Indeed!" snapped the captain. "However, while you carry my name, there are those who might not agree and I therefore will request you to remember, ma'am, that you *are* my wife!" Why did it matter? Hell, because he wasn't going to have a woman flaunt his name about town and make eyes at bucks like Sir Blaize!

Mr. Brumby's jaw had dropped as he witnessed this marital dispute. "Just a moment . . . please captain," he said, having to raise his voice in order to get the young couple to look his way; they were absorbed in their militant glares at one another. "I didn't think I had to remind you . . . but perhaps I had better."

"Yes . . . what is it?" said the captain, his dark brows veering together.

"Delicate . . . very delicate," mumbled Mr. Brumby. "Good God! That I should have to be . . . but then, you were ever a headstrong girl . . . always taking your fences flying with never a thought to the footing on the other side."

"Mr. Brumby, that is not quite fair . . . in this particular matter. As you know, as we have explained, my father constrained us beyond our control into this . . . marriage."

"Aye, and extracted a promise from you that you would not look for a way out. I do know. It is what he told me he was going to do, and I *told* him no good of it would come! Well, now just see how matters stand."

"How do they stand?" inquired the captain quietly, bringing the attention to himself.

Mr. Brumby considered him. "Well now, it can be done, though as I have already stated—"

"It's delicate. Yes, I am aware," cut in the captain.

Mr. Brumby cleared his throat. "Are you also aware that in

order to obtain this annulment you will both have to sign a document swearing that you have never . . . er . . . consummated the marriage?''

Silkie's eyes dropped to her lap and the intricacies of the black design of her half-gloves. She sensed rather than saw the captain's deep blue eyes glance her way and something inside of her twinged when she heard him answer. ''Of course. I think, Mr. Brumby, that both of us would at this point sign our souls away to achieve the goal which we seek.''

''That is, of course, for your consciences to bear,'' said the solicitor gently but uncompromisingly. He relented in light of Silkie's gloom. ''However, putting this consideration aside, I can not stress enough how important it will be for you both to conduct yourselves with . . . er . . . reserve.''

''Your meaning, sir, is not clear,'' returned Silkie, her head arching, her eyes inquiring.

''What the good Mr. Brumby is trying to tell us, my bride,'' said the captain with a sardonic smile, ''is that we shall be expected to occupy separate living quarters.''

''That's right . . . and during the voyage to America . . . separate staterooms . . . and it would help if a trusted servant were witness to the fact that you . . . are avoiding . . . your conjugal rights,'' said Mr. Brumby, and his cheeks were scarlet. This was not the sort of employment he had any liking for.

The captain answered for his wife and himself. ''Of course.'' He was turning to find his lovely wife blushing becomingly. She remained quite silent as she contemplated her clenched hands. A beauty. Such a fair-haired, hot-blooded beauty. Fleetingly he thought of the morning he had taken her to himself and he felt a rush of desire spring through him. Never mind! Forget it. Damn, but she was an intriguing little creature.

Silkie felt him eyeing her and she summoned her courage to look up defiantly at him. A twinkle of amusement lit his dark blue eyes and for a moment she was taken off guard by his intimidating good looks. Oh faith! He was taking her away to America. Away from Marksbury cottage, away from Rye . . . from Blaize. How could she bear it? It was unfair, so unfair . . . but who said life was fair? No one, in fact. It was one of the few things she was not naive about. Well then, buck up. You are no shrinking thing, she told herself bracingly. At least you will be escaping Wade Ashford just as your father wished, and so shall make up for the broken promise.

Zara Marksbury's nails were long and neatly manicured. It was the fashion to paint them, but this was something she no longer did. She stood at the library's huge diamond-shaped, lead-paned picture window and gazed on the wide stretching lawns, fading now with the promise of winter. The leaves of autumn were gone and the sad willow tree that Blaine had just reached looked forlorn in its bleakness. Blaine! Really, there was no reasoning with the girl. She was pining over that dratted boy, Werth!

Zara watched her daughter continue down the red-brick path towards the stables. No doubt the child would ride off her depression. Hopefully she would do that, for Zara was sick to tears of her daughter's moping around. She turned and found her husband still perusing the *Chronicle* and she said with some impatience, "What can you be reading? My word, Tyler, I have been waiting patiently these fifteen minutes and more to speak with you!"

Tyler's blue eyes looked up absently from the newspaper; he had been too engrossed with the news of the day to notice his wife's ill temper. "Listen to this, Zara," he said with some excitement. "There is this fellow, Morse, and the man has perfected this thing . . . read about it once . . . a telegraph, you see, and damn if it didn't work . . . sent a message from Washington to Baltimore."

"Sent a message?" she returned doubtfully but interested in spite of her irritation. "What the devil do you mean? Sent a message, how?"

"With this thing . . . the telegraph . . . through the air . . . most astounding really."

"Through the air? 'Tis impossible! Just what do you mean believing such rubbish?"

"Zara, do but listen,"—he smiled patiently—"he used a sending device in Washington and tapped out the message, 'What hath God wrought' and it was received in Baltimore the same day . . . the same time. Truly remarkable."

She regarded him. "I suppose, though I don't for a moment really believe it. What else does it say?"

"That he needs a financial backer," said Tyler thoughtfully.

"Aha! Of course." She took the paper away from her husband and set it aside. "Now, enough of such things. Tyler, we must do something to get Dare home as quickly as possible!"

He sighed. It was not the first time he had sustained this particular line of conversation with his wife. "Yes, my love," he answered placatingly. "What do you suggest?"

"Good lord! Can't *you* think of something for a change?"

"It is my belief that if Dare is not already on his way across the Atlantic, he soon will be," answered Tyler with a smile. He reached out and took her arm, pulling her into his lap.

She was out of humor, but other than smoothing over her gaily printed day gown and lightly cautioning him not to wrinkle it, she did not object. "Tyler, do you think so? Really, do you?"

"Yes, my darling, for we already know when he left the Orient. If my calculations are correct, he should be weary of London by now and getting ready to sail."

"I hope so . . . for I tell you, Tyler, I don't like Blaine's mood. I have never seen her so low."

" 'Tis that lad, Werth. This departure has her pining, not Dare's absence," said Tyler cautiously.

"Oh, pooh. Pine she might for that stripling, but Dare is just the one to put the color back in her cheeks!"

Tyler's hand strayed and found the small pertness of her breast inside the low scoop neck of her gown and he fondled, discovered the nipple, and teased it gently. "Do you know, Zara . . . how much I always want you . . . how much I want you at this moment?" His other hand was reaching for her neck, gently drawing her into position.

She pulled away. "Oh Tyler, not now, for heaven's sake!" She was up and off his lap in a thrice, moving across the library's oriental rug, reaching for the door. "I've got so many things to do." She was gone.

Without getting up, without sighing—Tyler had learned long ago to accept such treatment from his wife—he reached in his pocket, bent to his bottom left drawer, and inserted the key. A moment later a bottle of Irish whiskey, his favorite, was withdrawn and his glass was filled. He raised the glass as though to a friend and then downed it, quickly, thankfully. It was only ten in the morning, but he had a long day to get through and this would help. Oh, God, it had to help!

# Part Three

*Ay me! for aught that I could ever read,*
*Could ever hear by tale or history,*
*The course of true love never did run smooth.*

—A MIDSUMMER NIGHT'S DREAM

# Chapter 1

*The* sun came up glowing nearly orange, filling a portion of the eastern sky with its full color. It was a warm day and though the winds blew with their promise of winter, there was still a hint of autumn in the air.

Silkie's long, white gold hair was caught at the nape of her neck but the wind blew it round her enchanting face as she stood on the deck of the *Seamaid* and said goodbye to the land of her ancestors. Kora touched her shoulder and as Silkie felt the pressure beneath her serviceable dark wool cloak she turned and smiled. "Well, Kora, my love, the sails are full and we are off." It was quietly said, with resignation, and slightly, ever so slightly touched with the excited anticipation a spirited child would feel.

"So we are, m'dear, but don't you be fretting none, 'tis for the best. Lord love ye, Mrs. Trent . . . when I think of how that Ashford dared his last—"

Silkie cut her short. "I have asked you repeatedly not to call me Mrs. Trent"—she put up a finger forestalling Kora from comment—". . . and I . . . I don't want to speak about Wade Ashford now. Not just now."

"Don't you? Well as to that, you are Mrs. Trent and what I am supposed to call you is more than I can ken," said Kora, taking umbrage. She was herself unnerved by the fact that she could see England fading away. "And as to *that* devil, whose name I won't again mention, but you know who I mean, well, it was a good thing Captain Trent was on hand yesterday. He meant mischief, that man did and . . ."

Silkie laughed and put an affectionate arm round Kora's

plump shoulders. "My, but you do rattle when you are feeling sorely."

Kora's mouth set and her chin went up. "But I'm not feeling sorely and why you should think I am is more than—" She stopped herself. "Am I bleating like a silly old woman, then?" She shook her head. "I suppose I am. Fact is . . . never took to the sea and . . . well, there is less and less land and more and more water."

Again came Silkie's laugh, a musical sound full of invitation. "Do you know, Kora, I haven't unpacked. . . ." She gave the woman something with which to occupy her time.

"No, and why should you? 'Tis for me to do and so I shall, right now," said the woman turning round and making for the companion stairs. Her gait was none too steady and there was a moment when she lurched and thankfully found the captain. He steadied her, put her hand on the rails, and then turned to discover his wife leaning over the bulwarks with her back to him.

An odd, almost contrary sensation touched him. He frowned, for his mind never seemed to coincide with his feelings these days. She was inscrutable. She avoided him. She would laugh suddenly, turn, and find him looking at her—only to turn away coldly. Why? He hadn't ill treated her, damn it, and she had misused him from their first meeting!

He was pondering this when his first mate came up to him and told him he was required at the helm. Sharply he put all thought of Silkie away and turned to his men and his ship. Here was something that could dissipate his frustration and make him forget her gold-flecked grey eyes.

She heard him behind her and turned round to find him going off with Master Forbes. Look at him! He never spared her a moment. He was always busy with something, someone. She was leaving England, her home. She was here on this marvelous sailing slice of timber but did he offer her his arm? No. Did he give her a tour? No. Did he give her any attention at all? No. A gentleman would have. Yes, but he had been there when Ashford came yesterday and . . . and . . .

She closed her eyes and the scene came flooding back to her. How bad tempered Dare had been. He had seen her sign over the deed to Marksbury cottage for Mr. Brumby to sell, and instead of sympathy he had roughly said to her that she wouldn't be needing the old place anymore. . . .

Oh! She had wanted to slap his face. He didn't stay long enough for her to do more than give him a sharp set down. He only laughed harshly and said she had better write her puppy a farewell note.

"A note? I think not, captain. My farewell to Blaize shall be given in person!" she answered tartly. Her grey eyes flared as she tossed a stray lock of flaxen hair behind her shoulder.

He looked at her long and his eyes quieted with his silent thought. There was a moment when Silkie thought he was about to reach out his hand and lay it on her cheek. He did not. Instead, he shrugged his shoulders and said lazily, "You will, of course, do what you think appropriate to your relationship with your neighbors. I have no objection in that regard."

She felt hot ire surge through her. "No objection?" Her bosom heaved. "Haven't you any at all? Well, by God! Perhaps you should!" With this she picked up the grey of her wool riding skirt and slammed out of the cottage. She was in a rage—she couldn't even think why. She only heard her mind's voice screaming. How dare he? Just who did he think he was? Your husband, another voice answered. The devil he is!

She went into her stable and there her rage suddenly froze. It was very nearly empty. Ajax, her father's chestnut hunter, had been taken by Joseph to Sir Blaize, who would perhaps sell him. Their dog-cart and carriage had been sold in Rye on the previous afternoon along with a bevy of tack and tools. She closed her eyes and composed herself. Over. This life was over. No, she told herself. What was over was the life she had left. It was spent and now she had a new life ahead of her. That was how she had to think.

She took a curry comb and brush to Rocket and quickly cleaned off the evidence of his morning's roll. Hurriedly she slipped on her sidesaddle, put on his bridle, and led him outside to a mounting block. As she jogged him down the drive she felt rather than saw a movement at her back, and quickly looked round to see Trent mounting the hack horse he had left in the barn. What was he doing? Following her? She cut across the lawn to a wide open field, paced herself for the three-foot jump across the post-and-rail fence into the next field, and took it flowingly. She landed and looked behind her as Rocket cantered forward. Dare wasn't there. She slowed to a stop at the top of the hill and waited a moment. He still wasn't there. No doubt he was just returning to Rye then. Good. So he wasn't following her, after all.

What was that she felt? Relief? No, not exactly. However, there wasn't any more time to pursue this question for it was then that she saw a rider on a flashy steel grey gelding coming towards her. She saw the set of the shoulders in the many-tiered dark riding coat. She saw the angle, jaunty and rakish, of the dark top hat, and then she saw the face. Her heartbeat increased rapidly and for a moment she thought of turning her horse round and rushing off. Where could she go? This one would follow for sure. Wade Ashford would in fact enjoy the sport of hunting her down!

She waited for the inevitable meeting and gave herself silent words of encouragement. Buck up. After all, he can't attack you out here while you are on horseback . . . can he? No, of course he can't. All the same she wished she had brought her crop.

Wade Ashford saw her take the jump and his jaw set. Damn but she was a minx he meant to have! Even in her mourning grey, she was a stunning piece. Look at her stand her ground and defy him. Blister it! He would bring her down and make her beg . . . as her mother should have . . . would have . . .

He inclined his head as he brought his horse to a halt and faced her. A slight curve to his set lips lightened the harshness of his expression. "Well, Silkie Marksbury . . . your father is dead."

It went through her painfully but though she flinched she managed to look directly at him. "Yes, and you are beaten." It was softly said and without the triumph he wanted for himself.

He went rigid and his sneer once again marked his dark expression.

"Do you think so? Then you haven't yet learned what I am capable of accomplishing."

"Oh, but I am aware, fully aware. You forget that my father would not have been on that miserable voyage if it hadn't been for you and your hateful wager. He might now have been alive. . . ." She looked away at the sudden glint of satisfaction that had come to Ashford's hazel orbs.

214

"That's right!" said Ashford, cutting her off. He had never quite seen it from this angle before. "But that was too quick, too easy. I am not done yet."

"What more can you do?" She shook her head. "You called me Silkie Marksbury, but you should know I am now Mrs. Trent. I shall be off with my husband for America."

"So I have heard. Oh yes, I have already presented my notes to Mr. Brumby. Perhaps the sale of your cottage will go a good distance to satisfying those notes, we shall see. But that still won't do for me."

"What is it you want?" she returned in a flash of desperation.

*"You,* Silkie. I want you." Suddenly his gloved hand was gripping her round the waist and she was lifted off her horse. She struggled and with a painful thump found herself on the ground. She gasped, unsure of what he was going to do, and as she got to her feet she reached for the reins of her nervously prancing horse. The sharpness of her movement spooked Rocket and he reared before he bolted, head and tail held high.

Silkie, startled, uncertain, and just a bit breathless from her tumble, turned in outrage to discover that Ashford had dismounted and was once again reaching for her. Her top hat had come flying off during her skirmish and ridiculously her eyes alighted on it as it lay on the ground. She wanted to discover and hold a certain semblance of normality. She wanted to tell herself that this was not happening, so she found herself walking towards the hat, bending to fetch it up, when Ashford's gloved hand closed round her upper arm.

She turned and her eyes flashed at him. "Don't you think you have done enough for one morning?" What was she doing, pretending he meant her no harm?

"No, my sweet bird, not enough," he said on a low but meaningful note. Part of the pleasure was the fear he could instill and he saw it there behind her bravado. The reins of his horse were loosely held through his arm as he drew her roughly to him.

"Stop it, Ashford, I warn you . . . Trent will have your blood if you touch me!"

Ashford laughed and it was a hard, cold sound. "He might try, but in the end he would find I have none to shed. No, my dear, I must always come out the winner, it is inevitable."

It was quietly said but it sent a shiver through her body. He felt it and it spurred him on. She was held tightly against him, both her hands pinned at her back with his large fingers pressing hers together until she winced. His other hand caught her neck and forced her into position as his mouth sought her pretty lips.

Oh God, how he crushed her to him, but it was not with ardor. No, there was no passion in his kiss, at least not the sort of passion a man normally feels for a woman. What then? Bitterness, rage? Ah yes. She recoiled at the hatred she could feel exuding from him. His touch was brutal—but it was not the violence that made her feel chilled and frightened. It was from his hatred, his resentment. Why? Why should he despise her so? She managed to stretch her neck and turn her face away. As she did her words were a quiet but dominant breath all the same.

"Do what you will, for I tell you, Ashford, I have already paid the price!" She readied herself for what she thought was the inevitable, what all men seemed to take on their terms.

He pulled up short and held her shoulders so that he could look full into her eyes. As soon as he had, he realized his mistake. Damn, they were Serena's eyes . . . so grey, so filled with gold. No! Here was something Serena had never felt. Defiance! Silkie's eyes were lit with flames of rebellion. Oddly enough, he was touched by the fight in her, but he thrust it away.

"No, not yet, little woman! I will though. I will come and whisk you away when you won't expect it . . . and when you least wish it. Right now you are miserable over your father's death, unhappy with this marriage, for don't think I don't know . . . I do." He shook his head. "I will have my way when you are full with some new and wondrous joy, when you feel most protected. And then will I strike! Remember that." Again he pulled her up, but this time his touch, though aggressive, displayed more expertise and less brutality; his voice softened. "But for now . . ."

She attempted to pull out of his hold. She was angry at his threat and she struck at him with her small fists, kicked out at him, but he laughed and caught her tightly. They were at that moment interrupted by the sound of pounding hooves, and they looked up to see a devil of a man riding hard and fast.

Dare had been taking the pike towards the village when his

horse picked up his head and gave a series of whinnies. It was then that Rocket came trotting riderless out of the brush, his reins trailing and his head and tail well up. He was lathered from his fearful bolting across the field and the whites of his eyes showed as he nervously inspected Dare.

The captain felt a moment's anxiety when he realized this was Silkie's steed. She must have come off taking one of her fences. She had been in the devil of a mood . . . they had argued . . . Certes! He calmed himself and approached the animal slowly so as not to spook him. "There now, Rocket . . . that's a good boy . . . there, where is your lady? Now what can you have done with her?" His voice was soft and soothing as he reached for the loose reins. This done, he patted the horse's neck. Assured by this time that Rocket was sufficiently settled to follow in tow, he began retracing the horse's tracks.

It was something he had learned to do when he had first begun hunting. In the wilds it was very nearly necessary for survival and he had learned the art well. He had this as well as the knowledge that Silkie had no doubt been on her way to Sir Blaize's estates. So it was he came to the scene in the open field, and with a harsh curse and a strong desire for blood he heeled his horse onward.

Dare Trent was a man of action and decision. He didn't jump off his horse and whip off his glove to challenge Wade Ashford. He leapt off his horse but it was his fist that came up and planted Ashford squarely.

Wade went reeling backwards before he was able to catch his balance and his temper. The darkening look was there but so too was his sardonic smile. "Do I take it, captain, that you wish to meet me at dawn?"

"Here and now will do for me! Come on, Ashford, you have been longing for this, so just come on!" the angry reply came bowling out of Dare's gritted teeth. He was in a rage. He was livid with fury, very nearly unable to think. He only wanted to mill his man down.

"A brawl? No, I think not." Ashford turned to Silkie, who stood riveted, unable to speak. "Shall I beg your pardon, my dear? Yes, perhaps that will serve for now. You understand, don't you, *Mrs. Trent*? I mean to have my way, on my terms, in my time."

"Go to hell, Wade Ashford," Silkie managed on a contemptuous note.

"Yes, I think I shall, but I mean to take you with me." With this he bent, took up the top hat that had dropped to the ground a moment ago, and turned to face Trent. "There, captain, you may unclench those large fists of yours, for you shan't get to use them on me anymore this day. Content yourself, for I think you have done some damage to my jaw."

"If you ever come near my wife again, you won't breathe long enough to wonder what damage I have done!" snapped Trent. He had gone to put Silkie behind him as he watched Ashford mount his horse.

Wade Ashford's sneer marked his features as he inclined his head, tipped his hat, and rode off in silence. Even now he was making his plans. Dare Trent would suffer long and hard for all he had done. Oh yes. And Silkie? She was Aaron Marksbury's daughter. She could have been his child if Serena had . . . but no, Serena had chosen to spur him for Aaron. How Silkie would pay!

Kora's words had reminded Silkie of the encounter. England was fading away in the distance, swallowed up by the sea and sky. How Dare had turned on her, lectured her about riding out alone. How cold, arrogant, unfeeling he had been, as though it were all her fault that Wade Ashford had kissed her. Oh God, when would she be free of Dare Trent? He was overbearing, unjust, self-assured, and probably a womanizer. She had seen the way the village girls had flirted with him and how he had responded. How dare he tell her how to go on, or how to behave!

The captain stared for a moment at his wife. She stood a beauty in the wind, troubled, unhappy, and alone. He felt a wave of compassion strike him. He hadn't been very understanding these two days. After all, she had agreed to the annulment. Perhaps they could be friends . . . and damn, she had lost her father, she was being taken away from her home. He stepped forward and though an urge to touch her came through, he managed to keep his hands to himself as he spoke.

" 'Courage, lass. The hurt cannot be much.' " It was a line

from Shakespeare. It came to mind and he said it softly, hoping to dally her out of her gloom.

She heard the strong male voice. It came to her gently and she responded immediately. In spite of her mood, she turned and with the smallest of smiles, answered in kind, " 'No, 'tis not so deep as a well, nor so wide as a church door; but 'tis enough, 'twill serve.' "

He chuckled. "What's this? Have I taken on a blue stocking as wife?" He shook his head in mock concern. "Lord preserve my sanity."

She laughed. "You have no fear on that score, Captain Trent. Blue stocking? Faith, but Mama would have laughed to hear you say so." She gathered a stray wave of golden hair that had whipped round her face and threw it back over her shoulder. "No, in fact, I was never really any good at my studies. I do enjoy reading and I can't tell you how many times I've read *Romeo and Juliet*. It's a favorite of mine and it was easy enough to answer your quote."

"Then 'tis a romantic I have on my hands." He was so near to her now that her sweet, fresh fragrance drifted round his head. He had a sudden, almost overwhelming desire to take her into his arms. She was in nearly every manner quite intoxicating. He brought himself up and snapped off the sensation. What was this? He was no schoolboy!

"Perhaps I am . . . or at least I was . . ." She frowned then and turned away from him to contemplate the ocean they were slicing through.

He touched her shoulder. "Come Silkie, you are young and you have your whole life ahead of you."

She turned a stiff chin to him. "Is that what you told yourself the morning you forced yourself on me?"

He stiffened. "I had been tricked . . . and you were a part of it all." He shook his head. "You are not loading me down with that one, madam, and so I tell you to your head!" His words came out sounding harder than he meant them to be.

Silkie's gloved hand went to her forehead in a gesture of extreme irritation. "Faith!" she exclaimed in some indignation. "Not load you down, indeed! Tell me, captain, for I really would like to know just how deep your mind runs, as I suspect your power of rational thought to be as shallow as your consideration. Who do you think should take the blame for what happened after the marriage ceremony? Who, captain, you or I?'' She didn't wait for his answer and indeed, she would have had to wait some time—her words had the effect of momentarily stunning him. ''You will walk away a free man in the end. That's right, you know . . . but plague take your soul, for I shan't. What you forced on me will remain always . . . so then, who was the victim, you or I?''

He felt a thrust of insensible anger take over. How dare she behave the innocent. ''You are coming on a bit too sweet and helpless, aren't you?'' He shook his head. ''What do you hope to gain by it? A comfortable marriage settlement? That's it, isn't it?'' His sensuous lips formed a sneer. ''Let me remind you that I found myself in *your* room, in your bed, and with my arms around you! Don't try and fob off the blame to me! You and your father caught me in as treacherous a ploy as ever I thought possible and''—he inclined his head disdainfully—''I thought myself entitled to my rights.''

She fretted over this and her hands tugged at one another though her ire was up and it helped her through the moment. ''I had nothing to do with—''

''What then, tell me your father drugged you, laid you in my arms! Tell me that!''

''You . . . you are an insufferable boor!'' was all she could answer. ''I don't care what you think, what you believe, as long as I find myself rid of you in the end!'' She turned away from him at that and stomped off towards the companion stairway. She was all too close to tears and wouldn't, couldn't let him see that.

In too much of a rage to contemplate the sincerity of Silkie's statements, he too strode off in a hard mood. He had the ship's work to attend to. That would occupy his time and his mind and to hell with the little spitfire. She was, though, a beauty of a vixen. She fired up at him in his mind's eye and something tugged at him. Hell, she was nought but a rebellious, traitorous, untrustworthy female. Who was the victim indeed!

# Chapter 2

*The* sun was bright in the east and the wind was gentle. Blaine's mood was dreamy and faraway as she stepped over knotty tree roots on the wooded shortcut into the village. Dried brown leaves floated gracefully on their journey to earth and squirrels made ready for the coming of winter.

She stopped a moment at the top of a roll in the hill. At her back the two large mansions of Trent and Marksbury stood, both regal, each in a different way. Below, the rows of quaint village homes with their picket fences and their individual character . . . and then the docks. The bay was calm but the people were in a flurry of excitement. Earlier that morning the call of "ship in the bay" had brought them all out. So she had, at the insistence of her mother, donned her blue silk redingote with its silver frogging, secured the matching blue confection on top of her auburn curls, and left the house behind.

"Go visit with Angie," her mother had ordered in some exasperation. "Why, I don't know what is wrong with you, miss, and so I tell you to your head. Go on now. You haven't been to town to see your friends in so long . . . I'm sure I don't know why they put up with you."

"Yes, Mama," she had answered as much from habit of obeying as from a desire to be away from her mother's constant nagging. She didn't know why it was, but all she wanted was to be alone and remember. Remember the feel of his arms, the sweetness of his kisses, the hot hungry desire he had aroused in her . . . Oh God, Denny . . . Denny . . .

"Praise be! I dunno how long I been waiting on you to

get out of sight of yer house, Miss Marksbury," said a small voice from a ragged clump of low evergreens.

Blaine was startled out of her daydream and her dark blue eyes focused on a small, familiar street urchin. He was dressed in loose-fitting sailor's garb and she recognized him as one of the young lads who worked at odds and ends round the docks for her father,

"Why, Matty, what are you doing up here?"

"Miss . . . if you please." He withdrew a sealed ivory envelope from his pocket and thrust it at her. "He wanted me to give this to you and paid me extra to be sure no one saw me when I did. So here . . . take it." This accomplished, the boy evidently felt his job had been done, and he took off with some speed back towards town.

Blaine looked at the envelope in her hand and frowned before she recalled her wits and attempted to call after the lad. "Matty . . . wait, Matty?" He was either out of earshot or chose not to hear, for he was soon round the bend in the path and out of sight.

"Now, who?" she said out loud as she tore open the seal and removed the folded paper within to read:

*Dearest love,*

*Torture was a word that had no meaning until I was separated from you. I woke each morning with you on my mind and trudged through each day until my sleep brought you to me again.*

*Fate is with us, Blaine. When I arrived in New York, my father had already made arrangements for another captain to sail our whaler on its planned expedition, as he needed me for another effort altogether.*

*You will remember our talks regarding the "underground railroad," to which my father and I are totally committed? As it happens, it is this venture that has brought me to Sag Harbor. We have worked out an interesting and, I think, viable plan to its further development. Mr. Garrison of the* Liberator *is staying in Southampton, and after my visit with him tomorrow,*

*I shall be sailing my schooner to Virginia. I need to see you before I sail. Don't, I beg of you, darling, deny me.*

> Your adoring and obedient
> servant, ever,
> Denny

Denny? Denny was in Sag Harbor. He was here. Oh God. *Here!* She remembered their last time together and it sent a thrill through her. Denny. She had expected he would be out on his whaling expedition, gone from her for four, perhaps six months, but here he was already! With a joyful laugh, she had her skirts in her hand and was rushing towards the village.

Mother? Mother would be furious if she knew . . . yes, but mother didn't know. Blaine and Denny could have a few hours together before Mother even realized he was here! This problem put aside, she laughed again. With her heart and head full of youth's early love, she put turf behind her.

The *Seamaid*'s masts were full with the evening's cool rushing wind as the clipper cut through the Atlantic Ocean on its steady path home. Above, the velvet darkness of the sky was alight with stars and the whiteness of a full moon brought a longing sigh amongst the crew. There were wives and sweethearts waiting for them in Long Island and they were feeling the need this night with the heavens reminding them of romance.

Below deck in the captain's stateroom, dinner had been served to its two occupants, but the mood was far from romance. Kora had taken one look at the food and nearly swooned; she was suffering from a touch of seasickness. With one hand to her head and the other to her tummy she had rushed out of the captain's stateroom and just barely made it to her small cabin at the end of the companionway.

This left Silkie concerned over Kora and then uncomfortable for herself as she turned in her chair and realized she was alone with her husband. Her grey eyes went to her lap and her fingers played with the taffeta of her gown. She was all too aware of the masculinity of the captain's cabin. She looked towards the porthole and discovered the moon peeping at her. She looked away and found the four-poster bed with its rich brown velvet quilt coverlet and its swagged hangings. She looked up and discovered Dare Trent's deep blue eyes, and they were ever so slightly touched with amusement as he watched her.

"I shan't eat you," he said softly, "though, the thought has just this moment crossed my mind . . . once again."

She attempted to enact the part of an offended maid. "Indeed!" she said sharply. There, she thought, that should depress his presumptuousness! How can he? Really, this morning he behaved a cad and now he is actually trying to flirt with me. 'Tis the outside of enough.

He laughed out loud, reached over the prettily set table and flicked her nose. "There, are you still angry? Don't be. We shall deal so much more comfortably if we call a truce. After all, we are after the same end. We have some twelve days we must spend in one another's company, and in fairly tight quarters. We might as well make the best of it."

"Why, how very gracious of you, captain. Will it be very difficult for you, do you think . . . passing the amenities with me?" She could not help the sarcasm that crept into her voice.

He felt his ire tickled but maintained his composure and his temper. "Perhaps, especially if you take a hard line with me, but I mean to try and be pleasant in spite of our differences."

She wanted to smack his face. Instead she smiled sweetly and asked him to pass the salt. His brow went up but he put the silver shaker into her hands. Well, she could play his game. She looked up from her plate and asked casually, "You said twelve days . . . how can you possibly reach Long Island in twelve days?"

"The last clipper out made it across the Atlantic in twelve days and nine hours. I mean to match or beat that time," he said with some animation.

She was interested. Her father had infested her with his love of the sea and ships and she had read something about the new clippers.

"They are graceful things, your American clipper ships. I remember Papa speaking of them. They were fashioned after a schooner famous for speed, weren't they?"

"In a manner of speaking." Damn but there was something in her voice that was all too sultry, something in the gold flecks of her grey eyes that drew out desire and left him aching to touch. Forget it! He returned to the subject at hand. "The Baltimore clippers served as a model for the early clippers. My *Seamaid* has a far more daring design."

"Yes . . . you are talking about the bow. 'Tis more concave than anything I have ever seen before."

"That's right. When I first worked on the model I was told that she would plow right under the water. Well, I didn't listen and fashioned her with long, clean lines from bow to stern. Her spars reach far out over the sides, her masts rise higher than most, and are kept taut. My *Seamaid* is the most modern of the clippers and I mean to build more like her."

"More? Why?"

"Because one day my son will be a man and the whaling industry will be over. It's inevitable. Trade, however, will prosper and grow and that means there will always be a need for faster and better ships."

Amused and intrigued with the man in spite of herself, she chuckled lightly. It was a musical sound. "Your son? You already have his future planned and he hasn't even been born yet."

"Ah, but he will be," he said with the self-confidence that was a part of his nature.

"Yes, of course. How could I doubt you? Have you a mother picked out yet . . . or doesn't that matter?"

His blue eyes were shaded a moment by his dark lashes and when next he brought them to her face they were inscrutable. She regarded him in that moment and was all too aware of his dynamic sensuality. Just what was he thinking? Who was this man? What made him, what moved him? She felt herself quietly drawn in by his aura and held fast. His words were, when they came, quiet, yet they resounded in her ears with a meaning she could not quite catch.

"Oh, it matters . . . as all things I apply myself to. . . ."

They were at this point interrupted by a knock at the cabin door and the captain called out gently for the young steward to enter. Tommy had been in Trent's service for little over a year. He was just barely eighteen, thin, wiry, and boyishly good looking with his fair hair in disorderly curls round his bright-eyed countenance. He was quick, efficient, and all too obviously shaken by Silkie's presence. Shy, darting glances were cast her way as he cleared the table and set the coffee cups. When she chanced to meet his gaze she very naturally rewarded him with one of her open, warm, and reassuring smiles. He nearly spilled the coffee in his captain's lap.

Captain Trent was not amused. He should have been tolerant but instead found himself depressingly irritated. He wasn't having his wife flustering every young male who came her way. He waited only until the door had closed behind Tommy before he turned a stern expression on his young bride.

"I will thank you, madam, to be more circumspect in your behavior with my crew."

"What?" Understandably she was startled. "Just what do you mean?"

"I will not have my wife flirting with every young buck who chances to find favor in her eyes!" He snapped in way of explanation.

"And when, captain, did you find me doing that?" she demanded, her own temper quick to take flight.

"Damn it, woman! You had that poor boy in hives just now and well you know it!" He flung his napkin onto the table. "You can't go about beaming those grey eyes at lads like Tommy. He is no match for you."

She was moved to rage. How could he? Her hands worked one another in extreme agitation and the grey eyes he spoke of were flashing wildly as the color came flooding into her cheeks. She was a rare beauty with her breasts heaving against the scoop of her low-necked gown, but when she spoke, she managed to coat her words with low-keyed sarcasm. "I do beg your pardon, captain." One hand flung a stray lock of flaxen gold over her shoulder as she raised her chin. "I suppose the trap's down and I have been caught at it again!" She clucked at herself. "Next time I shall remember you are up to every rig and manage my flirtations more discreetly!" With this she was up, turning on her heel and starting towards the cabin door.

She wasn't fast enough. The captain's coffee cup went over and its contents stained the white linen tablecloth as he shot up. Within the moment his large hand closed over her upper arm and she found herself pressed against his hard lean chest. He felt her breathing wildly and through his rising temper it excited him as did the fresh fragrance of her body and the cherry of her parted lips. His voice was low and menacing and very much an expression of the frustration he was experiencing.

"May I remind you, madam, that while you carry the name of Trent, there will be no carrying on, discreetly or otherwise . . . with anyone other than myself!" Thus commanding, he didn't bother to wait for her response. His head bent and before she knew what he was about his lips were on hers and his arms were around her supple body.

It was sudden and so intense that she lost a sense of herself. An overwhelming sensation tyrannized her. She wanted to push at him but discovered instead that she needed to hold tight to his arms if she didn't wish to crumble to the floor. What was the matter with her knees? They melted and she felt herself sinking. His kiss exploded in her mind. Stars as bright as those that shone in the velvet sky transported her until she felt herself floating.

This was impossible! She tried to regain composure of her wayward senses and her mind grappled for control. Impossible. It was her first discernible thought in a mind muddled with desires she hadn't been aware of. She shouldn't, couldn't be feeling this way. She couldn't even contemplate what it was she was experiencing. It was wicked! Wicked to want a man this way. She managed to bring her hand to his chest and push hard but ineffectually. She discovered that the touch of his lips on her ears, her neck, on her heaving bosom sent her blood temperature into fever pitch. Was that her voice that huskily requested him to stop?

He didn't answer her feeble entreaty. His hands had already undone enough of the buttons at her back to slip her gown off her shoulders. Gently, bewitchingly he brought his head lower and raised one breast to his lips. He suckled and felt exultation as she gasped. He had to have her. It was all he could think, all he knew as he deftly wielded her, sweetly aroused her with his touch.

This had to stop! He was going to put her aside in the new land he was taking her to. How could he make love to her in this manner when he meant to leave her? "Stop it . . . Dare . . . stop it . . ."

"You are my wife," he whispered as he nibbled her ear and lowered her to the floor.

How did she get to her knees? Onto her back? How? This was humiliating. She was behaving like a tart. This man meant to use her and leave her. She wasn't an object to be handled. "Dare . . . please stop . . ."

"You don't want me to?" His voice was full with his hunger and his mind was too overborn with desire to consider the import of his words. "Ah Silkie . . . you were made for this."

She felt a trickle of anger seep through and slap her coldly. "Dare, we are going to have the marriage annulled! Dare . . . remember."

"I remember," he answered softly as his hand slid up her slender thigh.

She pushed at him. "Then you will do well to remember that we mustn't."

"Who is to know?"

That was it! She was wide awake and frozen at that. She pulled away and didn't even realize how very easy it was to escape his arms. Had he been forcing her down or had she gone willingly into his arms? No time to consider this question. She was on her feet, holding her gown to herself, glaring down at him. "You keep your distance, Captain Trent . . . just keep your distance and your hands off me!" She was furious. With him? With herself? She didn't really know.

He was hungry still, unsatisfied with the tease of the taste, wanting more. He got up and attempted to seduce her back with his smile as he reached for her waist.

"Come Silkie . . . enough of this nonsense. We could make this voyage enjoyable for us both."

She wanted to slap him. "Nothing could make this voyage enjoyable for me . . . nothing, especially you!" Again she turned her back on him, heading for the door, and this time he made no attempt to stop her exit. However, as she opened the door he called her to a halt, his voice sharp enough to bring her head round.

"Silkie!"

She frowned at him and the gold flecks in her grey eyes glinted.

"Yes, Captain Trent?" There, formal, that would show him.

"You had better lock your door," was the quiet response she received.

228

She frowned at him and hurried out. Just what was going on? What was he doing to her? How could he read her a homily one moment, rant nonsense at her about what he expected of her behavior, and then the next moment attempt to make love to her? Her hands trembled when she reached her cabin latch. She felt as though her body was on fire. Once within her own quarters she leaned back against her cabin door. Lock it? He had told her to lock it. Against whom? Member of the crew or himself? She hesitated, and then resolutely bolted it firmly in place.

## Chapter 3

*Rain* fell heavily on Marksbury land, creating puddles in the flower beds. Its steady, sad sound could be heard as it pounded away on Blaine's stone terrace. She stood at the sheer, pale yellow hangings of her glass terrace doors, her dark blue eyes staring at nothing in particular and refusing to look at her mother standing at her back.

"Will you turn around and answer me?" demanded Zara Marksbury. She was in a rage and very nearly out of control. In her hand she held Denny Werth's note. She was waving it in the air. "Blaine, I want an explanation of this." She crumpled the note and flung it at her daughter's back.

That brought Blaine's face around and with a small cry she dove to the oriental carpet and scooped up the wrinkled slip of paper. Her lashes met her cheeks a moment as she composed herself and when next she opened her eyes they were defiant. Oh God, why hadn't she burned it? "You went through my drawers," she said on a whisper. It was a melancholy accusation, a sudden realization of her mother's ugly capabilities.

"Of course I did!" snapped Zara. "Do you take me for a fool? You came in mooning yesterday like a halfwit, my girl. Did you think I shouldn't notice? My word. Put it together with the fact that I was well aware that a ship sailed into port yesterday morning. Yes, I went through your things. My daughter stoops to lying, for hiding is tantamount to lying . . . and that gives me the right to invade her privacy!"

"I love him," said Blaine quietly. It was a statement, not yet a plea.

"You love him?" scoffed her mother. "You are a child. You

know nothing of life. What can you know of love? And this man
. . . this abolitionist . . . my word! If you father knows what I
know now . . ."

"Mama . . . no . . . please, you don't understand," cried
Blaine.

"Not understand? By his own statement, he proudly declares
himself in league with Garrison and the underground railroad!
Blaine, he would put your father in prison if he could."

"Papa . . . no . . . Papa has nothing to do with slavery."
Blaine puzzled up at her mother.

Zara bit her lip. That was a slip. No one knew, not even Dare.
It was illegal to import African slaves but the law was poorly
enforced and the black ivory market was a money-making one.

"Never mind. What I want to know now is how far have you
gone with this man?" Her brow rose as Blaine looked away.
Why, her daughter was coloring up scarlet. She stepped forward
and took Blaine's chin. "Blaine . . . never say . . . you? Oh no
. . . Blaine." It took a moment to sink in. Zara closed her eyes
and stood in silence.

Still sitting upon the floor, Blaine stared into her lap, the
crumpled note clutched in her fist. She couldn't look up and find
her mother's disbelieving eyes. She didn't want to contemplate
the harsh reality of her position and face her mother alone. How
could she?

Zara's shoulders sagged a bit with a sudden weary sadness. "I
see. So, things have gone that road? Well, well."

Pleadingly Blaine went to her mother and took hold of Zara's
hands. Softly she tried to explain, not yet realizing her mother
had no heart left for such things. "Mama . . . I love him."

"Love?" Her mother's laugh was short and scornful. "It is a
virulent thing that I sincerely hope you do not feel for very long.
Love indeed! What you are feeling is desire for a pretty boy with
pretty ways, nothing more. He has charmed you and you want
him. It is natural. You are both beautiful children . . . children."
For a moment her thoughts strayed against her will. She was
again sixteen, soaking wet from the fall she had taken into the
lake, and Aaron was pulling her out, pressing her to him. His
green eyes glinted as he lowered his flaxen gold head to kiss
her. . . .

She brushed this memory angrily away and returned to the

231

present, hard, cold, and calculating. "What you feel for Denny is a passing thing that will not last. Do not tell me you have never felt an attraction for Dare?"

"Oh . . . . as to that, mama . . . I always loved Dare . . . but it is not the same."

"Dare is ten times the man Denny is and Dare will make you an excellent husband," said her mother. "That is how you must see it in the end."

Blaine took an agitated step. "I won't marry anyone but Denny. I mean to marry Denny and have his children."

That snapped Zara up and she brought her eyes sharply to her daughter's face. "Mark me, little girl, you will not marry your Denny Werth and pray to God that you are *not* carrying his child, for I swear to you, if you are, he will never live to see it born!"

"Mama," breathed Blaine, her eyes open wide in fear. "What are you saying?"

"This, and understand me well. There is nothing I won't do to prevent your union with your Captain Denny Werth. Nothing! I am capable of much, Blaine, and I mean for you to marry Dare Trent."

"Are you . . . are you actually threatening me?" ejaculated Blaine in disbelief.

"You? Of course not my love. You are my daughter and I mean for you to have the best. That is not a threat. What I am saying is very simple. I will remove whatever obstacles in your path, using whatever means necessary." She touched Blaine's frigidly pale cheek. "Now, why don't you have a bit of a rest before dinner. There's a love." So saying she glided towards the door, smiled sweetly before exiting, and then left her daughter alone.

Blaine stared at the closed bedroom door. This was her mother. What the world had always said of her was true. Here was a cold, cruel, and ruthless woman. If she continued to see Denny he would be in danger. There was nothing her mother would not do to put an end to their dreams. Her mother would have him killed! My God. That was what she had actually said. *She would have him killed!* A tear formed and trickled down her face. Oh Denny . . .

\* \* \*

Silkie's long flaxen hair was tied loosely at the nape of her neck with a black ribbon and as the force of the westerly wind picked up some might and tossed her tresses about her face, she took up her hood. She tied the dark string, her grey eyes lit with amusement, and she clapped her gloved hands for Tom, the young steward. He then missed his shot on the shuffleboard he had constructed at the rear of the deck that very morning.

"You are over the line!" she called at him gleefully and went to take her position. He called out a grumbling rebuttal and she giggled. Her black disk had slid some distance and she moved to retrieve it when a low male voice in the distance caught her attention. She looked up. Dare. He had been on watch until very late the previous evening and then he had been closeted in his cabin for most of the morning. Now here he was filling the eye with his impressive form.

Six days had passed since that first evening they had spent together. Since their harsh words scarcely a sentence had passed between them. Her husband had been carefully avoiding her at all turns. This should have pleased her, but contrarily enough she found herself irritated by it. His aloof behavior she found insufferably rude and, looking at him now, it was inexorably, perversely brought home to her that the width of his shoulders was quite marvelous. How wonderfully broad, how powerful the line of his back in the dark wool seacoat he was wearing. No captain's hat covered his shining locks of long black hair. Their silky waves were tossed about by the wind, shading in part his handsome profile. He turned and she nearly gasped when his bright blue eyes met her grey and she knew that he was aware of her interest. Immediately she turned away.

"Come on . . . do you mean to take your shot?" She heard Tommy calling to her.

How pleased she had been when he had appeared at her cabin door that morning and told her he had put together the shuffleboard game she had described to him. She smiled at him now and pushed her disk, gently landing it in the number seven frame. "Ha ha!" she cooed. "What do you say now, Tommy? Do you own yourself beaten?"

"What, by a female? Never!" he returned. Close quarters had put them in one's another's path in the last six days and this had promoted a fast and informal friendship. He had adored

Silkie from the start and she had very wisely taken his worship and channeled it into friendship. A moment later he had knocked her disk out of the seven box and sent it out of bounds. He laughed merrily over this fact.

"Beast!" she countered in mock anger. "I shall teach you to behave like a gentleman."

"Never you mind. I'm a sailor and doing very well at it, thank you," he answered happily.

"Thats a truth." She laughed.

*"What the devil is the meaning of this?"* Dare's voice was low and yet strangely thunderous, cutting through the gaity so that the young steward was immediately sent into hot blushing discomfort, while Silkie was momentarily stunned into gaping silence.

"Beggin' yer pardon, Captain Trent," Tommy managed to squeak out in a scarcely audible voice. "But . . . I did check with cook . . . and with Master Forbes and they both told me I could have a few hours to myself . . . well, so I thought . . . well . . ."

Silkie flung a stray long strand of white gold hair out of her eyes and cut in, though her legs felt shaky and her heart was beating wildly. "Tommy was kind enough to put together a shuffleboard game for me. It is all my fault . . . I put the notion into his head yesterday when I told him how Father and I sailed his yacht during the summer months and how we enjoyed playing at shuffleboard during a calm." Damn this man! Why was she rattling in this style? Why was she intimidated by him, by his bright glaring blue eyes? What harm was there in what she had done?

Dare Trent's dark brow was up and his countenance was stern when he looked at his steward. "I don't enjoy having to remind you, Tom, that you are not cook's steward, *not* Master Forbes's steward, but *mine*, and therefore it is *I* you should have applied to for free time. As it happens my cabin is cluttered with navigation maps and documents."

Tommy's color drained. Rarely had Captain Trent ever spoken to him so coldly. He had always liked working in Trent's employ and he meant to continue for as long as Trent would have him. He did not demure at this juncture but accepted the reprimand in silence, saluted, and with a quick "Yes, sir" turned to Silkie, made her a courteous bow, and hurried off.

Trent waited only for the lad to get out of earshot before he turned on his wife and in frigid accents advised her that he thought her conduct totally unbefitting her position as his wife.

"My . . . my . . . conduct?" riposted Silkie, shocked into wide-eyed disbelief. She directed a look of scorn at him. "I have never considered myself dull-witted, Captain Trent, but I believe I am going to have to ask you to explain just what you mean by your singularly odd observation."

"Be done, woman! You have been fluttering your lashes at that poor boy all week so that he doesn't know whether he is coming or going. Then what must you have him do but paint this thing on my deck . . . and what do I find but the two of you playing and laughing for my entire crew to witness . . . why, it is the outside of enough!"

"That is as fusty a viewpoint as ever I have heard!" snapped Mrs. Trent. "Do tell me, sir, must your wife not only give you children, but also promise never to laugh with anyone else?"

"That's right!" He already had her shoulders. Damn but she felt good to touch. He had vowed to keep his hands off her—now here he was and damn it to Hades if he didn't want to crush her to him, kiss her, stroke her. . . .

"Then if you mean for her to be able to keep such promises, captain, you will have to see to it that you don't neglect her, for even the best of wives need some attention."

"And is that what I have been doing? Have I neglected you, Silkie, my little beauty? Did you mean to show me the error of my ways by openly dallying with poor Tom?"

"Why, captain, don't mistake me or my words. I don't consider myself your wife and therefore I don't look for your attention. Show you the error of your ways?" She gave a short laugh. "Indeed . . . so long as I end up free of you, your errors do not in the least interest me. Dally with Tom?" She pulled out of his hold and started off. "No, captain, I wouldn't do that . . . for I don't mean to have him and wouldn't hurt him."

He took a step towards her. "Madam, there is more I would say to you on this subject—"

She cut him off. "Is there? It will have to wait. Your interruption of our game was most timely. It is nearly noon and I promised Kora I would take lunch with her.'' She gave him her back and started off.

Captain Darrow Trent watched his wife's departure and was filled with irritation. For the last six days he had managed to devote his time to the smooth running of his vessel and to work on a design for another clipper he meant to put into the works when he returned to Sag Harbor. This had been easy enough, for Silkie had taken to having her meals with Kora in her own cabin. He had noted with some annoyance the easy friendship she had struck up with his young steward, but although it had irritated him, he had not seriously thought anything of it. This morning though, when he had seen her touch Tom's arm, when he had seen Tom make her laugh carefree and bright, it had moved him to blind jealousy. Jealousy, he asked himself now, how was that possible? He didn't want her for wife. He didn't want any woman just now for wife. Why then should it matter who made her laugh? Why, indeed?

## Chapter 4

*Thunder!* An unmistakable sound. It tore through the sky, blasting the heavens. It brought Silkie bolt upright, out of deep sleep and into startling awareness. She sat for a moment, holding the patchwork quilt to her neck as she contemplated nature's raging work outside.

It was not the first time she had met a storm at sea, but from the sound of it, this was certainly the most violent one she had ever encountered. Her eyes widened and in the darkness of the cabin she tried to think. It was the middle of the night and it took a moment to adapt to her surroundings. The ship pitched as she started out of bed and she went reeling backwards and clunked her head.

"Faith!" she exclaimed out loud and steadied herself. She then moved across to her grey muslin, draped over a chair, and quickly slipped out of her nightdress and into her gown. The buttons were not as easily handled but after she had these done for the most part, she slipped on her cloak and started for the cabin door. Again the storm's wrath slapped at the ship and sent it unmercifully into the rising breakers. Silkie was flung across the room together with odd pieces of furniture. She banged painfully into the wall, took a long breath, and edged against the wainscotted wall to her cabin door once more. This accomplished, she made her way to the companionway where seamen hollered and the first mate called, but it was Dare's voice which she heard clearly.

"Fasten the hatchways, lads, look lively." It was the sure sound of command bellowing over the roar of crashing waves.

Silkie had long ago acquired her sea legs and a knowledge of handling a boat during a storm. Yet as she made her way through the companionway and up its stairs to the top deck, she was struck at once with the seriousness of the present situation. This was not a boat, but a clipper. This was not the Channel, but the open ocean, and this was not just a storm, it was a full-scale hurricane!

In contortions of rage the gale swept through the shrouds, screamed through the rigging, and threatened to mutilate the *Seamaid*. Everywhere men were working fast and hard to save the clipper from going under. In the very midst of hail and freezing rain they worked the sails while the *Seamaid* drifted uselessly.

The sound of her husband's voice at her back brought Silkie's head round. "What the devil are you doing up here, madam?"

She ignored this remark and the irritation it aroused. "Can I help . . . Dare . . . what can I do?"

"You can go below and keep out of our way!" he snapped.

Her chin went up. "But Dare . . . I know something about—"

He cut her off with a harsh growl and took up her arm, dragging her roughly along with him to the stairwell. "Get below!"

She looked up at him and their eyes locked for a moment—a brief moment full with emotion. What was this? What did she feel? What did he feel? Was he feeling something, or was she wrong in sensing that he did? Silently she left him and went below, where she nearly bumped into Master Forbes.

"Forbes . . . please . . . is there anything I can do to help?" she asked almost pleadingly.

He eyed her doubtfully. She was merely a sprite of a woman. What could she do? "Lordy, Mrs. Trent . . . I just don't know." He scratched his chin, thinking it would serve his captain if he could keep her busy at something relatively safe. It occurred to him that cook might need her. "Wait now . . . we have some valuable stores and cargo below . . . cook is there now."

"Yes, of course. Crates will have to be secured." She beamed, pleased enough that she would have something useful to keep her busy. "I will just have a look in on Kora and then report to the cargo room for duty."

"Right," he answered, "Now I've got to make sure those lads have managed the mailsail."

"When last I looked, Forbes, it seemed to me that it was hanging in the buntlines ready to be set if necessary," she returned over her shoulder.

Forbes's head snapped with surprise. The lass knew something of a ship, eh? Well, well. He did not have much more time to contemplate this, however, for he could just make out his captain's roar above the crashing waves on top deck and he hurried to his post.

Silkie went to Kora's cabin and found the older woman huddled in her bed and groaning pitifully.

"Kora . . . what is it, Kora?"

Kora had never liked the sea. Even its view from land was not something she took in with pleasure. If it had not been for Silkie, she would not now be on the open ocean. She hadn't been able to desert Silkie though, so here she was, and had spent most of the last six days with her head reeling and her legs wobbling and feeling drained and weak. This state of being was so foreign to her that it left her depressed and much unlike the resilient woman Silkie had always known. It was with some shock that Silkie discovered Kora trembling. "Kora . . . please . . . are you ill again? My poor Kora."

"Lass . . . lass . . . the sea means to have us . . . we are going to die . . . and you such a babe still."

Silkie laughed and it was a bright sound filled with the exhilaration she was feeling. Their predicament, the storm, brought her senses alive. While it awakened a certain fear, it had not terrorized her—no, rather it brought her to life. She chucked Kora beneath the older woman's plump chin. "Kora my love, you have seen me through all sorts of trouble. Are you going to cave in now?" She shook her head. "No, of course not."

Kora put a trembling hand to her forehead. "Cave in, is it? Not for all the world . . . there now . . . go on. It is jest my head aches so."

"Try and sleep Kora . . . I must go below and help cook secure the stores," said Silkie gently as she tucked Kora into bed and patted her shoulder. "I don't think you should try getting up with the clipper pitching as she is."

"And you, Silkie my love?" cried Kora in sudden agitation. "You will be careful?"

"I am no Johnny Raw to an angry sea. I will be careful,"

said Silkie, smiling as she left. She held herself steady as the ship suddenly lurched. A moment later she was releasing a breath of relief and making her way to the lower deck. The storeroom was in a shambles of disorder and she found cook crying his woes with some eloquence.

"There now Master Cook," she teased in musical accents, "we shall set things to right, see if we don't."

"Mrs. Trent," whined the small, wiry man, "how can we . . . jest the two of us?"

She frowned. "Is there no one the captain can spare us?"

He shook his head. "Master Forbes called all the starbow lines ahoy! Every last man is working the rigging."

"Then let us stop jawing away and get to it, my friend." She took up a length of rope and began securing a heavy crate whose side had split down the middle. "What is in these crates?" she asked curiously of the cook as he worked on the water cans.

He glanced over his shoulder and smiled. "Jest like a woman to sniff out treasure."

"Treasure, is it? What kind?" she retorted with lively interest.

"Silks and pearls and what they call that . . . blue china. Real pretty stuff," answered cook just as the gale shook the clipper as though it were made of paper. "Lord have mercy," he whispered, "she is hauling hard."

"Aye," agreed Silkie, who ran to catch a smaller crate just wavering on top of a larger container. She set it in place and the two began working quickly and harmoniously at their chore.

The time went by harshly for the crew of the *Seamaid*. They were soaked through and frozen, but they worked the sails diligently and efficiently, their captain working right along with them. The sails were furled but they were stiff from the cold sleet and Dare could feel his fingers going numb. Suddenly the violent waves calmed.

Quiet. It came in slow degrees, but it came nonetheless, and the members of the crew looked at once hopeful and relieved. The Captain confirmed that the danger was past by ordering them to go below in shifts and change into dry clothing. A cheer was set up and Dare smiled with tired satisfaction; they had been battling against the storm for nearly seven hours. It was coming on dawn and there was a promise of a sun.

He had made his way below to his quarters when the thought

240

of Silkie tickled his mind. He frowned. Well, perhaps he would just have a look in on her and make sure all was well. He went to her cabin door and knocked. No answer. His fist came down with a bit more force. No answer. For no reason at all a sudden fear leaked into his heart and he opened the door, calling her name. "Silkie?" He stood for a moment in some surprise. Kora. Of course. She was with Kora. He moved down the companionway to Kora's door and gently knocked.

"Yes? Is that you, Silkie . . . come on in, child," called Kora, rubbing the traces of sleep from her eyes. She had finally managed to fall into a deep slumber some hours ago.

The Captain opened the door. "No Kora . . . so then, where is your mistress?" Worried in earnest, now he came right to the point. What if she were hurt? What if she had been swept overboard? Had he seen her go below? He couldn't remember. Yes, yes, of course she had. He had made certain of it. Then where the hell was she?

Kora blinked. "She isn't in her room?" Then she remembered and brightened. "Oh, that's right . . . she said something about helping with the stores . . . but that must have been hours ago."

"Thank you, Kora, I am sorry if I disturbed you. Get some rest. I think we have seen the worst of the storm." He turned on his heel, closed her door at his back, and made his way to the lower deck. So, she had not obeyed him. She was contrary and wild. Going below to the storeroom was not what a lady should do! And even as this came to mind, he was filled with a certain reluctant admiration for her.

Silkie and cook were just about finished with their work and she was stretching out her arms. She was tired and quite sore from the bruises she had sustained during the terrible lurching of the ship earlier. However, valuable cargo had been saved from breaking out of its containers. Cook had told her how during a storm on another vessel he had sailed, barrels and boxes had broken loose, spilling their contents of tea, coffee, sugar, and spices all over. He now looked about him with some pride.

"Aye, Mrs. Trent . . . we've done a fine piece of work, you and I have."

The storeroom door opened and standing in its frame was Dare Trent. He looked at that moment a wild demon of a man. His

Irish blue eyes were hard and bright, for he found his wife had indeed flouted his command. His face was set in a hard line not unmixed with the weariness of his night. He was wet through and needed a change of clothing—but first he meant to deal with Silkie!

"Just what the devil are you doing in here, madam?" Dare's words were clipped and there was no mistaking the steel in his tone.

Silkie's cheeks flooded with hot color. How dare he speak to her as though she were an erring child? She could see cook watching them doubtfully and her chin went up in defiance. "Now, just what would such as I be doing in the storeroom at this hour? Having a rare kick-up, thats what!" she answered on a low note of sarcasm.

"I want an answer, Mrs. Trent!" He was determined to bring her to heel.

Silkie was about to give him a sharp setdown as only she could, when fate decided to take a hand. A violent gust of wind came rushing round the clipper at that moment. As the ship rocked, Silkie went flying across the room and came knockingly hard into a set of wooden water barrels. Cook and the captain were at that moment wedged in between some wooden crates, but the captain looked up in time to notice that one of the barrels had worked itself loose from its roping and was wavering just above his wife's head.

He gave a shout and Silkie looked above just as the barrel came rolling over. Althought she attempted to duck out of its way, she wasn't quite fast enough and the heavy container crashed painfully against her shoulder before it took her down. The fall left her winded and a splintered piece of wood from the container had scraped open the sleeve of her gown, giving her arm a nasty gash. Water flooded out, soaking her through, and she lay for a moment on her side while she tried to collect herself.

"Silkie?" Dare called her name without even realizing it as he bent over her.

Silkie looked up in some surprise, diverted by the sound of genuine concern in his voice. She found an odd look in his blue eyes. It was a strange moment in which she felt irresistibly drawn into those eyes, and when he helped her into a sitting position, she suddenly felt shy. Perhaps because of the gentleness he was displaying towards her, she looked away from him and surveyed herself.

"How badly are you hurt?"

"Not very badly, I think." She started to stand up and winced as a shooting pain went right through her shoulder.

"What?" he asked at once. "What is it? Did you injure your back?" He had his arm supporting her round her trim waist and he leaned her into his tall and sturdy frame. Damn but she was good to hold! An incongruous thought at such a time.

"Not my back," she answered, "my shoulder, but I think I have only bruised it. I am quite alright." He scooped her up cradlelike into his muscular arms, and she objected more strenuously. "No . . . no . . . really, I can walk." He hadn't paid this any heed and she pursued, "Dare . . . if the ship lurches again we shall both be in for it."

"Never mind," he answered softly and went to the door cook was holding open for them.

"I'm that sorry you got hurt, Mrs. Trent," Cook was mumbling in some agitation, "after all the help you was." He shook his head. "That piece shouldn't a broke loose . . . I didn't have it tied down properly . . . it was my fault."

"It was not your fault. The ropes can take just so much tension," Silkie answered him as her husband swept past, taking the lower deck companionway to the short flight of stairs. At this point his wife once again voiced her objections.

"Please Dare . . . I can walk . . . you can't possibly manage these stairs with me like this."

"Can't I?" he answered as his jaw set and he took the stairs to the cabin deck.

A passing crewman hurried to the captain's stateroom, held open the door, and lit the whale oil lamp while Dare carried his charge to his own quarters. Silkie didn't speak until Dare set her on his bed and the sailor left them alone.

"Captain . . . why have you brought me here?" she asked in some surprise.

"You may not have noticed, madam, but your arm has a nasty slash. I mean to clean and dress your wound and I have what I need in my cabinet." He closed the door, moving quickly as he collected a basin, filled it with water, took out bacilium powder and soft clean wrappings from a sideboard drawer.

She watched him. Faith! What was she feeling? Shy? Absurd. It was ridiculous to feel this way, she chided herself silently. He was sitting by her side on the bed, smiling reassuringly at her when without warning he ripped open the top of her wet gown and grinned at her shocked reaction.

In her haste earlier to change her nightdress for a grey muslin day gown she had not bothered to don any of the usual undergarments. She now found herself exposed to him in naked glory. She released a short cry and dove for the enormous quilt folded back on his bed. Her hands drew it up to her chin while she glared at him, quite at a loss for words. As he chuckled and his blood warmed, she discovered her voice and demanded, "Just what did you think you were doing?"

He laughed. "My beauty." At this he cocked his head at her. "You are that."

"Never you mind. Just tell me why you tore off my bodice!" she demanded as she watched him soak a cloth in the basin of water he had set on his lap.

"Your arm?" he requested, and when she did not comply, his brows rose. "I can remove your cover, you know." She gave him her bare arm immediately and he smiled benignly. "That's better." Again the boyish grin appeared. "Oh, don't look so outraged, my love, the gown was quite ruined, you know." He cleaned the wound in gentle strokes and frowned to see her wince.

"You didn't have to tear it off like that . . . you could have asked me to remove it."

"Which you would not have done without an argument. I am in no mood. It has been a long night and I haven't the patience to put up with your missish modesty!"

"Missish modesty? You odious brute . . . you miserable boor, you . . . you . . . oh!" she exploded in some heat. "Missish modesty, indeed!"

"Have you another label for it, my sweet?" He had already dusted the open wound with the bacilium powder and wrapped the treated area with the white cotton bandages. He now attempted to examine her shoulder as she pulled away from his touch. His eyes, such blue eyes, were at that moment filled with amusement. "Silkie . . . just let me have a look." She sat rigid while he touched the bruised area. "You have some swelling and it's bound to turn colors by morning, but nothing serious." He let her go, and with something of a weary sigh began discarding his own salty wet garments.

"Just what are you doing?" she demanded after watching him drop off his drenched seacoat, superfine blue coat, and open-necked white linen shirt.

He looked at her and grinned and she could not help but notice that his vivid blue eyes were twinkling. Their lights nearly blinded her as did the charm of his smile. "I am, as you can see, getting out of my wet things." He pulled off his boots.

How far did he mean to go with her in the room? In some agitation she hurriedly offered, "If you will but hand me a wrapper . . . anything you have here will do . . . I will retire to my own quarters and you may get comfortable in private."

He was unbuttoning his breeches but he took the moment to turn round and throw her a long and calculated glance. All the while, his blue eyes glittered, brimful with his intent, entertained by her reaction. She was all too conscious of the magnetism of the man, all too aware of the shortness of breath she was experiencing and of the buried longing within her heart. She was drawn by his eyes, momentarily silenced by a current that passed between them. He had cocked his head as he moved slowly towards her and his fingers were reaching for her chin.

She knew what he was about. She knew what he was going to do and even so, even as her mind commanded her to put a stop to it, she also knew that she didn't want to. He took her chin and tilted it in place for his kiss. He only knew that he had to have her. It was against all resolves. It went against the grain. It put all his plans for the future in doubt, but he had to have her! He didn't know when he had decided this—he only knew that he wasn't letting her out of his bed today.

"Ah Silkie." His voice was a low song of promised honey. "Comfortable? No, my pet, if you left me alone now, I would be anything but comfortable."

She was spellbound by the husky note of his words, by the softness of his expression, and by the gleam of desire in his deep blue eyes. She couldn't resist and was, even in that moment, honest enough with herself to silently admit she didn't wish to resist. What was this? Did she have the soul of a courtesan?

He saw the gold flecks in the recesses of her grey eyes become darts of flame and knew that he had aroused her. The knowledge excited him to a fever pitch but he restrained himself, careful now not to frighten her. Damn, how he wanted her! His free hand moved round and found her waist and slowly, cautiously he pulled the remainder of her damp gown away from her body, discovering the full swell of her breasts. Christ! He was on fire! He took her cherry mouth now, controlling himself from devouring her all at once. He managed to kiss her softly, deftly, gently. He managed to tease her with the tip of his tongue, to nibble at her lips even as he kissed her.

She couldn't move as he took her into his arms. Were those her hands that pushed her gown away? Was she helping him to free her body? The touch of his mouth on hers was sweeter than anything she had ever experienced. It was tender beyond belief and she discovered unexpectedly that it teased her desire in a way that made her feel wanton. What was happening? Was she moving into his arms on purpose? Was she thrusting against his hard bare chest? Oh faith! The quilt was lost as was her control over herself. Did it matter?

He was whispering her name, saying words that titilated her blood into frenzied action. Was she bewitched? Every nerve end was alive and in tune to his touch. She couldn't resist . . . or perhaps she didn't want to. At that moment she only knew that she wanted his touch, she wanted to fall back against the pillows and feel the strength of his body covering her own. She wanted him to make love to her.

"Ah Silkie . . . you feel so damn good . . ." he groaned as his hands explored her sensual form with an expertise that brought them to white heat. He cupped her breast firmly as his mouth moved down the length of her neck in slow tantalizing degrees, until he had her nipple. Sweetly, hungrily, oh so delectably, he suckled a while before his mouth continued its downward journey to her midriff, her belly white and flat, further still to where he parted her thighs.

She groaned in total abandon, wild now beyond sane thought. She only knew she wanted him more than she understood, and rational notions had no place, no chance for survival. She called his name as he manipulated her senses. She whispered to him, no longer shy, "Dare . . . your touch is magic. . . ."

"Ah babe, you were made for me." His passion was out of

control as he separated her legs and positioned himself for his thrust. He longed to hear her say she wanted him, "Say it, Silkie . . . say you want this now, as much as I . . . please, babe." He teased her with the hard tip of his penis at the opening of her warm and ready womb.

"No . . . I won't say it." Even in her frenzied state she found her contrariness pushing forward.

He laughed in some exultation as she rotated beneath him, seducing him to take her, and he did. She groaned with pleasure as he moved within her and his hands took her hips, teaching her, showing her just how he would have her move. She met his thrusts with ardor and he initiated her to an abysmal region where sensation reigned supreme.

"So tight, my sweetness . . . you are so wonderfully formed," he moaned as he gyrated within her lovely body and played havoc with her mind.

What was she doing? She couldn't stop herself. She was touching him, loving him with her body . . . where then was her heart? She only knew she was responding to needs she hadn't really known she had. Then he was bringing her to a peak of pleasure and very soon afterwards she knew he too had climaxed. It was a satisfying thing to know she had pleased him. Why? That was a question she did not want to think about.

He held her for a long time, then propped himself up on his elbow, smiling down into her grey eyes, fingering her cherry lips, refusing to allow her to look away from him when she seemed to want to. "No, my pretty bird . . . don't blush . . . you were perfect." Damn, but what did he feel? Satisfaction? Yes, but something more. What? A question he didn't wish to explore. Contentment? Yes—why? No time for these queries. He set them aside, and his voice was low as he felt himself stirred once again.

"But it was too soon over. Never mind. This time, little beauty, it will be different. You brought me to it far too quickly . . . but I promise you . . . we will take a bit more time with it now." He pulled her on top of him, chuckling beneath his breath as she objected. He held her face, nibbling at her earlobe, silencing her with his hungry kisses.

She managed weakly, "Dare . . . stop . . . Dare . . . think . . . we shouldn't, we can't."

"We can . . . and, my sweet, we will," he answered almost roughly as he took her breasts in his hands. "Hush Silkie . . . just hush and let me . . ." Already his fingers found the pleasure points and deftly began to seduce. ". . . there . . . ah babe . . . let me love you."

Love her? Was that what he was doing? No, he didn't love her. He wanted to be free of her. It was just her body he wanted now, but even as this thought presented itself and pinched at her heart, she cut it off. That was something she would consider tomorrow. Not now. Logic was something she would examine later because now . . . now his Irish blue eyes enchanted and his hands bewitched and . . . oh God, she wanted him. Love? What was love?

# Chapter 5

*Wade* Ashford had spent the last few weeks arranging his financial affairs. His Rye lodgings had been leased to another bachelor. His country estates had been placed in the hands of his capable agent and solicitor, leaving him confident that he could leave things for a protracted length of time without returning to find his holdings in ruins. Pleased with himself, he sat in a wharfside tavern in the seaport of Hastings, a resort of some social standing where he had managed to book passage on the American packet ship. His man, Tatem, was on board setting things in order in his stateroom. He had nothing to do now but enjoy himself, for in the morning he was off to New York and Silkie!

A passing barmaid caught his eye and he swung out his arm, catching her round her trim waist. His bumper of ale was set aside in deference to worthier game as he placed her fully on his lap.

> *"If lovers, Cupid, are thy care,*
> *Exert they vengeance on this Fair:*
> *To trial bring her stolen charms,*
> *And let her prison be my arms!"*

He recited this ode merrily before dropping a kiss on her earlobe.

The maid giggled as he proceeded to kiss her neck. "Fie then, covey, what would ye be doing with yer fancy words? Turning a poor girl's head?" She pushed at his hard chest but her coyness of manner was very nearly professional.

"As long as I turned it in my direction . . . ." He had her now very nearly stretched out and ready to receive further advances. ". . . eh then, sweetheart, make a lonely man happy?"

She smiled and fingered the lapel of his dark brown velvet cutaway.

"Lord love ye, guv . . . oi gets paid nicely for the time oi puts in this ken . . . serving ale to thirsty men. Oi'm not in a position to throw away me wages, ye know." She looked at him full.

"Ah pet, you wound me," he said in mock hurt. "Did you think I wouldn't compensate you for the loss of wages you would incur while you were with me?" He took her chin. "There's a pretty . . . for before we seal this bargain of ours, I should like a sample of what I mean to pay for." His mouth closed over hers as his hand went into the low-necked bodice of her gown and found her full-blown breasts. His fingers took her nipples and played while her hand went hidden under the table to the growing muscle in his breeches.

It was at this moment that three young men exploded into the tavern. Sir Blaize and his cronies were in jolly spirits after having been larking about for some hours. However, Sir Blaize pulled up short when he saw Wade Ashford at his game. "Whoops," he said, or rather slurred, for this was not the first tavern they had patronized that evening. "Fred . . . look there."

Fred felt it incumbent upon himself to attempt to comply with his lifelong friend's request, so he pulled himself up to his full six-foot height, swayed, held an empty chair back for support, and focused his light brown eyes in the direction of Sir Blaize's pointing chin.

"Eh?" He saw Wade Ashford's hand go into the barmaid's gown. "Oh." And then he saw the girl move her hand over Ashford's crotch. "Damn!"

"Know who that is?" Sir Blaize was nodding in Ashford's direction.

Even through the fog in his mind, Fred heard the grave quality in his friend's tone of voice and he was moved to gaze at Ashford with solemn intensity. As this scrutiny gave him not a clue, he gave it up with a shrug. "You've got me, Blaize, ole boy."

"Well, I know who he is!" returned Blaize, his habitually sweet expression becoming marred with a sneer.

Fred's bushy brows went up and he leaned into his other

friend's shoulder. "He has got a bee in his bonnet . . . see if he don't."

"Eh?" returned Earnest, coming out of his reverie. He brought vague, blood-shot brown eyes up to his taller friend's face and attempted some logic. "What's that? Can't have it right, Fred ole man . . . Blaize don't wear a bonnet."

"No, no noddy . . . not in his bonnet," corrected Fred, "though, seem to remember that's the way it goes. . . ."

"Where?" riposted Earnest, promptly attempting to show his friend he was up to every rig.

"Where? How the devil should I know . . . which reminds me . . . that fellow,"—he indicated with a thrust of his chin—"over there . . . know him?"

Earnest's grin was as absent as his present state of mind, which was understandable as all three had imbibed enough for a week's pleasure.

"Haven't a notion . . . but seems to be enjoying himself." This observation sent him off into unholy mirth which was not cut off until Fred pointed out that Blaize was acting strangely. Indeed, Blaize was moving in on the couple with something of the devil in his eyes!

"Oh-oh!" commented Fred, "something is afoot."

"Right then," agreed Earnest. "Perhaps we had better find out who the chap is and . . . lord but will you look at Blaize! He is as hipped as ever I have seen him."

Fred lunged forward, driven by an instinct and a deep-seeded knowledge of his friend's temperament. They were in for trouble if Sir Blaize were not headed away from his quarry. "Hold there, Blaize ole boy . . . tell you what. Let's sit and have a bumper of ale."

Earnest considered this with a frown. "Ale? Now why would you want to do that? Came for their brandy . . . told you . . . this inn has the best brandy in the—"

"Sneck up, Ernie!" returned Freddy sharply, for Blaize was pulling out of his grasp and he sensed trouble.

"Fred. That is Ashford," said Blaize in way of explanation.

Fred knew something of the circumstances that had led to Silkie Marksbury's departure from England. They had been friends. Fred looked long at Ashford for a moment and it seemed to sober

251

him a bit. "I see." However, he quickly added, "Let it rest. 'Tis done, man, 'tis done!"

"No." Blaize was shaking his head. "Don't you realize . . . his being here . . . at this port . . . with that American packet ship harbored out there . . . don't you see what that means?"

"And even if I do, what can you do about it?" answered Fred, really worried now. They had assumed when Ashford had sold his holdings in Rye that the rake had returned to his former haunts in London. Blaize was probably right in his present assumption. Ashford was no doubt on his way to New York . . . but just what could they do?

"Damnation!" cried Blaize in sudden frustration. "Don't you see? I let her down. I was all she had after her father died . . . and I let her down. She didn't want to go off with that American . . . but she did, and I did nothing to prevent it."

"Certes! What could you have done? She was married to the fellow," answered Fred reasonably.

"You already know that was not a marriage of her choice . . . blister it, Fred . . . I should have gone with her to New York . . . seen her free of him . . . brought her home . . . married her myself."

Fred shook his head. "It wouldn't have answered . . . and starting a row with Ashford now just won't answer either."

"It will tell me what his intentions are."

"You are badly foxed, man, and well you know it. Can't question the fellow . . . you don't have the right . . . and he'll plant you a facer." Fred eyed his friend. "Could probably draw your cork for I'd swear you are not fit in your present condition to take him on."

In answer to this he was roughly shoved aside and before he could do anything to prevent him, Sir Blaize had gone boldly up to where Ashford was still sitting.

"Mr. Ashford," said Blaize loudly. "Want a word with you."

Ashford turned from the wench in his lap and studied the tall youth, one brow going up. He looked familiar. A sneer tickled his lip. "As you might have observed, I am otherwise engaged," Ashford said coldly before returning his attention to the barmaid who giggled and stroked his neck.

Sir Blaize's color rose and he felt heat flood his cheeks, but he had a purpose in mind and tenaciously meant to see it through. "I must insist, Ashford."

Wade Ashford had put older, wiser men to the dust in similar circumstances. The lad was in his cups and no doubt jealous over some maid they had perhaps both been interested in. He glanced contemptuously at Sir Blaize and then resumed his nibbling on the barmaid's ear.

"Damn you, Ashford, I mean to talk to you about Silkie!" It was a low growl and it had its effect. How could it not? The very mention of her name was enough to make him go rigid with emotion. Ashford put the barmaid aside and quietly patted her rump.

"Later, sweetheart." He then waved a hand to the chair opposite him. "Well then, what has Silkie to do with you?" Then it dawned on him. Here was Sir Blaize. A friend of Silkie's . . . that's right . . . well, well. Now, what was all this about?

Sir Blaize drew up the wooden chair and straddled it, deciding in that moment to play a cool game. "I thought perhaps you could take her something she left behind . . . seeing as you will be leaving for New York in the morning."

So that was it. Relief that it was nothing more trickled into Wade Ashford's eyes and Sir Blaize saw it and went pale. It was true then—Wade Ashford was on his way to New York and Silkie. Oh God! He meant her mischief. In that moment and in his drunken state Sir Blaize made a decision.

"I would be delighted to take her anything you please," answered Ashford carefully.

Sir Blaize stood up. "Good. Then I shall get it to you as soon as possible." He nodded, leaving Ashford abruptly to return to his friends who stood watching in some fidget.

"Well?" asked Freddy.

"Well?" echoed Earnest.

"Come on," was all the answer they got as Blaize pulled them along. "I've got to hurry!"

# Chapter 6

*Silkie* awoke with sunlight filling her cabin. She moved in her bed and groaned. Her body ached all over. *Her* cabin? *Her* bed? Oh God . . . she remembered now, and remembering brought a sharp constriction to her throat. Her grey eyes clouded over and Dare's image made her close her eyes and bury her head in the crook of her arm deep in her pillow. She was hit with a welter of emotions, top on the list being blue deviled with a sense of rejection, slighted, hurt, used, and just a bit broken. No anger yet to help pick up her pieces. No resentment to solder them whole. No pride at that moment. Somehow during the night it had been flung to the winds and there had been no time to find it.

She opened her eyes. A quotation from *Much Ado About Nothing* rang sharply in her ears:

> *Sigh no more, ladies, sigh no more,*
> *Men were deceivers ever;*
> *One foot in sea, and one on shore,*
> *To one thing constant never.*

Faith, but he knew his own kind when he scribbled those lines, and Dare Trent was just such a man. Whispering sweet words in the darkness, taking her body, giving her his own, enchanting her with his deft skill and then? Deuce take it, she had only herself to blame! She had played the game willingly, hadn't she? Her father had always told her to "play and pay" . . . and she had, with her heart. This was no time for maudlin tears. Early this morning she had felt a contentment in his arms she had never imagined possible to experience. She had been fulfilled in a new and wondrous way, and if he had broken the spell, she had no one but herself to blame for allowing him to take her. What had he said? Oh yes: "I had better get you back to your own cabin."

It pierced her soul, a gentle believing thing, and even so, she had waited, not understanding him fully. In the darkness of his room, in his arms, as he tenderly kissed the tip of her nose, he had continued, "We don't want Kora to be in a position where she must find herself swearing to a lie. There is the annulment deed to be signed and witnessed, so come along, my sweetings."

It had been a slap, so hard, so unexpected that she had been unable to speak, unable to move. He must have sensed her confusion; he didn't wait for her to stand but scooped her up, quilt and all, and carried to out his door, down the corridor, and across to her own room. All the while she had clung to him. Why? Waiting for him to profess himself a cad for uttering such words? Waiting for him to somehow scatter her doubt? Look at him, she thought as he deposited her on her bed, he stands there in naked glory and talks about annulment! But she had been too stunned to feel anything but the hollowness in her gut and the havoc of her threatened heart. He had dropped a light kiss upon her lips and oddly enough she had allowed it. Why? She should have summoned her ire to the fore. She should have slapped his face. She should have . . .

Now, in the bright afternoon light, nothing made any sense and there was only one thing she knew for sure—she was hurting, badly, and she just didn't know how to deal with it. How would she face him? How would she go on? What did he think her? Some common slut, to be used and put away? Didn't he care beyond his own plans, his own needs? She felt scorched to the core, and when Kora knocked at her door she found herself sending the woman away.

Kora stood outside Silkie's door, a worried expression commanding her features. Now, what was this? Silkie, tired? Why wouldn't she give her admittance? That wasn't like Silkie. But, perhaps the child was tired from the efforts she no doubt put forth during that harrowing storm. Yes, of course. That was it, thought Kora, giving herself an answer that would serve to calm her nerves. She needed to do that, for life had suddenly gone topsy-turvy and she wanted things back in order. Thus, having assuaged her fears rationally, she made her way to the stairs and to the topdeck where she meant to get a whiff of fresh air and think about their future.

Inside her cabin, Silkie's future loomed darkly and poor Silkie's hurting heart cried.

In a decently appointed stateroom on a swift American packet in the same morning sun but at some distance and days behind, Sir Blaize was opening his eyes with a hand to his head and a low, confused sound on his lips. His first thought was a questioning, "Where the hell?" He said it out loud as his head came up and he made a feeble attempt to scan his swaying surroundings. At the same time he became aware of the fact that while nothing around him actually moved, neither did he feel quite level. There was a sensation of motion, of dipping, plunging, and a fear began to form. His eyes rounded and he was suddenly bolt upright. "Holy!"—a dawning realization. Disbelief gripped his soul and then in some mixed emotion he spotted his friend sprawled out on a settee in a corner of the pitching room.

"Freddy!" he called and lunged towards him, fell, cursed, and on his knees made it the remainder of the short distance. "Freddy!"

A memory, hazy and slightly unreal, flitted into his mind. Wade Ashford. Something about Wade Ashford had brought him to this pass. That's right. Ashford was sailing on an American packet for New York. Silkie. That's right. He'd had it in his head to warn Silkie. "Oh no," he groaned, then took up his friend's rumpled coat and shook hard. "Freddy . . . wake up . . . Freddy . . . we are done in . . . Freddy!"

Freddy opened his eyes and moaned, "Go away."

"Listen to me, Freddy . . . we are in trouble . . . Freddy, we are on a ship. . . ." What he thought his friend could do, he didn't know. He only knew he had to share his misery immediately.

Freddy snapped into position. "What? What's that you say?"

"For mercy's sakes . . . you heard me!" returned Blaize, understandably out of patience. "Damnation and hell, Freddy . . . how did you let me do this?" His hand went through his tousled hair.

Bloodshot, brown, and bewildered eyes stared without seeing. He'd heard what he'd been told, but it couldn't be true, could it?

He then heard the ocean slapping time against the sturdy and neat lines of the ship. The fact that he was swaying in rhythm with the room added additional conviction to his flashing fear. He and Blaize had suffered the trials of their adventures during their days at the university, but never before had they landed themselves in a situation that had no ready solution.

"But . . . this is impossible," was what illogically came to his lips.

"Blister it, Freddy! You know what I am when I'm foxed. I depend on you . . . on Ernie . . . how could you let me do this?" demanded Blaize, much incensed.

"Indeed . . . it isn't like me at all," answered Freddy, attempting to recall how such a thing came to pass. He jumped to his feet with the flash of memory. "Got it now . . . you took off for the purser's office. Bought yourself a first-class passage . . . tried to stop you, couldn't do it . . . you charged Ernie with seeing to your affairs and you packed some things from your hotel room. Ernie wouldn't even come to see you off. Said it was too damned dangerous, said you would have him sailing with you if he weren't careful. Asked me what I was going to do and told him I would knock you on the head if I couldn't talk you off the ship. That's right. I was going to knock you on the head. So along I came with you to see your cabin . . . and didn't have to after all because you saw it reasonably after a time."

"What? But . . . then what are we doing here?"

Freddy frowned over this. "I remember. We talked it over . . . said it wouldn't be any good your coming on the same packet with Ashford coz he would know you were coming to warn Silkie. No good that. We said we would sail on the next packet."

"Oh God"—Blaize was pulling at his locks in some frenzy—"then how came we to be here?"

Freddy spied the empty bottle of brandy. "Drank a toast to the wisdom of your decision," he said in some gratification, pleased to have the explanation and his memory in order.

Blaize paced. "Blister it to hell!" he hissed out loud. "We must have been foxed beyond belief. Stupid! Damn if we didn't fall asleep . . . and here we are sailing for New York!"

Freddy stared hard for a long while and as his nature was such that he accepted his fate with deliberate resignation, he turned instead to the immediate realities of the problem. "Know what, ole boy?"

Blaize was just the opposite sort of character. Nearly everything he did was touched by emotion and he was now in a state of supreme agitation. He gazed at his friend sharply and his tone was testy and impatient as he wondered how Freddy could be so calm. "No, I don't know what but I am damn sure you are going to tell me!"

"Thats right, didn't think it occurred to you . . . but awkward, you know."

"Awkward is an understatement of the situation!" snapped Blaize. He frowned for he could see he hadn't quite caught his friend's drift. "What are you trying to tell me, Freddy?"

"Well . . . thing is . . . you might not have realized . . . but my position here . . . not clear."

"What the devil are you talking about?"

"Stowaway, ole boy . . . stowaway . . . don't feel like being put adrift somewhere in the middle of the Atlantic, you know."

Blaize stopped and stared at his friend in disbelief a moment before the ridiculousness of the situation struck him. This hit him so soundly that he burst into indecent mirth, during which Freddy watched him uncomfortably before Blaize had recovered long enough to assure his friend that he had enough of the ready cash to shell out on his behalf.

"Good thing," answered Freddy. He then sighed, happy to have this out of the way, and looked about him. "Now, what we need is tomato juice and soda water . . . devil of a head, you know."

Silkie's long, white gold hair framed her face and blew gently round her neck in the salty wind. Her grey eyes glistened even now, touched as they were with sadness and confusion. She leaned against the bulwarks and looked out at nothing in particular. She had been reading Byron earlier and one stanza kept dully repeating itself in her mind:

> Alas! It is delusion all:
> The future cheats us from afar,
> Nor can we be what we recall,
> Nor dare we think on what we are.

How true this was for her. Oh faith, life had turned upside down in the space of weeks and the last five days . . . Had she ever suffered so? Had man ever brought her so very low before? What was happening? What could she do to take her life in her own hands and right the wrong? For something was wrong, terribly wrong, and it was all because of Dare Trent.

His blue eyes haunted her dreams. His kiss kept her yearning, hungry for more. The memory of his touch, his caresses, his deft skill, and his charm was something that was eating away at her heart. Five days had passed since the morning he had taken her and made exquisite love to her. Five days of wondering whether it had been her imagination. That was it. Yes, of course. She had only dreamed that he had kissed her, touched her, wanted her. There was no trace of that time together left in his manner. He had scarcely come near her since and when he addressed her it was purly impersonal. He didn't want her anymore. Those hours had been enough to satisfy his animal needs and now she was discarded. The realization brought shame to her soul and flooded her cheeks with heat. How could he have done that to her? Didn't he realize how vulnerable she was? Didn't he realize that she had given herself out of love? Love. Oh God, how she loved him. She hadn't wanted to admit it before, but there it was staring her in the face. All she had left to rescue her spirit was her pride.

Pride brought her chin up when he would pass her, behaving as though she were some rare disease to avoid at all cost. Pride kept intact her sophisticated air of aloofness whenever he was near. Pride kept her from showing him that her heart pounded, ached, yearned for him. Doesn't he want you? Doesn't he care? Why isn't he even trying to bed you again? Weren't you good enough as a lover? Didn't you please him? Why? Oh damn, why won't he even try to bed you so you can ease some of your pain by refusing him?

"*Land ho!*" The call went up first from one seaman and as the sighting was confirmed, the call was suddenly picked up from all parts of the deck. "LAND-HO!"

Silkie was momentarily diverted from her soul searching and peered out with renewed interest. Indeed, she could just make out the dark irregular shape of a coastline. She looked round to find Dare, spyglass in hand on the quarterdeck. The sailors had gathered on the forecastle, most of them hopping around like butterflies. For the briefest of moments, Dare's blue eyes lit on Silkie's face, and they exchanged a look that went through her like electricity. What it did to him, she couldn't know, he quickly looked away!

Well, Silkie . . . Trent . . . Marksbury . . . there it is. America, Uncle Tyler, and Aunt Zara. Your new home and the door to your freedom from your husband. Right, then. It is what Dare wants and so must you.

Sag Harbor was already alive and active when the *Seamaid* was sighted. As it happened, two days earlier a Marksbury-Trent whaler had docked and the town was happily busy with the ship's valuable cargo. The cooper's shop was situated at the edge of the village and there was the usual gathering of menfolk. They came to watch their heavyset cooper wield his trade, a fascinating pastime, while they gossiped and exchanged philosophy. Outside the cooper's door, near his store of finely made oil casks, a jaunty set of lads hopped and played over pyramids of staves and lumber. Their school day had ended and there was still some hours before their mothers would call them in for dinner. But when the cry went up all activity ceased.

"SHIP IN THE BAY!"

"SHIP IN THE BAY!"

Everywhere people stopped and listened. Yes, again. "SHIP IN THE BAY!" It was confirmed. Expectation brought them into a frenzy of excitement. What was this? Another whaler so soon after the last? Work stopped, and suddenly everywhere people were flocking towards the docks, asking questions none could answer and speculating about the new arrival. A sight indeed as children leaped over the jawbone of a whale set in a corner of the dock and adults rushed the wharf in high gleam.

"The *Seamaid*," said a seaman excitedly. "By damn . . . she's in . . . Darrow Trent's *Seamaid* is in!" This was picked up and repeated through the crowd and thus the news traveled through the town.

Even so, it was nearly an hour later when the house of Marksbury received the news and Zara happened to be passing. "What?" she asked a giggling chambermaid whose beau was a sailor on the *Seamaid*. "What's that you say?"

The young maid dropped a curtsy, this time sure her mistress would be pleased, for it was common knowledge that Zara anxiously awaited the arrival of Captain Trent. " 'Tis the *Seamaid*, ma'am, she is pulling in to harbor."

Zara's dark eyes opened wide with pleasure. "Has she docked?"

Just then the front door flew open and Tyler, his countenance flushed with his news, burst forth, "Zara, collect our daughter. Dare has landed!"

## Chapter 7

*Silkie* was the last thing he should be thinking of, but damn if she weren't the first! There she stood, clothed in somber grey. Lord, but she was an elegant beauty with her flaxen hair piled high beneath that simple grey silk bonnet she wore. Everything about her attracted the eye, caught the imagination, touched the soul. Why? He had enough to do to keep himself busy. They were docking, there were customs documents to attend to, last-minute instructions to his men, his ship to oversee . . . and Tyler. Tyler would soon be arriving with Zara and Blaine in hand. Blister it all, it was his fault for giving in to his desire that night!

Certes, but he had wanted her. With every fiber in his being he had wanted her—so he had taken her. She had responded in a way that set every other consideration aside. She was a woman, fully grown and ripened for such passion. From all he had witnessed of her, she was capable of handling herself. He had seen that after that first time he had taken her. She wasn't even affected by their encounters. She stood apart from him with her twinkling grey eyes, appearing unconcerned with his aloofness, giving him a dose of it herself.

Hell and fire! His nerves were frayed. His head was filled with conflicting emotions and his mind's eye was filled with Silkie. This little bit of woman with her gold-flecked grey eyes, her bright smile, and her vixen impish air had him thoroughly confused and all too bewitched. He had to put her out of his thoughts and he would, damn it, he would! Devil a bit! What was she doing now? Hell, if she weren't touching Tommy's arm!

Why was it that every single time he looked, the young steward was at his wife's side? He wouldn't have it.

He started forward and then stopped himself. What was this? He was behaving absurdly. She would soon be in her uncle's home, signing the annulment papers that would wipe out their farcical marriage and set them both free. He had no rights to Silkie. His dark brows flew upwards. *Like hell he didn't!* He moved in on the pair and there was the hint of impending storm in his bright blue eyes.

Tommy looked up to find his captain bowling down upon them and uttered a low "Oh-ooo?"

Silkie turned halfway to discover much the same. In stern defiance her chin went up and her grey eyes glittered as she squared for the encounter. However, it was the captain who spoke first and not to his wife.

"Tom, I believe you have some duties to attend to in my cabin. I wish all my clipper drawings neatly packed and ready for shipment with the other papers I have prepared on my desk."

"Yes, captain," answered Tommy quickly as he bowed himself away.

Interested in spite of her irritation with him, Silkie broke the momentary silence that ensued. "Clipper drawings?"

He found her eyes. Such flames in their recesses. A man could get lost there. A man . . . any man . . . but not he, oh no, he knew better.

"Yes," he answered, almost coldly. "Designs I have been working on."

"Oh, how exciting," came the instant response. "Are they fashioned after the *Seamaid*? Do you plan to put together a fleet of clippers?"

Her simple interest tore away at his cloak of frost and he softened. He took her arm and walked her towards the bow of the ship and his voice took on some of the intensity he always felt whenever the subject came up. "As a matter of fact, that is precisely why I made this trip. I would like to talk your uncle into moving into the China trade . . . get away from whaling, or at least not depend on it wholely as a means . . ."

"And doesn't my uncle agree with that line of thinking?" she puzzled up at him.

"Well, he doesn't agree with me that whaling will soon be on the decline." The frown that had lifted from his face flitted back a moment, for he could just make out the form of his partner as Tyler descended from his carriage and gave his hand first to his wife and then to his daughter. Softly he said, as he watched her face for a reaction, "There is your uncle now."

Silkie nearly jumped. She was excited about meeting her father's brother. Excited and just a bit uneasy about it. There was something about it that stirred a fear in her—and then she saw Zara Marksbury and a chill shot up her back.

Zara Marksbury's welcoming smile as she picked up her mauve silk skirts and dropped lightly from the carriage steps to the wooden dock below was quite genuine. She was in a flurry of high spirits. Her cheeks beneath their carefully applied rouge were actually filled with color and her dark blue eyes glistened. Tyler was pointing up towards the *Seamaid*'s quarterdeck and she followed that line, ecstatic to have Dare finally home and within reach. All her plans for the future were centered on him. She wanted him for Blaine. This time, ah, this time, she would not be thwarted!

On deck, Dare felt some absurd instinct to shield his young bride when he found Zara Marksbury's face. He took hold of Silkie's elbow. "Courage, my minx, I fear this will be harder than either of us have anticipated."

Silkie looked up at her husband's face. Oh God. Sometimes, at moments like these, she very nearly felt he truly cared. His blue eyes stroked her—she daren't believe they caressed—and his smile reassured her. At their backs they could hear the clucking sounds of Kora and it brought a twinkle to Silkie's eyes. She also had the satisfaction of finding that twinkle reflected in her husband's eyes, but then she gazed down at Zara Marksbury once again.

Zara's smile had slowly died and her waving hand stopped in midair as she encountered the vision of Silkie, at that moment in close contact with Dare. Stunned. It was her first reaction. *What in blazes was this?* "*Tyler*?" she demanded in a tone of sharp asperity, for already her plans were being challenged. She could feel it and her composure was lost in that space of time. "Who the bloody hell is that creature standing in Dare's arms?"

Blaine had descended the carriage steps and had been adjusting the ribbon of her pale blue bonnet. Rarely had she ever heard her mother give over to emotion in public and she was shocked. "Mama," she whispered in scandalized accents, "people will hear you."

Her mother chose to ignore this reproach and though she lowered her voice, her words were hard clipped. "I will have an explanation, Tyler."

Tyler seemed amused. He too had seen the beauty at Dare's side and very much the same question had come to mind. He attempted, however, to assuage his wife's fears with a gentleness he should have realized would only serve to irritate her. "Dearest, now how can I answer that?" He patted her kid-gloved hand. "There, Zara, I am certain Dare will have an explanation for the girl's presence on his ship, though the truth is he need not explain to us or to anyone what he does . . . or with whom he does it. . . ." There was a soft note of warning behind his words. He was reminding her that while she was used to ruling the roost in their own clime, she could not do the same in Dare's. Ah no, Dare would never tolerate such a thing from Zara or anyone else.

She was irritated by his easy acceptance of a situation she found most unnerving, but his words rang true and she was wise enough to consider them. Indeed, she would have to be careful. Dare would not be pushed. Rather, he would move in the opposite direction, if only to be contrary! "Well, I will not have some tart foisted on my family, and so I shall tell him," she declared, the battle in her dark blue eyes.

"We have not one reason to believe she is anything but a respectable girl," chided her husband as he gazed openly at the lovely woman clothed in somber grey at Dare's side. At Dare's back he could make out the plump form of a middle-aged woman and correctly he assumed she was a duenna of some sort. He pointed this out to his wife as they moved forward to meet Dare. He had taken Silkie's arm and was now leading her down the planking.

Zara Marksbury considered this as she stepped along in her husband's train and with a sigh of impatience turned to take up her daughter's hand and push her forward. "There . . . you look just as you ought. Darrow will be sure to take notice."

"Oh, Mama." Blaine sighed with a gentle shake of her head.

However, it did not miss her attention that Captain Trent was in fine fettle.

Dare came up to his partner and took that man's hand warmly before clasping him in a fond embrace. "Tyler! You look well."

He was cut off by Tyler's enthusiastic laugh. "Swashbuckler! We expected you home a month ago . . . and, my lad, while I may look well enough, good God! You look fitter than ever I have seen you."

". . . and Zara . . ." Darrow smiled and there was just a touch of reserve. Too much had happened since he had been a small child adoring Zara Marksbury; too much to ever be set aside and forgotten. He was leaning forward, taking her hand, kissing her gloved knuckles, and then finding Blaine peeping across at him. With something of a chuckle he called out the childhood name he had for her, "Cookie!" He took her up in his arms and swung her round. Because she laughed, giggled, and demanded her release he teased, "What's this, have I been replaced by another love while I was gone?" He was surprised by the sudden stillness, but there wasn't time to consider its meaning as there was the business of introducing his bride. He stepped aside and took up Silkie's hand, drawing her forward, for he had made something of a decision. He would not now, on the open wharf, introduce her as his wife. That and its lengthy explanation could come later when they were all alone.

"Tyler," he said on a graver note, "I want you to meet your brother's daughter, Silkie." He allowed a moment for this to sink in before he turned to his bride. "Here is your family, Silkie, your uncle Tyler, your aunt Zara, and your cousin Blaine."

Dumbfounded for the moment, Tyler was quickly overcome with a flicker of the past. In genuine affection he took his niece in his arms.

"Why, my child, how very pleased I . . . we . . . are. . . ." He turned to his wife who stood rigid, stricken by sudden memories. Aaron. Here was Aaron and Serena's child. How dare Aaron send her here? Why? And then sure knowledge flooded into her mind. Aaron was dead. Oh God . . . Aaron was dead. She went pale, but she accompanied her daughter to step forward and greet Silkie.

While Blaine and Zara made Silkie's acquaintance, Tyler, in a low voice, leaned towards Dare. "Do not spare me, Darrow. What can this mean? What of my brother . . . his wife?"

"I am sorry, Tyler, from what I understand, your sister-in-law had passed away some time ago . . . a year or so."

"And my brother?"

"Recently . . . as the result of injuries he sustained in a storm at sea . . . and Tyler, there is more, a great deal more we must discuss . . . in private."

"Of course. What a dolt I am to keep you standing here on the wharf. Come . . . come all of you."

## Chapter 8

*December* was proving itself a mild time of year. A flurry of light snow had fallen, giving the quaint village of Sag Harbor a fairy tale appearance, but the sun felt warm and the breeze gentle as Dennis Werth hailed the town's one hackney carriage and directed it to the Marksbury estate.

Once inside he took out Zara Marksbury's letter to him and reread it, for he found it difficult to believe she was actually agreeing to receive him. When he had written to her, he had done so out of desperation, without any real hope that she would see him . . . and now this? And Blaine? Why had Blaine refused to meet him? What had gone wrong? Darrow Trent was back in Sag Harbor. He had, in fact, spent a pleasant evening in his old friend's company the other night and Dare had given him reason to think that Blaine still returned his love. Why then hadn't she responded to any of the notes he had smuggled to her? Had they been intercepted? If so, why the friendly epistle he had this morning received from Zara?

A week had passed since Dare had arrived with Silkie on his arm. May the saints preserve her sanity, thought Zara, for she had nearly lost it when he had announced to them that Silkie was his wife! Well, at least they were in the process of annulment, yet? Silkie was staying under their roof, *not his*. He would soon be free to marry Blaine, yet there was something in the way Dare would gaze at that girl, and it worried Zara to no end. And then there was Blaine.

Thus far, she had managed to keep Blaine away from Dennis Werth. This she had managed neatly with her threat some weeks ago to have him "handled" if Blaine were to attempt to see him again. Blaine had taken her at her word, but recently was showing definite signs of weakening, or reconsidering. After all, if Blaine got it into her head to elope with Dennis, Dare would never have her afterwards.

Such a coil. However, Zara believed she had a sure way of pitting Blaine against Dennis, sending her into Dare's presently empty arms! It was good that Tyler was in New York on business. She slipped the black lace of her dishabille attire off her shoulders and stretched out on her damask settee in front of the blazing fire. Within a short space of time Dennis would be here, and Blaine? She smiled to herself. Yes, she had taken care that Blaine would be as well!

Darrow Trent was taken into Tyler's library to await his wife's arrival. She was out riding the handsome grey gelding her uncle had provided for her amusement. On the bright yellow brocade sofa was an open book. It was Silkie's copy of Byron, and he flipped the leather-bound pages to where she had marked a passage. Out loud, he read:

*I speak not, I trace not, I breathe not thy name,*
*There is grief in the sound, there is guilt in the fame;*
*But the tear which now burns on my cheek may impart*
*The deep thoughts that dwell in that silence of heart.*

Hell, but didn't that also describe his state of mind these days? Did she feel that way? Guilt. It flooded through him when he chanced to meet her the other morning. He was out walking his grounds when suddenly there she was with two of Tyler's hounds. Her eyes were filled with her loneliness and it had made him feel like taking her in his arms and comforting away her sadness. Had he broken the child in her? She seemed a different person here in Sag Harbor. Gone was the bubbly, vibrant, defiant beauty he had first met. She had been shrouded by a loss of confidence, by an overwhelming sense of emptiness, and it showed in her large grey eyes. Damn, but he had certainly hurt the child in her and there was a certain grief in that knowledge. He had felt the cad and had extended himself to make pleasant conversation, a thing he had avoided since that night on board his ship when he had made love to her.

"Silkie?" he had said merrily enough. "I see you have already met Tyler's best hounds, Resonant and Actor. He has great hopes for these two, though at present they are just a bit too fast."

She smiled. "Yes, and he tells me he hasn't managed to deer proof them yet."

"Ah, but he will. Have you heard some of the methods he has developed to break them of the habit?" He was grininng, for Tyler meant to go the gammut and make certain all his hounds chased only fox.

She laughed and it was a bright sound. "Yes, but if it is true that these two outrun the pack and the huntsman, it won't matter."

She looked away from him, for suddenly she remembered England and that last fox hunt they had been on together. Why, it seemed one hundred years ago . . . and afterwards he had kissed her in the study . . . and then her father had put them on a course that had changed both their lives.

Dare saw her draw into herself and stopped, calling the hounds firmly to stay within range as he took her shoulders and drew her to him. "Silkie . . . believe me . . . I want you to be happy. . . ."

How could she bear it? She looked up and found those blue eyes of his sincere, ineffably bright with warmth and concern, but was it love? Why wouldn't he love her? "I am happy, Dare. Really. My uncle is very kind to me and my cousin is very sweet." She looked away. "Kora goes on very nicely and fits right in. She seems to like America."

"And you?"

"I haven't seen much of it yet, but my uncle tells me we shall be fox hunting next week and that will make all right with my world."

"Yet you pine for England?"

"A bit," she answered softly.

He sighed. "Soon you will be free of me and there will be routs and balls. Zara is quite a social hostess."

"Yes, it should be fun," she answered noncommittally.

The thought of some young buck coming along to sweep her onto the dance floor suddenly irritated him. "No doubt that is all you need, a beau to set your world right." He still had her shoulders. For some reason he couldn't seem to let her go.

"Oh, not just any beau could do that. He would have to be very special indeed to replace you. . . ." There, it was out. The words had been scarcely audible and they had flowed before she had been able to prevent them.

He was taken aback, but pleasurably so. Did she really think so well of him? Did she care? Oh hell, all he wanted was to scoop her up and taste that honeyed mouth so deliciously pursed at him. He couldn't speak, so he did bend and tenderly kiss her.

The moment was shattered by a crisp harsh voice at the top of the hill. It had been Zara. Blister it! She was always about these days. She said something about Tyler needing him up at the house and Silkie, her face averted, had taken the hounds and hurried off.

Now, here he was, once again lost in thoughts of Silkie. She haunted his dreams, played havoc with his emotions, taunted his desire. He wanted her in his bed, he wanted her youthful, supple body, he wanted her parted thighs and the fire which she was forever stirring in him with only a glance.

The door opened. Silkie. Her flaxen hair fell in cascading waves beneath a top hat of dark grey. Her body moving slowly in a riding habit of the same; she was exquisite as she glided towards him, her gloves hands outstretched. She was graceful, she was elegant, and he was hungry for her touch. He took a step forward to meet her, dropping the volume of Byron on a nearby table to take up her gloved hands.

"Silkie," he said on a low note.

What was this? What was happening? After his abstinence on board his ship, his recent behavior was coming to her in waves of pleasurable shock. Did he want her? She couldn't breathe? Why couldn't she breathe? She managed, softly, "Hallo, captain. I didn't expect you until tomorrow. That is when our appointment with your American solicitor was scheduled for . . . or is there some problem?"

He nearly groaned. "There is a problem, my sweetings, most definitely there is a problem, and it has nought to do with my solicitor. . . ." He pulled her into his arms, pressing her delightful body against his own. All resolves had been shaken off. Time had not served to heal, only to agitate towards this moment. He discovered her mouth and it was as sweet as he recalled. Aroused beyond thought, he felt her response and knew he had to have her.

Oh faith. She couldn't think. She shouldn't allow this. He would only cast her aside again. They should talk before she allowed him to touch her, kiss her, caress her . . . but it felt so good she didn't want him to stop. All she wanted at that moment was to sink into the comfort of his arms, for all doubts disintegrated while she was there. He was removing her hat, pulling at the pins in her hair, groaning her name, telling her how much he needed her.

"Ah babe, all I have thought about is having you in my arms. . . ." His kiss was magic on her forehead, her nose, her ears, her neck, and then again deliciously on her lips.

"Dare . . . someone could walk in on us . . . Dare." He scooped her up into his arms and strode towards the sofa. She could see the determination written on his face and it thrilled her.

"You are my wife," was all he said in answer and he felt himself exult in the statement.

"Dare please . . . you mustn't do this . . . I can't stop you, I don't want to. . . ."

"And you think I can stop. Do you, sweetings, for if you do, you are indeed an innocent. In spite of all that has happened . . . I do believe you are an innocent." He unbuttoned her jacket, his hand was moving to cup her breast.

She had to put an end to this. With every bit of willpower she possessed she brought herself up and pushed at his skillful hands.

"No . . . no more . . . we can't." She shook her head but there was a plea in her grey eyes. Why didn't he say he loved her? It was what she had been waiting to hear. She loved him with every ounce of hot blood that now pumped through her veins. "I may be your wife right now, but by tomorrow that will have changed."

"Tomorrow is the future, Silkie. It holds no place here and now."

"You wrong me then, for what you can walk away from I cannot," she said sadly.

He pulled himself together. It was a draining thing that brought his lashes to his cheek and so he did not see the flicker of hurt that swept her countenance. All she could think was, even now, even in his passion, he will not give over and say that he loves me, wants me as his wife.

When he had collected himself, he managed to give her a smile and flick her nose before he got to his feet. "Right then . . . I had better leave you . . . for God only knows what I might do if I stay." He turned abruptly and a moment later she was alone and staring at the door he had closed behind him.

Dennis met Dare in the central hall as Dare was taking up his hat and greatcoat.

"Denny." Dare smiled though he was in no mood to make amiable conversation with anyone. "What brings you here?" Then he winked. "No doubt my little cookie, Blaine?"

"Ordinarily you would be right, but not this time. I have an appointment with her mother this morning."

"Good Lord, I don't envy you!" Dare grinned as he patted Denny on the shoulder and bid him good luck.

"Thanks, I think I might need it to get through this session," said Denny. The butler was already leading him up the grand staircase to Zara Marksbury's quarters.

Zara heard him enter and moved slyly as she turned to greet him. She read the frown on his face when he noted her state of dress and quickly attempted to set him at ease. "La, but is it eleven o'clock already? You must forgive me for receiving you like this, but I am a . . . er . . . late riser."

He felt a hot rush of embarrassment as he looked at Zara Marksbury. Here was the mother of the woman he loved and it was absurd that he should be noting how well formed she was. Hastily he answered, "No, I am probably early . . . I was most anxious, you see."

She laughed and moved towards him, and when her voice came, it was low and at its most seductive. "Were you Denny? Were you indeed?"

In Blaine's room, her devious mother's machinations were already in full swing as Zara's black maid carried out her mistress's instructions.

"Well now, honey, iz a good thing you done left off that boy of yers."

Blaine had been seated at her vanity, brushing out her short auburn curls. She turned now, puzzled. "What? Are you talking about Captain Werth?"

"Uh-huh, I sure enough am . . . why . . . no sooner yer back was turned but he was making up to yer mama."

"Stop it! How dare you say such a thing!" snapped Blaine, jumping to her feet.

"Well, ya don't know then? Huh! And I thought that's why ye throw'd him over."

"It's a lie!" cried Blaine.

The black serving girl shook her head. "Ain't no lie . . . why, bless me chile, he's in there wit yer mama right now."

Blaine waited for no more. She rushed to her door and down the hall. Zara had, in her deft way, managed to get close enough to Dennis so that when her door was flung open to exhibit Blaine seething in white heat, she was neatly holding Denny's shoulders and giving every impression that she had just been in his arms. The fact that Denny turned guiltily around and ejaculated Blaine's name was all the more proof to the lie and Blaine needed no more.

"Denny." She shook her head. "Oh God . . ."

"Blaine . . . dearest . . . I did try to warn you," said Zara soothingly.

"Warn me? Look at you! Just look at you!" To Denny she said on nearly a hiss, "You disgust me! Do you hear . . . I never want to see you again." With this last anguished cry Blaine fled the scene and left Zara pleased enough with its results.

Furious, Denny turned on Zara. "So, that's what you were about. I will go to her and explain."

"She will never believe you. Don't you see, I am willing to lower myself in her eyes and swear that you made love to me."

"She must know what you are . . . how low you would stoop . . ."

"She has always worshipped me. No, she will think only that I seduced you to keep you away from her, but it will serve to keep her contemptuous of you and that is all I need for the present. Good day, Captain Werth."

He inclined his head. "It doesn't end here, ma'am. I swear, it does not end here."

She laughed as he made his departure for she believed otherwise. She had seen the look in her daughter's eyes and understood the child well enough to know that Blaine would have no more of Dennis Werth.

# Chapter 9

*Wade* Ashford had lost himself through the years and what he was now was a man obsessed. Revenge had early implanted itself as a thing he must have; his whole being was centered in it now. He would whisk Silkie away from Dare Trent, out from under the man's nose, and he would leave her degraded on the streets of London. Such would be the fate of Aaron Marksbury's daughter, of Dare Trent's wife. People would point her out as a whore no longer fit for any gentleman's house. He would see her beauty marred, he would see her vitality drained, he would find satisfaction at last!

Ha! Did that infant, Sir Blaize, think to outwit him? More fool he! He had seen Blaize on board the American packet even though the lad had taken his meals in his room and had taken some pains to keep out of sight. Well, he had played his cards like the gamester he was and had literally put a spoke in the lad's wheels. He had waited until they were on the road from New York and then skillfully arranged for Sir Blaize to have a traveling accident. Ha, that should stall him a day or so. Enough time for him to get Silkie into his hands and be off with her. He had chartered a schooner and crew to take them back to England on his return to New York. No one would believe that Silkie had not gone willingly. His meeting with Zara would insure that.

His meeting with Zara. He sat in his room in the American Hotel on Main Street in Sag Harbor and fingered the quill he held high. Yes, he was sure she would lend her aid. She must hold Aaron's daughter in some loathing, and word was that she had been put out to find Dare married when she wanted him for her own daughter. He had not been at the hotel more than a few hours but he had already picked up the local gossip. The sun was in the midday sky as fickle mare's tails gathered and obscured its rays. He wondered fleetingly if they were in for some rain, and then he was putting pen to paper and smiling as he thought of Zara's face when she would read his letter.

Would she look the same? Perhaps the years had mellowed that vicious streak she had in her. No, he thought not. Word was that Tyler was more often than not to be found in his cups. If Tyler were not happy, well then, Zara was the cause. . . .

A moment later he called up a lackey and put the epistle and a coin into his hand with instructions to wait for a reply. Then once again he was contemplating the sky. By tomorrow night he meant to be on the road once again, this time with Silkie in hand. Nothing would stop him.

"I tell you, Freddy, this was contrived!" ejaculated Sir Blaize as he considered the broken axle of their hired carriage. "Damn but just look at it."

"Who?" started Freddy. "Oh! But . . . he didn't know we were even on board, did he?"

"Hell and fire, but he must have. I always wondered . . . you know that morning when I rounded the corner and thought he saw me? Well, he gave me no indication . . . but he must have . . . and then he planned to waylay us on the road, stall us so we couldn't warn Silkie." He shook his head in some irritation of nerves. "This is bad, Freddy!"

"Yes," Freddy agreed. "I think it is going to rain."

"Will you stop about the rain. I mean, if he wanted us out of the way . . . well, don't you see?"

"Afraid not . . . but I am sure I shall as soon as you explain," said Freddy, wondering whether there was a blacksmith nearby.

"He must mean to take immediate action . . . get to Silkie right off, before we have a chance to see her and warn her that he is in town."

"Right then. Best be off," said Freddy, reasonably.

"Noddy!" Sir Blaize said in supreme exasperation. "How? We can't just walk off and leave the horses!"

"No, don't want to walk . . . boots weren't made for it . . . and limited wardrobe, you know, unexpected trip."

"Stop jabbering at me!"

"Well, thing is you wanted to know how we should manage."

"That's right, don't tell me you know how?" asked Sir Blaize dubiously.

Freddy coughed deprecatingly. "Thing is . . . have a notion . . ."

"Then for God's sake, tell me!"

"Unhitch the horses . . . hop up and ride to the nearest village. Hire another carriage . . . send smithy back for this one. After all, you came with enough of the ready—" He frowned. "Yes, and while we are at it, might buy me another pair of boots . . . and a shirt too . . . can't go on wearing your things. They don't fit."

He was seized joyfully by the shoulders and shaken. "Damn if I couldn't kiss you!" Blaize started the necessary work of unhitching the horses. "Boots, is it? You may have any number of boots . . . shirts . . . anything your heart desires, Freddy . . . only let's hurry!"

Silkie sat for a long while trying to make sense of what was happening to her. He wanted her, badly. She was sure of it, but then why wouldn't he keep her for a wife? Well, fool, she answered herself, you know that a man can want a woman without loving her.

Yet she sensed he had strong feelings for her. Even when he was avoiding her deliberately, she sensed that she was at the center of his heart. She got to her feet and wandered outdoors, these thoughts making a muddle of her mind. She stopped to chat with the Marksbury groom holding Dennis Werth's hired carriage. She was stroking one of the horse's noses when she asked idly, "Have we company up at the house? I didn't see anyone come in."

"Aye, that captain . . . the one sweet on Miss Blaine." The youth holding the horse's head grinned. "Said he wouldn't be long . . . and coo . . . here he is now."

Silkie turned to get her first glimpse of Dennis Werth and smiled amiably as he approached. However, her smile was nearly swept off her countenance, so stern was his face. Curious, she dove in as was her habit at such times. "Hallo . . . I am told you are my cousin's friend, Captain Werth. I am . . ." Should she introduce herself as Mrs. Trent or Miss Marksbury? She settled it by giving her first name. ". . . I am Silkie."

278

Not lost to all manners, he managed to smile though it was of short duration, and he tipped his hat. "I am honored," he said, but his agitation was clearly written in his hazel eyes. ". . . however, I believe you mistake . . . I don't think Blaine would now describe me as her friend."

What was this? Blaine had spoken of him only a few times but it had always been with something akin to reverence. "Now, what is this, captain, a lover's quarrel?" Impulsively and because he looked so sad she reached out and patted his arm. "Don't you fret it, all will be better in the light of a new day. What the two of you need is a moment to consider how silly it is to waste your time arguing over trivialities."

He groaned. "Would that were the problem." He had a hungry look in his eyes. "It is not, however, so simple . . . and the only remedy I can immediately conjure up is to push Zara Marksbury over a cliff of some considerable height!" With that, he made as though to get into his carriage, but as he climbed up its steps, Silkie, once again acting on impulse, dove in after him.

She apologized with her smile. "I can be a bit of a nuisance, but you cannot lope off with such a parting line. Would you mind taking me for a drive? It is, after all, an open carriage and we cannot be accused of misconduct." Teasing, she was surprised to see a strange expression pass over his face. What was this?

"No doubt, that is what will be said, but certainly . . . do sit beside me. Why not? I might as well be accused of this in addition!" So saying he whipped the horses into a jog and guided them down the long drive.

"Captain Werth . . . whatever has happened . . . and of course it is none of my business, but perhaps I may be able to help."

He studied her for a long moment before sighing. "I don't think anyone can help . . . but here goes. Zara is against a match between her daughter and myself"—he again shot a look at Silkie—"indeed, she has other plans for Blaine."

"So I have gathered from Kora." Kora had already informed her mistress that the servants whispered about how Zara wanted Dare for Blaine.

"Who is Kora?" he puzzled up.

"She is . . . was my housekeeper . . . is now my everything . . . but please do go on."

279

"Right. Perhaps I should tell you. Indeed, I think I must if only to set you on your guard."

"What do you mean?"

"Zara has as much reason to resent you as she does me. More, in fact." He eyed her sideways. "Dare . . . mentioned something about the circumstances of your marriage in England when we dined together the other night. I know too that your uncle has set in motion an annulment decree which seems to have Dare fidgety. Odd that, he seems to be more than a little vexed about it when he should be pleased that you will both soon be free to pursue your separate lives."

She caught her breath, but avoided the subject of her marriage. "So then, captain, set me on my guard." She was well aware that Zara disliked her. She had discussed it with Kora, who had told her only that Zara fancied she had reason. That was all Kora had said.

"The master plan was that Zara would show Blaine how unsuitable I was so that Blaine would make a push to have Dare . . . who is . . . about to be free."

"Yes . . . so I have heard in the nether regions of the house. It is all the servants can talk about these days. They find it very shocking."

"How they can be shocked at anything Zara sets out to do is more than I can fathom. The woman is without scruples!"

"Why do you say so?"

"Oh, she is discreet enough . . . one never knows when she is moving from one affair into another. Unless one looks at Tyler, for I'd swear he knows."

This time Silkie was shocked and she opened her grey eyes wide. "Oh captain, I do hope your annoyance with my aunt isn't pushing you to say such . . . dreadful things?"

Gravely he answered, "You don't know me, but I am not that sort of man. The only reason I mention it . . . is so that you will be prepared for what I am now about to disclose to you."

"Steady, captain, I don't want rumors . . . for I only deal in facts," she cautioned.

"Then have these facts, ma'am!" he said sternly. "Your aunt had me up to her room for the express purpose of convincing Blaine that I was having an affair with her!"

Her hand flew to her mouth. "No . . . never say so . . . but . . ."

"You are wondering how she contrived to have Blaine arrive upon the scene of her making?" He shook his head in some exasperation. "I too should like the answer to that question. It doesn't signify. Blaine came in on us at a moment designed to make my poor darling think the worst and—"

"Please do excuse me for interrupting you, captain, but could you tell me how you happened to lend yourself to such a . . . scene?"

"I swear to you I don't know. I was standing there . . . my hat in my hands one moment, and the next, she managed to get in my arms and put hers around my shoulders. It looked bad . . . but it was not .. . do you know what I mean?"

Silkie considered this. "Yes . . . yes, I can see how it might have happened . . . and of course Blaine ran to her bedroom in tears?"

"Not until her mother made it plain to her that I was her lover. Just in case her eyes deceived her, you see, she admitted to having an affair with me. She slandered herself in her daughter's eyes . . . to ruin me!"

"Faith!" exclaimed Silkie, "that is a coil if ever there was one."

"So, you do see . . . there is no hope." He sighed.

Silkie gazed at him a long thoughtful moment before replying, and she was answering herself as well as him. "Do you love Blaine?"

"I do, madam, with all my heart," was his earnest reply.

"Then there is always hope. . . ."


Zara was well pleased with the results of her morning's work. She was dressing to go into town and do some shopping when a servant arrived at her room with a note and advised her that a lackey from the American Hotel awaited her reply downstairs. She was intrigued and tore open the envelope to read:

Zara sweet,

After all these years, we have the opportunity to re-venge ourselves on Aaron and Serena and make them squirm in heaven. Indeed what kind of heaven can they have knowing their treasure suffers here on Earth!

Don't think *your* plans secure. I have it on excellent authority that Dare Trent finds himself falling in love with Serena's daughter.

However, I have an answer and this time I shall not be thwarted. Meet me in one hour at my hotel and I shall be pleased to tell you what I have in mind.

> I am, as ever,
> fondly yours,
> Wade Ashford

Wade Ashford had known just what he was doing when he wrote about Dare being in love with Silkie. It was a gamble he chose to take just in case Zara believed herself to be home free—just in case Zara felt she could do without him in this instance—and he was right. This was just what Zara had been afraid of. More than once she had glanced from Dare to Silkie when neither had even been aware that they were gazing into each other's eyes, and she had felt more than a twinge of irritation.

She would meet Wade Ashford . . . indeed, how could she not? Precious life! Imagine, Wade . . . here in Sag Harbor. A flicker of memory skirted her mind. There had been one pleasant afternoon spent in Wade's arms. He had been an accomplished lover and it would be amusing to see him after all this time. More than twenty years. Egad! Twenty years? She quickly went to her looking glass. Traces of age had touched her, but even so, she was well aware that the image reflected was quite attractive still.

Tyler? He was in New York, poor darling. What would he say if Blaine were to tell him about the incident with Dennis? Never mind. Blaine would not do that and even if she did . . . Zara would tell him it had only been a trick to wheedle Dennis out of their daughter's heart. And what would Tyler say about Wade Ashford . . . here in Sag Harbor? Would he suspect that Wade was up to mischief? Tyler could, even in his cups, see much more than she was wont to give him credit for . . . just like that statement before he left for New York. He had said that he rather thought Dare was head over heels in love with his brother's daughter. Said he wouldn't be surprised if the two didn't come to their senses before the courts declared the marriage null and void. She had scoffed at the notion, but it had nagged at her afterwards. Well, here was Wade Ashford . . . with a plan that would secure her own!

What sort of fetch could Ashford be up to? After all this time he still harbored hatred towards Aaron and Serena. Dead. Aaron was dead. What did she feel about that? When she had first heard the news it had been with something of an ache. Aaron was dead, but that was a hope that had died long ago. Here was Ashford still seeking his ounce of blood, right into their graves.

Would she help him this time? There was a definite pleasure in the thought of obtaining some measure of revenge. Yes, it was nice to think of Serena—who was no doubt, as Wade wrote, in heaven—squirming for her child. Aaron. It was Aaron's soul she was attacking as well. That's right, damn him!

Famous! She would meet with Ashford and if he were reasonable and it were not too risky this time, they would deal . . . She smiled, for at this juncture, she wondered if he were still the same dashing blade he had been in their hot youth.

On this last, she took up her quill, dipped it, and quickly scribbled an answer to Ashford.

Well then, the final cast was set.

## Chapter 10

*The* perversity of Zara's disposition did not allow her to see more than her own version of any event. Therefore, it was not a surprising thing that she did not recognize how severely her morning's endeavors would hurt her daughter. Zara did most certainly pity what she felt was her child's momentary suffering and disillusionment, but she shrugged it off, saying that it would strengthen Blaine's character, harden her to a world that would hurt her if it could. By the time she was done with her rationalizing, she could only see that she had done her daughter an immense favor. What was a little pain to that? Zara did not understand that she had given her daughter not a cruel world, but a crumbling one, and that Blaine was incapable of standing amongst its ruins.

Until that morning Blaine had always admired her strong and willful mother. Until that morning, Zara could do no wrong. She would excuse Zara's harshness, even in the matter of Dennis, saying to herself that her mother just didn't realize how good Dennis was. Ha! All that was over in the passing of a few moments. Her mother had been seducing Dennis. She had seen it with her own eyes . . . Dennis, in Zara's room, Dennis? The earth trembled, the skies darkened, and she was struck by a hurt that was overwhelming.

What was her life worth any more? She had no home—her mother had destroyed it. She had no future—both her lover and her mother had slashed it to pieces. Oh God . . . her mother, Zara . . . no better than a common whore, selling herself, for that is what she did, sell herself to ruin Dennis in her eyes. Blaine knew that was why Zara had Dennis in her bedroom. She knew Zara had no love for Dennis . . . poor Papa . . . how many others had her mother trifled with? That was why Papa drank so heavily; it all made sense now.

It was too much to her naive soul to withstand. She tore out of the house without her cloak. She ran past a surprised groom, across the rolling lawns, and towards the east woods. She ran and she ran, never noticing how much ground she had put behind her, never noticing that the skies were indeed growing grey and the weather altering for the worse, and she never noticed that she had crossed a point forbidden to her and entered *Sterling Woods*!

The wisps of clouds in the afternoon sky had already scudded out to sea, pushed by heavier, darker cumulus. There was a stillness peculiar to a snowstorm; the damp winter grey gave warning of what was sure to come. Silkie had for some minutes noted the change in weather. During her lifetime in Romney Marsh they had never had to withstand many snowstorms, but even so, she knew that the darkening sky portended much and remarked upon it as she frowned.

"What do you think, captain, should we be turning back? Silly goose that I am, I neglected to wear my top hat, and while this riding habit of mine is sturdy enough, I am beginning to feel the damp."

He smiled and begged her indulgence while he pulled up the folded top canvas and secured it. "There," he said, "that should do until I get you home."

Even as he clucked, a soft winter breeze brought them the first of the flakes as drops of flurrying snow fell to earth. Their faces and lashes were tickled with the white dew and Silkie giggled. "Oh look . . ." she pointed at the evergreen woods they were passing for they had already collected a lovely, sparkling foam of white.

"Pretty, aye . . . but those woods have a bad history . . . no one in Sag Harbor trespasses those thickets," he said with the twinkle lighting his hazel eyes.

"Oh goodness, what can you mean? Tell me . . . oh do please."

"I warn you, it's gory," he teased.

"The gorier the better," she returned promptly, her eyes

widening. He laughed. "Right then, you asked for it. I am told . . . and have nothing to prove the tale for I am not a Sag Harbor citizen."

"Never mind, just tell me."

He chuckled again. "Once upon a time, there was a man named Cornelius Sterling. He was a broth of a man and there wasn't a maid in the village who didn't want him for a husband. Poor Cornelius, what did he go and do but choose a girl from New York and bring her back here to live. Well, he built her a house on the edge of those woods . . . Sterling Woods . . . the remains of that house can be found scattered throughout the thicket. Was she happy? No, not she. Within the year she took on a lover and one day Cornelius came home and found them together. He went mad. Took an axe and . . . well . . . their parts are buried all over Sterling Woods, and they say the swamp was born out of her heart which was buried at its center."

"How perfectly dreadful." She thought about it for a long moment and then asked, "What happened to him? Cornelius?"

Captain Werth laughed grimly. "He put a bullet through his head. His ghost is said to lurk about looking for his beloved."

"Whom he cannot find as he didn't leave enough of her in one place. Thank you, yes, it is quite a gory tale."

They had by this time pulled up in front of the Marksbury's double Georgian doorway and as a groom rushed to take the horse's heads, Denny hopped down and came around to give Silkie his hand.

"Madam," he said uncertainly. Here was a new friendship, and with it came hope once again for Blaine and himself. Perhaps this cousin of Blaine's would help them.

She smiled. "Silkie . . . please, you do make me feel ancient. Madam, indeed!" Her smile belied the severity of her tone.

"Silkie then, I . . . I can not tell you enough . . . how honored I am that you had the patience to hear my story."

"Which one?" Silkie teased, dimpling at him.

He grinned and felt himself and his spirits quite lifted. She made everything seem so very natural and surmountable. "The first of the two." He bent to kiss her gloved hand as the front door opened and the Marksbury butler stood aside, his chin well up as was his custom.

Silkie smiled at the man and bade Captain Werth adieu gently as she touched his arm. "Remember now . . . I mean to set things straight . . . somehow. I shall let you know. Where may I address any message I may have for you?"

"I am staying at the American Hotel in town, though my boat is docked at the wharf and I spend some time there as well."

"Everything will work out right and tight, sir, see if it doesn't," she assured him though she was certainly concerned about just how she was going to manage this. Zara was already set against her and this would only serve to give the woman something to sink her fangs into. Ah well, never mind, somehow she would see it through.

She saw him off and turned to find the elderly butler still standing awaiting her. "Ah Gatsby . . . I have kept you standing in the cold doorway. Come . . . let's close it up and be comfortable again." She twinkled up at him. "Whatever is the matter?"

She had, in the short space of time she had been installed in the Marksbury household, managed to endear herself to many of the house's staff. Gatsby was one of her silent admirers and they were wont to pass quips here and there. She saw at once that he was troubled and as he did not answer her, she persisted.

"Gatsby . . . tell me. What is wrong?"

He was of English birth and breeding. His father and father before him had served in the awesome capacity of butler as well and he knew his place. One did not, under any circumstances, gossip with one's superiors, yet he had watched Miss Blaine grow up and was worried sick over her prolonged absence. Her behavior was most odd. She had never run out of the house without a cloak in the middle of winter ever before . . . with such a look of anguish on her face that it near broke his heart. What, just what was he to do? He stood there in a frenzy of indecision.

Silkie stamped her foot at him. "Gatsby . . . now what is it? Tell me, do."

Kora came clucking her tongue from down the long corridor and answered instead. "He can't, m'dear Mrs. Trent, and that's a fact . . . but I don't hold with his scruples in this instance, so I'll be telling you."

"Right you are, Kora, my love," said Silkie, giving the

plump woman a hug for she hadn't seen her since that morning.
"What has happened?"

" 'Tis Miss Blaine. She ran out of here some hours ago . . .
with no more than her day gown on . . . her head uncovered and
her face streaked with tears.''

Silkie grew grave all at once and sent Gatsby after her hooded
cloak. This donned, she put up a hand to stall Kora's flow. "I
shan't be long."

"But child," objected Kora, "it's getting dark . . . there is a
snowstorm of some bluster blowing out there. Where do you
think you are going?''

"Just to the stable. Maybe one of the grooms knows her
direction. I shan't be gone long," she repeated.

It didn't take more than a few minutes for Silkie to find the
groom who had seen Blaine leave the house earlier. He stood,
scratching his unruly dark hair, and begged Silkie's pardon.

"S'cuse me for saying so, but Miss Blaine . . . she looked
upset like. She took to the woods''—he pointed out the stable
door—"and her pa, well he would be none too pleased as ya can
wander off into Sterling Woods right easy.''

Silkie waited for no more. She was already moving, calling
back to him to get a saddle. "And not a sidesaddle, if you-
please, for I may have to ride hard through the thicket." She
threw the saddle pad over the grey gelding, and reached for the
bit. "And you had best give me whatever warm blankets you have
handy, just in case I do get lucky and find my cousin.''

Some moments later she was astride and tightening the girth as
she walked the gelding down the bridle path towards the east
woods. It was already very near five and dusk was settling. Even
so, the white blanket that now covered everything gave off a
bright glow and Silkie could not help marveling over the winter's
frosty setting as she trotted through the woods. The gelding
knew his way about and managed for the most part to stay on the
trail that swirled through the woods. Silkie called out her cousin's
name from time to time, and then she crossed the road to stare at
a stretch of pine trees that lined Sterling Woods.

He didn't know why it was, but he found himself mounting
his black and riding across the wide lawns to the Marksbury
house. You are a damn fool, Dare Trent, he told himself cyni-

cally as he handed the reins to the Marksbury groom and walked the distance to the front door. What you are doing here is more than you can answer. What good will it do to see her again? Tomorrow you will sign papers that will forever separate you. That's right . . . but now, now Zara is in town. You saw her go into the village earlier and it will afford you some time alone with your wife. Your wife? Why do you think of her that way? She is not . . . well, not really . . .

Damn if he knew what he was doing. He very nearly turned on his heel without touching the knocker when the door was opened. Gatsby stood to one side as Kora attacked, "Oh mercy, 'tis you, captain. That thankful I be . . . for 'tis a rare set-to we have here." She drew him inside.

"What is it, woman? What has gone wrong?" For some irrational reason he felt a sudden chill of fear. "Where is my wife?"

"That's just it," answered Kora. "When I told her that Miss Blaine was overdue . . . she was only supposed to inquire after her cousin . . . but the groom says she tacked up the grey and headed for the east woods . . . in *this* snowstorm . . . and it's that worried I am."

Dare Trent waited for nothing more. He was now most definitely turning on his heel, but there was no notion of returning home. Indeed, his Silkie was out after dark in a snowstorm and he would not have it!


Freddy considered the situation he presently found himself in. His steadiness of character, his open, amiable disposition suffered a severe attack. Though Blaize had seen fit to provide both of them with serviceable winter greatcoats, he felt their style and design were notably lacking. Though they had managed to find a small village and a public stable, the conveyance they had hired was little more than an open gig whose springs should have been replaced years ago. Though they traveled now the correct road— for some hours they had not, for Blaize had inadvertently missed the turnoff—this same correct road, this main pike was little better than a miserably rutted dirt bridlepath, on which Freddy expected at any moment to find a tribe of savage Indians. He had read enough about them in this heathen land. If all this were not enough to put his gentle soul in danger, there was one more thing that threatened his placid nature. *It was snowing!*

It was not a soft, mild flurry of pretty white flakes, but a swirling, raging whirlwind of wet, very nearly hard, bright snow that landed and collected. He felt it dampen his cheeks and he pulled up his collar.

"I say," he managed at last. Sir Blaize seemed oblivious as he drove the horses onward in staid tenacity. "Blaize . . . I say . . ."

"Well, then, confound it, Freddy, say it!"

"Snow, you know," said Freddy, putting out one gloved hand as though to collect proof.

"Blister it! I know it's snowing," answered Blaize, ever impatient.

"Right. Thought you did," returned Freddy sadly. He attempted to peer through the darkness and discovered that it was certainly going to be hard to get through if much more snow accumulated. Mildly he suggested, "Might be a good thing to take shelter at the next inn." Deep in his heart he knew this was not something Blaize was ready to do.

"Can't," came the expected reply.

"Why?" Freddy's discomfort urged him to pursue.

"*He* won't stop!" answered Blaize. "Must see that."

Freddy did not see that, but what he did see quite clearly was that Blaize would not at that moment give in. With a sigh, his eyes heavenward, and a silent prayer for mercy, Freddy relapsed into silence.

Zara Marksbury was pleasurably stretched out beneath the covers of Wade Ashford's bed. He had risen to pour the remainder of a bottle of champagne they had opened earlier into their glasses, but now he stopped by the window and was gazing out on the blustering snowstorm. She looked at him for a long moment. He was certainly a dasher, even now with the years adding those lines of dissipation to his face, even with that bitter hatred glinting in his hazel eyes. What a bold, demanding lover he had been in bed and how very satisfying it had been to please him.

"What are you thinking, Wade darling?" she asked at length

to bring his attention back to herself. She didn't really care, but she did wish he would stop staring out the window with that cold, hard look of his. It was most disconcerting.

He turned halfway and studied her a moment. "Have you thought about it, Zara? Tomorrow you will be bringing Serena's daughter to me."

There was an expression on his face that frightened her. "That's right, but unlike the past, you *will* manage to pull it off this time and keep my name out of it."

He sneered. "Unlike the past, I will pull it off and Silkie will be mine to destroy . . . which I mean to do . . . in slow degrees."

She stared at him. "Do you so hate the child?"

He shrugged. "I care nothing for her . . . it is Aaron . . . Aaron I wish to reach, even in his grave!"

For a moment Zara wondered about Ashford's sanity. He was certainly obsessed. For her part she wanted Silkie out of the way to insure Blaine's future with Dare Trent, but she decided not to comment on this. "Come on darling . . . come back to bed," she coaxed, patting the quilt beside her.

He was still somewhere else, back in time, facing Aaron whose fists pounded at him. Serena was there in the background. He had very nearly made Serena his, but something had gone wrong. Not this time. No one would get in his way. He didn't hear Zara. He didn't see her lovely naked form get out of the bed and amble to him until she was separating his silk robe, wrapping her arms around him.

"Don't fret my lover . . . you'll have her . . . soon enough and now, now you have me."

He curled his lip, but Zara was a delightful tease and his hand went to her small pert breast and cupped it deftly. His mouth took hers and their tongues tempted one another to further play.

Zara laughed triumphantly, pleased with herself and her skill as she led him to the bed. "No doubt, darling, this will be our last time together . . . until we meet in hell, that is."

"Zara . . . don't you know? I rather thought you did," he whispered as his lips strayed over her ears, as his hands parted her thighs.

"What's that, lover?"

"We are in hell," he said and plunged deep within her.

## Chapter 11

*Silkie* was scarcely able to see as she wielded her grey gelding through the thick stretch of pines and birch and made her way deep into Sterling Woods. The going was slow for the ground was bad and the trees dense. The snow had only just begun to accumulate and the glow was simply not enough to lead her safely on. She had just made up her mind to retrace her tracks and head home when she heard it.

A cry for help. A low sobbing sound, very much more a moan than an audible call. In some excitement Silkie cried out, *"Blaine?* Blaine, is that you? Blaine?"

"Y-es . . . y-es . . . here," Blaine called feebly.

Silkie urged her horse in the direction of her cousin's voice. What was the matter? What had happened? And then she saw the girl in a heap on the ground with a metal trap clamped around her ankle and bright red blood staining the snow.

"Faith!" cried Silkie, jumping off her steed and nearly slipping as she ran to her cousin's side. Blaine was soaked through, she was shivering, her lips were blue, and she looked as though she were about to faint. Silkie inspected the trap and cried in some heated irritation when she could not get the teeth of the trap apart. She touched Blaine's forehead and tried to reassure the girl.

"Hold on love . . . I am only going to my horse to get you a blanket." With which she scurried back to the gelding she had neglected to tether and undid the blanket she had secured to the saddle. This she wrapped tightly round her cousin and once again began with all her might to try and undo the trap. Suddenly she heard her name brought on the wind: "SILKIE?"

It was Dare. What was this? A miracle certainly, for silently, idiotically, she had been calling his name. Now, out of nowhere, a godsend, here he was. Joyfully she responded, "Dare . . . oh Dare . . . hurry!"

All at once he came crashing through the brush and he was upon them, taking command in his firm, quiet, and marveously effective way. He bolstered Blaine with his teasing as though she had done no more than taken a spill into the local swimming hole and cut herself slightly on the rocks.

"Cookie! What's this, girl? Damn but you are good and wet . . . and ruining all this pretty snow with that purple blood of yours." He ripped the trap apart as though it were no more than paper, taking it and flinging it high and far.

"It isn't purple," she countered feebly, "it's . . . blue."

"Right, and it matches your lips!" teased Silkie. "That's a brave lass, we'll have you home."

"NO!" cried Blaine, sharply interrupting. "Not home . . . not to *her* home."

Dare exchanged a quick, surprised look with Silkie but immediately answered her. "That's right, why should you go home when you know you can get away with so much more at my house. I daresay you staged all this just to get an invitation." He lifted her up and carried her to his horse, straddling her across the saddle while Silkie made certain Blaine held the blanket close around her.

He turned to his wife. "Silkie . . . you will accompany us?"

"Of course," she answered at once and to herself she said, What do you think, you big dolt?

Nearly fifteen minutes later, with Blaine very near to losing consciousness, they rode up the long winding drive to Darrow Trent's house. Silkie found herself curious, as she always was whenever she had chanced to look across the sweeping lawns and see the colonial-style home that Arthur Trent had built for himself and his son. Though not enormous, it was quite a beautiful example of American craftmanship, with its intriguing elliptical windows and its ornately molded doorway and covered portico.

Dare called to his groom who came running out of the stables and sent him off after the doctor.

"Take the fresh chestnut and ride carefully, but as swiftly as the weather permits," he said as the boy took charge of their horses.

The front door was opened by a middle-aged butler and he stood aside to allow the captain carrying his light burden to enter.

"Have a hot bath prepared in my room and a fire in the blue guest room," Dare said. He proceeded to take the stairs while his man went about the business in his train.

Fleetingly Silkie wondered why a bath in the captain's bedroom, but there was no time to consider this properly for he needed her to open the door to the guest room. This she did, entering before him to pull down the coverlet of the four-poster bed, take up a tinder box, and light the branch of candles on the nightstand. While she did this he had deposited his charge.

"Silk . . . you will get her out of those wet things . . . I think you may find a man's nightdress in the wardrobe cupboard. It will have to do."

"Done." Silkie smiled. "Go on . . ." She waved him off but he lingered a moment to take up her hand and bring it up to his bent head, where he placed a most affectionate kiss upon her gloved knuckles. She felt a warm thrill rush through her as she discovered his Irish blue eyes. Faith, how she loved him!

As Dare left the room, however, he met the butler who came in carrying logs. Together they piled them in the hearth and set it ablaze while Silkie took off Blaine's shoes and set to work on the gash on the girl's ankle.

Silkie fetched some fresh water from the basin, tore the slip of her undergarment, and began bathing Blaine's wound. The room was warming from the roaring blaze in the hearth and once again Silkie ushered Dare out of the room. Once alone with her cousin, the door closed at their backs, she began undressing her.

"That's a girl," Silkie said softly, wondering why Blaine had lapsed into such pitiful silence, hoping she would release her pent-up emotions, make it possible for her to assuage her hurts by bringing them out into the open. "You know, I don't think that gash you received from that miserable trap will scar you."

"It doesn't matter," said Blaine, not looking at Silkie.

"Oh? Doesn't it? But then, you are right. Dennis Werth is not the sort to allow a scar or two to affect his love for—"

"Stop it. Dennis is a . . . a—"

"No, he isn't, Blaine," said Silkie quietly, interrupting her. Here was the opening she wanted. "What you witnessed this morning was not what you think."

Blaine turned her head to stare at Silkie, "You don't know . . . you couldn't know."

"Oh, but I do. Shall I tell you what you think you saw?"

"No, no . . . I don't want to talk about it."

"Of course you don't, but what stands is a lie and I think you should have the truth. Then if you don't want to talk about it, we won't."

"Silkie. My mother and Dennis . . ." The girl sobbed in anguish.

"Nonsense, though that is what your mother wished you to believe. You see, she wants Dennis out of your system. What better way to accomplish that than to make you think she and he were having a—"

"Stop it! She wouldn't contrive something like that . . . make me think she is a . . . a . . . doxy so that . . . ."

"Oh but she would. Do you think it was an accident that you came upon them?"

"Yes . . ."

"Tell me, why did you go to your mother's bedroom at that time?"

"Well . . ." And then Blaine remembered. It had been her mother's black maid who had told her that Dennis was with her mother. She closed her eyes and groaned. "You mean . . . ?"

"Thats right," answered Silkie.

"But . . . why was Dennis in her room?"

"He says that she sent for him and he went thinking she was finally giving her consent to your marriage."

Blaine shook her head. "No . . . oh no . . . ."

Silkie had helped her don the huge white nightdress, pulled the covers up to the girl's chin, and now stroked her head. Blaine was dreadfully pale and it was no wonder, she had been caught in that trap for nearly an hour. "You get some rest until the doctor arrives. Shall I send up some tea?"

295

"No . . . no . . ."

"Right, do you take it with milk and sugar?"

Blaine managed a smile. "Yes, you badger." She watched Silkie move towards the door. "Silk?"

"Yes, love?"

"Thank you . . . so very much."

"Drink your tea when you get it and that will be a real thank you. Words never count unless they are backed by action." So saying, Silkie smiled and left her cousin to rest alone.

In the dimly lit hall outside she was met by her husband who came forward to take up her hands. She had in the interim shed her cloak and gloves, but she felt damp through the riding habit she still had on and her boots were also wet. She didn't want to return just then to the Marksbury house but she needed a change of clothing.

"Dare . . . if you don't need me now . . . I will just run up to—"

"You will do no such thing and I will need you," he said, touching her nose lightly.

"Yes, but I shall return as soon as I change my things."

"No, my sweetings. What you are going to do"—he was leading her down the hall to a set of double oak doors, one of which he opened to gently urge her within—"is get into that hot tub my people have prepared for you."

She looked up at him in some surprise, though truth was she dearly wanted to dive right into that tub and soak away her aches. "Dare, I can't do that."

"You can and, my dear, you will." He closed the door at his back. "Now, will you get your wet things off . . . or shall I perform that office for you?"

She laughed and held him at bay. "Agreed . . . I will take my medicine and climb into your bath . . . and I can undress myself, thank you."

A knock sounded at his door and his man opened it at Dare's invitation to advise him that the doctor had arrived. Dare sighed. "*This* time, I suppose I shall have to let you." He bowed to her, his bright blue eyes twinkling as he left her to the tub which sat in the middle of his bedroom on a green woven rug. Silkie looked around with keen interest. *This was Dare's bedroom.* A titilating circumstance. Nonsense, she chided herself. Why should she be feeling goosebumps? Because . . . look at that bed! It was huge and its overhanging ceiling was draped in rich brown velvet. In swagging folds trimmed in gold the hangings fell to the floor from each of the four posters. The coverlet was in a matching material. She looked away from it to the fireplace on the wall opposite. A large stone affair with a long, lead-paned window flanking its far corner. The room was sparsely furnished; only a wardrobe cupboard was propped up against the quiet design of the faded yellow wallpaper, and its opposite wall at her right side held a small, dark wood writing desk of classic design. It was a handsome room and, she thought, it needed only a touch here and there to make it perfect. . . .

She shook her head. What was she thinking? Absurd girl, stop your dreaming. The bath awaited her and she went to the fireplace, undressed, and draped her things out to dry before she got into the soothing hot water and relaxed. Blue eyes. Such bright blue eyes. They drew out her soul and played havoc with her will. Devil. He was, of course, a devil. What was he doing tonight? Preparing her for his bed? Had he decided it was time again for a bit of . . .

Stop it! Your fault as well as his. You allowed him to take you on board the ship. You allowed him before that . . . your fault. You could have said no. Ha! How could I have stopped? My heart was pounding then as it is now and my limbs moved on their own. The memory of his touch stirred her now and she felt her nerve endings tingle. There was a hungry feeling deep inside of her but it was more than desire. She wanted him to love her, to need her, to say what every woman wants the man of her choice to say. She sank deeper in the tub and soaped herself with the body brush he had left her. Oh Dare . . .

Dare paced in the library. He had shed his dark brown riding coat, his waistcoat, and cravat. He stood in his shirt sleeves and buckskin riding breeches by the fire, his black hair in handsome disarray and his blue eyes staring at the flames. Ah Silkie. Why had it taken him so long to see? Why? Because you had been forced into the match and that went against the grain?

The doctor entered the library, leather sachel in hand, spectacles low over his narrow nose.

"I've left the child sleeping, Dare . . . best be keeping her here a week or so. No sense moving her across the way."

"Is she going to be alright?" Care asked, going forward.

"Eh? Fool thing to do, go running off into Sterling Woods, could have gone down in one of the bogs, but yes, she will mend well enough. Mind though, she might come down with a head cold . . . but her lungs seem fine enough now, and there is no fever."

"What about her ankle?"

"She was lucky. It didn't get the bone, but she has one hell of a bruise and will be sore for a few weeks. It's swollen but only slightly and that's natural."

"No stitching?"

"No . . . it wasn't deep and she didn't cut the artery. She'll do."

A moment later Dare saw the elderly doctor out and raced to the stairs, taking them two at a time. He was in a heat rush for Silkie. Relieved about Blaine, there was nothing for it but to attend to his own pressing need! *He loved her.* With all his mind, with all his heart, he loved her. It had dawned on him overwhelmingly when he had been searching for her in Sterling Woods. Why hadn't he seen that before? Was it too late? No, it couldn't be, he wouldn't allow it to be! He had been wild with anxiety earlier that night when he had thought she might be in danger—and now he felt an effervescent sense of relief.

He got to his room and stood a moment before going in. Was there a chance she wouldn't have him? Hell, she was his wife! He meant to keep her that way. His wife, oh God, that felt good! With something close to violent determination, he went inside quietly and moved towards the tub. She lay there, her head back, her eyes closed. He surveyed her and then she felt her lips caressed.

Her eyes fluttered open and she saw those blue orbs of his.

"Dare, what are you doing?"

"Kissing my wife," he answered glibly. "Damn but you are a sight for the soul. Silkie . . . do you have any idea what you do to me?"

She had crossed her breasts with her arms. "Turn around at once." When he did not comply she said, "Dare . . . turn . . .''

Instead he dipped into the tub and picked her up out of it as though she were little more than a babe in arms. As she protested he carried her dripping wet body to the fireplace rug and laid her down. He was on his knees, pressing her flat beneath him as he dropped a kiss on her nose, on her forehead.

She squirmed and objected and then he was saying something she found difficult to believe.

"Hush, my love, my only love . . ."

"Dare . . . don't."

"Don't what?"

"Don't do this . . . don't say things you can't mean." She was grave, suddenly sad.

"Silkie, hear me well, for I don't like to repeat myself. I love you. I adore you, I want you and damn it, woman, I mean to have you." He was now kissing her ears, her neck, dipping lower, taking hold of her breast and suckling at her rose-tipped nipple.

She couldn't believe it and it was hard to think with him teasing the hell out of her body. "Dare . . . you . . . you . . . love me?"

"With all my heart and soul. Didn't you hear me?"

"I always hear you . . . but . . ."

"Confound it, woman. You are Mrs. Silkie Trent and so you shall remain." He found her hips with both his hands and tenderly stroked, and then his hands slipped beneath and took up her buttocks. "Here . . . let me show you what that means." His knees had separated her legs as his mouth took hers and their tongues met. They were lost in the magic of one another as sweetly he molded her to him, hungrily whispering in her ears, gently urging her to help him with his breeches as skillfully he discarded his boots.

And then he took her to another kingdom. His hands, his lips traveled the length of her supple body, and as he kept her thighs parted he encouraged her to hold the hardened rod of his manhood. He taught her how to please him as he drank her honey and listened to her groan with pleasure and then he was teaching her just how to use her mouth around that rod of his while he exploded her bubbling blood with his own very deft arts.

What was happening? It had never been like this before. She loved him, but oh faith, how could she be doing this? To please him, yes, but it also pleased her . . . and then he was pushing her back down on the rug, mounting her, placing his hard, pulsating manhood between her legs, gently inserting it in her heated flesh, sweetly saying her name, "Ah Silkie . . . so tight, my love, even now . . . ah babe . . . give it to me."

She felt him enter her and climaxed very nearly at that moment. As he rotated her hips and moved hard and hungrily inside of her, she felt herself peak over and over again. She couldn't think, she didn't wish to. All she wanted to do was lay there, take him as he said over and over that he loved her. And then he was groaning as he reached his high. He lay there holding her, not withdrawing from her womb for some moments as he kissed her lips, her eyes, and softly told her how well she had pleased him.

"Ah woman . . . won't you tell me?"

"Tell you what?" she teased for she knew she had withheld telling him she loved him. She had said other things, but this she had kept still about.

"You know what," he answered, a frown drawing his dark brows together.

"Ah, yes of course. Dare . . . you are . . . a most perfect lover . . . though, of course, never having had anyone else, I have no measure to judge by."

"Damnation! You'll just have to take my word for it, woman. You've got the best lover in all this kingdom, but you know that is not what I want to hear."

She relented. "Love? The word isn't adequate to describe how I feel about you."

"Always?"

"Yes, always," she whispered.

He was lifting her up cradlelike and carrying her to his bed. "Silkie, my love, I mean to keep you to your word."

She gathered that at the moment, he had something else in mind, and she attempted to object as he laid her down and began manipulating her body. "Dare . . . oh . . . no Dare."

"Yes, oh Silkie, yes." He grinned.

## Chapter 12

*It* was morning. The snowstorm had abated and the white wintry fluff covered lawns and roads alike. Wade Ashford cursed silently as he headed towards the village carriage house. Nothing was going to stop him. Damn, there was no more than three or four inches. He would buy a sleigh if he had to, but he would see this through right on schedule!

Zara had left him during the night. Their plans were set, the hour was approaching, and he would have to hurry. This time, this time nothing was going to stand in his way. Even if he had to storm Trent's place and put a bullet in the man's head, that was what he would do. From all that Zara had said, however, Trent did not seem to hover around Silkie these days, so it should be a fairly simple affair of whisking her off.

He smiled to himself at the thought. All the village would know that their great man Captain Trent had had his wife stolen from under his nose, and all the village would think she had gone willingly. Why not? She did not even live with her husband. Why wouldn't they believe she had run off with another man? Ah, true, revenge would be sweet, so sweet. He moved into the carriage house swiftly, briskly, and a few moments later, a suitable carriage was purchased. They were to hitch to a team he had waiting in the stables and bring it round to the hotel. Damn, but he could hardly wait!

Dare sat up in bed and watched his wife get dressed. "I don't know why you feel you must ride over yourself . . . I will send a servant to collect your things . . . for that matter, Kora will manage the entire affair for us."

She smiled at him. "That would be most rude. Now, you told me earlier you had to run into the village today. Why don't you take care of your . . . er . . . affairs, and I shall attend to mine and we can meet here in the afternoon, at which time, my dearest love"—she came over to wrap her arms around his neck and his hands went to her trim waist—"you can take me for a sleigh ride and show me some of this marvelous island of yours."

"You mean we can meet here and . . ." He drew her into his lap, kissing her mouth.

She fought him and laughingly pulled away. "Stop it, fiend!" She lightly stepped out of the room. "Later, my love . . ."

He watched her go and sighed. Was it possible for man to be so happy? Was it dangerous? It was something his father had said to him a long time ago when his mother had died. Arthur Trent had been grieving sorely and he had sworn at the heavens for being jealous of his happiness. Hmmm. A thought, for just recently he had read much the same in the poem of Edgar Allen Poe's, "Annabel Lee":

> I was a child and she was a child,
>     In this kingdom by the sea;
> But we loved with a love that was more than love—
>     I and my Annabel Lee;
> With a love that the winged seraphs of heaven
>     coveted her and me.
>
> The angels, not half so happy in heaven,
>     Went envying her and me—
> Yes!—that was the reason (as all men know,
>     In this kingdom by the sea)
> That the wind came out of the cloud by night,
>     Chilling and killing my Annabel Lee.
>
> And so, all the night-tide, I lie down by the side
> Of my darling—my darling—my life and my bride,
>     In the sepulcher there by the sea,
>     In her tomb by the sounding sea.

What was this? Why should this poem hit him now? What was this foreboding he felt? Hell, there was certainly one thing he knew—he meant to protect Silkie against the world, against night chills, against the angels if need be. No one and nothing was going to take his Silkie away from him!

He got up hurriedly at this point and began getting washed and dressed. He would get his business over with in town and go up to fetch Silkie from the Marksbury house. That's right . . . it was Zara . . . he was worried about how Zara would take the news that Silkie was coming here.

Zara did not take the news well. It went through her like a knife. Silkie and Trent? No. No, Trent was for Blaine. She had planned it. Oh, thank God for Wade! She would have to think fast. Alter things just a trifle. But getting Silkie on the road to Southampton was something she meant to do, one way or another.

"I see . . ." she said slowly. "And you are very sure that is what you want to do?"

"Of course, Aunt Zara"—she started for the stairs—"now if you will excuse me, I want very much to change these things." She touched her well-worn riding habit with a smile.

"Yes, but dear, don't you want some . . . time to consider before you leave your uncle's protection? Isn't this rather drastic . . . moving into Dare Trent's house?"

"Aunt Zara, I know because of the circumstances of my arrival, it is difficult for you to understand, but . . . Dare and I love each other. His home . . . is my home."

Zara stiffened. She could scarcely keep herself in check, but she did. Indeed, she altered her face to one of gaiety. "Right you are, and a new bride must celebrate." She put her finger to her lips as though in thought. "I know. You and I will drive over to Southampton, such a lovely little village with some of the finest shops . . . there is this quaint china shop. I will take you there and you will pick out a pattern . . . no, no, do not object. It will be your wedding gift from your uncle and myself."

Silkie was surprised by this sudden change in Zara. She was, in fact, surprised by Zara altogether, for the woman had hardly mentioned Blaine at all. She seemed satisfied that Blaine was recovering in Dare's home. That appeared to be all that Zara cared about when they had first discussed Blaine's condition, and now, now Zara was taking her shopping? This did not make sense. She knew that Zara had to be upset—after all, Zara had gone to quite a bit of trouble to separate Blaine and Dennis, with Dare in view for Blaine.

"How very kind of you . . . but really, Aunt Zara, I think we must leave it for another day. I should help Kora . . . and I would like to get back to Blaine."

"Nonsense. Blaine needs her rest and Kora is quite capable of packing your luggage. Besides, you will soon be out of mourning and will be choosing a livelier wardrobe. Now, hurry . . . go upstairs and choose your prettiest grey and I will call for my carriage."

"Oh, Aunt Zara . . . I don't know."

"Tut, tut, I won't hear another word . . . and you know what you might like to do?" She didn't wait for an answer. "Pack an overnight portmanteau so that I may drop you off at Trent's house . . . rather *your* house, when we are done with our shopping, for that will give Kora all the more time to do a thorough job." She smiled, but bitter resentment welled within her. Damn the girl! Damn her to Hades! *Her* house, indeed! By all rights it was Blaine's house, it was Blaine's man! How dare this girl come along and usurp . . . just as her mother had done! Well, she wouldn't have it!

Silkie had no choice. She didn't wish to insult her aunt and perhaps make an enemy. She smiled weakly and took the stairs, hoping that her aunt didn't have a long day planned for Southhampton. Oh Dare . . . you were right again. When they had first discussed it, he had insisted he come along with her to break the news and be able to quickly whisk her off before Zara got her "claws" into her, but she had laughed at such a notion. Now see what has happened.

"DENNIS!" Dare called to his friend from across Main Street as the young captain left the American Hotel, and quickly he stepped towards him. After a moment's greeting, he said quietly, "My wife, Silkie, charges me expressly with an errand on your behalf."

"Oh?" said Dennis and there was something of hope in his hazel eyes.

"You are to go to my house and pay a visit to Blaine."

"What? What can you mean? What is she doing at your house?"

"It is a long story, part of which Silkie tells me you know, and since that is the part *I* don't know, we shall one day have to go over it. However, now I am to tell you that Blaine had something of an accident in Sterling Woods and is recovering from her injuries in my"—he smiled to himself—". . . our guest room. Silkie says that Blaine will see you, though why she should is more than I can fathom, for anyone can see you are the devil himself and not worth the ground she walks on. Hold there, Dennis, where the blazes are you off to so fast? I'm not done."

Dennis had grabbed his friend's arm in his excitement and then had turned on his heel and headed for the horse he had tethered at the curbing post. He shouted over his shoulder, "I'm going to see if she will accept to switch roofs as soon as she is able . . . that's where!"

Dare grinned to himself for a long moment as he watched his friend mount and ride off, but then the frown he had been wearing earlier descended. On the road to town he had passed a neat carriage driven by a darkly clad man who looked impossibly familiar. He had allowed it to pass without seeking to stare at the fellow, but he had the distinct feeling the man kept his face purposely averted. Who it was he just could not think . . . but it had him bothered. Well, put it aside, he had business to dispatch with his carriage builder and then he wanted to visit the cooper.

He hailed the elderly man as he entered the carriage house. "Tates, hello old fellow . . . do you plan to bargain with me today, or do I turn around and walk out?" He smiled and shook the white-haired man's aged hands.

"If it is a bargain you want . . . off with you, youngster, for what I have here is the best and for the best . . . you pay!"

"Hmmm. So I have been doing for more years than I care to count."

"Right, you have, and there's no one I'd rather do business with. You are a fair man, Captain Trent, that you are."

"Cut the gammon, my friend. I want a light carriage, something suitable for a lady."

"A lady is it? Well, well?" said Tates curiously. This was the first time the captain had extended himself in this fashion for one of his fancy pieces.

"It is for my wife," said the Captain gently as he read the elderly man's mind.

"Wife? Well, congratulations, for I'd swear you weren't saddled with one when you left Sag Harbor."

"That's right." Dare laughed. "But I am now. She is English."

"English, is she. Well, well. Had an English fellow in here this morning . . . traded carriages with me. I had one designed for speed and he had a well-sprung barouche. Made a nice deal."

"An English fellow? New in town?" Why did this trouble him?

"That's right. Said he was just passing through . . . called himself"—he took up a card from his desk—". . . that's it . . . Wade Ashford." He looked up from the calling card to find Dare's back—the captain was off. That was all he had to hear. Wade Ashford was here in town. It had been Wade Ashford he had seen in that sleek carriage! Damn, he had to get to Silkie . . . he had to get to her before Ashford did!

Zara motioned for her driver to stop as they reached the main pike. She could see Wade Ashford's canopied carriage and felt a moment of excitement. Her driver had been paid to look the other way and that was just what he would do. She turned to Silkie.

"La, darling, I see an old friend I should dearly like you to meet." She threw the door of her closed curricle open, pulling at Silkie's gloved hand. "Come on, dear, don't be shy. You must meet all the right people if you are to take your place as a Sag Harbor hostess . . . which you will be as Dare's wife."

Silkie sighed and allowed her aunt to lead her to the other carriage—and then she was looking up at Wade Ashford's smiling face. Stunned. She went rigid with disbelief and then knew that she had to get away. She turned to Zara but the woman's sneer told a story. This had been planned! How, she couldn't tell. She started to run, but Wade was already down, his arms round her like a vice. While he held her, Zara reached for the coils of rope he had prepared and neatly fixed them round Silkie's wrists.

"The laudanum . . . quickly . . . in my pocket," Wade ordered.

This produced, Silkie screamed as Zara put it to her lips. "No . . . no."

Zara knew the trick of it though and pulled at Silkie's mouth and tongue until they were raw. She saw her chance and against her will Silkie was gulping down the mixture.

"Just enough to keep you quiet, my dear," said Wade into her ear. "You'll sleep nicely, with your head propped up against my shoulder for any passersby to see . . . we will look a happy couple, don't you think?" To Zara, "Put her overnight bag in the carriage."

Silkie was coughing, but her eyes glared fire at him. Finally she got her breath. "Dare will kill you!"

"Will he? I think not. He will be told by your aunt that you went willingly."

"He won't believe it. He knows I despise you."

"He will believe it. Zara has a nice enough story for him. Don't you, dear?"

"You see Silkie, I have facts, half-truths to give him about your mother and father, and when I am done, he will believe that you two had a lover's quarrel because of your father, but that your separation had you convinced that you couldn't do without your Wade . . . and then, like a hero, he came to rescue you. Off you went and I, I simply could not stop you." She laughed wickedly.

"No. He won't believe you . . . he won't . . ."

"You had better pray that he does, for if not, he is a dead man!" growled Wade, lifting her into the carriage. She was kicking, so he took a length of rope and bound her ankles roughly. He turned, took Zara into his arms, and gave her a long, warm kiss.

"There . . . you have kept your bargain, Zara. Now I shall keep mine."

"See that you do . . . but Wade," she said as an afterthought, "Dare, I don't want Dare killed . . . if he chances to follow . . . I mean . . ."

"Then see to it he doesn't!" was all the reply she had. Ashford, taking the reins in hand, sent his horses forward.

Dare's black gelding loped easily through the soft snow as he took the Marksbury drive up to the house. There he dismounted and rushed up its steps, but before the door was opened a young groom had come up to hold his horse, calling out, "If yer lookin' for Mrs. Marksbury, Captain Trent . . . she took Miss Silkie with her in her curricle.''

Dare turned sharply and his voice was clipped. ''She had Miss Silkie, you say? Where were they headed? I did not see them on the road to town.''

''Thats right . . . heard her tell Mac, her driver, to take them to the main pike . . . to Southampton.''

Dare waited for no more. He was up a moment later and taking on a heady pace in his frenzy. This boded ill. He didn't know why, he just felt it deep inside his gut. Silkie was in danger. Every thought burned the words. Silkie was in danger. Wade Ashford, Zara Marksbury. There was a connection there, and it wasn't good.

He rounded the bend in the road and there coming towards him was Zara's closed curricle. He motioned for it to stop, and as he brought himself to Zara's window he bent to look within. His heart beat furiously and then stopped.

''Where is she, Zara?'' It was calmly asked but there was a warning underneath his tone.

''What can you mean?'' returned Zara, stalling for time.

''Silkie! Damnation, you know exactly what I mean.''

''Oh . . . but . . . I didn't realize. Why, she wanted to shop in the village, so I left her there.''

''You never went and returned from Southampton already. Don't try to pitch your gammon at me!'' It dawned on him then. ''Certes . . . you gave her over, didn't you?'' There was nothing in her expression that gave her away yet even so he knew. He shook his head. ''You haven't gotten away with this. I mean to go after my wife and I'll have her back, safe and sound. And Zara, I will see you later!''

She watched him ride off and then moved back to close her eyes. It was happening again. All over again. This was how it happened before. She had given Serena over to Wade and then out of nowhere Aaron and Tyler had appeared . . . Aaron had rescued Serena . . . oh God, oh God! She started to laugh, but it was the sound of high hysteria. Her hands were trembling and her vision blurred. The carriage was moving towards the house, but what good was it. Aaron wasn't there waiting for her. He was with Serena . . .

\* \* \*

Dare undid the leather holster that held his horse pistol. This he took out and stuck into the cumberbund around his waist. He rearranged his riding coat so that his hand would be able to move freely, for he meant to have his wife—and Wade Ashford's blood! It was not long before he had Ashford's carriage in view and he set his jaw as he closed in.

Leaning into Wade's shoulder was Silkie, the effects of the drug just beginning to make her groggy. She fought to stay awake, keep her head erect but he would reach up and roughly pull her to him, push her head down on his arm. "Let me go . . . Wade . . . please let me go," she whispered at last.

"Begging? I am surprised at you, Silkie. I didn't think you had it in you. Your mother never begged . . . and she was no fighter, as you are."

"What do you know of my mother?" Her lids closed and she tried to open them. They wouldn't, they just wouldn't.

"Didn't she ever tell you? No, of course. Serena would not. I was forgetting." His eyes found another space in time and his voice took on another quality, very nearly wistful, unguarded. "She was almost mine and if she had been . . . everything would have been so very different. Zara helped me then : . . as she did today . . . but your father played the hero and ruined"—he gritted his teeth—". . . but there will be no hero today. Not this time!"

Dare's horse made no sound in the snow as he came up on the carriage and reached out for the reins at the horse's head. Ashford, however, was quick to pull out the small pistol he had in his boot. He aimed, but it was far too difficult with Dare moving. He waited until Dare had pulled them all to a halt and was turning his horse to face them.

Silkie opened her eyes. Dare! Oh Dare . . . and then she saw the gun in Ashford's hand. She wanted to scream, but instead she pushed at Ashford with all the strength she still possessed. It was enough to throw him off balance at the moment of firing. The gun went off but he had missed his mark.

By then Dare was off his black and taking hold of Ashford's coat, pulling the man out of the carriage, dragging him up to meet his closed fist. Ashford was a good deal older and slower and was scarcely able to ward off the blows when he spied the gun in Dare's waistband. He went for it.

Dare took hold of Ashford's wrist and attempted to get him to release his hold on the pistol, but Ashford held to it as he would his life. He wanted to kill Dare, had to kill Dare. The captain was just able to twist Ashford's hand slightly so that the barrel of the pistol went up . . . and then suddenly it was all over and Ashford was slipping to the ground, his blood flowing freely from his belly and a cry from his lips: "No . . . no . . . damn you all . . ." It was the last breath he took, but Dare could have sworn Wade whispered, "Serena . . ."

Then Dare was looking up to find Silkie falling out of the carriage. He called her name as he ran to catch her up. "Ah Silkie . . . my own sweetings." He was chuckling now for she was once again falling asleep. He kissed her forehead, her eyes, her nose, and she mumbled pleasurably, "Savage American . . . but just in time." With which she went off into the deep realms of induced slumber.

Hours and hours had gone by and Zara paced like a caged animal. She poured another shot of brandy and gulped it down. Her vision had been blurry all afternoon and the brandy had not helped . . . anything. What was wrong? Her palms were sweating and her body felt chilled. It was ridiculous. Not well, she wasn't feeling well. Oh God, why didn't she hear anything from the Trent household? Could it be that Dare never found them?

Aaron. Aaron had found them that day . . . so long ago . . . Aaron and Serena. Now it wasn't Aaron . . . no it was . . . who was it? Yes, that's right, Arthur's son. Arthur? What a pleasant interlude he had been after her heartache over Aaron. Aaron . . . there was that name again. Where was Blaine? Her baby . . . her baby hated her . . . Blaine would forget. Yes, of course she would.

Zara heard a commotion downstairs and ran out of her room, tripped on the hem of her mauve silk skirts, and tumbled to her knees. What was wrong with her? Why couldn't she function? She looked to the hall below and in the dim light she saw Aaron there.

"Aaron?" she said on a hushed whisper. What was this? Had he come to haunt her?

Tyler was a broken man. The years weighed heavily this day for he had been to Trent's house. Ashford's body had been brought into town and the rife gossip there was the first thing that had confronted him when he stopped by his offices. Ashford and Zara had been at it again. He knew it all and even so he hoped he was wrong. He looked up and saw Zara getting to her feet, holding the railing for support, and what, what did she call him? He shook his head.

"It's all true, isn't it, Zara?"

"Oh God!" It was Aaron. He was angry with her because he knew what she had done to his child. "I'm sorry . . . Ashford . . . Ashford said . . ."

Tyler turned away but his wife's scream brought his head up and around.

"AARON!" she cried in a frenzy. "NOT AGAIN." She moved on her knees. "Haunt me then . . . please . . . only stay . . . please stay."

Tyler frowned. What was this? He took the stairs to reach her, bent and brought her up by her shoulders. She was shrinking beneath his touch. "Where is he, Tyler?" she asked, looking around doubtfully.

"Not here, Zara, not here."

"But he was. I tell you . . . he was." She insisted in the voice of a child. "And he will come back. Tyler? Stay with me until he comes back. I love you, Tyler. You are my friend . . . but you know . . . Aaron . . . Aaron was meant for me."

"Yes, my dearest . . . come, let me take you to your room."

"Thats right. We'll wait for him together. . . ."


Silkie awoke to find herself in her husband's bed and she smiled. The light from the whale-oil lamp told her she was alone, although a roaring fire was ablaze in the hearth. She stuck her toes into her pink silk slippers and shrugged herself into the pink silk wrapper draped over the quilt coverlet. Kora must already be installed in the house, she thought as she made her way to the hall and down the stairs.

Had it really happened or had it been a dream? Wade Ashford? Zara? Oh faith! Had Dare killed Wade? She had to know and where was he anyway? She found a lackey in the corridor at the foot of the stairs.

"Where is the captain, please?" she asked quietly.

311

"He must be in the library still. I jest showed out the magistrate and that's where they were."

"Magistrate?" she repeated. Oh God, so it was true . . . quickly she went to the library door and opened it wide. Within stood Dare by the fire. He was alone and sipping a glass of cognac. It had been a long grueling day, telling the facts and attempting a low profile where his wife was concerned. He didn't want scandal attached to her name. He looked up and across as the door opened and his smile was a caress. "Well, woman, it is about time you were up!" he greeted her.

She flew across the room and into his arms. "Dare . . . oh Dare . . . it did happen then?"

He kissed the top of her flaxen head. "I am afraid, my sweetings, that it did . . . but never mind, it will all mend."

"Will it? Will it really?"

"Indeed . . . and you will be happy to know that your cousin and Captain Werth have set a date. The wedding will take place in New York and I mean to take you on a shopping spree while we are there, so we have some festivities ahead."

At that juncture they heard something of a commotion outside the library door. Evidently the captain's butler did not wish to admit whomever was out there. The door, however, flew open and two young, thoroughly disheveled, weatherbeaten, determined young men stomped forth and came up short to find Silkie in the arms of her husband.

Freddy coughed and mumbled something inaudible about the intrusion. Sir Blaize exclaimed, "Silk . . . Silk . . . came as fast as we could."

She called out their names and ran across the rooms to clasp both of them and bob up and down excitedly. "When did you arrive? How did you get here? What are you doing here?"

"Came to warn you," said Freddy portentiously.

"It's Ashford," said Blaize in way of an explanation. "Silk . . . he is here and up to no good!"

Silkie and her husband exchanged glances and it was Trent who first dismissed his butler with a request for refreshments and for the two remaining guest rooms to be prepared. He then turned to Blaize and said, "Do you mean you sailed across the Atlantic to lend your protection to Silkie?"

"Of course," answered Blaize, pulling himself up to his full height.

"Honorable thing to do," explained Freddy.

"Then on behalf of my wife and myself . . . thank you. You will be, I think, pleased to know that Ashford is no longer a problem."

"Eh? How's that?" asked Blaize.

"He's dead," put in Silkie quietly. "Dare killed him."

"Gadzooks!" ejaculated Blaize. "Did you hear that, Freddy?"

"Ay," said Freddy sadly. "Know what, Blaize?"

"No. What, Freddy?"

"Could have stayed home. . . ."

At which the assembled company burst into a round of laughter. Trent poured out four glasses of wine and passed them round before raising them in tribute to Silkie's friends. He drew her back into his arms and whispered softly, lovingly, "It seems, my dear, all my life you will lead me an interesting measure, for if you have inspired such friendship, think, oh babe, think what you will manage from me."

She went to her tiptoes and kissed his ear. "You may count on it, Dare . . . you may certainly count on it!"